CATHERINE CARSWELL

(1879-1946) was born in Glasgow, on ⋯
George and Mary Anne Macfarlane. ⋯
English literature at Glasgow University ⋯
days be admitted for a degree. Thereaf⋯
studied music for two years at the Frankfurt Conservatorium.

In 1904, after a brief engagement, she married Herbert
Jackson. When, in 1905, she told him of her pregnancy, he tried to
kill her. Declared insane, he spent the rest of his life in a mental
hospital. Catherine returned to Glasgow where her daughter was
born and worked, first in Glasgow and then in London, as
dramatic and literary critic, for the *Glasgow Herald*. In 1907 she
began legal proceedings for the anulment of her marriage. She
won the case, making legal history.

Her friendship with D. H. Lawrence was kindled by her
favourable review of *The White Peacock* (1911). They began
corresponding and their relationship lasted until Lawrence's
death. In 1915 she married Donald Carswell, with whom she had
one son, and in the same year she lost her job at the *Glasgow Herald*
for praising *The Rainbow*. Soon after this the Carswells moved
briefly from London to Bournemouth. She became an assistant
dramatic critic at the *Observer* and continued working on the
novel which would become *Open the Door*! In 1916 she and
Lawrence exchanged manuscripts of *Open the Door*! and *Women In
Love*. Her novel was completed in 1918 and won the Melrose Prize
on publication in 1920. Her only other novel, *The Camomile*, was
published two years later and she then devoted herself to *The Life
of Robert Burns* which made her name in 1930. This was quickly
followed by a biography of Lawrence, *The Savage Pilgrimage*
(1932), a number of anthologies and a life of Boccaccio, *The
Tranquil Heart* (1937).

After her husband's death during the black-out in 1940,
Catherine Carswell lived alone in London. She worked with John
Buchan's widow on his memorial anthology, *The Clearing House*
(1946) and on her own autobiography which was published,
incomplete, as *Lying Awake* in 1952. Her friends included Vita
Sackville-West, Edwin Muir, Rose Macaulay, Storm Jameson,
Hugh Macdiarmid, John Buchan and Aldous Huxley. Catherine
Carswell died in Oxford at the age of sixty-six.

VIRAGO
MODERN
CLASSIC

NUMBER

201

OPEN THE DOOR!

CATHERINE CARSWELL

With a New Introduction by
JOHN CARSWELL

Virago

Published by VIRAGO PRESS Limited 1986
41 William IV Street, London WC2N 4DB

First published in Great Britain by Andrew Melrose 1920
Virago edition offset from
Chatto & Windus fourth edition 1931

British Library Cataloguing in Publication Data
Carswell, Catherine
    Open the door!—(Virago Scottish classics)—
    (Virago modern classics)
    I. Title
    823'.912[F]   PR6005.A749
    ISBN 0-86068-564-0

Printed in Finland by Werner Söderström,
        a member of Finnprint

INTRODUCTION

Although the latter part of *Open The Door*! is mainly set in London, and the clue to the book is an episode in Italy, the roots of the novel are in, and belong to, Glasgow.

One must think of those Victorian terraces and the monumental centre of the city as fairly new, offering a sense of enterprise and confidence in the middle of danger and poverty. It was an energetic city, with its waterways and its shipping, its chemical plants and its neighbouring hills and moors, its dramatic new Gothic university building beside the crevasse of the Kelvin. Gilbert Murray became Professor of Greek there just ten years after Catherine Macfarlane was born in 1879. He was twenty-three. It was one sign among many that Glasgow was on its way to becoming a cultural as well as a commercial metropolis. Soon its School of Art would burgeon under Charles Rennie Mackintosh. All her life Catherine felt herself to be "a citizen of no mean city".

At one level, no doubt, the title of her novel suggests an escape from the world in which the author grew up—a world of Calvinist religiosity, oppressive conventions and smothering family life. She describes them, and her resistance to them vividly: but lovingly and with sympathy. Much of Victorian Glasgow is repudiated in the book, just as it was in her later life, but never with hatred. The clue to the title has much more to do with entering than with escape, and the "door" is "the little sunken door in the wall" which Joanna, the subject of the novel, sees in Italy and is told admitted a lover to the house of the Renaissance courtesan "La Porziuncola".

Most novelists, if they decide on an attractive heroine, either describe her attractiveness or arrange that it shall be taken for granted. The unusual thing in *Open The Door!* is the heroine's own knowledge of her attractiveness, mingled with senses of power, risk, guilt, misery, fear of failure, pleasure in success, and a measure of mischief: all set against the austere, deeply imprinted consciousness of the family life created by the United Free Church of Scotland.

Open The Door! was a first and a mind-clearing book drawn from direct experience. Joanna's family—especially her elder sister and her lovable but infuriating mother—are taken from life. So is Phemie, the baby-draper's daughter, whose original, after many adventures, paired off with one of the author's brothers. Joanna's lover Louis is modelled on the portrait painter Maurice Greiffenhagen, and Lawrence Urquhart, with whom the book ends, reflects my father Donald Carswell, whom Catherine married in 1915. Even the relative ages of the principal characters are preserved from their originals in real life.

But to what extent was Joanna Catherine? For this one must look at Catherine's life and the genesis of the novel.

Catherine was the second of the four children of George and Mary Anne Macfarlane, God-fearing middle-class Glaswegians and Wee Frees: both her grandfathers had been ministers who sacrificed their livings in 1843 and "came out" to form the Free Church rather than accept patronage and "intrusion". Though she was converted to socialism by reading Blatchford at the age of seventeen, and later espoused many left-wing causes, she could never quite abandon the idea that "underneath were the everlasting arms" or bear the depreciation of private charity.

Some of the most lively parts of the novel describe Catherine's family life with her elder sister and two younger brothers, and in many ways the "hens of gold," as they loved being called by their mother, were surprisingly free. As the most talented of the four, she was the only one to attend a university—Glasgow of course—and she read English, though in those days she could not be admitted to a degree. She also spent two years at the Frankfurt Conservatorium and became a respectable pianist. Her mother's side of the family had relations in Italy, and there too Catherine spent some time. The Aunt Perdy of the book is not a fiction. But the engineer Rasponi, Joanna's first husband, is an almost complete invention substituted for Catherine's first, and disastrous, marriage.

In September 1904, when she was twenty-five, she met a man called Herbert Jackson while she was staying with her former Glasgow professor, Walter Raleigh, at Farnham in Surrey. Herbert Jackson was Mrs Raleigh's brother, and some ten years older than Catherine. He had fought in the South African War, and his occupation was now that of an artist. There was a whirlwind courtship, and they were married in October. Whether the Raleighs could have prevented the marriage, one cannot know. Certainly they were placed in an appalling situation, for they knew that for some time past Herbert Jackson had shown clear signs of mental instability. He had causelessly assaulted people, issued challenges to duels and complained of imagined slights and persecutions, though most of the time he seemed normal enough. They kept their counsel. Perhaps they hoped marriage would steady him.

In this they were quite mistaken, for the key to his paranoia was a delusion (and delusion it was) that he was impotent, and the consequent conflict imposed by the need to abandon his delusion produced not an amelioration but a crisis which grew rapidly worse. From claims that he was being watched and spied upon he moved to accusations that Catherine was secretly betraying him. In March 1905, when she was pregnant, he swore the child could not be his and its father was probably the Prince of Wales. A few days later he produced a revolver, which she took from him and threw out of the window. He was taken to a mental hospital, where he remained under a certificate, too dangerous to be discharged, for the rest of his life. He would see neither his wife nor his daughter Diana, who was born in October 1905.

Catherine returned to Glasgow to live with her mother, and was received with a mixture of sympathy and reservation. Her husband was thirty-six, and as the law stood there seemed no way she could avoid being married to him for the rest of his life.

Soon after coming back to Glasgow she started on her writing career as dramatic critic and fiction reviewer for the *Glasgow Herald*. This renewed her contact with Donald Carswell—the Lawrence Urquhart of the novel—whom she had known when they were studying together at the university, and who was now a sub-editor on the *Herald*. The Louis of the novel had come to Glasgow about the time of Catherine's return. This was Maurice Greiffenhagen, who became Professor of the Life Class at the Glasgow School of Art—then at the height of its fame—in 1906. Greiffenhagen was already a well-known artist who went on to be an academician and, in his time, a fashionable portrait painter. He had painted what is perhaps the picture by which he is best remembered as long ago as 1891, when he was thirty. This was "An Idyll" which shows a brawny shepherd enthusiastically embracing a reluctant but not wholly unwilling shepherdess in a woodland setting. It hangs today in the Walker Art Galley, and must have been a rather bold purchase at the time. D. H.

Lawrence, then teaching at Croydon and still an unknown schoolmaster, saw it in 1908 and was so impressed that he made copies of it and wrote to one of his friends: "As for Greiffenhagen's 'Idyll' it has moved me as much as if I were fallen in love myself." Later events in Catherine's life add a strange poignancy to this coincidence.

Greiffenhagen was forty-four when he met Catherine, and she fell lastingly in love with him. He was married, with a family, and seventeen years older.

At that time, deeply committed to Greiffenhagen, Catherine embarked on what most people must have thought was a hopeless attempt to free herself from her own marriage. She could not divorce Jackson, as the law then stood; and he, being certified insane, could not divorce her. Her unprecedented case was that because of his developing mental illness he could not have fully grasped what he was undertaking when they were married, and so the marriage was null and void.

Jackson v *Jackson* came to court in May 1908 and lasted six days, during one of which Catherine gave evidence about her extraordinary honeymoon, facing strict cross-examination. Several doctors were called, one of whom, challenged on the point that he had examined Herbert Jackson only after the marriage, compared the forest tree he had seen in the disease with the sapling that must have preceded it. It was powerfully urged on Jackson's side that a nullity would make the child illegitimate, which no court should allow—least of all on the request of the mother. Jackson himself, his counsel said, was too ill to appear. "The respondent," said Mr Justice Bargrave Deane, "was not at the time of the marriage a raving lunatic: outwardly to people he was competent. The question is, whether he was really insane." It was for her to prove it, and he found that she had, so establishing a leading case.

Three years later, in 1911, she received D. H. Lawrence's first novel, *The White Peacock*, in her pile for the *Herald*, and declared that she found in it "a new voice". Soon afterwards, on the death of her mother, she moved to London (where Greiffenhagen was now living) and established herself in a cottage in Hampstead with Diana. The dramatic criticism for the *Herald* naturally had to stop, but she continued to review their fiction every other Tuesday, so their columns included favourable notices of *The Trespassers* and, more enthusiastic still, *Sons and Lovers*.

It must have been about this time that she began writing the novel that became *Open The Door!* Her relationship with Greiffenhagen was collapsing under his resolution to follow his own path, and Donald Carswell had also taken the plunge to London with a post on *The Times*.

Diana, never a well child, died of pneumonia in 1913 after "eight happy years", as her mother wrote on her grave in Hampstead churchyard. Soon afterwards Catherine and Donald became engaged, and he was to prove an utterly devoted husband—but the name of Greiffenhagen could never be mentioned between them.

One must suppose that some correspondence, now lost, with D. H. Lawrence preceded her first meeting with him in June 1914, since it was clearly prearranged and their friendship ripened very quickly. Lawrence, who had come to England with Frieda to get married, did not reach London till the latter part of June, and by the end of that month he had not only met Catherine but was half-way through her novel. They were to remain close friends for the rest of Lawrence's life, as some two hundred letters testify: one of the largest bodies of Lawrence's huge correspondence to survive. Since he never kept letters, her side of the correspondence is lost; but two things are evident. She was never either the recipient or the victim of the wounding fury which Lawrence showered so liberally on and about most of his other friends. She was devoted to him, and perhaps saw more clearly than most his extraordinary originality. But as she records in her own life of him: "From beginning to end I had for Lawrence, as he well knew, a special kind of love and admiration which I never had for any other human being . . . But I felt also the need to save myself." Lawrence knew about Greiffenhagen, as several passages in the letters make clear, and that may have entered into and stimulated the development of their early relationship; but they met at a moment when both were on the point of getting married. There was an instinctive puritanism in them both which each was quick to recognize (and sometimes to reproach the other for straying from). Lawrence married Frieda in July 1914, and Catherine married Donald early in 1915.

The novel which Lawrence read in the summer of 1914 was an early version of *Open The Door!*, not the book we now have. He covered the manuscript with annotations and criticisms, discussed it with her, and called for extensive rewriting. "Nearly all of it is *marvellously* good. It is only so incoherent . . . My stars, just you work at it and you'll have a piece of work you need never feel ashamed of." Beside this encouragement, his criticism of the style as "indirect and roundabout, stiff-kneed and stupid" merely seemed an invitation to try harder.

Lawrence, at that time, was working on *The Rainbow*, which came out in 1915 and was promptly prosecuted: but not before Catherine had reviewed it for the *Glasgow Herald*. She found it "a difficult review to write", and although it contained a measure of criticism the praise in it caused her to take the precaution of seeing that it went to the printer without passing under the editorial eye. So she promptly lost her job—continuing in journalism, however, as assistant dramatic critic of the *Observer*.

She was also pressing on with her own novel, and many

references in Lawrence's letters show the interest with which he had followed its progress. By the autumn of 1916 it was finished, and she took it with her to Cornwall where she and Donald stayed some time with the Lawrences, and it was much discussed. Lawrence was by then working on *Women in Love*, and as a result the name of one of the characters in *Open The Door!* (Sholto Bannerman) found its way into his novel until she made him alter it, and it became Donald Gilchrist.

This was when the manuscript of *Women in Love* reached Catherine and Donald a month or so later. Donald read it for libel (he had now qualified as a barrister) and Catherine altered Gudrun's clothes as well as making a number of stylistic points, all of which Lawrence accepted. But she did not like the novel, and reproached him for writing about "people so far removed from the general run, people so artistic and 'spoiled', that it would hardly matter what they said." Lawrence's defence, that it was only by the study of upper-class putrescence "that one could discover whither the general run of mankind, the great unconscious mass, was tending", did not convince her. The difference led to her itemizing his new friends of Garsington and Bloomsbury (friendships the novel in fact destroyed) and telling him he would have to work "for those who could not understand him till long afterwards, and he would have to be alone, all through and in the end alone".

This difference did not end their friendship, and he continued to encourage her about *Open The Door!* "Don't hate Joanna," he wrote, "she is young. She will grow up. But the hideous wasters who will only rot in the bud, how I hate them. But Joanna is all right. She is a kind of dead-nettle, who looks like a pure weed, and comes out with very quaint and bunchy flowers at the last minute."

Thus *Open The Door!* was finished five years after it was first thought of and was submitted to Lawrence's publisher Duckworth, who refused it on grounds of length. She then sent it to Melrose, who not only took it but gave it a prize, half of which she offered to Lawrence, who declined it.

The novel was published in 1920, but if, as is usual, one takes the First World War as a Great Divide, it belongs both in conception and flavour to the pre-war world; although oddly enough it owes nothing of its structure or feeling to the conventions of Victorian or Edwardian times. Its characters are not imprisoned by anything but themselves, and the liberation they seek is not social but personal.

Catherine was now committed to a writing career—the more so as Donald's ambitions at the Bar were quickly disappointed. He was a gentle, scholarly, quite unpractical man, who worked slowly and with infinite care. His two books—one a collection of essays on nineteenth-century Scotsmen, and the other a study of Sir Walter Scott and his circle—broke new ground with their careful research and impeccable writing. They earned respect, but little money. Her small inheritance was soon spent.

Her second novel, *The Camomile*, which came out in 1922, was much more light-hearted than her first, and more tautly constructed. Two more were planned, one of which was to be shared with Lawrence, who sketched it on lines which later emerged as those of *The Plumed Serpent*. But what that novel would have been like with the Scottish setting Lawrence projected for it ("the Maclure, who claims to be chief of the clan and has bought the ancestral castle of his native isle . . . a man of about forty-five, rather small, dark-eyed, full of energy, but has been a good deal knocked about") has to be left to the imagination. Neither of the collaborators could see how it would end, and it was abandoned.

The difference over who were Lawrence's friends was the underlying theme of the celebrated dinner party he gave at the

Café Royal, at which the world from which he had drawn *Women in Love* was conspicuous by its absence. Soon afterwards he left England, and Catherine saw him only rarely, though they continued to correspond. Her decision to turn to biography was very much her own, though she was encouraged in her choice of subject by both Donald and Lawrence, and she dedicated the *Life of Robert Burns*, published in 1930, to them jointly.

There had been no life of Scotland's national poet for many years, and his memory had become institutionalized in a curious mixture of sanctimoniousness and booze. Catherine's book is in no sense an exercise in iconoclasm but a carefully researched rescue of the real man, and almost every page records her sympathy with what she was discovering about him. It remains today a very sound biography indeed. The book was bitterly denounced by orthodox Burnsites. It was even preached against from the pulpit of Glasgow Cathedral by the Rev. Lauchlan Maclean Watt. Many were shocked that a woman should write the life of Burns. But the book made her name, and brought her many friends, among them John Buchan.

Lawrence died in the year the Burns biography was published, and almost at once she was plunged into the controversies over his memory with a letter to the press denouncing the obituarists who had condemned him as a "dark and sinister failure". She put her collection of letters at the disposal of Aldous Huxley for his edition of Lawrence's correspondence, and in 1932 published what is probably her best-known work: the memoir of D. H. Lawrence which she called *The Savage Pilgrimage*.

It would never have been written but for John Middleton Murry's strange "destructive hagiography", *Son of Woman*, against which she felt bound to mount a defence. Of all the early biographies of Lawrence hers is the most clear-headed in that it assesses him as a man, not a prophet. But at the same time she was one of the very few to emphasize the new key that Lawrence had struck and the probability of his lasting literary—and social—influence as a writer.

Catherine was fifty-three when *The Savage Pilgrimage* was published and a well-known writer with many friends. But of coteries and circles she had an instinctive fear. Her closest friends were Scotswomen with whom she had grown up and who had engaged in professional careers: two doctors, Maud McVail and Isobel Hutton, the sculptress Phyllis Clay, and Maggie Mather (the Phemie of *Open The Door!*) who became a professional musician. So far as she was concerned they had as much claim on her as the newer friends she made through her work—Vita Sackville-West, Storm Jameson, Athene Seyler and Rose Macaulay.

When one contrasts John Buchan with Hugh MacDiarmid her friendships were indeed wide-ranging. She shared neither the cautious conservatism of one nor the eccentric nationalism of the other, but was a friend of both, as correspondence shows. What is more, both Catherine and Donald were close friends of Edwin and Willa Muir, whom MacDiarmid regarded as his arch-enemies.

During the 1930s Catherine produced three anthologies, much literary journalism, and a third biography: a life of Boccaccio, which she called *The Tranquil Heart*, chosen, as she said, because Boccaccio was the first author to write avowedly for women. By now she was earning almost all the money that came into the house.

Her closest friend during these years was Daniel George, the critic and publisher's reader, whom she came to know when he was still Daniel Bunting, the talented, self-educated manager of a firm of geyser manufacturers. He was already an accomplished writer and critic, and in the middle thirties became literary adviser to Jonathan Cape. With him Catherine collaborated on two of her anthologies—*A National Gallery* and *The English in Love*.

She belonged to the unlucky generation that had to live through two world wars—one in youth, and the other in old age—and the outbreak of the second, which as a passionate anti-fascist she had long foreseen, pressed very hard upon her. Donald was killed in a street accident in the blackout early in 1940, and soon afterwards I was sent abroad.

She wrote and wrote. Much of her time was spent with John Buchan's widow, working on the two volumes commemorating him—*The Clearing House* (1946) and *John Buchan by His Wife and Friends* (1947)—both of which owe much to her. She began collecting materials for a life of Calvin. She also worked on an autobiography which she did not live to complete but which was published in 1950 under the title *Lying Awake*. She died in 1946.

Although, as I have said, she was a woman of many friends and kept her friendships alive by the systematic and copious writing of letters, she rather avoided what might be called the routine of social life. More and more, in order to get her writing done, she would hire some out-of-the-way room into which she escaped from chance visitors and phone calls, keeping its address secret even from those she knew best. And much as she venerated her craft of writing, and dedicated as she was to it, she was singularly free of the feeling that writers deserve any special respect. To have a name, she accepted, was important, but in no more important a sense than a shop needs a name if it is to have customers. And she was much happier (despite her fondness for company she really liked) prowling round Kentish Town for odd books, curious furniture or second-hand pieces of costume than at a party.

One can detect a great deal of this in the Joanna of her novel, who is more interested in the strange, sad Mr and Mrs Moon and their family than in her smart cousin Irene. She never really considers what is going to happen to her hopeless commitment to Louis, and the final scene on the moor could not better express the absence of calculation that was so characteristic of the author. Although Lawrence had doubts about the closing passages of the book, and felt that they really belonged to a different novel, they seem to me to bring together the book's many themes in a final scene of great force and power, equal to the best she ever wrote.

That Catherine was Joanna appears from this recollection I have of Catherine when I was eight years old. She had taken me with her into a church in France which, because of some festival, was crowded with worshippers. Just inside the door an extremely shabby man blew his nose on a dirty rag, thrust it into his pocket and sank down, quite alone, in prayer. Catherine sank down behind him and gently picked his pocket of the rag, which she replaced, with equal gentleness, by a completely clean handkerchief from her handbag, neatly folded. Through it all he remained, I am sure, quite unconscious of what was happening. Taking me by the hand she led me out of the church, and when the door had closed behind us said, "I hope he'll think it was a miracle. He needed one so much." That was Joanna speaking.

John Carswell, London, 1985

BOOK I

"... Open the door, and flee."—2 Kings ix. 3.

CHAPTER I

I

FOR Juley Bannerman to leave home was in any case a heavy undertaking. Even without her four children, even with the admonishing help of her husband, the occasion was one for which complicated plans—gallant but not availing —had to be laid weeks beforehand. And on this morning neither alleviation was hers.

As always she had done her best, of course. The night before she had not undressed, had not so much as taken the hairpins from her aching head. Then since breakfast her two daughters, aged twelve and fifteen, had rushed about the house, strapping and unstrapping luggage, and exhorting her. Her confused servants had done what they could. Even her little sons had tried to help, and as the four-wheeled cab went lumbering over the granite setts of the city, they strove unskilfully to knot up her bonnet strings between them.

But it was all no use. The morning express from Glasgow to Edinburgh, said the porter, had been gone these two minutes. Now there was no train until ten minutes past twelve.

Smarting, not for the first time, under this kind of public ignominy, the children precipitated themselves upon the pavement before Queen Street Station, and Georgie, the eldest, a stout and lively girl, addressed herself with violence to the open door of the cab.

"It's always the same when Father isn't here," she stormed. "I told you we'd miss it, didn't I?" In her rage she could have struck her mother.

It exasperated the children that the culprit still stayed sitting in the cab, untying and retying the black ribbon strings of her bonnet with a little defiance in her face ; and they knew she was avoiding their eyes when she leaned forward smiling at the porter, seeking his sympathy, speaking in her warm, pleasant voice.

"Oh ! But I feel sure there must be a train before then," she urged, as if by sheer hopefulness she could belie the time-tables. "Let me see the board." And she began a cumbered descent from the cab.

For a woman of but forty-two, even allowing for the fact that at this time she was some months gone with child, Juley moved heavily. Not even the loss of a night's rest could rob her face of its girlish freshness, but this very youthfulness and ardour of expression served to emphasize her physical ineptitude. It was as if she had never grown used to her body. Often enough had her children heard her sigh impatiently for wings.

Yet Joanna, her younger daughter, looking on, could not believe that swiftness and grace were not mere matters of goodwill, and that therefore this clumsiness was deliberate. "Why will mother move like that ? " she questioned in childish vexation. And driven by a strong craving, she stared away from the imperfection facing her, and set her eyes instead on a patch of the blue, perfect sky of May which had shone out suddenly between showers above the house-tops.

"The man must know about the trains, Mother," Georgie scolded, and turning to the porter she asked him when the twelve o'clock train reached Edinburgh.

"But Aunt Georgina's lunch is at one ! " declared the elder boy, Linnet, when he had heard the reply ; and spinning on his heel he seemed to find a zest in adding to the family misfortunes. "Aunt Georgina *will* be cross ! And what about the carriage ? It'll be waiting at the station for us."

At this a disconsolate exclamation came from Sholto, the youngest. Sholto did so love to sit by Mackintosh, his Aunt's coachman whose fur cape smelt of naphtha, as they drove along Princes Street.

Georgie glared murderously at her mother.

"It's all because Father isn't here," she repeated.

But the time-table had showed a train that would leave the Central Station in half-an-hour. So the luggage was put back on the railed top of the cab, and the children crowded into it for the five minutes drive. Their last difficulty lay in getting their mother to break off a conversation with the porter. She had discovered that as a lad he had attended her husband's Bible Class for Foundry Boys : and now she was telling him about the Evangelistic tour Mr. Bannerman was making in the United States of America. She had to be pushed and pulled, protesting, into the cab. Then some one remembered that a telegram must be sent to Aunt Georgina. But at last they were set out on their way again, and they were soon arranging themselves in the train.

II

Though the third-class compartment which the Bannerman family had secured to themselves would have seated ten full-grown people with comfort, it now appeared so to overflow with animated life that other travellers, valise in hand, passed it after one hesitating glance through its windows. Certainly the children from the moment of their entrance did everything they could think of to repel fellow-passengers. Not only was this by tradition essential to the joy of a journey, but if strangers got in, Mrs. Bannerman was sure to talk to them. She loved and idealized strangers, eagerly furnished them with reading matter, and was swift in leading the talk to eternal verities—all of which was a severe trial to her daughters in their sensitive teens. In most ways leading quite detached lives, and feeling a good deal of contempt, each for the other, Georgie and Joanna were at one in this : they hated any publication of their mother's peculiarities.

And so young Sholto was posted at one of the platform windows and told to grimace with all his might at anyone who seemed to have designs on the door-handle, while behind him, Linnet, disguised as an invalid, lay at full length, propped slightly by a hold-all and covered to the chin with his mother's shepherd's-plaid shawl. In another window, an umbrella, crowned with Sholto's glengarry and draped with Linnet's reefer coat, served as an additional scarecrow.

In all this the leader was clearly Georgie. She gave her orders in Double Dutch, a secret family language much used and treasured by the four, and the younger ones did her bidding more or less. To the mother's fiftul supplication for quiet, no one paid much attention. But really Juley was as youthfully elated as any of her children at the adventure of travelling, and they knew it. Her satisfaction, together with great pride in her unmanageable flock, beamed from her. She enjoyed, too, arranging the hand-luggage on the racks and beneath the seats, and was joyfully looking forward to opening the letters of that morning, one letter bearing the Philadelphia postmark. She had a day-old newspaper to read as well, and had brought with it several issues of *The Believer* and of *Distant Lands*—some of these still in their uncut wrappers of weeks ago and showing marks of dust. In the current number of *The Believer* she knew there was a breezily up-to-date article by her husband, entitled "Are Miracles Essential?" To read with a clear conscience was a luxury Juley never enjoyed at home, where calls on her time and strength were unending, and household duties, in spite of her three servants, ever in arrears. Already on this journey she had expressed some of her pleasant anticipations to the kind guard who sympathized with their loss of the other train. Next, to her daughters' distress she confided in the ticket-collector. "We are going," she told him, "to the Assembly of our dear Free Church."

"I do wish, Mother, you wouldn't tell every one where we are going," objected Georgie the moment the door was closed again. "People only laugh at us. That man was laughing. I saw him. What's the use of telling *him* that Grandpapa came out at the Disruption? He's probably a U.P. anyhow."

"Dear, dear, how sensitive you children are," replied Juley undisturbed. She was annoyingly accustomed to such rebukes, and feeling suddenly hungry she opened a small paper bag and began to eat from it with relish. She had thriftily saved half a buttered roll from their hasty breakfast.

"What if he did smile, Georgie?" she went on between bites. "It will do him good to smile, and us no harm."

Georgie blew an irritated breath, and settling herself with a wriggle in the corner where the umbrella had been, she resolutely opened the book she had brought with her. It was *Sartor Resartus*. She did not understand it, but it exhilarated her with a sense of superiority to the rest of the family. She glanced scornfully across at her sister who was reading *Tit-Bits*, indulging an inferior appetite for mere bits of curious information.

The train had moved out of the station, but just then it slowed down and stopped on the high bridge which there spans the Clyde. Joanna, from learning how many times a sovereign beat finely out would engirdle the earth, looked up and out of the window. Below her, framed in the great transverse shanks of the iron grille, the water looked so beautiful that she could have called out. Yet something kept her quite still and mute in her corner.

It had been raining half an hour before, but now the sun gleamed on the brown surface of the river and on the wet, grey granite balustrades of the Jamaica Bridge. The bright red and yellow horse-cars flashed as they followed each other northwards and southwards along shining rails, and the passing craft on the water moved in a dun-coloured glory. By one bank some paddle steamers were being re-painted for the coming season. Joanna with the others had often sailed in them for summer cruises, and she knew by the number of funnels and their colours to which line each boat belonged. She knew the dredgers too, obstinate in mid-stream, with their travelling lines of buckets trawling glittering filth from the river-bed, while passing them, a string of half-submerged barges and rafts hung behind a little panting tug. Less familiar was a giant liner that made her slow way seaward. Her decks were deserted. Only a negro leaned, gazing, upon a rail astern.

This picture, cut into sections and made brilliant by the interposing trellis of black metal, appealed not so much to the little girl's untrained eye, as symbolically through her eye to her heart which leapt in response. The sunshine on that outgoing vessel and the great, glistening current of brown water filled her with painful yet exquisite longings. She did not know what ailed her, nor what she desired. She got no further than thinking that she would like to be a stewardess when she grew up.

With a warning cry and a long shudder the train, which had only stopped for a moment, started again. But before it had passed over the bridge, Georgie too, glancing up from her reading at the disturbance, caught sight of the river.

" O, look ! Just look ! Look at the river, all of you ! " she shouted, rushing across the carriage. " Mother ! Joanna ! Isn't it simply lovely ? Isn't it exquisite ? " And in her enthusiasm she dragged her mother to the window at which her sister was seated. " Only look there ! "

Juley leaned to look back at the retreating vision. She

had laid her hand on Joanna's shoulder, partly to steady herself, partly in affection.

"Yes, dears, beautiful!" she agreed with warmth. "God has put us into a beautiful world. Let us try and make our own lives to match it!" And after a pause she quoted words which had risen in her mind at the sight: "They go down to the sea in ships, and see His wonders in the mighty deep."

Joanna felt miserably inclined to shake off her mother's touch which had increased to a meaning pressure on her shoulder. It seemed to violate her, and she guessed with hatred at the pleased, ready tears in her mother's eyes. Even while her own tears pricked painfully behind her eye-balls at the beauty of her mother's words, she threw up frantic defences against their bid for her sympathy. Not for the world would she have yielded, not for the world could she have told why. The familiar, absurd thought came to her that she was perhaps a changeling or foster-child in the Bannerman family, no real relation to any of them. How else explain this trouble, this obstinate aloofness that was so common with her?

As for Juley she sat in her place and reviewed her little family, her "hens of gold" as she loved to call them. God, in His infinite mercy, she mused, had seen fit to give her the charge of these four immortal souls; and she would, with His help, try not to fail in so great a trust. In the scurry that morning she had not found time to kneel as long as usual by her bedside. Without constant and secret prayer she knew herself unable to face the difficulties of daily life. So now she closed her eyes and prayed. She prayed for each of her children, including the one yet unborn: for strength and wisdom to guide their feet in the way of peace: for her husband in Philadelphia, and the work he was doing among souls there between the intervals of his business. Lastly she prayed for the whole family of mankind. But prayers embracing the human race are so generous that upon the soul that offers them they have the soothing and releasing effect of a wide landscape or a river which has quietly overflowed its banks. And this is what happened to Juley Bannerman. A sense of extraordinary peace lapped her about. The white *Believers* and the blue *Distant Lands* she had thought to enjoy, were destined to travel back to Glasgow a week later in their unviolated wrappers. She slept.

III

The train ran on with a throbbing rhythm that was grateful to the sleeping woman. Linnet sat in a lethargy as usual, twitching his pale blue, delicate eyes in a way he had ; and Sholto who wanted to fire off a new penny pistol, searched his sporran for pink percussion caps. With his glengarry off the child showed a bullet-like head covered with short, dark fur, a head that looked as if it could ram enemies out of its way. And the strong knees beneath his tweed kilt were always covered with bruises which were his pride when the first pain of them was past. Already he was more than a match for Linnet, and his sisters had been compelled to abandon physical reliance in their dealings with him. When he was whipped he bellowed, but shed few tears, unlike Linnet, who overflowed at a touch. Indeed it was enough to address Linnet teasingly as " President Lincoln " (his namesake) to see the corners of his mouth go down. Though he was now ten, his mother had not yet had the heart to cut the fair effeminate ringlets which reached the collar of his sailor suit. The others, all straight-haired, were proud of Linnet's curls.

Georgie and Joanna seemed deep in their reading. Joanna, seeing her mother asleep, had kicked off her shoes without untying the laces : her brown beaver hat lay beside her. Both girls were dressed alike in porridge-coloured coats trimmed after the fashion of the nineties, with panels of terra-cotta plush. Ugly garments they were, but they had a special quality in their wearers' eyes because Aunt Perdy from Italy had chosen them. About a month before, Aunt Perdy, Juley's sister, till then known to the children by name only, as " poor Aunt Perdy," who led a vaguely romantic, vaguely unmentionable existence on an Italian hill-top, had seized the chance of her disapproving brother-in-law's absence to pay them all a visit in Glasgow. During her short stay she had turned the Bannerman household upside-down. It was a household where personal remarks were not made, but Aunt Perdy's talk had consisted chiefly in personalities. She had turned from her soup at dinner to tell the housemaid that her hair was glorious, but her face stupid : had assured Georgie that her neck and hands were her only good points in looks : had drawn up impromptu horoscopes unasked for each member of the family from Juley to the cook. It was on the occasion of the choosing of the porridge-coloured coats that she had announced with all the gravity and force of prophecy that Joanna promised to be a beauty in the course of time. It was a prophecy rebuked by Juley, but both Joanna and Georgie had heard it; and since that day the relations between the two girls had changed subtly. Till then the elder had been a secret bully. When they were dressing together she would often throw Joanna's clothes on to the dusty top of the wardrobe, and she had enjoyed watching her suffer. But even then she had sometimes felt a curious spasm in herself seeing her younger sister asleep in the bed they shared. Joanna's skin made her think of wild roses, and there was a suggestion of fragility in these undecided contours that roused something besides her contempt. Not so very long before, at a Christmas party at Aunt Georgina's, when their mother had arrived very late, bringing her whole flock—though only two had been expected—Cousin Irene, newly returned from "finishing" in France, had swept the apologetic little Glasgow group with her tortoiseshell lorgnette (Irene was terribly fashionable).

"What stu-u-r-dy children!" she had drawled.

Juley, proud of the robust bodies she had brought forth and reared, had smiled delighted at the compliment. But Georgie had been lashed by her cousin's patronage. She had stood out crimsoning and looking in that moment sturdier than ever.

"That shows all you know!" she had exclaimed. "Linnet's extremely delicate—he has to wear a trust. And Joanna is not a bit sturdy. She has to have Malt Extrack with every meal, and it was all mother could do to rear her at all!"

What Georgie had not realized before her Aunt Perdy's visit was that Joanna's look of fragility held a promise of future beauty. Now without question she knew and accepted it. She felt not a trace of envy. The contempt did not go, but the bullying ceased.

Juley still slept. She had in full measure the capacity for making up arrears of sleep; and it was well that she had, for failing to get to bed in the ordinary way and at a reasonable hour of the night was one of the sins that did most easily beset her. She acknowledged it, fought and prayed against it, but with little avail. And her children were as ashamed of it as if she had been a drunkard.

To herself Juley's weakness was a baffling mystery. Night

after night, soon after ten o'clock had struck, however strong her resolve of the earlier evening had been, she was beset by a vision of duties undone. There were letters that should have been answered weeks ago, the accounts needed making up, cheques ought to be signed. Throughout the day interruptions, to which she was ever a victim, had prevented her from attending to these things ; and now, between ten and eleven, they collected to form a dark cloud about her. Scratch, scratch, would go her unready pen ; and she took great pains with her erasures, always having a fine pen-knife by her in her japanned pencil case, and finally rubbing the place quite smooth with the back of her finger-nail. When her husband was at home he had the authority to drive her to bed, but now that he was away the girls would wake with an unhappy start hearing the clock strike two, and would steal in to remonstrate. Never in after life could they hear the sound of a quill pen squeaking along paper without a vision of their mother by candlelight, her face wearing a look of innocent craft, mingled with guilt at being found out. True, even then she usually maintained the defensive. So long as she was at her chaotic desk she was upheld by the sense that she was fulfilling duties, however belatedly. But there were times when in the delicious quiet of midnight she would be ensnared by the unread newspaper of that morning ; and this, whether discovered in it or not, she held to be sinful. At other times again, on some slight pretext, such as a fresh box of matches, she would with many precautions creep down the basement stairs and prowl about the kitchen, peeping into jars, sniffing inquisitively at their contents, testing Ellen's saucepans with a forefinger to see if they were thoroughly scoured—finding a dozen things amiss. Ultimately, the housewife in her rampant, she would spend three-quarters of an hour cutting up bars of soap into even squares for the economy of drying before use ; and when she came to place them neatly in rows on a high shelf, she would find that the shelf wanted dusting. On these occasions she reverted entirely to the careful, secretive, peasant stock from which her family had sprung on her father's side—a strong stock that had risen and married far above itself. In spite of a pricking conscience Juley enjoyed her stolen visits to the kitchen like a truant schoolgirl, and during such raids her mouth would be set in lines of obstinate naughtiness.

When her husband was at home, however, there were but few adventures below-stairs for her. Her uupunctuality, her muddle-headedness and her slowness were very trying to a facile and naturally precise man as he was, and she was achingly aware of her own shortcomings. Not that Sholto treated her harshly. He was forbearance itself, and she knew he recognized her constant struggle to please him. Greatly she craved his affection, and he gave it to her. But not like a spendthrift. He doled it out, while she devoured it hungrily. She was conscious without vanity that he had a fixed perception of her goodness, her inherent purity of heart and motive, and that he consciously kept this in mind when she tried his patience. And for this she was humbly grateful, often telling herself how blessed she was in such a husband. But without knowing it she thirsted for something Sholto did not give her, as he had it not, and when this thirst attacked her she suffered a sick loneliness of heart that drove her to her knees. There, by her bedside, many a time, with tears she would ask forgiveness of God for having married.

For when she was twenty-five there had come very definitely to Juley Erskine, as she then was, the call to a religious vocation. Had she been a Roman Catholic she would undoubtedly have entered some working Order such as that church provides, and under its strict rule and constant spiritual exercises might have thriven. But to her the Church of Rome was the Scarlet Woman. So her call demanded simply that special kind of consecration, which, so long as there are Leper Islands abroad and slums at home, will always remain open to ardent souls of any denomination. Juley had taken her decision, but not yet a definite post for service, when she met Sholto Bannerman. And very soon after their meeting he asked her to become his wife.

Sholto with his immediate charm had become accustomed to women's admiration, and up to a point he was susceptible; but no woman had ever appealed to him so strongly as this one. Miss Erskine was not pretty, but her physical freshness, notable in itself, was made arresting by some spiritual quality in her which Sholto did not attempt to define. And she was just difficult enough to make the winning of her a pleasure. She would have refused anyone else; but Sholto's chance lay in the fact that they had met in mission work, and in a particular Vineyard where he was already an experienced labourer.

In 1881 there had swept over Scotland a wave of religious revival—the second and lesser wave set a-going by Moody and Sankey—and in Glasgow alone the registered converts numbered over thirty-two thousand. There were stupendous after-meetings which made the City Hall resemble a vast fishing ground, with the blind, sweet-voiced singer and the nasal, humorous Yankee orator as the skilful casters of nets. Both Sholto and Juley had readily lent themselves as helpers and it was thus that they had met.

Juley had hesitated long and seriously, but in the end she had taken Sholto instead of her dream of holiness. He was so handsome, so masterful, yet so gracious—so full of sunshine, and apparently so warm. He was so sure too that as his wife she would be fulfilling her true destiny. Every argument was on his side. The idea of a home of her own had always worked strongly in Juley. She loved children, and seemed made to care for them. So she recanted. But she never forgot her dream. And when her babes came, she told herself that surely the beings born of such a marriage would give themselves in due time to the Work from which their mother had turned back. Nay, they would do it far better than she, with her many drawbacks of temperament, could ever have done. So one by one she dedicated them, and prayed for them, and was content to be obliterated from the Book of Life itself, if only her prayers might be answered.

With her husband she had a measure of happiness. To the end she idealized him ; to the end hid her hunger under self-censure. In the intimate chamber of their married life she was never really awakened. Sholto in the early days used to tell her laughing that she compared favourably with other women in her wifely demands, which he declared were for an almost fraternal affection. She believed this, and was flattered by it as he had intended she should be—impressed too by his air of worldly knowledge. But it was not the truth. She wanted utter union with him, and as he could unite with no one, she remained wrapt within herself. When she felt the stirrings of passion in herself she was dimly ashamed, and had to reason that after all this world was peopled by God's own ordinances. Only the yielding up of oneself to mere delight was sinful.

As for Sholto, he too was faintly ashamed of his sensual self, but it was not so strong that he could not keep it fairly easily in hand. The baffling truth about him—known to no one, least of all to himself—was that at the very heart of him there was an emptiness. He was a fine, gracious figure of a man. But at the centre of his being there was a falling away. This—though he gave other reasons, and believed them—was why he shunned intimacies. Sometimes when life pressed hard on him, a look of vague fear would cross his face. But it always passed quickly, and the guarded, sunlit emptiness returned. He subscribed to the Evangelical system, not passionately like his wife, but because it saved him from thought. He had the faith of a little child; he had also the spasmodic terror of a little child that its faith may be misplaced. Indeed he was in twenty ways a child. He liked all games and played them well without taking special pains— he liked laughter too, and could never resist a pun. Being with his children gave him pleasure, and he took them out for long walks of a Saturday afternoon, when they had much ado to keep up with his strong, springing steps. To them it seemed that the earth shook a little under his tread, and they looked up to him as to a god. To women it was his habit to speak banteringly; and they liked it, smiling on after he was gone.

But what Sholto loved best of all was public speaking. Better than games, better than being with his children, better than shooting capercailzie and rabbits at Duntarvie, their house in Perthshire, better than his curbed enjoyment of his wife's virginal freshness, was to him the elevation of a platform. This for him was the unique sensation of existence. He had the gift of winning and holding attention, and he was supremely conscious of the upturned faces of his audience drinking in each word as he made point after point with a shallow, limpid charm. So long as he was speaking to an assembly that secret emptiness of his did not matter.

IV

Juley had wakened, and was rummaging in her stuffed hand-bag for Sholto's letter. To find it, she had to turn everything out upon the seat beside her. There were various purses and pocket-books—part of her complicated system of accounts—also several handkerchiefs, a good pair of gloves to put on when she reached Edinburgh, some tracts—pink and yellow—and the paper bag in which the breakfast roll

had been, now folded and neatly encircled by an elastic band.
Linnet pounced on a piece of toffee he had given to his mother
a week ago.   But he and his brother at once stopped fighting
for the sweet when at length Juley began to read aloud from
the sheets of crackling paper written over in the father's fine,
flourishing hand-writing.

" . . . The blessed work goes on famously here, thank God,"
he wrote.   And his wife raised eyes shining with solemn
hilarity—eyes none of the children cared to meet. ". . . Pray,
Juley, that our little ones may all become workers in His
vineyard—Bannermen and Bannerwomen of that *Better
Country* to the end !   I have had a troublesome *cold* this last
week, but hope to shake it off in a day or two, D.V.   We are
having *severe weather* ; and although in other respects superior
to ours in Glasgow, the Y.M.C.A. Hall here has a *very draughty
platform*.   Tell Georgy-Porgy that Father wears the woollen
comforter she knitted for him, and has found it a *comforter*
indeed.   But it would hardly do to appear in it while addressing a meeting of 2,000 souls, now would it ?   Kiss her and
Joanna and the boys for me, and tell them Father expects
them to look after you in his absence, particularly as to getting
you to your bed in decent time . . ."

"A-ha !   Do you hear that, Mother ? " interrupted Georgie ;
but her mother lifted a forefinger for silence.

"Remember," she continued reading, "that the *Body*,
ordained as the earthly temple in which the *Soul* dwells
during our brief sojourn here, needs reasonable rest and care
until that joyful *Day* of our *Release*.   To die in harness has
always been my prayer, but we have been given certain *Rules
of Health* on the most sacred authority, as also the *Common
Sense* enabling us to observe them.   May God guide you,
my dear wife, in all wisdom, and give you ever more deeply
that Peace which passeth all understanding.

"Your affectionate husband,
"JOHN SHOLTO BANNERMAN."

Before she was quite finished, Juley's voice broke, and she
wiped her eyes with simple ostentation.

"Thank God, children, for such a father as you have ! "
she exclaimed.   Then finding that Sholto had added a postscript to his letter—"Since writing this," she read out, " my
cold has become worse, and seems now to be on my chest

(not chest of drawers, tell Linnet!), but Mrs. Ross here is a kind body and a great *poulticer*, so I expect, D.V., to throw it off shortly."

"If Father died, would we have a cablegram by the line laid by the Great Eastern?" asked Linnet with unusual animation.

"Linnet! How can you!" cried Georgie. Whereupon Linnet subsided. But his imagination had been captured by the idea of the cable, and he had been thinking of it while his mother was reading. Two months ago they had all gone to Liverpool to see their father off, and the children had been taken over the Great Eastern which lay there as a show ship before being broken up. Linnet had been impressed by the story of how the cable had been laid under the sea; and now he half hoped that his father would die, so that he should be able to see with his own eyes what a cablegram looked like. He wondered if it got much nibbled by fishes on its way.

*   *   *   *   *

It was, after all, a united little party that was driven an hour later to Aunt Georgina's imposing front door in Moray Place; the more so because certain humiliation awaited them there. Unpunctuality was a weakness with which Mrs. Balmain had no sympathy; and from their cousin Mabel, who alone had met them at the station, they knew that their telegram had not arrived in time to prevent inconvenience. Mabel with Irene, Aunt Georgina's only daughter, had already started in the carriage to meet the missed express, whereat Irene had been greatly annoyed. She and the carriage were now paying calls, so that the Bannermans must be content with a common cab. Mabel, who was a Bannerman, not a Balmain, and was not an inmate of the Moray Place household, was sympathetic, as always, in a misfortune. But neither Georgie nor Joanna failed to notice the sly grin which their orphaned cousin could never wholly restrain when the family from Glasgow got into trouble with their Edinburgh relations.

v

To the Bannermans from Glasgow the worldly grandeur of their father's eldest sister did not make for comfort. They would far rather have stayed, as Mabel did, with the gentler spinster Aunt Ellen, in her rambling house at Colinton that had been worn shabby by generations of the family. True, even at Aunt Ellen's there was nothing like the freedom of Collessie Street, but at least one did not suffer from constant strain and terror. Mabel was double-faced, but she put on no airs like Cousin Irene, whose recent engagement to a rising young member of Parliament had caused a stir in Edinburgh Society. Mabel was only too glad to be invited to Duntarvie in the holidays and to wear Georgie's outgrown muslins. Though her mother had been a Bannerman, her father had come of less desirable stock. But Aunt Georgina's husband was Lord Westermuir, a judge of the Court of Session ; and her prune-coloured silk gown that rustled, her long, gold ear-rings that dangled, and the profusion of old lace which was displayed on her handsome bosom, all proclaimed that in her the high-water mark of the Bannerman house had been reached.

The same ineffable standard was set by Aunt Georgina's luncheon table, at which on the following day the Glasgow Bannermans took their places. At Moray Place every meal was a ceremony. But luncheon with its decked sideboard, its gloss of perfect damask, its array of polished crystal and crested silver, and its ormolu-handled fruit dishes of apple green and gold, was for the children the supremely disconcerting event of the day. Joanna had always connected its restrained lavishness with a verse of Scripture often quoted by her mother, bidding us to " seek first the Kingdom of God . . ." It was the " all these things " of the latter part of the text, which were to be " added unto " the obedient seeker, that seemed embodied to the carnal eye in Aunt Georgina's table at precisely one o'clock each day. And it was a puzzle to the child, considering her mother's fine enthusiasm for God's kingdom, that the Collessie Street appointments should remain so lacking in elegance.

That morning Juley had taken the four children and Mabel to the opening of the Free Church Assembly. For her it was the treat of the year, and she was so genuinely aglow with it that the children had to share in her elation. Besides, the big ministerial gathering on the Mound was an impressive sight, especially to those who had a traditional part in it, and had not both their grandfathers " come out " at the Disruption of 1843 ? Had not Grandpapa Bannerman been so famous that wherever they visited they saw his engraved portrait hanging in people's entrance halls ?

So the young people had been thrilled as they took their seats in the large, square building, and they had loved standing up when the compact body of black-coated men, ringed about by their womenfolk and children, rose to receive the venerable Moderator. But the climax was reached when the Assembly, without the accompaniment of any instrument, had lifted up its voice in the Old Hundredth. Then Juley, as she sang loudly, had wept with unconcealed joy ; and Georgie and Joanna might also have yielded to the surge of emotion had it not been for the smirking scrutiny of Mabel.

When Juley shed tears because of God's amazing goodness, her face became enraptured ; yet at the same time one knew that she rejoiced in her capacity for rapture. The emotion was valid, but she hoped it would not go unremarked, and in the way she looked about her with wet eyes, there was a hint of reproach for the apathetic world in which her ecstasy found itself singular.

To her daughters the perception of all this was bad enough in public places : when it was shared by Mabel it was torture. Mabel, so pretty, dark and sidelong, (when she walked, she actually seemed to advance sideways) would look lingeringly at her Aunt's face. Then dropping her eyelids she would smile to herself. Soon she would send a liquid glance either way to Georgie and Joanna to make sure that they had observed her amusement. She would know at once by their stony expressions that the shaft of ridicule had gone home.

And now Aunt Georgina had helped them all to soup from a silver tureen. Georgie was sipping hers in what she knew to be the correct way, from the side of the spoon instead of from the tip as she did at home ; and Joanna had nervously raised a glass of water to her lips, when she caught her aunt's eye upon her.

" We don't usually drink water before our soup, Joanna," said Mrs. Balmain quietly. " At least," she added, " I don't know how you do in Glasgow. In Edinburgh it is thought vulgar to drink immediately before food. Besides it is bad for the stomach."

Joanna crimsoned and put down her glass untouched. Neither her mother's kind, grieved glance nor the message of sympathy sent across the table from Georgie's eyes could

salve her wound. Though a murderous hatred of her aunt
rose in her, she unhesitatingly condemned herself. She
had not known any better than to drink water before food,
and now she sat disgraced before them all—particularly before
Cousin Irene, for whom that very morning at breakfast she
had conceived a violent admiration. Oh ! why were she and
her family not in keeping with the elegance around them ?
Why were they not cool and at ease at the luncheon table
as Cousin Irene was ? Joanna and Georgie had long ago
agreed that Cousin Irene was a " softie " and a snob. But
at this moment Joanna with her craving for exquisite-
ness was passionately envious of Irene's endowments. She
felt ashamed, not only of herself but of the others. She looked
across at her mother who was encouraging Sholto to
finish his soup by blowing upon each spoonful ; at Linnet
who lounged back in his chair ; at Georgie who was being so
careful with her tablespoon. And there was Mabel smiling
hatefully, with her eyes on her plate. Joanna reminded herself desperately that the Erskines, on one side at least, were of
a far more distinguished history than either the Bannermans
or the Balmains. But this consideration only added the sting
of unfairness to her present sense of inferiority. And she
suffered.

VI

Three days later came the news of their father's death from
pneumonia.

They were all five sitting in Aunt Georgina's little morning-room, the only room in the house where the children
felt at ease. The boys were on the floor making a paper
fire-balloon ; and Joanna, with the book of directions open in
front of her, was at a table cutting out and glueing together
the more delicate parts for her brothers. They were very
happy and busy amid a litter of tissue paper. But Georgie,
sitting by the window, would insist on discussing the verbal
inspiration of the Bible, a subject mentioned that morning
in the Assembly. And Juley had laid down her *Asias's
Millions*, the better to refute her daughter's argument.

"It says in Genesis, Mother, that Adam and Eve were
the first man and woman ; now, doesn't it ? " demanded
Georgie.

"Yes, dear," Juley admitted, but doubtfully, suspecting a trap.

"Yet," pursued the girl with increasing truculence," when Cain was sent to wander about after killing Abel, he got married and had children. Now who could marry him, if he only had brothers and sisters ? There couldn't even have been cousins ! "

"Besides," put in Joanna as she neatly blew out a section of the balloon on which the glue had dried, " it says that God told people not to kill Cain. What people can these have been ? "

"You must admit it looks a bit fishy, Mother," wound up Georgie.

"Georgie ! " her mother reprimanded her, here on sure ground, "I cannot have such words used of God's Holy Word ! "

"Oh, well ! Anyhow you can't get over the contradiction, can you ? And that's only one of heaps. Now, what I say is . . ."

But no one was ever to hear this important saying of Georgie's, for at that moment Aunt Georgina entered the room. Tight in her hand she carried a slip of greenish paper, and though her grip on herself was equally firm, even little Sholto knew instantly that she was the bearer of grave tidings. At her low-voiced, startlingly kind bidding, the children trooped out by the door she had left open. But before it had shut behind them they caught the magic word —*cable*, and were terrified by the even more unusual expression on their Aunt's lips—*My poor sister !* "

Instinctively the four moved to the end of the passage and huddled close together there, like sheep before the storm breaks. Not a sound came from the little morning-room. Linnet durst not ask his sisters the questions about the cable that trembled on his lips.

It was thus that their Aunt found them when she came out again, softly closing the door after her as if upon a sick-room. On her proud face was a look none of them knew— a look of stricken passion that altered her and frightened them. Sholto had been among the few beings his sister had ever loved, and when they were boy and girl together she had been madly proud of him.

She laid her hand now on her young namesake's shoulder.

"My poor children," she said. "You will have to be very brave for your mother's sake."

Georgie was the only one to speak. The others seemed petrified. "It's not anything wrong with Father?" she questioned. And on a rising key at her Aunt's low reply, she cried out—

"No, no! . . . I won't have it . . . I can't bear it . . . I tell you it isn't true! Father, Father! Let me go. Don't touch me!"

There was horror for Joanna in the noise Georgie was making. Georgie's voice sounded all over the house, while Aunt Georgina was so quiet. And how quiet it was in there where Mother was! With a quick movement the child broke from the others to run to her mother. But Aunt Georgina caught her by the arm, still gripping Georgie also.

"Control yourself, Georgie, and think of your mother," she commanded with grievous severity; and her fingers felt like iron on the young flesh. "Remember you are the eldest. Think of how your father would wish you to behave."

"I'll try, I'll try!" sobbed Georgie. "Don't speak to me." And presently their Aunt left them, telling them they might go to their mother.

In the morning-room they found Juley strangely uplifted. And when each had clung to her in turn, she addressed them starry-eyed and lyrical.

"My beloved children," she said quietly, "it has pleased Our Heavenly Father to lay His hand upon us all, and to try our faith, whether it be faith indeed. He has taken your earthly Father to Himself. We can only pray for strength, and look for our refuge in Him. For He is our Refuge and our Strength in time of trouble. Let us pray to Him now, together, that I, my darlings, may be given the strength to be to you father and mother both, until it pleases Him in His great mercy to take me also to Himself. Let us pray to the Father of the fatherless."

Upon this the tears gushed from her eyes; and she would have knelt down with them at the sofa. But Georgie refused.

"I *won't* pray to your God!" she cried out at the pitch of her voice. "If it pleases Him for Father to die, like this, away from us all, I don't love Him. I hate your God! *My* God is quite different. I'll go and pray to *my* God. He'll

know that you can't ever make up to me for Father.   Oh !
I can't bear it ! "   And she rushed from the room.

"Poor Georgie ! " said Juley. "God the Maker of our
hearts speaks to us all in different ways." And with the
remaining children she poured herself forth in prayer.

When at length she had left the boys in Joanna's charge,
none of them spoke for a few moments.   Then in the gaping
chasm of silence Linnet moved diffidently to where his interrupted work still lay on the carpet, and he picked up a streamer
of blue paper.

"I suppose we may as well finish making our fire-balloon,
Sholto," he remarked.

Now the tears sprang to Joanna's eyes and rolled down her
cheeks. It was not that she felt any real, personal loss.
But something in her little brothers' aspect made her see them
suddenly as fatherless.

"Oh, Linnet ! " she exclaimed, striving for a degree of
realization. "Think ! We'll never hear Father blow his
nose again like a trumpet in the lobby when he comes home
at night."

"And he'll never be Lord Provost now, either," appended
Sholto morosely, "with the two lamp-posts in front of our
door."

Linnet nodded, seeing the tragedy in this. And in deference to it, he kept to himself his bitter disappointment about
the look of the cable.

VII

But it was Georgie who was wakened in the small hours
of the morning, and taken to her mother's bedside to play the
daughter's part there. They had had to send for the doctor
at midnight ; and Aunt Georgina had not been able to lie
down, nor even to take off her dress. She was grim with
weariness and sorrow.

Henceforward Georgie wore a look of satisfied importance,
as of one who has been momentously confided in. But it was
some days before Joanna could get her to share the secret.

"You must promise faithfully not to tell Mabel," Georgie
stipulated, giving way at last.

Joanna promised faithfully.

"Well then," said Georgie, lowering her voice to a searching
whisper, "we were going to have had a baby ; but now it's

not coming, because of Father. And that's why Mother is ill in bed and seeing the doctor. She only said it was a *Disappointment*. It was Aunt Georgina told me the rest. She said at fifteen I was old enough to know. All the same, remember you have promised not to tell Mabel."

Joanna, gratifyingly awestruck, gazed at her sister. The collective "we" in Georgie's mouth impressed her strongly. Had she sought in her mind there were a thousand questions to be asked. But at twelve one is still used to accepting mysteries without challenge.

And so this strange new loss which was in some indiscoverable way connected with her father's death in America, was stored in the dark lumber-room of the child's mind.

CHAPTER II

I

A S soon as Juley was well enough she returned home with
the children to Glasgow. And there, when they were
got past the first excitement of condolences, it looked as if
things would continue much as they had been in Sholto's
life-time. Every one said that the widow bore up wonderfully, that she was an example of Christian fortitude.

Sholto's affairs were in good order though people were
surprised at the smallness of his estate, and business acquaintances shook their heads a little, murmuring the word " speculations." But Juley herself made no complaint. She was
indeed relieved at having to give up her husband's cherished
project of moving to a grander house in a more fashionable
neighbourhood.

Collessie Street, at the top of its precipitous, roughly
cobbled hill, had at one time been a residential quarter of
distinction. But in 1896, the roomy, solid, black houses—
deep-bitten by the carbonic deposits of half a century—
with their square-pillared porticoes, and their stone areas
guarded by rusty spear-head railings, had a forsaken look.
Their domestic curtains were more and more giving place to
the ground-glass and perforated metal screens of institutions ;
and where once a famous surgeon had brought up his family,
there was now a dingy training-home for fallen girls. The
place, however, was not without dignity. And to Juley and
her children, the ugly, well-built house at the corner felt like
a part of themselves. They all hated the idea of leaving it,
even for the excitement of a West-End mansion.

From the big day-nursery windows on the top story which
commanded wide, grey views to the south and west, the girls
could remember watching the distant ascent of their first
fireworks—rockets soaring in honour of Glasgow's earliest
Exhibition. From the same windows they had seen with

26

rapture the first lighting of the city by electricity. And three times they had hung out great flags over the sills for Royal Processions. Once Georgie was quite certain that Queen Victoria driving up Sauchiehall Street, had waved her hand in special acknowledgment to their high window.

Within the house, as one entered, the first thing to meet the eye was a richly illuminated scroll bearing the words—

AS FOR ME AND MY HOUSE, WE SHALL SERVE THE LORD.

It had been Sholto's first act on returning from his wedding-trip, to hang this text. And Juley often looked at it now, remembering vividly how her bridegroom had stood on a chair to nail it in its trumpery frame full between the marbled pillars of the lobby so that nobody could miss it. He had laughed and had kissed her afterwards. And the sight of it in these, the early days of her widowhood, always filled her with resolution.

But as time went on it began to be evident that Sholto's widow and his children were variously disposing themselves to serve the Lord in ways which Sholto himself would have dealt with summarily had he been alive. More and more Juley's resolution when she looked at the house-text became linked with a stricken conscience : more and more she saw that to play the double part of father and mother was not going to be so easy as at first she had imagined.

"I wonder," said Joanna tentatively one night as she and Georgie were getting into bed—"I wonder what Father would say if he knew you missed out 'for Jesus' sake' in your prayers now ? "

But Georgie was ready for such questions.

"Father isn't the same now as he was," she told her sister. "He understands everything now, and knows just what I feel about God and all that."

II

It was at this time, within a year of her father's death that Joanna had a dream about him.

She was sleeping that night with her mother (in spite of many disadvantages it was still regarded as a treat among them to sleep with Mother) and had wakened suddenly at three in the morning with a familiar pang of misery at finding no bedfellow. Juley had not even got so far as to fall asleep at her prayers by the bedside. So Joanna arose, and shivering with fury and cold went barefoot down to the parlour. There, as she expected, she found her mother seated before her untidy roll-top desk with her head fallen on her papers. She had dropped asleep over a letter in the middle of an erasure, and she wore the old squirrel-lined cape in which she always ran out to catch the midnight " lifting " at the corner pillar.

When at last they were both upstairs, Joanna climbed back into bed, and, having exhausted herself in bitter reproach, lay wide awake and silent while her mother undressed. No matter how tired she felt, Juley was meticulous over her toilet. Always she had to dip her brush in the ewer so as to dampen the front part of her hair before plaiting it separately from the rest. Her creamy neck, covered at other times, and her raised, unconscious arms, so astonishingly soft and youthful, gave the watching child a deep thrill of pleasure. Soon the thin, sleek plait was ready to be tossed back, and Juley turned out the gas. Then did Joanna creep immediately into her mother's arms, and in that warm, lovely encircling, her thin little body was flooded with well-being.

When they were both asleep, Joanna dreamed that a visitor was standing on the outside doorstep, ringing and ringing at the bell for admittance ; but that she alone of all the house heard the summons. Going downstairs in her dream to open the door, she peeped first through the ground glass which formed its upper panel. Engraved on the glass was the head of a man with a curly beard, long believed by the children, for some inexplicable reason, to be a portrait of Satan ; and by putting an eye level with Satan's eye they were accustomed to spy through upon visitors. Joanna did this in her dream, and saw what froze her with horror. It was her father that stood without. He was unmistakable, though in some indefinable way horribly altered, and his presence filled her with repulsion. Father was dead. They had had a cable to say so, had mourned him, and he had no right to come back in this way. In terror, but under a kind of constraint, she opened the door one small inch. And that dreadful stranger who was yet her father tried to push his way into the house. But now hatred overcame every other feeling and, shutting the door with all her might, Joanna fled upstairs. As she went, all her determination was never to let the others know who had called.

On waking, which she did immediately afterwards, the child was first conscious of immense relief that no such return need in reality be feared. "For," said she to herself in that conscienceless moment, "we can do as we please now he is gone." But with complete awakening, all and more than all the repulsion of her dream turned upon herself. How could she have acted so wickedly in sleep, thought so unkindly on waking? She lay listening to her mother's quiet breathing, picturing her mother's eyes and Georgie's, could they have seen into her unloving mind. And for days afterwards, until she had done penance, her heart was heavy.

III

The opportunity for penance came in this way.

On the road to school, Georgie and Joanna had to pass a wind-swept corner where a disfigured woman sat all day on a camp stool. Slung from her neck was a stout piece of cardboard on which the words KIND FRIENDS I AM BLIND had been scrawled. And sometimes—though their father had always condemned what he called "unorganized," "indiscriminate," or "spurious" charity, particularly in any case so clearly marked as this one was for the Blind Asylum of which he was a director—one of the girls would slip a penny into the beggar's hand. Once Georgie had spoken to her, asking if she had any children at home, and Joanna had been smitten by the toneless negative of the reply. "Do you think anybody ever kisses her?" she asked her sister after they had walked on some way in silence.

"I don't expect so," had been Georgie's answer. And as an afterthought—"She wouldn't be very nice to kiss, would she?"

It could not be denied. Even while Joanna was feeling obscurely something of that strangest envy of the human soul—the envy of utter misfortune—she shuddered at the thought of touching the afflicted face with her lips. Yet she was sure she ought to. The unkissed woman with the terribly prominent, closed eyelids persisted in her imagination. Night after night, when the figure of sorrowful censure visited her bedside, she said to herself—"To-morrow I will do it. To-morrow I will make myself kiss her!" But day after day, passing to and from school, she had shrunk from the deed which the night before had seemed so possible and right. And gradually she was becoming used to the denial.

Under the fresh reproach of her dream, however, Joanna conceived of this kiss, so long withheld, as the appointed expiation. At nights she had anguished moments in which her father on one hand and the blind woman on the other levelled at her an accusation the less tolerable for being unspoken.

And on the following Sunday she was finally urged to the act. A strange minister was preaching in their church. He spoke with kindling eloquence about the woman who was healed by touching Jesus in the crowd; so that suddenly Joanna, strung to an ecstasy, took her resolve. It would be more correct to say that there flashed in her in that moment the absolute knowledge that she would accomplish the deed next day.

On Monday she and Georgie passed the woman as usual. Georgie, who was holding forth on the iniquities of her form mistress, did not even glance towards the camp-stool. Nor did she look round, when, a few yards further on, Joanna murmured something unintelligible and ran back.

Now that the first step was taken, only desperation held her to her task. Her breath went from her, her lips felt parched, and as she stooped to the sightless head a clang of bells sounded in her ears. For a moment she lost all consciousness of her surroundings.

On feeling the nearness of another human being, the poor creature on the stool instinctively held up her little tin mug; and as Joanna drew back after giving the kiss, she saw this gesture. There had been no other response. The face was vacant and unlovely as ever.

Joanna felt deeply ashamed. In her self-centred anxiety about the kiss she had forgotten to bring a penny.

"I'll bring you one to-morrow," she assured the beggar hastily. Then turning away she sped after Georgie.

"Were you giving her a penny?" Georgie asked but without interest.

"No."

"What were you doing then?"

"Nothing, fastening my shoe-lace. Go on with what you were saying about Miss Dunbar."

IV

All her childhood Joanna had been a fugitive from the realities immediately surrounding her town existence, and her intenser life was lived in her flights. She had many avenues of escape ; but of these the best was provided by her passion for the country.

And for her " The Country " and every one of its joys was summed up in the single word Duntarvie.

The children owed Duntarvie—which was a real place as well as Joanna's home of dreams—to their mother. For Juley, if she yearned principally after her children's souls, cared shrewdly too for their bodies. She would not allow them to have dancing lessons, but she believed in young legs running wild. Above all she insisted that a free country life for at least four months out of the twelve, was necessary to counteract the early delicacy of Linnet and Joanna. The old farm-house in East Perthshire had once belonged to the Erskines, though it had passed half-a-century ago into the hands of strangers. But when Joanna was five Juley learned that it was to be let, and she gave Sholto no peace till he had taken a lease of the place.

To the children there was music in the very name of the village from which Duntarvie was three miles distant uphill. And the square white-washed house—with its red-tiled steading (a paradise for climbers), its ponds, its ruined saw-mill, its haphazard garden full of gooseberries, currants and wizened tea-roses,—became a far dearer home than the one in town.

Their last summer at Duntarvie was that before Sholto's death. For some reason there could be no renewal of the lease. Loud were the expressions of sorrow in the household, and Juley, in spite of the enormous addition the place made to her domestic cares, was as sad as the children.

As for Joanna, her love for the place as the end of the time drew near increased to an agony, and more and more she withdrew her voice from the chorus of regret. Instead, when she could, she would leave the others, and run up and up the moor in front of the house, not once pausing till she reached a secret lair of her own finding—a dry, pale, golden

bed among the high heather, close by the little firwood boundary with its rotting silvery fence, and there flinging herself
on the ground she would bury her face in the sunwarmed
moss and draw deep breaths of the earth.

Among these embraces lavished by the child on the earth,
embraces more fervent than any she had given as yet to a
human being, there was one that stood out for ever from the
others.

One September morning during the last week of their stay
she had slipped out a while before breakfast, taking her way
through the fringe of beeches which ran up behind the house
between steeply sloping fields till it enringed the upper pond.
The lower pond, near the outhouses and the swing, was a
homely puddle nozzled in by ducks and navigated by a raft
made from the doors of an old shed with Joanna's stilts as
oars. But the upper pond, besides being twice the size of
its neighbour, was a mysterious water. It was fed by a
natural spring ; and a legend of the neighbourhood told of a
golden cradle in its depths containing the body of a King's
babe immune from mortal decay. It was rush-bound, betraying its treacherous surface in glints only, and wild fowl
of many kinds made it their habitation. Foxes in the moonlight slunk to its edge to drink ; and on an islet in the middle
season after season a pair of herons reared their young.

To this haunted pool, with its girdle of beech trees, on
which Joanna knew every foothold and every untrustworthy
branch, she stole that morning. Lying concealed among
the drenched reeds of the margin, she waited until the
disturbed coots and waterhens went reassured about their
interminable business. For what seemed an age she stayed
motionless, listening intently to each tiny splashing and div-
ing, to the whisperings among the bearded rushes, to the
sudden plump of the frogs, to the chuckling of the water-
fowl under the banks.

At that moment the twelve-year-old child entered deeply
into Nature's heart, and for the first time it came to her that
she might make of her rapture a place of retreat for future
days. It was a discovery. Henceforth she felt that nothing,
no one, would have power to harm her. For all her life
now she would have within herself this hidden refuge. Even
if she were to be burned at the stake, or flayed alive like the
people in Foxe's *Book of Martyrs*, she would be able to fly in

spirit from her torturers to this reedy water ; and they would wonder why she smiled amid the flames.

So she lay on till she was bodiless ; and only the cold, penetrating through her clothes to her skin, reminded her. She moved, and only in moving realized that she was wet through, and cramped. Her stirring startled the old heron. He rose noisily, first trailing his feet a little way along the surface of the tarn, then made away westwards till he became a far speck over the hollow where the nearest farm lay.

Stretching herself and shaking the water from her hair, Joanna felt glad at the thought of breakfast. It was good that the others were waiting at home, sitting at a table spread with the floury baps that came each morning fresh-baked from the village ; and coffee, and bramble jam, and fresh butter, which she loved to greediness, from their own cow's cream. But before turning homeward between the beech trunks, she stooped once more to the ground, and leaning on her two palms kissed the moist grass till the taste of the earth was on her lips. "If I forget thee, O Duntarvie," she whispered, "let my right hand forget its cunning." (She was not clear about the meaning of this phrase ; but she loved working with her hands, and the words expressed her emotion better than any other words she knew.) Then she picked up some odds and ends—a small lichen-covered twig, a skeleton leaf, and the untimely fallen samara of a sycamore—to keep as remembrancers of her vow, and racing back to the house she arrived in a glow, bright-cheeked, her short skirts dripping from the brackens.

v

Mingled with these raptures were the early stirrings of Joanna's womanhood, and at seven she had fallen deeply in love with her cousin Gerald Bird, who was then twenty-five.

Gerald, only son of Aunt Perdy, was a soldier, and he was recovering from fever caught in India when Juley invited him to Duntarvie. She was sure that he would quickly get strong in that wonderful air. And strong he did get in spite of his aunt's perseverance in probing him for what she called "the root of the matter" ; in spite also of his having left his susceptible heart in the keeping of a blue-eyed jilt in Calcutta.

He travelled with the Bannermans from Glasgow, and on the little local line which ran from Perth to their village, the compartment was so crowded with people returning from a cattle-show that he took Joanna on his knee. Gerald was far from being aware of the bliss his careless contact gave to the small girl. But so it was. For the last forty-eight hours Joanna had been his passionate slave. Now the loved one held her in his arms, and that she might stay there as long as possible she pretended to fall asleep, leaning her cheek against the rough coat he wore. Ever afterwards the smell and texture of Harris tweed recalled the delirium of that journey in the embrace of a god.

To Joanna cousin Gerald was indeed a god. He transgressed against all her standards. He even shot chaffinches and robins with his revolver and afterwards skinned them. Yet she asked for nothing better than to stand watching while the plumage was slit down the breasts and slipped deftly from the piteous little bodies of Gerald's victims. The young man's lean wrists and his long fingers, so dark and merciless, thrilled the child to the soul. Secretly she imagined herself a little fluttering bird in their cruel yet skilful grasp ; and she felt she would gladly have let them crush the life out of her for their own inscrutable ends.

Actually one wet afternoon it had looked to her as if her fantastic wish might come true. She and Gerald were in the coachhouse, where the stanhope and dogcart were kept among a litter of odds and ends—gardening tools, empty flower-pots, wheelbarrows, and rolls of wire netting for the chicken runs which Sholto was always making—and for perhaps half-an-hour she had been watching in rapt silence while a pearly-breasted chaffinch was stuffed and sewed up. But, suddenly tired of his finicking task, Gerald threw down his work and stretched his arms above his head with a groan. He was sitting on the worn bench by the door, with his back to the dripping eaves, and presently to amuse himself he drew Joanna between his knees. Smiling, he pointed his penknife that was still blood-stained against the child's breast, almost cutting through the wool of her faded, tightly stretched jersey, and he threatened to skin her like a little wild bird. To his surprise—for he expected her to wriggle or protest— Joanna stood dumb and quite still and strange in his grip. So he soon stopped teasing her. But he had provided her with a theme which she afterwards embroidered out of all recognition in many an erotic rhapsody.

Joanna admired everything about her cousin. She idolized his brown face and bright grey piercing gaze, vibrated at the sight of his hands, and at any time, night or day, could see with her mind's eye the wave with which his hair crossed his brow. She had tried hard to make her own hair lie like his ; but where the line of growth began round her forehead there was what Georgie called her " baby fringe," and this crop of short new hairs, fairer than the rest, would do nothing but curve downwards in obstinate, fine half-hoops of gold.

There was, however, one secret about Gerald which terrified while it fascinated her.

It happened one afternoon that, climbing about the old sawmill, he slipped and hurt his foot. Some stones in the crumbling walls had given way, and when he picked himself up he limped with a screwed-up face to the burn that flowed from under the ruin. Joanna was there in the boggy field picking marsh-mallows and some reeds to make a rattle, and Gerald sat down on the bank near her. Already his foot was beginning to swell, and he wanted to dip it in the water. Joanna stood beside him clutching her heavy-headed yellow flowers, and the beards and sharp points of the reeds tickled her chin. She watched the young man take off his shoe with a grimace, and peel the sock from the bruised ankle. And as he rolled back the grey flannel of his trousers half-way to the knee she saw with a pang of delicious horror that his leg was hairy. From the ankle upwards it was covered with black silky hairs that clung to the gleaming skin.

The child's first thought, that her cousin was the victim of some terrible blemish, passed almost at once. There could be no mistaking his unassumed indifference. So in a moment she knew she must accept this strange thing as normal. Men—grown-up young men—were like this. Later on she often visualized those amazing ankles guiltily. But she would not for the world have spoken of her discovery, not even to Georgie.

VI

Yet another incident which made its mark on the still folded woman in Joanna, belonged to this time at Duntarvie. And like the ecstasy by the upper pond it happened during

the Bannermans' last summer there, when the girl was entering her teens.

She and the others—with Mabel, who always spent July
with them—had been making blaeberry wine down in front
of the house by that same burn which farther on flowed
beneath the saw-mill. It was late afternoon on one of these
endless midsummer days of childhood in the North when the
sun puts off its setting till long, long after bed-time. The
children had been up on the moor for hours past with mugs and
baskets, picking the new-ripened fruit which grows so fragrant
and near the ground, its leaves showing dapper among the
heather. Their faces and hands, their bare legs and under-
clothes, were stained with purple. They had eaten their
fill, and had rolled afterwards on the green, richly-decked
table of the moor. And now using their handkerchiefs as
strainers, they were crushing the gathered berries till the dark
juice ran through into jars beneath. Three times a sounding
call had come from the house, and at last Georgie and Mabel
lingeringly climbed the bank towards the road, dragging the
small boys with them.

"Come on to supper, Joanna," they cried over their shoulders
in their young high voices, as they came to the rickety one-
legged gate of the garden. But Joanna, though she cried
in return that she was "just coming," made no movement
to follow them.

Instead she began to trail her dyed handkerchief in the
water, startling the little shadowy trout that were so hard
to catch ; and every now and then she tossed back the long
loosened strands of her hair, the better to see her own reflec-
tion in the brown mirror of the stream. Dreamily, she wished
she were as pretty as the little girl in the water.

But a shadow passed, blurring the magic, and Joanna
looked up quickly to see Alec Peddie standing on the opposite
bank. Alec, the lad from the nearest farm, was a handsome
rascal of fifteen, supple as an Indian and almost as brown,
with a skin as soft as the corduroy of his breeches. He often
came across the hill to help with odd jobs at Duntarvie, and
in a sense was the children's playmate. He was great at
birdnesting, at draining ponds and damming streams. And
in the Easter orgies of whin-burning he was the acknowledged leader. Himself in the grip of a curious still excitement, he would dare the others to jump after him over bigger

and bigger bonfires; and Joanna especially would fly in a frenzy at his bidding over the great crackling bushes, her eyes tight shut, her hair full of sparks and her clothes singeing amid the smoke. Afterwards, when the flames had died down, they would all rush about stamping on the embers, kicking up fiery spouts with their scorched shoes, and screaming like curlews in a gale. Only when the fires were quite out and black, would a certain estrangement in their relations with Alec reassert itself, and this would remain more or less until Easter came round again. He was useful to them, and in a way they loved him, but they did not trust him.

As he stood now looking across at Joanna with careless, glinting eyes that were the colour of the water below, Alec showed his white teeth in an impudent grin.

"Hullo, Alec!" said the girl shyly.

In reply the boy jumped over to her side, and immediately helped himself royally to her blaeberry wine. Then unasked he plunged his fingers into one of the baskets and empurpled his mouth widely with a great handful of fruit. "You look awful bonny, Jo!" he said thoughtfully with steady eyes on her, and again he crushed a mouthful of berries against his palate.

It was the first time Joanna had ever been called pretty to her face. She was moved, and did not know what to say.

"So do you!" she countered, bashfully; and at this Alec burst into a ringing appreciative laugh.

After that there was a silence between them, and Joanna gathered her things together and stood up. But the boy put out his hand hastily and touched her wet arm. He was looking at her oddly when she glanced into his eyes.

"If ye'll come up yonder on the moor wi' me, Joanna," he said, rather fearful but with a word of cajolery in his rich voice, "I'll show ye what lads is for."

A minute later she entered the house, while Alec unabashed by her shy denial went whistling and cutting solitary capers across the darkening moor. But the thrill of the boy's touch remained with the girl, and the shameless young pagan look he had given her took its place also in her dreams.

CHAPTER III

I

FOR in town Joanna led almost wholly a dream-life. The indoor existence, the hard streets which she hated though they made a good playground, the petty boredom of school, and the growing disharmony at home, all drove her in upon herself. In two respects only was the child's being vivid—in the activity of her body, and in her dreams.

At twelve she was the reckless rider—a menace to foot-passengers—of a maimed tricycle horse which had once been dappled, and fiery of nostril. And when nursery shows were got up, with Sholto as "Handy-Andy," and Linnet as the performer of transparent conjuring tricks, Joanna, dressed in tights suspiciously recalling woven underwear, always performed upon the trapeze.

But what satisfied her most deeply was climbing. Climbing involved a mental and physical equilibrium which was a delight. She welcomed the cool excitement that possessed her in dangerous places, up high trees and on the windy edges of roofs. She learned to walk steadily, balancing with her arms along the top of a narrow paling, and knew how to trust only half her weight to a weak foothold, passing in a swift, predetermined rhythm to one more secure. At such moments she was the queen of her own body, and not of her body alone, but of a whole system of laws she could not even begin to formulate.

Joanna, however, was afraid of jumping. She always felt terrified of a jump beforehand; and afterwards, practise as she might, it jarred her painfully. Often when her companions had leapt unhesitatingly one after another from the rather high back garden wall at Collessie Street into the stony lane beyond, she had to stay behind for long minutes. To have sat on the wall and scrambled down with a twist would have been easy enough. But this the child would not do.

And she always jumped in the end, though no one looked on and she was sick with fear. Once indeed of her own accord she set herself a jump that was mere foolhardiness. There was a legend in the nursery that cousin Gerald had jumped from the parlour window across the area at the back of the house—a considerable feat even for a young man—and the time came when Joanna got it into her head that she must do it too. It was weeks before she could bring herself to the point, and often she would stand by the window looking at the forbidding stone drop, some six feet wide and twelve deep, which separated the house from the sloping green below Then one day, in the middle of the Latin lesson at school—a lesson through which Joanna habitually dreamed—it came to her that she would do it that evening.

When she got home she went straight to the parlour. It was empty ; and she opened the window and quaking climbed out upon the sill. Suppose she managed the jump, but did not land high enough on the slope ? That would mean over-balancing into the awful area, and suppose she slipped on leaving the sill ? Her palms, wet with fear, clove to the pane behind her. She had a prickling agony all over the front of her body. She was lost if she jumped. Yet she knew she would have no peace till she did. She shut her eyes, opened them again, leaned back for impetus. " If I'm killed it can't be helped ! " was the thought that flashed through her mind like a solution. Why had she not thought of that before ? And springing with all her strength she landed on her hands and knees well up on the grass.

It had been easy as easy, she told herself when she picked herself up. But she was shaking all over as she went up the dark kitchen stair. And she never attempted it again.

II

As a dreamer, the child was of that sort whose imaginings are never without some touch of the practical, and the material and the ideal often went curiously linked. One night, not long after her thirteenth birthday, just as she was dropping off to sleep, an idea flashed in her mind and it so worked upon her that she lay awake for hours. Perhaps it had been suggested to her by the description of the Tabernacle which her mother had been reading at evening prayers.

Anyhow her notion was herself to build a temple, using as
her materials, candles and a wooden box. She thought of
the vistas of pillars this temple would have—beautiful white
pillars, more beautiful than the alabaster ones in the City
Chambers—rising out of a floor of wax which was to be scored
and scored across while still soft to make it like a marble
pavement. Tossing from side to side on her bed, she wondered
whether the pillars should be left plain, or fluted by an excori-
ating finger nail. As the possibilities of her design grew upon
her she became more and more wakeful, with a touch of fever.
She would have, she determined, a tiny Ark of the Covenant
made from a wax-coated match-box, and at either end, guarding it, she would put the two little stucco angels Aunt Perdy
had brought her from Italy. She would gild them ; and a
vision floated before her of kneeling cherubim gleaming between
aisles of flawless marble—all the work of her own hands !

Next morning was a Saturday, and Joanna, hardly able
to bear her excitement, ran with her weekly sixpence down
the hill to the grocer. Though he gave her the cheapest
candles to be had, there were only twelve in the packet,
and they looked disappointingly unlike marble. On the
other hand they were longer than she had expected. And
forgetting for the moment the considerable size of Aunt
Perdy's angels, Joanna thought she might reduce the scale
of the Temple by making two pillars out of each candle.

When she got back to the house breathless, her mother
opened the door to her and could not help noticing her bright
countenance. Questioned, the child poured forth an incoherent tale about match-boxes, marble pillars and angels.
Juley did not attempt to follow it. She only comprehended
an unusual excitement, and she noticed with a pang that at
such moments her daughter bore a strong likeness to poor
Aunt Perdy.

"Would that I could see my dear child as much concerned
about spiritual things ! " she lamented with a grieved shake
of her head.

When Joanna set to work upstairs with more doggedness
now than enthusiasm, the result was a conflagration which
left a large hole in the nursery carpet. Then and there the
remaining candles were confiscated for household use. But
Juley, always scrupulous in money matters, gave the Temple-
builder as many pence as they had cost.

III

Even during Sholto's life-time there had hung over Juley's dressing-table a rival text to the one in the lobby. No richly illuminated scroll, this, but a simple square of glossy, maroon-coloured cardboard, silver-edged, and showing up in silver letters the words—

TO THE JEW FIRST.

The importance of the Jews had been a subject on which Juley and her husband had differed, sometimes painfully. Juley, try as she might—and she never gave up trying— had not been able to convince Sholto that God's promises in the Prophets had been particularly to His Chosen People. The curses, Sholto would admit, must apply to Israel; but everything else he appropriated to himself and those like-minded with him. Nor would he admit his illogicality in the matter. It was without his approval therefore that his wife had gone regularly to a seedy and unpopular Jewish mission on the South Side of the river.

Juley's belief was that the scattered nation had been ordained to preach the Gospel in all parts of the world, thus hastening the return of Christ. She could not help regarding the most unattractive Hebrew as a second, or at least as a third cousin of her Saviour. And the lustrous-eyed men in greasy clothes who had cringed before Sholto, expanded— sometimes alarmingly—in the sunshine of his widow's frank sympathy. More and more often they were to be seen at her table.

As for Sholto's attitude with regard to the Second Advent, Juley had found it still more puzzling. As an evangelical, he had perforce held theoretically correct views on the subject. But Juley had only to mention what to her was the most joyous topic of the Gospels to realize that he considered the actual prospect highly inconvenient.

In this as in the Jewish question Sholto had had the discreet backing of his minister Dr. Ranken, and Juley had come away worsted more than once from visiting her pastor with a request that he would lend his pulpit to one of her Hebrew *protégés*. But Sholto had been dead over a year before the idea of leaving St. Jude's occurred seriously to her.

It was a bold idea, for till then the Bannermans' church

had been as much a part of themselves as their house.   Indeed it was more deeply connected than the house with their family tradition.   Their grandfather had made it famous among Glasgow churches, and in the eyes of many among the congregation their father, as a prominent elder, had been a more important figure there than Dr. Ranken, the minister, who had begun his career merely as the great Dr. Bannerman's assistant.

From the gallery, whither they were banished four times a year on Communion Sundays, the children used to lean forward with awe in their hearts, and in their throats a choking sense of their father's dignity.   Sholto always led the other elders in their solemn progress through the napkin-decked body of the church to the choir rails.   And there, after the grave order of the Scottish service, they partook of the broken bread from Dr. Ranken's thin hands before they dispensed it, pew by pew, to the waiting congregation.

The children of course had all been baptized at these same choir rails.   They were known individually to each member, and every detail of the building was as familiar to them as the interior of their nursery.   How well Joanna knew the pattern of the coloured, diamond-shaped panes in the high rectangular windows : there were two yellow diamonds, then a blue, then two more yellow, and a red square at each corner.   Then there was the dark, highly varnished pulpit with its canopy of mahogany spires.   Often she had half hoped, half feared that the great bristling lid would fall by its own weight on Dr. Ranken, extinguishing him in the middle of his sermon like a jack-in-the-box.   Yet it remained poised ; and certainly its intricacies provided a maze in which a child's imagination could run riot.   It was one of Joanna's fantasies to picture herself and her cousin Gerald (conveniently reduced to scale) playing a madly amorous, yet innocent game of hide-and-seek amid the wilds of this Gothic forest.

But a period of changes had come in which Sholto was prime mover, and the canopy had been done away with.   At the same time offertory bags were substituted for the plates at the door, a paid quartette was added to the choir, the congregation was requested (with very partial success) to join in the Lord's Prayer, and the whole church was upholstered in blue-grey repp, instead of in crimson as formerly.

Sholto had always advocated what he called "a bright

service." "The only way to keep a hold on our young people ! " he would say breezily in the face of conservatism. Certainly, at the time of his death the decoration of St. Jude's vied with its service in sprightliness. With its white and pale blue paint, its gilding, and its palm trees in niches, it resembled a Casino rather than a church. And the paid vocalists never for one moment allowed it to be forgotten that they were paid. A stranger could have picked them out as they stood shoulder to shoulder in the van of the choir—the contralto as manful and almost as moustachioed as the bass—singing the praises of God right into the faces of those who were fortunate enough to occupy the front pews.

The only thing not in keeping with this airy spirit of renovation was the minister himself. Dr. Ranken was bleak-faced, with hard-bitten features, and a smouldering misery in his deep-set eyes. And he so constantly sought his text in the Pauline Epistles that the children came to fancy him a reincarnation of the Apostle. Georgie in particular conceived a violent dislike toward St. Paul in the person of Dr. Ranken, and within six months of her father's death she began to wander from St. Jude's on Sunday evenings. As Juley herself paid tentative visits to other places of worship in her search for some richer milk of the Word, she could not well forbid her daughter, but when Georgie began to attend openly the church of Mr. Nares—a Congregational pulpiteer and strenuous moralist from England who was reputed little better than a Unitarian—things were serious. Since Dr. Ranken had refused Juley's request that he would preach at least once a year on the Millennium, she had not felt able to call upon him for his pastoral advice. She longed to consult him about Georgie, but she could not forget the manner of his refusal, nor the way he had looked at her, making her feel herself peculiar. What was to be done ?

After much prayer Juley summoned all her courage, and once more visited her minister. She entered the dark study feeling painfully shy and forsaken, and when Dr. Ranken rose in his unsmiling way to shake her by the hand and bid her be seated she was smitten by a keen consciousness of widowhood. The truth was that shyness was his own affliction. Juley could have knelt before him, covering his hands with her tears, begging his counsel in her many difficulties, pouring out her heart to him. But his own forbidding reticence made of any such action a ludicrous impossibility ; so she sat down in silence, praying within herself desperately that she might be given the strength to see her task through. She must try to put her case without exposing the needs of her soul in any way that he would shrink from as undignified.

So, restraining herself and in an agony of faltering, she told him that unless he could give her and her children greater spiritual nourishment, she had prayerfully decided to leave St. Jude's. His forbearance when she had said her say brought her nearer to breaking down than ever. No one knew better than she what it meant to Dr. Ranken to lose the Bannerman family in this way, yet he uttered no reproach. He merely said she must do as she felt best, advised her to send Georgie to a boarding-school, and expressed a hope that at least his family and hers would remain on friendly terms. Bob, his fifteen-year-old son, was a constant visitor at Collessie Street ; and it would be a pity, the minister said with a wintry gleam of humour crossing his face, that the children should cease to enjoy each other's society because Mrs. Bannerman could not conscientiously enjoy his sermons !

So yellow-haired Bob Ranken came about the house as much as before, and for a time he struck up quite a friendship with Joanna. But Juley became subject to fits of depression which no wrestlings of the spirit seemed to avert or allay. Indeed the attacks grew denser in quality and longer in duration till her old conviction of sin in marrying became almost abiding. Her children suffered seeing their mother's increasing difficulties in the routine of life, but as yet they did not guess at the depths of her dejection nor at her heroism. Scrupulously she went on with her duties. But sometimes the God she worshipped appeared less like the Father to her than like the stupendous Tradesman of the universe Who slowly renders His accounts.

In her wanderings from church to church she sought her ideal pastor in vain. Ministers began to fight shy of her, and she became increasingly nervous of them, though her convictions never wavered. Her severance from St. Jude's told both on her and on the children. Church-going became spasmodic and a matter for individual decision. Sometimes of a Sunday the Bannermans would have extra long family prayers at home instead of going to any outside service ; and as likely as not a Jew from the South Side mission would officiate.

But Juley never felt perfectly easy about such shifts. The household seemed dishevelled. Besides, in any other place of worship than St. Jude's Sholto Bannerman's widow found herself a nobody. She began somehow to lose caste a little, and shrank from the greetings of her husband's old acquaintances. As time went on she would once in a while steal in on a Sunday evening to the very back of Dr. Ranken's gallery, taking all precautions to avoid observation. And there she would listen to his arid discourse carefully and with tears, to know whether she might not return to his fold without violating her conscience. The children could always tell by her face at supper when she had been to St. Jude's.

CHAPTER IV

I

EACH year the family fell farther apart. Shortly after the interview with Dr. Ranken Juley took his advice, and Georgie was sent to a boarding-school at Bristol. But though the school was only decided upon after much prayer and careful inquiry, the girl returned for her holidays less manageable at the end of every term. Both Juley's daughters had derived from her in full force the capacity for ecstasy. But she seemed powerless to direct their energies, and with increasing grief she saw her prayers apparently unanswered. Her faith was sorely tried, and often she wept in secret. But she always renewed the attack, and with a peculiar obstinacy, maddening to them, attempted to force her vision on the children. Once they had been ready to drink in their mother's words as the essence of truth, and she had flashed veritable heaven at her babes from her apocalyptic eyes. Now it needed all her courage to maintain her beliefs in the face of their entrenched hostility.

Also Juley failed them socially, and the girls felt this more than they knew. They were no longer invited to Aunt Georgina's. Soon they hardly went anywhere. Sholto's acquaintances dropped off one by one, and most of Juley's "friends in the Lord" were either freakish or out at elbow; so that Joanna came to think that Heaven must have a predilection for ill-looking oddities. Some of them turned out to be rogues as well. One, a negro revivalist to whom Juley's efforts had opened two Glasgow pulpits, was discovered to be a bigamist on a brilliant scale. Another, a Polish-American Jew who had paid long visits to them in Collessie Street, and addressed many drawing-room meetings there, absconded with the money collected for the establishment of a Hebrew mission-church in New York. Even the more deserving were feeble creatures in any earthly sense, and Juley herself sometimes mourned the days of her youth when God's people made a better show in the world of mammon. She never put down the change to her own growing eccentricity. Though always perfectly cleanly and careful in detail she was dressing herself with increasing dowdiness, and she sorely grudged herself a new garment. Her income was strained by the children's growing needs, but she none the less continued, as Sholto had done, to set aside one-tenth of it "for the Lord," and never did she refuse an appeal for help, whether made to her purse, her time or her strength. She was loved by the poor. But Joanna and Georgie, just as they would have given all the spiritual qualities of their home for material graciousness, would gladly have exchanged their mother's unselfishness for dignity and tact.

II

It was therefore natural that both the girls should turn for help to the fine arts. It was a misfortune that neither was greatly gifted, but Georgie at any rate had no hesitation in accepting her own enthusiasm as marked talent if not genius. The only thing she was uncertain about was the field in which this talent was to have play. She had thought of writing, and once actually started a novel in which Mr. Barr, the organist of St. Jude's, with whom both she and Joanna were in love, was to be saved from his unfortunate weakness for the bottle by a heroine remarkably like Georgie herself in everything except appearance. But in the second chapter unexpected difficulties arose, and at the same time Georgie heard Madame Neruda play at one of Sir Charles Hallé's concerts. From that day the girl decided that music was her natural means of expression, and the violin her instrument. It was dreadful to think how much time she had already wasted over the piano.

So Georgie was given violin lessons at the school in Bristol, and when, at nineteen, she came home for good, she wandered from teacher to teacher much as her mother wandered from church to church. Each time she meditated a change there were the best reasons for condemning her present instructor, and before very long it came to this, that no one in Glasgow could give her precisely what she needed. There was a man in Dresden . . . she was certain that if she could only go to Dresden . . .

"But, dear, you seemed to be getting on so nicely," Juley pleaded when Germany was first mentioned. "Mrs. Boyd was charmed with the way you played *Simple Aveu* the other day at the Canal Boatmen's P.S.A."

"Mrs. Boyd!" cried Georgie in loud scorn. "What does Mrs. Boyd know about music? She *would* like *Simple Aveu*! And that's exactly what I'm trying to tell you. *Simple Aveu* is the kind of piece Miss Findlay gives to all her pupils because she thinks it will please their friends to hear them play it in the drawing-room at night—because it's *tuney*! Don't you see that if I'm ever to do anything with my violin—anything real—I must go somewhere where they take music seriously?"

This discussion—one of many—happened one Sunday evening in spring. Juley and her daughters were returning after church from a walk along the Great Western Road, and Joanna seeking a refuge from the distress by her side, found it in the beauty of the world about her. For the Great Western Road at sunset on a fine Sunday is a romantic highway. Once a stranger had stopped Joanna there, and sweeping off his hat, had asked in broken English how soon, continuing westwards, he should get to the sea. The question, though geographically astonishing, gave some expression of the magnanimous charm of the road. Now troops of church-goers, their faces illumined by the glow on the horizon, sauntered westwards; and others with their faces in the shadow returned to the town. Innumerable couples—Highland servants chattering loudly in Gaelic, strings of very young girls in their Sabbath finery, young men with buttonholes and whirling canes, who eyed the girls as they passed—all used the whole breadth of the road for walking, and only moved aside deliberately to make way for a jogging Sunday horse-car.

Joanna steeping her mind in vague dreams tried not to hear what Georgie and her mother were saying. But the argument continued even after they had got home and were waiting in the parlour for supper. Joanna's silence was taken for granted, and she sat by the window looking out. She still tried not to listen, though it was harder indoors.

"But you said only the other day, dear" (it was the pained yet patient mother's voice speaking) "that Miss Findlay was a splendid teacher and thought so highly of you. Besides, poor thing, you know her circumstances and what the loss of a pupil means to her, quite apart from the hurt to her feelings."

From the window now Joanna was watching two pigeons, burnished on their high perch by the hidden sunset. They sat on the ledge of a house opposite, one motionless as a carved bird, the other making his toilet. With gentle yet precise movements the male arranged his breast and back feathers, unfolded, folded, and refolded his wings; and when at length all was to his liking, he sidled caressingly up to his mate.

" Of course," shouted Georgie, " if you are going to sacrifice my career to charity ! "

At that word, as at a signal, both pigeons took flight. Joanna followed their swift passage across the clear cube of sky, then sighing turned to face the dark interior.

III

Georgie had her way and went to Dresden. The photographs of Joachim and Neruda vanished from the bedroom mantelpiece. The motto, " Genius consists in an infinite capacity for taking pains," which had been pinned up also, went along with them in Georgie's trunk. And at first the family felt a strange blank in the mornings, no longer being awakened by the thin scrape of exercises in the third position.

Though Georgie did not realize it, her victory was due, not so much to her own forcefulness as to her mother's desire that she should be provided with the means of earning her own livelihood. Secretly Juley disbelieved in Georgie's dreams of the concert platform. But if the girl really loved music she would be the better equipped for having studied abroad. Matrimony in Juley's eyes was not a thing to be sought for its own sake, and if her daughters neither married nor felt the call to be missionaries, they would have to do something for themselves. Sholto's estate when divested of his legacies to charity, had not amounted to more than £7,000 ; and when this should come at Juley's death to be divided, equally between the four children, the portions would not be large.

With the same practical end in view, Joanna was allowed to forsake her High School for the School of Art when she was barely seventeen, and not yet in the sixth form. For some time it had been understood at home that Joanna should become an artist. She was neat fingered. Her mother always

counted on her to print the invitations and decorate the collection card for the monthly Jewish meeting held in the drawing-room : and at school she generally carried off a second
prize for drawing. What sort of an artist she wanted to become she did not yet know, but that could be decided later.

Another change at this time was the coming of Mabel to
Collessie Street. Mabel, faced even more urgently than her
cousins by the necessity of earning a living, had decided to
become a hospital nurse ; and before starting her regular
training she came to spend a winter of study in Glasgow.

Juley told herself that this was a happy arrangement for
Joanna during Georgie's absence. The two boys, now fourteen and twelve, lived apart in a world of their own. School
claimed them all day, and lessons most of the evening ; and
on Saturdays they went off to football, returning mud-coated,
and arguing about "half-backs" and "scrums," "fouls"
and "forwards." But in reality it was Juley herself, in
dire need of sympathy, who fastened on Mabel when she came.
Mabel was nothing if not sympathetic, and her aunt poured
into her ready ears much that had better have remained
unspoken, while in return Mabel imparted many of the
confidences she had at various times received from Georgie
and Joanna. Juley, already admiring her niece's choice of a
profession, was impressed by a maturity in the girl quite
lacking in her own daughters. She attributed it to the fact
that Mabel was an orphan, and she rejoiced in the good influence Mabel was bound to exercise over Joanna, whose bedroom she was to share.

IV

The remarkable thing was that Joanna, receptive as she
was at this time, remained immune to this same influence.
Seven years earlier both she and Georgie had taken a passive
pleasure in Mabel's fertile invention in the field of childish
indecencies ; but in their later girlhood they had provided
a disappointing market for her primitive ancedotes. Georgie
in fact had warned her sister that there were others like their
cousin at the school in Bristol, and that all that kind of thing
was detestable as one grew older. And now Mabel at nineteen, returning to the charge with a smattering of physiology,
a great store of bald tales, and some grotesque confidences
of the hospital, found Joanna unresponsive.

It was not that Joanna made any prudish objections. In a sense she even listened. But while she continued as in childhood to hoard the correct and the incorrect together in the dark chambers of her mind she by nature ignored all that made the telling savoury to Mabel. If she was still amazingly ignorant about life it was not exactly from lack of information. At Duntarvie she had been in close touch with nature. In Glasgow she had been allowed to play in the streets. Juley was no believer in ignorance for young people. She had even approached Joanna once or twice with an attempt at definite enlightenment. But Joanna had shied so badly and so persistently that at length she was left to herself. She would not have it that her very considerable knowledge of natural processes should in any real way affect the love-fantasy in which she now had her being. Constantly and to the full she indulged herself in the drug-habit of maidenhood ; but her waking dreams were quite as innocent as they were sensuous. What she learned from Mabel therefore was kept jealously shrouded. It was no more true to her than it was true that members of the Young Men's Christian Association, because they were men, were potential lovers.

Yet all the time a lover was what she unceasingly sought. In the streets, at church, on tram-cars and steamers, at concerts, even at religious meetings, Joanna was for ever seeking faces that would suit the hero's part in those dreams of which the constant heroine was herself. In any kind of assemblage there was sure to be one such face at least, and when she had found it she knew a dozen ways by which to induce immediate delirium. She need only, for instance, recall with closed eyes a moonlight cruise on the Clyde the midsummer before. The paddle steamer loaded with embracing lovers had churned phosphorescently through the black lochs. The band had played dance music. At intervals the spray of fainting rockets had been shaken down the dark sky.

No one seeing her aloof eyes and still face would have guessed at the eagerness of the girl's search. Young men feared her, knowing she hardly saw them. Yet at eighteen, a little weary of fruitless emotion, a little dream-sick, the conviction had begun to force itself on Joanna that she was without attraction. For the past ten years she had lavished unreciprocated passion on individuals of both sexes. She had worshipped Gerald Bird, had longed to reclaim the boozing organist of St. Jude's, had trembled in the presence of her geography teacher at the High School—a plain, middle-aged woman with mysterious eyes. And these were but three out of many. But never yet, so far as Joanna knew, had she figured for an instant in the dreams of another human being, and she was beginning to give up hope. Clearly she foresaw a dismal stretch of life to an unloved old age.

CHAPTER V

I

TWO years passed in this way; and when Joanna was twenty and full of desperation, she heard that Bob Ranken was coming to Glasgow for his Easter holiday.

She had been seventeen the last time she saw her old playmate, he eighteen. Two years after his interview with Juley, Doctor Ranken's health had begun to fail; and after struggling on gallantly for a while with a "colleague and successor," he had retired as "minister emeritus" to Tunbridge Wells, where he had a married sister. He himself had been long a widower. He had hoped rather than suggested that Bob should enter the ministry. But the boy was set on being a mining engineer, and on leaving school went to South Kensington to study at the School of Mines.

Thenceforward his visits to Glasgow had been rare. But on the Easter immediately following Joanna's twentieth birthday Dr. Ranken was sent to Bad Nauheim and Bob came to stay with one of the oldest families of the St. Jude's congregation, the Boyds of High Kelvin Place.

From the moment Joanna heard from Mamie Boyd that Bob was expected, her imagination busied itself with the coming meeting. In her condition any excitement was welcome. But most welcome of all was an excitement that promised to bring nearer to her that great and solid world, in the existence of which she believed as only your dreamer can believe.

Would Bob be much changed? she wondered. And gazing into her mirror she tried to see herself with his eyes. Would he tease her about her long skirts and her hair done up? (She wore it in a fine shining knob now on the top of her head.) It was wonderful how suddenly her lassitude gave place to gaiety.

She recalled the little constraint that had arisen between Bob and herself during his last school holidays in Glasgow. How clearly she was able to re-live it! They had started romping, as in the old childish days; but Bob's touch on her had brought a giddiness. He had tried to snatch a sketch-book from her; and she, half pretending, half really shy of letting him see her drawings, had fought to keep it. They had wrestled for it—Bob grunting with laughter when in the tussle they upset a small table covered with books—until he got her pinned against the wall and she had to own herself beaten. A tremor of pleasure went through her now at the feeling of his yellow tousled head, so near to hers as it had been, and his red, laughing, triumphant face. There had come a sudden steadiness into his blue eyes, as if he had observed something new in her or in himself. Then his eyelids with their pale lashes like veils had drooped, and he had let her arms go. She had felt like water that runs swiftly over an edge of rock, that shivers in mid-air before falling in a shaken dazzle of delight down into nothingness.

And now she was to see him again.

On the evening he was expected, she spent a long time over her dressing. She took a hot bath—everything must be perfect, and though it was only Wednesday, she put on every stitch clean. She hoped Bob would not think her dress too odd. She had designed and made it herself at the School of Art, and it was of thin crinkly apple-green silk quite untrimmed. She could not help feeling elated when she ran into her mother's room to see herself in the long wardrobe glass. She felt sure the narrow apple-green ribbon looked well round her hair, but it was a trial that her cheeks became so easily scarlet. She was thankful Mabel was not to be in that night. And the boys had gone to Aunt Ellen's for Easter. There would only be her mother.

While still in her mother's room Joanna heard the door-bell ring, and she listened throbbing while the visitor hung up his hat and crossed the tiled lobby to the parlour at the back of the house. How was she to go down—to enter the room?

But after all it was astonishingly easy! And when they had shaken hands firmly and were talking hard, she asked herself what she had been afraid of. It was like the jump out of the parlour window long ago—the same relief, the same slight trembling afterwards. Bob's hair wasn't so yellow as it used to be. In this light it was the colour of ashes. His voice was the same, though soft, almost lazy. And he still grunted funnily when he laughed. His eyes—Joanna could not bring herself to look at his eyes after the first encounter. She looked instead at his hair, at her own hands, at the fern-case by the window, in which her mother cherished delicate little plants. And she heard herself chattering freely about the School of Art, and asking Bob all about London.

But in the depths of her confused heart she knew it was not like old times, however hard both might pretend it was. At the very first glance something must have happened between them. Otherwise why could she not look at Bob ? And why did he never for a moment stop looking at her ? She wondered at herself for having imagined he would laugh at her for being grown-up. She could not now have asked him what he thought of her hair. She had caught a glimpse of her new self in his eyes, and under her chatter she felt lost and troubled. But it was a sort of happiness too, this breaking of the life in her out of the old confines.

At tea the mother's presence was a respite. Joanna was like a child again, hiding in her mother's skirts and peeping out from that refuge at the too persistent stranger. She tried hard to collect herself. If Bob would have spared her only for one minute. But then all of a sudden her lips curved into a smile, and from that moment she smiled uncontrollably. She would have given anything to hide her burning, smiling face. There was panic in her breast. And to recover gravity she tried to think of the saddest thing she knew. She thought of the Crown of Thorns. But it was useless, especially when Juley was questioning Bob about the Presbyterian churches in London. Only when she looked up and found herself in Bob's waiting eyes did Joanna stop smiling, and then her breath went from her.

And after tea came prayers. Prayers at Collessie Street took place without respect of visitors, and generally Joanna resented this with bitter *ennui*. But to-night everything was different. She did not know what she looked for in the coming act of worship, but she felt it held something hidden for Bob and herself. Till then they would both be in suspense.

When the servants had come upstairs and were in their

places near the door, Juley opened her Bible on the half-cleared tea-table, and with a short prayer that God would not let His Word return to Him void, she began to read the passage for that evening.

Joanna, with her spreading apple-green skirts crinkled as petals that are folded in a poppy bud, sat very still on the worn leather sofa, and Bob in an armchair faced her across the hearthrug. She seemed to him like an early spring flower, and his eyes, young and disturbed, never left her. As for Joanna, though she gazed steadfastly aside at the crumbling coals, the young man's presence was putting a spell upon her. The space between them vibrated unceasingly, and there was magic for both of them in the familiar, unheeded poetry the mother was reading.

Even Juley's interpolations as she read the Bible had no power this evening to irritate her daughter; and as if knowing this, she lingered to her heart's content on the precious phrases, explaining them to the servants, and drawing the sweetness from each word before she passed on. Poor Juley! After a day of small desperations she now came to refresh herself at God's footstool with an eagerness that made her quite blind to what was passing beside her. Half an hour hence she would be staggering once more under her burden; but for this blessed space she was laying it aside with deep-drawn sighs of content.

"May God bless to us His holy Word. Let us pray!"

At this signal the servants rustled starchily from their seats and Joanna and Bob stood up. It was the moment, Joanna then knew, for which they had both been waiting. As her mother and the servants knelt before their chairs, she raised at last her full eyelids, and with his whole being Bob held her glance. It was only an instant that they stood thus, but to Joanna it seemed an age. Then Bob crossed to her side, and trembling they knelt down together at the sofa.

As soon as they knew by the modulations of her voice that Juley's prayer was in full flight heavenwards, the boy and girl, so far as they could for nervousness, began to look into their new situation. In her own agitation Joanna made no allowance for Bob's, but his was the greater. She felt rather than saw that his right hand lay palm upwards close by her left elbow on the rubbed leather sofa. It lay waiting there dumb and humble for hers. She was thrilled by this, but at the same time a little spasm of disappointment passed through her. Why could not Bob take her hand simply, boldly ? Was it not the man's part ? Here was she, ready at a touch to give all that could be asked for.

But swiftly that moment passed. After all this was Bob's way of asking, and she had never been asked before. Besides, though she did not guess at his shy terror, Joanna could read aright the urgency of his desire. The knowledge of this set an abrupt flame leaping in her. She became wooer as well as wooed. With averted face, and eyes obstinately closed, she shifted her weight wholly on to her right elbow, and her left hand, released, slid down and laid itself on the patient hand beneath. Timidly she gave herself, yet with fullness, palm to palm. And Bob clasped her in a rapture of gratitude. With his first touch she was flooded with happiness. But at his kiss she became dreadfully conscious of her knuckles which she felt must stick out hard against his lips. If only she had hands like Georgie's, with soft dimples instead of knuckles ! How she wished to be perfect for him !

II

After all she had only a few minutes alone with Bob before he left the house an hour later, and even then they were not secure from interruption. Hardly had they risen from their knees, when Mabel came into the parlour ; and though Joanna tried afterwards she could never recollect her cousin's excuse for this unexpectedly early return. All she could recall was the picture of Mabel looking up at Bob with her coy, curiously liquid gaze from under the brim of her hat as she took it off. But Bob had no eyes that evening for any-one but Joanna, and after some talk suddenly, as if he had that moment remembered something, he said he must be off.

Joanna went with him to the lobby and stood watching his rather blundering actions at the hatstand. In his acute self-consciousness he fumbled like a blind man. The two did not speak for a few minutes, partly from shyness, partly because Mabel had only just disappeared round the bend of the staircase, leaving the parlour, where Juley still was, with the door open.

But to Joanna's delight, Bob in a low voice began talking to her in Double Dutch. That she herself, or Georgie, or the boys should ever forget their old secret language was of course unimaginable. Yet she had not dreamed that Bob would remember it—Bob a grown man who had gone out into the world! Joanna loved him for it, and she blushed at him, bright with grateful surprise.

"Joey," he whispered as he tugged on his waterproof, "can't you come out for a minute?"

"I'll try," breathed Joanna in return, and she wondered at her calmness, making this her first appointment with a lover.

"I'll wait at the corner of Burns Street where we used to play peever," said Bob. "How long will you be?"

"I'll come as quick as I can."

"I'll wait half an hour. Promise you'll come!"

"I'll come within ten minutes."

"All right. But remember I'll wait half an hour."

She opened the door and he went out. They had not touched each other since they knelt at the sofa. They were waiting.

Joanna shut the door, and for a moment stood suspended, uncertain. Her pulses raced and her brain was working swiftly. She was afraid to follow Bob at once. From the outside the front door could only be shut with a bang, and she knew her mother would run out at the sound, and standing on the steps would call to ask her where she was going. That, she could not have borne. But she feared still more to go into the parlour or upstairs, lest her return to the lobby should be somehow prevented. So she hovered in the dim hall, resting on tiptoe ready for flight. She listened with sharpened hearing to the sounds in the house. She ought to go and change her thin slippers, but Mabel was still in the bedroom. Joanna could hear her moving, though she was two floors distant. Scarcely half a minute had passed, but in despair she was sure Bob must be tired of waiting. He would be gone. He would think she didn't care. It was terrible.

Half frantic, she pulled on a blue woollen tammy which was on the hatstand and threw a short old tweed cape round her shoulders. Then passing the bottom of the stairs, and slipping quiet as a shadow down the long tiled passage, she looked into the parlour.

Juley was there, standing burdened by the table. With one uncomfortable hand she clutched some little flower-glasses which needed fresh water, with the other she held up a newspaper. Something on the printed page had caught her eye just as she was leaving the room, but not for the world would she relinquish duty for enjoyment. It was like her thus to tax self-indulgence with physical discomfort.

"Mother, I'm running to the post. I'll be back in a minute," Joanna rattled out the old, old formula in a colourless voice, and was off, not waiting for an answer. Before her mother had taken in her words, she had fled the house. She went the length of Collessie Street like the wind. Then feeling safe she made her way more slowly towards the place where Bob would be waiting.

III

Some clock was striking the last strokes of eight, but dark had scarcely fallen. It had been a wet afternoon, and though the streets were drying rapidly now under a sounding wind, they still held pearly reflections of the pale, torn sky. Where the moisture stayed in shallow pools, it was like the high light on round white pearls, where the shadows of the tall houses congregated it was like grey and black pearl. Soft clouds, grey as doves, drove slowly across the luminous sky. The universe was washed clear of colour, and the world through which Joanna sped light-footed might have been one of those dim pictures in which children take delight—pictures that lie scattered by the thousand on the seashore, and are so cunningly painted on the pearly inward of each deserted shell.

And though along the whole vista of dark stone street there was no tree, the emergency of spring made itself felt as surely as in any country woodland. Certainly the young woman in each pulse and duct and pore of her body was alive to the season's clamour. She was unfurled like a flag to the wind of spring. For the first time since she had lain by the margin of the upper pond at Duntarvie, she found herself able to look full upon beauty without grieving. In the interval there had always been a discord between herself and her apprehension of beauty outside herself. Sunsets, the faces of flowers, the evening star raised steadily like a torch above a screen of cloud—these had been hardly endurable, always lacking the consummation they called for. But to-night she felt at one with the whole earth's loveliness, for she was desired, and her lover awaited her coming.

At the appointed corner Bob in his shabby waterproof moved to meet her.

"Let's go down there, shall we?" he suggested. And with a nervous movement of his chin he indicated the hill that plunged downwards on their right. There was no one else in the quiet street but a lamplighter who scurried on in front of them, lighting the yellow lamps one after another, till he turned a corner; and with the coming to life of the lamps, as by a miracle the world was flooded with transparent, wonderful blue. "Now"—thought Joanna, as they reached one of the flights of stone steps which in places eased the steepness of the hill—"Now he will tell me he loves me." Surely the moment had come—the moment for which all her life she had been waiting.

When they were gone down the first flight, Bob jerked out his arm and just touched the back of her cape. It was as if he meant to enfold her. But instead, losing courage he dropped his hand and took hers, pressing it with an abrupt terrified action against him. With the back of her fingers Joanna could feel the hard outer muscles of his thigh through his waterproof. Thus joined they went on more slowly across the paved landing to the top of the next flight.

"Joey, do you really care?" he whispered.

This was something altogether different from her imaginings, but not for anything would Joanna let Bob think she judged him. Besides, there was an appeal in his muffled voice and in his dimly seen face which moved her.

"Yes," she returned in small, bereft tones. "Of course I do." Then fearing this might be the wrong answer, she added, "If I didn't, I shouldn't let you hold my hand." And she gave him a timid beseeching look.

Bob stopped, glancing swiftly up and down the steps. Still never a soul! Far, far below was the foggy incandescent track of the New City Road, with its crowds, its passing cars full of light, and its sordid glare of shop windows made beautiful by distance. But up here the two of them clinging together in the dark-blue middle air, seemed suspended on a ladder between earth and sky, a frail ladder that was shaken by the travelling wind.

"Will you kiss me—just once?" he pleaded drooping his head towards her.

This again was not of the pattern of Joanna's dreams. Had

she been all wrong about love ? Well, if she had, it was her fault, not love's. She must still believe, and follow where love led. So she turned her obedient face to Bob, and he bent shyly down to her. He was completely surprised by the rich surrender of her lips, she no less amazed by the bashfulness of his.

" Is this the first time any one has kissed you ? " The question slipped instinctively, jealously from him.

The girl's heart leapt in response to that. " Yes " she replied with joyous truthfulness. " The very first time."

" I'm glad," he said.

In the little pause that followed, Joanna felt that it was her turn. " Is it the first time you have kissed any one ? " she asked, ignoring as he had done, the fact that all the virility of their first intimate touch had been on her side.

" It isn't the same for a man," Bob told her, and a smile flickered across his face.

" You mean you have ? " Joanna was intent. And her real unconscious hope was that he had kissed many women.

" Only once, and it was not like this at all. It didn't count really."

Joanna was silent for a moment. She tried to feel disappointment that she was not the first.

" But now you'll never kiss anybody else ? " she exacted. " Never, never again ! "

" I shan't want to," Bob assured her.

" No, but promise ! "

" I promise. There ! And now kiss me again."

" You kiss *me* this time," ventured Joanna with a daring that shook her. She felt a new recklessness of response, and this time as he pressed her lips more manfully, a kind of drunkenness crept up behind her eyes. Yielding to it was like plunging down and down, forfeiting one's identity, losing the power of sight. Bob's features became indistinct and dreamlike.

" How wonderful your lips feel," said Bob solemnly, as if he were reading out a text in church.

" Do they ? " Joanna felt them with her finger-tips, wondering. " I love your hands, Bob. I was looking at them at prayers," she said in return. But she did not tell him that it was because they reminded her of Gerald's hands.

" Tell me," he asked her presently, when they had walked

some way on in silence. "How long have you cared ? "

And Joanna, floating in a rosy haze, was easily harmonious at the cost of truth.

" I must have cared for years and years without knowing it,' she replied, happy in pleasing him. " And you ? "

" I suppose I must have too."

" I wonder what makes you like me, Bob ? "

" I think it's because you are so gentle."

So they strolled homewards, lying sweetly to one another and their own hearts for love's sake, till they came to the bridge which led across to High Kelvin Place. Here Bob stopped, saying he would see Joanna home again. But before turning back they paused, leaning on the parapet of the high-hung bridge, and they gazed down into the wooded bed where the river was only betrayed from time to time by a snaky gleam. To their right rose a sheer escarpment of stone, and towering yet higher behind it, tier upon tier of flats full of windows seemed in the darkness to be a dense forest screen hung unevenly with barred, many-coloured lanterns. To their left ran the low crescent of shops, like a necklace of gold and brilliants curved in a velvet case and with the coloured lights of a chemist—a great ruby and emerald for its central gems. And above them, across the great moist arch of sky, so candid and pale, an endless volume of cloud streamed up like smoke from the horizon.

" How lovely everything is ! " murmured Joanna entranced, and she longed for Bob to take her in his arms, and with her all the wonder of the night which was in her heart. But he seemed in a dream, and as they returned hand in hand to Collessie Street, she felt there was a shadow over him. He himself could not have named it, but he was beset by that dread of young men, the dread that he would never be able to earn a living. He was working now, he told her, for an examination in the autumn, and much depended on his passing it. That he was going up for it at all he owed to his father's sacrifices. And what with this and with his father's illness Bob was oppressed and fearful.

He broke it to her that after the examination he would be going to South Africa. One got on faster abroad, and he longed to pay his father back without delay. It would mean, of course, that Joanna and he would have to wait for years to be married, but not for so many years as if he stayed in this country. The question was, could Joanna wait for him?

Yes! Joanna could wait: a lifetime if need be. She showed him shining eyes of assurance. She was gluttonous for sacrifice.

And would she not mind keeping everything a secret from other people for the present? To announce it would only distress his father needlessly. Besides, until he had some definite prospects he would rather have nothing said.

Joanna agreed almost rapturously to everything, though the situation as it unfolded struck some unacknowledged misery into her. She declared that he was not asking anything nearly difficult enough for her. She wished to be put to the hardest tests.

Indeed Bob was a little taken aback by her eagerness. Were women then so easy to win? Her capitulation seemed as complete as though it came at the end of a long siege.

When he gravely kissed her good night she surprised him again (though herself still more) by pressing her body with a swift wildness against his. It was only for a delirious instant that she leaned so. But later, as she lay awake thinking over what had happened, it was upon this instant that she dwelt most of all. For her it was the astonishing jewel of the evening. Yet even so she did not let herself look closely and directly into it. Her choice was to keep it vague and veiled. And she hid it forthwith in the inner shrine of a temple not made with candles.

IV

Though Bob had still a fortnight of holiday before him, the summer session at Glasgow University opened next day, and Joanna and Mabel went together to the Anatomy Class at three o'clock. Joanna had promised to meet Bob afterwards, and at ten minutes past four she was racing towards the gate of the Botanic Gardens where he waited. Escaping from Mabel had not been easy, but she had managed it somehow.

She distinguished Bob's figure from a distance, though he was standing with his back to her, and she wondered how it was that with all men so much alike, one's lover should be so unmistakable. He was at the entrance to one of the glass houses, which, with their squatting, opalescent bosses, are like breast-plates of mother-of-pearl. Under the bright lift of the sky, that seemed to have burst upwards through tatters of brown cloud, the world showed a shouting violence of colour.

Yet it was the lassitude of spring that assailed the two as they strolled about the hilly red paths of the garden. They talked disjointedly, and with uncomfortable silences in which Joanna found herself drifting irresistibly into solitary dreams. They passed some stunted stone pines that laid their dark heads together in a conspiracy, their black tufts and tassels showing in Japanese detail against the sky. And by the side of these bandit trees a company of beeches stood like nuns, so detached and pure were they in their pallor. Joanna, thinking these things, found herself again and again inattentive to what Bob was saying.

Still unlinked, they descended to the Kelvin by a long winding flight of timber-edged steps cut in the steep earth of the ravine. Quickly the sunshine was left behind, and they dropped into the damp, shrubby gloom. Then mounting the slight wooden bridge, so arched that it had slats nailed across for foothold, they stood in the sunlight once more and looked down at the stream. Among the willows leaning top-heavily over the swollen current, some of the longest twigs were already threaded with silver. The water kept catching at their drooping ends and letting them go again. Two greyish swans stayed themselves on the swirling surface. The rank grass was sprinkled with a few scraggy hyacinths. Joanna wished it was more beautiful.

" I say, Joanna ! " said Bob, and something in his abrupt voice made her search his face quickly. " After all I wrote to dad this morning to say that—telling him about you and me——"

" But I thought——" began Joanna in concern.

" Yes, I know. But afterwards I felt that if it got round to him and I hadn't told him, it would hurt him. Besides— well, I told George Boyd last night. We were sitting up talking by the fire. You don't mind, Joey, do you ? It was really because I'm so proud of your caring about me."

" I don't see why I should mind," replied Joanna unsurely. " It was you yourself that said——"

" I know," admitted Bob, " and I still think we ought to keep it to ourselves as much as possible. George has promised not to say a word to any one. But with dad so anxious about me, and ill and all that——" His voice trailed off weakly.

"I'm afraid he's pretty bad. The doctors don't seem too hopeful, though even at the worst it will most likely be a long business."

Bob gazed with gloomy, rather foolish eyes upstream at the anchored swans and bobbing willow-slips, and a nerve in his cheek twitched slightly as he spoke of his father. Joanna looked at him, and far down in her heart came the perception that he was no use to her. But never, never would she admit it! Her eyes rested on his sensitive, too short upper lip, and remembering the night before, she found she could conjure up again that curious drunken feeling behind the eyeballs.

"Bob!" she whispered, moving closer to him.

"Yes?" He slipped her hand with his into his pocket and looked aslant at her.

"Promise me!"—(why of course she must love him if his touch made her voiceless)—"promise me you won't stop loving me whatever your father says."

And Bob promised. But Joanna scarcely listened now. So long as they stood linked ever so slightly, the stream of her being ran full and sweetly, and Bob too was at peace.

v

Joanna had shown her drawings to Bob and he had admired them. And she had made tea for him in her new studio that she was so proud of, though it was only a little draughty attic wedged under the slates of a high block of offices in town. And now as they sat there at either side of the tea-table, a wicked silence sprang between them. It had not been wicked at first: it had simply been rather wretched. Neither had seemed to have anything more to say. And while Bob fidgeted with his cigarette, Joanna had let herself slip under a spell of inertness. But wickedly, after a few moments, she had begun to wonder how long, left to itself, the silence would last. At first she could not, now she would not break it. What would Bob do?

She waited, her hostility increasing instant by instant till she was perfect in hardness against him. And when he sprang up, as if to him the situation was no longer bearable, a little cold, satisfied flame shot up within her. But she was unprepared. And when Bob strode to the back of her chair, thrust his hands under her armpits, and jerked her roughly to her feet, it shocked her like an explosion.

For a second she stood outraged and quite still where he had put her ; then wrenching herself from his hold she walked to the window without looking at him.

Bob followed, and they both stood staring out in consternation at the chimney-pots and the knotted meshes of telegraph wires.

" You hurt my arms," said Joanna in a queer muted voice. " Why did you ? "

" I don't know. I'm sorry." He too sounded strangled.

She glanced at him, but could make nothing of his face. She had hoped to find strength there, but she saw him bewildered and quivering, cheated of his manhood.

" Truly I'm sorry," he repeated. " Somehow I couldn't bear to see you sit still a moment longer, never thinking of me at all. Kiss and be friends, Joanna ! "

He eyed her guiltily, and guiltily she went into his arms. They had not before felt so close to each other.

VI

When she was alone, however, Joanna remembered the exasperation in Bob's touch. What had happened ? She did not know, though in her self-infatuated humility she was ready to lay all the blame at her own door. If she were to be great in love, as she had dreamed, she would have to go some other way about it.

With her brain on fire she devised a plan—a fresh, surprising way in which to shine before Bob ; and that night before going to bed she posted a note asking him to lunch with her at the studio next day.

" Be sure," she wrote in the postscript, " to bring a *new penny* with you. It's for something special. Don't fail me."

After a restless night, she went out and ran in and out of shops spending her pocket-money with a perilous elation. She bought flowers, fruits, and the most tempting luncheon food that she could find. She even went to a licensed grocer for the first time in her life, and asked for a bottle of their very best champagne. Never having seen, much less tasted champagne, she imagined a ruby-coloured vintage in the tiny bottle all trussed up in gilt paper, for which the man asked twelve-and-sixpence. Willingly she would have given him all the money left in her purse.

The next thing was wine-glasses, for there were none at home, and Joanna bought two that caught her fancy in the window of a second-hand dealer. Set exquisitely on their octagonal stems, they were like the calyxes of water-lilies, and the ancient flint glass from which they had been cut seemed to imprison the faint green shimmer of river water and the criss-cross of reeds.

When Bob arrived he was dumbfounded by the extravagance of these preparations, and by the convulsive welcome in Joanna's embrace. She asked him at once if he had brought his new penny, and he showed it to her, wondering. Seeing her corybantic face, he felt afraid, even a little sheepish.

She would not answer any questions, but made him uncork the champagne, and cried out in amused distress when, instead of ruby, a pool of amber rose hissing in one of the wine-glasses. He laughed too, then making her sit on his knees, and some of her strange gaiety diffused itself into his veins also.

" As we are engaged," said Joanna radiantly, " I want you to give me an engagement ring. It's always done, you know!" And she paused a moment, rejoicing in her lover's clear discomfort.

" You see, mother and Mabel know now," she continued smoothly.

" They do, do they ? "

Saying this, Bob sat up, almost dislodging Joanna, but she clung to him, and with eyes full of cruel tenderness, watched his trouble grow

" Well, why not ? " she challenged gently. " You told Georgie and your father. I really only told Mabel. And Mabel, though I said she mustn't, told mother. It was mean of her, but is there any reason why they shouldn't both know now ? "

" Of course not, no reason. Only——" Bob broke off to begin afresh with " What did she say? Did she mind ? "

" Mother ? No. She was nice about it, especially when I told her it would be years before we could get married, or even tell people we were engaged."

" H'm, she'll want to speak to me, though."

" She does. Do you mind ? "

" Of course not."

But Bob did mind. Joanna knew it by his slackened hold on her. In the little silence she stood up and began to tidy her hair at the mirror over the mantelpiece.

" And Mabel ? " Bob asked presently.

Joanna turned, smiling broadly, with her arms still raised, and she had never been more attractive to him than at this moment. " Mabel asked me to show her my ring," she replied.

" So that's why you want me to give you a ring ? "

" Don't be a silly, Bob ! I only want to wear something you've given me."

" Do you think I haven't thought of it ? " said the young man wretchedly. " I haven't any money now, but as soon as I have——"

" O Bob, dear !" Joanna sang to him with ringing sweetness, " it isn't a *real* engagement ring with diamonds on it I want. A bit of string or an elastic band would do *perfectly* if it could be made to last. That's why I got you to bring the penny to-day. Show it to me again."

Coming close to him she collapsed softly on the floor with her hands on his knees, and she looked up at him with shining eyes of false worship.

" Now, this is what I want you to do," she told him. " Give the penny to George and get him to put it in the puncher down at the yard. He did one for Mamie once. You'll see what a perfect ring it makes, with the date inside and everything— just like a wedding ring—and then you'll put it on my finger, and I'll wear it for ever and ever."

Bob pulled her to him and hugged her between his knees, fond, but in misery.

" You are splendid, Joanna," he said. " I'm far too commonplace for you. You should marry a poet, or something or other of that sort."

Though she was flattered by it, Joanna did not like this remark. She became very still in his arms, then withdrew a little, sitting back childishly on her heels.

"You know what I said that day on the bridge in the Botanic Gardens ? " she began, not looking at his face.

" What, particularly ? "

" About your always, always loving me ? "

" Yes."

" And the first time you kissed me I made you promise never to kiss anybody else ? "

" Yes."

" That was all wrong," she insisted, beginning to glow again. " Last night I was thinking things over. If people love each other they shouldn't make bargains or tie each other down (much less of course if they don't love each other). I want you to feel quite, quite free. And if you should ever stop wanting me, you aren't to feel bad or anything. You are just to tell me straight out. That is to be *our* sort of engagement."

She took Bob's hand, but there was no response in it, even when she laid her cheek against it.

" I suppose you mean it's the same on your side too ? " asked Bob, taking his hand away

For a moment Joanna felt the impulse to unsay all that she had said. And with the slightest encouragement she would have thrown her arms round him, giving and demanding afresh the immemorial vows of love. But there was that in his downcast eye and twitching cheek which kept her isolated.

" Surely," she said dully, instead. " You wouldn't want to hold me against my will ? "

" You know I shouldn't ! "

" Well, neither should I you. That's all I mean."

So Joanna's carefully planned betrothal feast ended in flatness.

VII

Within the next week Bob received three letters from his father. They were grave and affectionate, containing no definite reproach, but flying unmistakable signals of distress. There was an appeal in their restrained exhaustion, and the son knew that the writing of them had cost something.

Bob had his talk too with Juley, and though she had been kind, he came away writhing. He had barely escaped having to kneel down on the parlour floor with her to pray for guidance in a matter of such moment as the joining of his life with another's.

As for Mabel, she had congratulated him with a sly touch of amusement in her eyes which made him redden uncomfortably afterwards, and often at Collessie Street he noticed her

calculating glance pass between himself and his betrothed as
though there were for Mabel some secret edification in their
connection.

He hated going to Collessie Street, and always tried to get
Joanna to meet him outside or at her studio.   But early one
afternoon he was caught in a heavy shower in town, and ran
in to the Bannermans' house for shelter.   Joanna was not
there, but Mabel was, and Bob and she sat talking until
Joanna should come in.

Before ten minutes had passed, Bob became aware that he
was enjoying himself as he had not enjoyed himself for weeks.
Mabel was wonderfully pleasant company.   She made none
of that emotional demand on him that he was conscious of
when he was with Joanna.   She neither exalted him into
something that he was not, nor pushed him into a mere pup-
pet's place.   His manhood expanded itself in Mabel's sensual
warmth, and it was a relief that she did not touch his imagination.   He began to have a glimmering of what was wrong
between him and Joanna.   She would not let him be himself.
She had no use for the man in him—the man he essentially
was.   She did not even see what he was, much less love it.
Mabel never got near his emotions : he felt no excitement
sitting here with her : yet she went straight to the male in
him, recognized it, made him feel pleased to be what he was.
She interested his mind too, and he found himself watching
her face.   Even when she was not talking, he found himself
wondering what were her thoughts.   Why had it never struck
him before that Mabel was clever ?   But just as he was asking himself this, Mabel invited him with a sigh to sympathize
with her stupidity.

"Joanna, now, makes me feel so commonplace and silly,
you can't think ! " she said.   " She's like a person in a book, I
always think, don't you ?   But I never succeed in being
anything but ordinary and stupid."

" I shouldn't have thought you were stupid, whatever you
were," replied Bob.   He was smiling at her, his eyes lively and
a little teasing.   If he had had a moustache he would have
twisted it upwards.

" Oh, but I *am*."   Mabel gave him a look of earnest innocence, leaning forward and hugging her knees as if for comfort.   "I shouldn't like you to know *how* stupid.   For instance,
do you know I haven't yet picked up Double Dutch, though

Georgie says it's easy as easy, and Sholto could do it when he was six."

Bob laughed. "It's only a catch. Do you mean to say you really don't know how to do it?"

"Really and truly," Mabel assured him. "If you'll try to teach me," she begged meekly, "you'll see for yourself what a little idiot I am."

Bob knew it was all humbug. But it was trifling, feminine humbug, and behind its shallow pretence Mabel and he understood each other and were at ease. He despised and rather liked her. Above all he was grateful to her. It was good to feel himself a man, even to feel a little manly contempt for a girl's trickiness. He could not feel contempt for Joanna even when she was most absurd.

When Joanna came in she found them chatting between bursts of 'laughter in the long-withheld language, and she knew at once how happy the two had been. Her greeting to Bob was forcedly casual, and soon Mabel, with an elaborate assumption that nothing was amiss, left the parlour. Joanna, who had walked over to the window, stood there biting her lips to keep from crying.

"What's up?" asked Bob. And he had persuaded himself into speaking rather truculently. (Why, from Joanna's manner one would think he had been caught kissing Mabel, when surely never on earth had there been a more innocent conversation!)

Joanna turned on him in passionate mortification. "You know perfectly well that we never allowed Mabel to learn Double Dutch!"

"But Jo! You don't mean to say you keep up a babyish thing like that, now we're grown up. I'd forgotten all about it. Anyway, what in the world does it matter, her knowing it, if she wants to?"

"Don't call me 'Jo'; I hate it! You knew perfectly well," the girl repeated.

"I tell you it never occurred to me that there was still anything in an old thing like that."

Meeting under Mabel's eyes, they had not kissed each other, and now it struck both of them at the same moment that if only they could kiss quickly all might be well. But they could not approach each other. Under Bob's wretchedness he was setting hard and triumphant against her, and Joanna while she could feel it could do nothing. She could only wait. But she had a fierce longing for him to lay things bare for both of them.

"I want to talk to you, Joanna."

"Go on," she muttered. She leaned by the misted fern-case, and behind her the grass in the back garden sloped vivid against the grey afternoon storm, and the newly laid path stood out ruddy with wetness.

"How can I, if you stand like that with your back to me?" His petulant voice was attractive to her, but when she turned and sat down to hear him, she was frozen again, seeing his propitiating glance.

Blind she was to his pathos and his decency. She could only hate him for being afraid of her, and she hated herself for having made him afraid. She would like him to have beaten her and made her his, but instead he was cringing now in expectation of punishment. So she sat aloof and forbidding, her hands folded, watching her power in misuse.

"I feel a beast, Joanna," he began at last; and she knew by his voice how his lower lip was trembling. "But you know what you said that day at the studio?"

For assent she could only look up. She could not speak. She knew now what was coming, and with all the energy of her egoism she was preparing to meet the shock without a cry. He should see how she could stand by her bargain!

"I find I'm not so sure of myself as I ought to be, which isn't fair to you," he continued. "Besides, you asked me to tell you if I wasn't, didn't you? And you said you'd tell me if you weren't? Bob knew this was an untrue beginning, but it came handy. The larger truth he was grappling with was too difficult.

"The fact is you are far too good for me," he said; and he stopped in despair.

But now it was out. That was something. He had only to wait for Joanna. Her eyes were downcast again, and she was so still that Bob longed for an explosion. A little cool excitement took him, as it often did in the laboratory when he watched a test-tube for the verification of some risky hypothesis. What would she do?

"Are you in love with Mabel?" she asked after a moment, and in the chasm of silence that followed, their glances clashed injuriously.

" No, of course not ! "   Bob's voice was sincerely indignant, but by the light of this indignation there flashed in Joanna a clear outline, like a map thrown upon an illuminated screen.

" But being with Mabel makes you feel you aren't sure about me ? " she said.

" Perhaps," Bob admitted slowly.   " But I'm not in love with Mabel," he added.   " You can take that from me. I'm *not*—never was, never will be."

Though he struggled nearer to the truth now, it still remained beyond his grasp that Joanna with her romantic cravings had sent him smack to the merely sensual Mabel, and that, as things were, a man's love could thrive with neither.

A sudden resigned sadness descended on Joanna, blotting out emotion for the time with its lassitude.   It was all too difficult for her to understand.   She felt a faint nausea, and only longed to be alone.   There was no inclination either to plead or to weep.   In a sort of dream she listened to her own voice calmly releasing Bob.   What was it to him that she saw the remainder of life stretching before her like a dull dusty road ?   There was not one kind thought in her for him.   He had failed her and made her fail.   Still in a dream she watched herself take him to the door and shake his hand mechanically.

But Bob lingered on the steps.   And as he looked at her standing there six inches above him on the door-mat, staring past him at the rain, the truth broke from him.   It hurt him, and he hoped it would hurt her.

" If only you had cared one bit for me, Joanna ! "

" *I*, for *you* ? " Joanna looked at him now.

" Yes, that has been it.   You've never cared a straw— only for yourself, and for something . . . Ideas, perhaps, I don't know what . . . never for me."

At this something seemed to snap in Joanna's brain, and the grey street danced scarlet before her eyes.   She raised her right hand, swung it far back, and putting strength into the open palm, struck the side of Bob's fascinated face.

His bowler hat bounded down the steps with an absurd hollow sound at each contact, and rolled across the wet pavement to rest on the grating of an overworked drain.   And after one petrified moment he followed it, his hand to his stung cheek.   But before he had picked it up Joanna was gone into the house and the door was shut.

VIII

She ran back to the parlour. For a minute she remained furious, glowing from her undreamed-of action, but this faded quickly and left her ill with chagrin. Who could have foreseen such an ending to heroic love ? What had happened ? She must think ! No. She must not think ! Not yet. Not for some time.

The noise of some one stirring in the room overhead interrupted her at her task of blindfolding thought. There was a sound as if a book had been dropped, and the crystals on the chandeliers tinkled from the vibration. Mabel ! Yes, it must be Mabel in the drawing-room. Mabel, sitting smiling to herself ! Perhaps she had been at the window—had seen what had happened. Joanna felt her vanity flayed.

It was a relief however having to call upon her energies, so as to escape the slanting, malicious sympathy of her cousin's eyes ; and stealing from the parlour she went on tiptoe to the hatstand where she had thrown her wet coat on coming in. As if in league with her action, there was a sudden, resolute reinforcement in the sound of the rain outside ; and some unconscious instinct of care made the girl take off the trimmed hat she was wearing, and pull on instead the old tammy in which she had met Bob the first time.

Once outside she ran in terror, turning uphill at the first corner so as to get quickly out of range of the windows.

The heavens were emptying themselves with determined violence, and Joanna rejoiced in the downpour. She gave herself to it, lifting her face to the drench. Soon she stopped running, but held to a rapid walk, as though bound on some definite errand. " I mustn't think ! I mustn't think ! " she told herself, making the words keep time with her footfalls—" Not till I get away. Not till I find a place to hide in."

Soon she was in a road where green tram-cars were running. She swung herself on to a westward-bound car between stopping places, and enjoyed the excitement of the spring. There were empty seats inside, but Joanna climbed upstairs.

The straight rain came down torrential, and recoiled hissing from the stone setts. The dark slate roofs gleamed against a slowly lightening pall of sky as if they had been varnished. On the exposed Kelvin Bridge a few shining umbrellas hurried and fought their way across to the comparative shelter of the houses at each end. Joanna, with fierce satisfaction grew wetter and wetter. Perhaps she would get pneumonia and die. Father had died of pneumonia. But she felt beautifully warm from her run.

When the car reached the terminus, she got down and struck off sharply to the right—her quickest way of reaching wooded country. After passing some unsightly tenement blocks and crossing the canal, she took an uphill bend between hedges in which last year's leaves rattled fretfully. It was a narrow lane, and for a while she was kept back by a horse and cart. The big, beautiful bulk of the horse was strained to the incline in a cloud of steam, and steam flew back in gusts from its nostrils. But Joanna must get on: so she ran up the slippery bank, and was soon far ahead. With every step she fled back to her childhood, back to the protection of dreams. She was seeking the woods as Juley would have taken refuge in prayer. She had failed and must find comfort. There was not yet in her the strength to face failure uncomforted.

And at last she was in the country, though it was all wrapped in cold clouds and mist. There were pastures now on either side, divided by grey stone dykes. A mare on the road shied badly at the lines of white water standing in the fields, and her rider, bowing before the arrowy rain, punished her reeking flanks viciously with his crop.

Still farther on, the road crossed a stream that flowed level with its banks. It was the colour of flint, and the white, angry little crests on its surface were like parings of horn. Joanna pulled off her gloves, took Bob's penny ring from her finger, and dropped it into the water. It disappeared without a splash. That was done, anyhow! Her gloves were too wet to put on again, so she flung them after the ring.

At the next turn in the road she saw what she wanted. Up to the left, beyond a hilly field, a fringe of trees ran along a crest of high ground, and they were like the trees on the way to the Upper Pond at Duntarvie. At once Joanna left the road, squeezed through an unlatched gate, and with her feet sinking at each step deeper in sopping cattle-tracks, she made for her wooded summit.

When she reached the trees she rejoiced to find that they were mostly beeches. Their trunks, wrinkled and sweating, were stained in dark patches with the rain, and the floor of dead foliage glowed purple and sodden. As the girl wound her arms round one of the strong, lovely trees, pressing her cheek against its wet hide, a thrush flew out from the undergrowth with a disturbed chuckling cry.

Now was the time to think things out clearly and bravely— to find out what had happened, and to face it. But she noticed a leaf that fluttered captive, pierced by a sharp twig, and first she must set it free. Next a blackbird distracted her attention. He sat grooming himself for some minutes, then flew off with a spatter of raindrops.

So instead of thinking, Joanna sat on the driest log she could find, and slipped moment by moment deeper into the familiar softness of dreams. Soon, very soon, the false image Bob had shattered pieced itself together again, and she saw herself again in the shape of her vanity. Was not this her supreme opportunity ? Could she not prove to Bob what it was that he had cast aside ? Yes, she would go on loving him in spite of himself—loving him and waiting. She had a vision of his returning, penitent and impassioned after many years, to find her true, unreproachful, angelically forgiving. He would return of his own free will, after long pining in vain for a word, a sign from her. Glowing, she imagined the moment when he would rush across continents to fling himself at her feet (the intervening years having flashed by like minutes).

But there ran as usual on the heels of Joanna's fantasy the necessity for concrete action. Bob was leaving the day after to-morrow. Her first notion had been neither to see him nor to answer any letter he might write, but to wait silently through the years. But suppose he neither came nor wrote ? Then he would never know of her heroic decision—a thing not to be contemplated. No, she must see him that night before she slept. But how ? If she called at the Boyds' house she was unlikely to see him alone.

This small but practical difficulty, with its demand on resource, was refreshing ; and even before her plan was complete, hope danced in Joanna's veins once more. Perhaps after all she would not have to wait for years ! Voluptuously she saw herself begging for Bob's forgiveness. She wallowed beforehand in their mutual abasement which was to end with fresh avowals and herself enthroned.

So she descended from her beech-grown height and made

for town again, tucking her wet hair up under the woollen cap that was heavy with rain.

In the tram-car a young man with a small moustache stared persistently at her, and when she alighted he followed her with his eyes as long as he could. This was by no means displeasing to Joanna, but she told herself how glad she was that Bob had no moustache.

At a stationer's she bought notepaper and a pencil, and without pausing, scribbled this note to Bob :—

"Come out and see me for a minute. I do want to speak to you. I'm waiting in the close next door.—JOANNA."

Having addressed it, she walked quivering towards High Kelvin Place ; and the first likely errand boy that passed, was waylaid by her and told how he might earn a sixpence if he were clever. Several times he had to repeat his instructions before Joanna would let him go.

And the plan worked smoothly ! The messenger had scarcely claimed his money when Bob stepped bareheaded out of the Boyds' house. He looked in his odd blind way to one side and another before he discovered Joanna, and watching him she felt faint with excitement.

"I say, you are wet, Joanna ! " was his first remark when they had met. Her skirts dripped on the stone flags, and Bob touched her soaked sleeve timidly. Rings of hair, curled and darkened by the rain, lay close against her cheeks. He found her freshened face splendid.

"Where on earth have you been ? How did you manage to send me this ? " And he flicked the note which was still in his hand.

Joanna told him how she had gone into the country and had thrown his ring into a river. But before she could disclose her intention of loving him for ever, she saw that Bob was looking on the ground, and she knew herself in the wrong again. It was all no use. His only suggestion was that she should change quickly into dry clothes. That was all then ! But what were his thoughts ? How unfair, that she could not—that she never would—know ! This unfairness it was that goaded her into asking him again if he loved Mabel ; and she really longed for his admission. But no. He still denied it ; and she believed him. He did not love Mabel.

Then why ? Why ? (How gladly would Joanna have put

him on the rack if so she could have wrung some damaging thing from him!)

But he would only say with maddening quietness that one couldn't argue about a feeling.

"Good night, then," said Joanna, unable suddenly for more; and she left him, going down the steps.

Yet when Bob uttered her name with pleading, she had to look back.

"Aren't you going to kiss me good-bye?" he asked.

She stood amazed at him; and the notion that he was an idiot careered through her brain. Either he was an idiot, or what he had just said was for ever inexcusable.

But instead of widening the distance between them, Joanna went on looking over her shoulder at him, and she saw how dejectedly he lingered in the dark entrance. He was going away the day after to-morrow, and was asking for a good-bye kiss. Why would she not give one?

In all simplicity now, she ran back to him. And in the shadow of the close she threw her arms round his neck and pressed her shell-cold face to his. To Bob it was the sweetest of their few kisses; but it was a farewell kiss, and short, and he let her go.

This time she ran from him without looking back.

IX

She did not see Bob again before he left, and with his going her life became empty. All charm and interest went from her studies; and before long her manifest indifference had its effect upon her teachers. They ceased to feel any professional responsibility where she was concerned. She became a notorious shirker of classes, and passed much time in listless dabbling at her studio. Sometimes she lapsed for hours into solitary idleness.

And at home it was worse. At home there was a jarring on the girl's exposed nerves at every turn. Juley's late nights were telling at last on her health. She was losing her wonderful recuperative power, and she suffered from swollen ankles. The children knew now when she had slept more on her chair than in her bed, by a puffiness that showed round her eyes in the mornings. But nothing they could do or say made any difference, so they were all cutting adrift from her.

Georgie in the autumn was going to London. She returned

from Dresden late in June, her dream of emulating Neruda gone, but her enthusiasm intact. A Dresden fellow-student, with a new system of teaching children, was opening a small music-school in Hampstead, and she had asked Georgie to help her. Georgie's capital—a sum of £400 which she and Joanna alike had by their father's will—would be involved. But what a chance after only one year's study abroad ! So Georgie got her way.

There remained the boys ; and though they were full of their own occupations, their activities brought the curves of their lives nearer to Joanna's than they had been since nursery days.

Linnet, with a mind to the Law, and a berth promised him in Mr. Boyd's excellent firm, was preparing for Leaving Certificates. He was studious rather than clever, and often he would come to Joanna begging her to " go over " an English essay, or he would ask her advice on a mathematical problem, the principles of which had first to be explained to her, so far behind had he left his sister in school subjects.

Sholto, on the other hand, dreamed Imperial dreams which wavered constantly between Canada and Australia. He loved open air, the exercise of his muscles, and all handicrafts. As soon as he left the Academy he was going to the Agricultural College, after which, before leaving the country he would apprentice himself to some farmer in the Lowlands. Meanwhile he spent his leisure in a shed in the back-green where he had a carpenter's bench. He made stools, and medicine-cupboards, and little tables, and afterwards poker-worked them to his immense satisfaction. And though Joanna from her Art School heights despised such a facile mode of decoration, she couldn't help growing interested when he asked her for designs. At Christmas-time especially, they turned out between them heaps of " blotters " and photograph-frames ; and in return for his sister's help, Sholto would gladly devote a whole Saturday afternoon to her when she was trying to turn the shed stove into a furnace for enamel-work.

But after Bob's kisses there was no more savour for Joanna in her brothers' companionship, and she had a miserable summer. She was glad of one thing only, that Mabel had gone back to stay with Aunt Ellen.

She was too dispirited even to protest against the small and hideous villa which Juley took for two months on one of the

Clyde lochs. And although the boys enjoyed the sea-fishing and knocking about in boats, all five got badly on each other's nerves during the holiday. Georgie resented not having been consulted in the choice of a place. They might at least have remembered that she hated the Clyde, and felt ill there. A cold and rainy season did not help. Georgie criticized unceasingly, and unceasingly practised her fiddle in the only sitting-room. Her diligence, as Janet the cook said, was "something awful." Now and then Georgie would demand of the others if they didn't notice the extraordinary difference in her tone, due to Dresden; and if the answer was doubtful, she argued the point till a definitely favourable reply was forthcoming. Once when Sholto stuck to his guns and insisted that it sounded the very same as before, she said, "Well, it can't be helped what you think; I know it's *quite* different!" Absence had made her very sensitive too to the failings of her family, and she girded particularly at her mother. Then Sholto, who could be as inimical to his mother as any of them, would step out as her champion. Georgie and he had always been peculiarly capable of irritating each other, and now they squabbled maddeningly over trifles. Linnet took to mooning. Joanna was quiet and wretched. Juley with many tears prayed for guidance and forgiveness.

Yet were there hours when for a quiet breathing-space the five seemed to regain something of their forgotten early harmony.

One promising afternoon Joanna and Georgie packed a picnic-basket, and with rugs and a kettle they all climbed the hill behind the house. Sholto pushed his mother up the steepest places with such vigour that she laughed like a school-girl with her clear bell-like laugh. Then when they had sat down and spread out their belongings, Linnet took her shoes off, and Joanna pulled out the toes of her thick cashmere stockings in the way Juley loved because it eased her poor feet. Next Georgie massaged the tell-tale ankles, remonstrating with them, but more gently than usual, while the others ran here and there, calling to each other in echoing voices, and collecting wood and dry bits of heather for the fire. Joanna was always happy tending a fire, and the boiling of the kettle was her special charge. After tea they even forbore to object when Juley read out to them from *Asia's Millions* how the Gospel was spreading among mandarins.

Yet another interval of reunion was to remain as a happy memory.

It had been raining since dawn, but towards evening the sky cleared, and Linnet suggested that they should all go fishing in the bay. It was a job to get started, but once down the steep lane from the house Juley was easy to manage. With encouraging cries the four hauled the rowing-boat down the stony beach; and Juley, very heavy and awkward, was helped aboard from the little jetty. When they had anchored over the fishing-ground, quarrelled amicably over the lines, and baited their hooks, the mother gazed at the lingering sunset and felt that Heaven was very near to earth. Memories of the early days of her motherhood brought happy tears, and she turned her swimming eyes from the radiant west to her full-grown sons and daughters beside her. Georgie was exclaiming excitedly as she wound in the jerking line. She was sure it was either three whiting at once, or an enormous dog-fish which Sholto would have trouble in killing. And when a very small but vigorous lythe appeared over the side they all shouted with laughter at her. Joanna caught three flounders running, through forgetting to pull her hooks a yard up from the bottom; but Juley said she liked flounders better than whiting, and was going to have these cooked for supper that very night. Linnet had no luck at all, and kept shifting his tackle from one side to the other, till at last he got settled in the bows with his Norfolk-coated back to his mother, and she noticed how like his father he was growing about the shoulders, one hitched a little higher than the other. Sholto astern, held his line between his knees. Both his hands were busy with a Jew's harp. It was, he said, the appropriate instrument for the son of a Mother in Israel !

Then as the deliberate Northern night drew on, and they began to feel cold, they shipped the anchor and rowed back, the four taking an oar each. Being used to boats since they could remember, all rowed well. At the end of each stroke the phosphorescence streamed from their blades simultaneously, and went swarming like millions of fireflies into the black water. And keeping time with their strokes the Bannermans sang. They sang " A Southerly Wind and a Cloudy Sky," and many old rounds and catches they had learned in the nursery from their father—for Sholto, in his youth had been a great choir-member. And their voices, on the quiet

stretch of hill-shadowed loch, sounded very happy, very youthful and plaintive.   Juley could not join in for tears ; besides,
though she had a pretty voice, she was apt, she knew, to go
out of tune, and she would not for anything have spoiled her
children's singing.

x

But in autumn, with Georgie gone, Mabel again in Edinburgh, and the old life in Collessie Street resumed, Joanna
sank into a kind of marasmus—a wasting without fever or
apparent disease.

She still found Bob's behaviour quite baffling, and spasmodically the hope still sprang in her that he would return at
length with some undreamed-of explanation.   But here was
no sustenance for life, and as the weeks dragged on she felt
so sore and lonely that she would even have welcomed the
return of Mabel.

CHAPTER VI

I

ONE day upon coming into the house she found a letter waiting for her on the lobby table.

She knew at once that it wasn't from Bob (her first glance on coming in was always at the lobby table in case there might be a letter from him, and anything else was a disappointment). But this letter—or rather package—had some interest. It was rolled up carelessly in a newspaper wrapper, stamped with an Italian stamp, and marked *Manoscritti*, to save in postage.

She would have opened it at once, but her hands were full, and she was tired. So she took it unopened to her bedroom, and threw it on the bed while she rid herself of her outdoor clothes. She kicked off her shoes in the way her mother never ceased to deplore, tossed her hat upon the chest of drawers, and her coat across a chair.

How tired she was !

Stooping to the mirror on the dressing table, and thrusting back her hair with both hands, she peered at her face in the fading light. She was certainly rather white, and there were blue, pathetic shadows under her eyes.

A wave of self-pity swept over her. People said youth was a happy time. She knew better. And there and then she determined that she would harbour no such sentiment in old age.

"Don't forget," she adjured herself—"don't ever let yourself forget that when *you* were young you were very, very unhappy." And throwing herself with the utmost dejection upon the bed, she lay there staring at the ceiling.

Oh, how familiar that ceiling was ! There in the middle were the plugged-up holes in the plaster showing where the trapeze had hung, in the days when the room was a nursery. And there in one corner was a network of cracks like a map. Long ago Joanna had connected this network with her

83

mother's weekly petition at prayers for " India, China and the Distant Islands of the Sea." And looking at it now, she wished vehemently that she had been born in one of these remote lands. She was certain that no one in China or the Distant Isles could be so bereft of life as she. Why, in India girls married at twelve. And we were asked to be sorry for them !

As she stretched out her arms in a gesture of weariness, the back of her hand came against the forgotten letter. There it was, still unopened !

She remained supine : she would barely admit the diversion ; but she lost not a moment in stripping off the wrapper. And in no time then she was sitting upright to smooth out the flimsy foreign sheets against her knee. They were so crossed and re-crossed as to be legible only with difficulty ; but she had glanced at the end, and with a queer little shock of excitement had discovered who the writer was.

It was a letter from Aunt Perdy in Italy.

After some re-shuffling Joanna found the beginning.

" My dear child and niece," she read—

" You will no doubt be surprised to hear from me, and possibly your mother will be displeased at my writing. But the *latter* cannot be helped ; and as for the *former*, Life is, and ever will be, full of surprises for *you* as for *me*. How, you ask, do I know this ? *Ebbene*, as we say here ; I will tell you. This morning (it is now evening, and from my lonely cot as I write I can see the sun dropping behind my beloved Carraras like a ball of fire) I was clearing an old trunk when I came upon a family birthday-book. To refresh my memory I began looking through it (the quotations for each day are from our dear Bobbie Burns), and what do you think I found ? Why, that the only two births in March for our family are yours and my own. Do you realize what that means, Joanna ? No, you do not. But your Aunt Perdy will tell you ; for she has devoted years of her life to studying the wondrous signs of *the Zodiac*. And *March*—the month of *Aries*—The Ram, i.e. *The Lamb*—is the most mystical month of the twelve. It is in *March* that the earth is born afresh every year. Our *Saviour* was born in March, not in December as is vulgarly supposed (though I will not go into that now), and the *Chosen of God*—those who are sent into the world to teach and to suffer—Ah! above all, my Joanna, to *suffer*—see the light under the celestial dominion of *The Lamb* which was from the foundation of the world. To *suffer*, but also to *rejoice*, as those born in any of the other months know not joy."

Here followed a rough diagram of the Zodiacal signs.

" This then," ran the letter again, " is why I write to you, of all my kindred. Though you are of a younger generation, and I doubt not that whatever you have heard of me from your deluded, conventional father and my poor weak sister, must have prejudiced you against me. Probably also you are stupid. But you were born in March ; and this gives me hope that my voice will pierce through all the falseness and deadness enclosing a sister soul. I believe that some day you will come out to this glorious land of liberty, and sunshine, this refuge of great-hearted exiles like myself, like dear Byron, like Shelley, and a host of others to whom freedom was life——"

The letter ended with a fervent if indefinite invitation.

Joanna's interest was excited. She resented her aunt's disparagement of her parents; the Zodiacal signs did not greatly impress her ; but she was roused because of the immediate echoing of her own nature to Aunt Perdy's. The letter meant to her far more than it said, and it did more than it meant. It opened an unsuspected door of escape. She remembered now, of a sudden, how her mother had sometimes sadly remarked upon a likeness between her and the strange aunt. This must now be verified, and instantly.

She ran downstairs to the drawing-room. And there, kneeling all eagerness before the inlaid cabinet, with its glass doors at either side displaying missionary trophies, she lifted out the family album. It had gilt-edged boards and brass clamps and clasps, and lay heavy on her lap as she opened it.

Yes, here was Aunt Perdy, one of a group of quaint little girls with long drawers showing under their funny dresses. And here she was, coquettish in a voluminous riding-habit looped up in half a dozen places, with her hair in a net, and a tiny billy-cock hat tipped over her nose. And here again she looked up from an open book, her chin in her hand, her pretty elbow on a fringed table, her soul in her eyes. In all the full-face portraits, the eyes—rather more deeply set in the head than Joanna's—were remarkable, oracular in their intensity.

Earnestly searching for a likeness to herself, the girl found it most clear in a carte-de-visite photograph in which her aunt was looking down at a baby on her knees, while a little boy (surely Gerald !) leaned against his mother's full skirts, his legs in their striped trousers mannishly crossed. Here the capricious sunlight had proclaimed the resemblance unmistakably, and Joanna saw that it was one of contour rather than of features. There was a faintly Japanese suggestion, a flatness of structure. It must have been this, thought Joanna, that had made Nilsson, one of the Art School masters, tell her once how like she was to a primitive Siennese painting.

Then, as she still searched the album, an idea blazed in her mind. She would learn Italian ! Why had she never thought of it before ? The word Italy had always held for her even more than the ordinary measure of romance. Juley's eyes had lightened when she talked to her children of Italy, much as they lightened when she talked of Heaven. Grandpapa Erskine, with his generous theory of education, had taken his motherless daughters, while still in their teens, to Rome. In Rome he had accepted the charge of the Presbyterian church, and had begun to write his life of Hildebrand. In Rome, later on, after forming many ties with the land of his adoption, he had died. There were cousins of Joanna's in Italy of whom she knew very little. Gerald had sisters, while another Erskine—Aunt Minnie—was married to a Frenchman, and had a large family at Turin. They never came to England ; but they sent cards and photographs at Christmas-time, giving glimpses of a life wonderfully different from the life in Glasgow.

And now had come this voice from Italy, claiming Joanna out of all the connection as a kindred spirit. Surely it was the voice of life ! Surely she would answer it ! And to begin with, she would go to the Italian class at the University. The session was just beginning. She would go to Gilmorehill to make sure, that very afternoon.

II

Still enlivened with her thoughts she approached one of the southern entrances of the park through which she was going to the University, and there it came upon her with surprise that she was walking amid beauty. The October day was yielding up its breath in faint, dun-coloured vapours, and the poor and harsh outlines of this region had borrowed for the time an appealing loveliness. Church-spires—St. Jude's among them—and tall houses, mysterious at their bases, rose triumphantly through the sullied lower air to the serenely brooding blue above, where they seemed suspended. And away to the left on its hill, dominating the park, the Gothic University stood high and black and alien against the sky.

Before entering by the wide iron gates, Joanna paused to look. Here too all was clothed with the magic of the hour. By day, a squalid, railed enclosure where growing things found a precarious life, the park showed itself now as a place of wonder, a dim paradise, which, as the evening deepened, would become murmurous with lovers.

In her full response, the girl drew an audible breath of delight and entered. After all it was good at this moment just to be alive, just to breathe. The desire came upon her for liberated movement—the deep-set human longing for wings. If only one could flit, swift and noiseless through the haze. She glanced behind her. It was barely the hour for lovers. No one was in sight.

She chose one of the higher terraces on her right, where many a time as a child she had bowled a hoop and started to run. Her feet made hardly any sound speeding along the path of hard earth, and her light balanced body was exonerated in its flight through the dusk.

But before reaching the flagstaff and the group of Crimean guns that threaten the University from their height, she sat down on a bench and stayed there motionless awhile. From here she overlooked the whole park. Behind her curved the topmost terrace, with its stone balustrade and its crown of steep French roofs. Below, lay the level murkiness where moving water was, and captive wild birds uttered disturbing cries. Triple globes marked where the new granite bridge spanned the Kelvin, and in places a pair of yellow lamps showed how a cab threaded one of the wider ways. It was a little world to itself, shut in and stuporose. But beyond it to the south, where a brilliant segment of light marked its confines, Joanna could see where the real world began. Nay, she could hear, coming from the Clyde across all that distance yet as if it were the beating of her own heart the dull, steady pounding of the yards.

But when the first quiverings of pleasure were subsided, the beauty and pathos of her surroundings became a trouble to her, and she wondered, as she had wondered countless times before, why this should be. Why was she not content simply to admire and enjoy loveliness when she had perceived it? Why must she suffer from the desire, herself, to be or do some loveliness? What was this ever-thwarted need of her being to give itself utterly to the achievement of she knew not what? She recalled her mother's words years ago, on seeing the Clyde shipping in sunshine, " Let us make our lives to match it." And passionately Joanna wanted to conform to loveliness. She longed to be in harmony with the beauty she had always worshipped. But how? Perhaps, as Dr. Ranken had so often used his pulpit to say, this desire ever unfulfilled, and this oppression, proved that her home was in heaven, not on earth. Her mother, she knew, believed this. And was there not something in one's soul which proclaimed it to be true?

She rose slowly. She was tired again, and unhappy and the evening was barren of magic. Still with a certain saving stolidity she persevered in her resolution and walked on to the University.

There she learned that she was too late, as the matriculation office was closed for the day. It was scarcely a disappointment.

On her way out, walking listlessly through the quadrangle where the professors live, she heard behind her the footsteps of some one gaining on her, and before she had reached the postern, a man passed her stepping quickly in the dusk. She saw that he was smallish and slight, that he wore no overcoat; and something foreign about his alert figure drew her attention. The next moment, as if in response to this, the stranger turned his head, and regarded her fixedly. Thereupon Joanna's observation ceased to be conscious. She had become too acutely aware of herself under his curiously frank scrutiny.

She carried home with her the impression of a white, small-featured face that seemed scornfully alive. The man must be a foreigner—probably an Italian. Who else should he be but Dr. Cellebrini, the Italian lecturer, whom, as it happened, she did not know by sight? The certainty that he could be none other quickened her failing resolve to join the class of which he was the teacher.

III

On the opening day, a week later, she arrived ten minutes before the hour of the lesson to find herself alone with one young man amid a shabby expanse of benches. Both fellow students were too shy to speak, and Joanna observing no more than that her companion was dark and bashful chose a place at some distance from him. The ordinary University youth did not interest her, even while he might embarrass her ; and she gazed with suppressed excitement at the dusty Gothic window-panes on which flaws of rain were appearing.

There was no doubt in her mind that the lecturer would be the stranger who had stared at her by the gate.

Presently a third person came in, and Joanna recognized a Mrs. Lovatt to whom she had been introduced not long ago at an evening entertainment at the Art School. Mrs. Lovatt, a great friend of the Director, was a patron of the arts and a well-known figure in the West End. Joanna blushed with pleasure now when the little woman greeted her unhesitatingly.

" I've forgotten your name," she said, " but I remember quite well being introduced to you by my friend Val Plummer." And she sat down by Joanna bemoaning the size of the class. She was a middle-aged woman, but girlish-looking, with very bright eyes in her wrinkled, pretty face. Under a soft grey felt hat, her grey hair showed in a becoming disorder, and with her grey, flowing clothes, she looked like a dishevelled but attractive and perfectly composed little grey mouse. She remembered admiring Joanna's appearance, and studied her now with bright approval, and also with what Joanna felt to be a touch of amused criticism. Without knowing it, the girl coveted the elder woman's ease and her general air of experience.

The next to arrive was the lecturer, and as he stepped up to the rostrum Joanna looked up eagerly. The disappointment was intense. There, standing above her was an emaciated, tall old man, bearded and rather bent. Surely there was some mistake ! Surely Dr. Cellebrini—the real Dr. Cellebrini—must be ill, and this old man had come to tell them so. So firm was her dream that it had to persist a little in the face of reality. But the next instant she knew that there had been no mistake except her own. She had believed, because she had so strongly desired the likely thing to be true.

There was no lecture that day, and Dr. Cellebrini told them that unless at least six students were forthcoming there could be no class that session. This had been decided by the Senate. He took down their names, however, and Joanna learned that Mrs. Lovatt's Christian name was Mildred. The dark boy, who mumbled his name with a Scotch tongue, was called Lawrence Urquhart.

He left the class-room while Joanna was helping Mrs. Lovatt to collect her scattered belongings. Some coloured beads had rolled out of a leather wallet on to the floor, and the two in picking them up became still more friendly. Mrs. Lovatt hoped that Joanna would come to one of her informal Friday evenings, and if no more students turned up she had the idea of having an Italian class in her own house.

They went out together, and as they passed from the darkness of the cloisters to daylight, the sound of a door closing made them both look back. Between the broad, stone pillars a man was hastening in their direction. Joanna could not see his face, but she knew him instantly for her foreigner.

" It is Rasponi, isn't it ? " exclaimed Mrs. Lovatt, screwing up short-sighted eyes. " The very man I want to speak to." And leaving her companion, she ran impulsively towards the Italian.

Joanna was shaken, and she became half dead with embarrassment. Should she go slowly on ? Should she wait ? Should she hurry off ? No doubt the right thing would be for her simply to disappear. But her fiercer longing chained her feet to the spot ; and in a few seconds she was joined by the others.

On the first meeting of their eyes, Joanna saw that recognition danced in Rasponi's, and something besides recognition. As her name was made known to him he smiled, showing a line of short, milk-white teeth, and his hand flew uncontrollably to his little black moustache. His face in the daylight was not so much white, Joanna saw, as ivory, with fine, carven features, and remarkable eyelids. There was something of the hardness of ivory in him too ; and under the loose grey tweeds he was wearing, she knew his body was like a coiled spring of steel. He was energy itself, but energy pent, not radiant. Joanna had never been so aware of anything : had never imagined anything so living. She was acutely disquieted by his nearness.

In the quadrangle he excused himself for a moment, as he wished to hand in a note at a professor's house. The two women walked on slowly.

"Isn't he beautiful?" Mildred Lovatt turned twinkling to her companion. "And a genius as well. It seems too much for one man!"

Joanna, startled, had no response ready. Did one call men "beautiful"? Women were beautiful, of course. But men—with their hairy ankles? And he was a genius as well. This meant an artist of some kind no doubt. To conceal her confusion she asked what he did.

Mrs. Lovatt was surprised at the other's ignorance.

"Don't tell me you haven't seen him racing about the roads on that diabolical bicycle of his?" she exclaimed. "I should have thought everybody in Glasgow must know him by now." And she told how Rasponi had fitted one of the new internal combustion engines to a specially strong bicycle of his own design, and how he was doing research work at the University in connection with a new machine for flying.

"People laugh at him," she ended "But I'm convinced, myself, that he'll succeed in time. He'll either fly or break his neck—perhaps both!"

After Rasponi had come up with them again, they stood talking for a minute by the postern at the very spot where Joanna and he had first looked at each other.

When Mrs. Lovatt had spoken of the small Italian class, he turned to Joanna.

"You already know some Italian perhaps, eh?" His English had the exaggerated precision of the foreigner. It was not broken, but over-perfect.

Joanna shook her head; and smiling he moved his eyes to Mrs. Lovatt.

"Yet Miss Bannerman looks more Italian than I, though so fair. Do you not see it?" he asked her. "Modern Italian, perhaps no. But of the Seicento. Why, there is her portrait in London in your National Gallery, by a painter of the Venetian School—Bernardino Licinio, I think it is. You know it? But surely? The portrait of a young man, it calls itself, but I have always doubted it, and it pleases me to have my doubts confirmed."

Mrs. Lovatt, her head on one side, looked at Joanna and tried to remember the picture he described. She was not successful, but agreed warmly that Miss Bannerman had struck her from the first as quite Early-Italian. Botticelli, she thought—or was it Luini ?—there was surely an angel wonderfully like her in one of Leonardo's groups ?

Unaccustomed to such talk, the young woman felt herself redden furiously. Nor was she spared by Rasponi. His eyes seemed to search her face : then they dwelt on her breast : then sought her feet. When Mrs. Lovatt had invited them both to have tea at her house one day soon, there seemed of a sudden no more to say.

Joanna took leave of them somehow.

IV

In spite of its meagre beginnings the Italian class prospered. There came to be seven students in all. But the original three remained slightly apart from the rest in a vague fellow-ship of their own ; and they greeted each other with a special friendliness.

Lawrence Urquhart was so manifestly glad to be included that Mrs. Lovatt, in the kindness of her heart, invited him also to tea, and she liked the shy eagerness of his acceptance. His oddly featured, dark face pleased her too, now that she came to look at it.

"Have you noticed what engaging eyes the creature has ? " she asked Joanna ; "they are pretty often turned in your direction."

But Joanna almost resented words that once would have flattered her. She was absorbed by the emotions Rasponi had aroused.

From the first he had sought her openly, and the whole face of her life was changed.

On the second day of the Italian class she had found him waiting for her by the gate. He had moved to meet her, sweeping off his hat with a gesture she would have found ridiculous in another man. But as he did it, it seemed beautifully to place power in her hands.

"It has cleared after the rain," he said. "Do you go down the hill and through the park ? If so that is my way also. My lodging is on the other side. May I go with you as far as our way lies together ? "

Joanna had meant to walk through the park ; but suddenly feeling flight to be imperative, she lied, saying that to-day she must take the nearer tram home.

Rasponi gave a faint shrug which combined disappointment with resignation.

" May I come then as far as the terminus with you ? " he said.

To this there seemed only one possible reply, and she gave an unskilful assent, trying hard not to appear as raw and school-girlish as she felt. The Southerner appeared to her a creature incapable of awkwardness. Passionately she wished that her upbringing had been more gracious.

At the park entrance, which was also the stopping-place for Joanna's tram, three street musicians were tuning up. There was a harpist on a camp stool, a standing fiddler, and a cripple in a wheeled chair, with a rug hiding his legs. They had settled themselves in the corner made by a church and the park railings, and instinctively Rasponi and Joanna paused, waiting for them to strike up.

Joanna glanced back towards the University. At the top of Gilmorehill where the road cuts the sunset across, two cyclists had that moment mounted from the far side. Their figures, poised in the golden air of the summit, stayed for a breath, suspended as by a miracle. Then their machines swept downwards. There was a rush of wind, a shrill whirring of bells, and they disappeared round the curve of the tram-lines.

And that same instant, as if by conspiracy, the little band by the gates broke into dance music.

In the girl something was set free, and her heart exulted.

" No wonder Pilcher chose this hill to test his gliders."

She looked at Rasponi to discover the meaning of his remark. He too was staring back up the way they had come, but his eyes shone with purpose.

" Perhaps you saw him trying them ? " he continued. "It must be about five years since his Glasgow experiments. A good man, that Pilcher."

But Joanna had not heard of Pilcher till now. She felt ashamed under Rasponi's incredulous glance, and was relieved when he put the subject aside.

There was still no car at the terminus. The harpist was thrumming diligently, the fiddler swayed as he tore the insistent melody out of his instrument, the deformed man in the chair gave forth the same air more delicately on a flute. They played well, and Joanna stood with Rasponi to hear the valse out.

"Ah! You see that?"

This exclamation, vibrating and jubilant, was drawn from her companion by an action of the busy little flautist. He had swiftly exchanged his flute for a handful of bound reeds lying concealed on his knees, and at a recurring phrase of the melody he blew into the Pan-pipes, drawing them sharply back and forward against his lips.

"Now we know why he has to hide his feet!" said Rasponi. And this time Joanna understood. He had moved closer to her under cover of the music. He spoke low, intimately.

She nodded, smiling too, and their eyes met. Elated the Italian was twisting up his moustache and for the first time the girl saw his narrow, rapacious lips. Ah, yes, Mrs. Lovatt was right. Beautiful he was—fine—gem-like. Yet for all his delicate, glittering quality, more male than any other man she had yet seen.

Immediately the car came she moved towards it, though before it could start, the trolley-pole would have to be changed round. Rasponi saw her into it, lifted his hat, and to her surprise went off at once. He did not even turn round. She would have given anything to be by his side, but was committed to her perverse choice. She watched him till he was no more than a speck near the central fountain.

V

Looking back afterwards she was no more able to trace the hurried sequence of events which led to her marriage with Mario Rasponi than one is able to relate the procession of incidents in a dream. Indeed it took its place appropriately in what was still a dream life. Outwardly there was an admirable semblance of intention, even of calm. But the girl was not yet near waking, and she proceeded in a kind of deliberate trance which brooked neither interference from without, nor direction by her own shrouded intelligence.

One of the strangest things in the strange business was that Mario never persuaded her into saying that she loved him. She was captured by his ardour; and after the first weak resistance worked, defiant of opposition, for their speedy marriage. But often she still cried at nights for Bob, and felt as if she must go mad in her renewed efforts towards understanding him. Twice she wrote to him. Surely if there was a scrap of real feeling in him for her, it would show now? But he remained aloof. He begged her to be sure of her own mind, wished her good luck, whatever her decision. In spite of this, Joanna would have gone to him had he been in England. She believed that a sight of his face might have held her firm against Mario. But while awaiting the result of his examination, he was with his father in Germany.

And all the time Mario's onslaught continued.

The researches which had brought him to Glasgow were complete. He wanted to get back to Italy where there was work after his own heart for the asking; and he was set on taking Joanna with him whether he won her love or not. His judgment told him that her quick consent was a likelihood: for love there would be time enough later. Actually he preferred it so. It satisfied an insane violence that was part of him.

To Juley he was attentive and affectionate in a bright filial way, which gave her great pleasure. He enlivened her, and she felt at home with him as she did always with foreigners. She loved airing her rusty Italian while he praised her intonation. His enthusiasm, his clear unworldliness warmed her heart. They had long and on her side impassioned talks about the persecution of the Jews in Russia. She was delighted with his interest in politics. She was still more delighted that he enjoyed her society. Here was a young, clever man who did not fight shy of her.

At first Joanna wondered that her mother made so light of Mario's frank irreligion. Was it possible that one to whom faith was everything, could overlook its absence in a son-in-law? Yet the explanation was simple. Rasponi came of a strict Catholic family (one of his uncles was a Cardinal), and the fact that he had broken with the Church of Rome was by Juley accounted to him for righteousness.

Then there were the rides he gave her. He had rigged up a wicker trailer, and attached it to that amazing machine of his which Juley would insist on calling the velocipede. She enjoyed every moment of the velocipede from its arrival at the front door. She liked to feel the neighbours at their windows while Mario was tucking her in. She smiled happily at the little crowd of children who gathered round ; and when he rang his bell, and took her slowly down the long slope to Woodlands Road and back again, she was in raptures. Each time they went out thus her wonder was new. She could not grow accustomed to it.

But she would not hear about his flying.

"If we had been meant to fly," she said, looking sorrowfully at him, "God would have given us wings." And she refused to listen to his ready arguments. So he let her be.

To Joanna he spoke little of his work, but much of woman's place in the scheme of things. He laughed to scorn her ideas of companionship between man and woman.

"Do you think I would choose you," he exclaimed one day, "if I wished for a companion ? You, a little, ignorant girl from Glasgow, with no experience of life, no knowledge of what most interests me—machinery : no intellect to speak of ? Why, you do not even know my language ! Some day— say twenty years hence—when you have learned all I have to teach you, you may be a fit companion for a man, and then only perhaps. But by then you will have lost what now sets my heart on fire. Companion ! My poor baby, you do not know what you are talking of, and what it is you want, you still less know. Would you be here with me now, dropping your eyes before the desire in mine, if we were companions ? I think not."

Joanna and he were having tea at a little wayside hotel to which he had brought her in his trailer. The country air had reddened her cheeks, but Mario was whiter than ever, and his eyes danced dark and fanatical in his head. The girl had no answer ready to his tirade, and he expected none. He continued.

"You and your Bob may be companions if you please. Both of you free to come and go, to take other companions— as many as you like—to live apart, to discuss this theory and that when you meet. Very good. You might have his companionship. Does it satisfy you ? "

Rolling her bread into balls on the table-cloth, Joanna tried to collect her scattered forces. She could never stand up to Mario in argument, and was so perturbed under his glance that her ideas seemed to melt like snow-wreaths near a bon-fire.

" Can't one have the two things together ? " she appealed to him timidly.

" In theory, perhaps," he replied, and as he spoke he buttoned up with an air of finality the high collar of his leather coat, " but not in practice. Not at least when I am the man and you the woman. There is at this moment a man at the corner table who has been looking at you, and I want to kill him for daring to do so. Is that companionship ? Na ! Let us go back. Waiter, the bill ! "

As the two left the room, Mario, holding the door open for her, glared at the man in the corner. He was an inoffensive young fellow, who had been struck, not really so much by Joanna as by the atmosphere engendered by the couple. The moment they had gone the other people in the room began to discuss them.

Another of their talks was in the park. It was strange how in Joanna's emotions the park came to be associated with Mario, as the Botanic Gardens were with Bob. And in the same way the two wooings were bound up with their seasons. Bob's young love, so confused and pathetic, had been in the early spring; Mario's was in the late autumn. And autumn even more than spring is disturbing to those who give themselves readily to Nature's impulses. For if in spring we are pierced by the innumerable points of flame which dart skywards from the ground, in autumn our senses are more subtly assailed. For passion's sake then the earth is laying aside her ornaments. There is a new restlessness and rapture of bird life, a new sense of disquiet and elation. The wooded places are full of the intoxicating smoulder of fecundity.

On this November evening, traces of a recent hail-shower still gleamed on the black railings, on the slopes of grass, on the dark-boled trees, each standing in the circle of its own lovely droppings. The naked sky, lofty and compassionate, flung its arch over a glittering world. And in that arch, incredibly remote, ineffably pure, hung the pale waxing moon like a beaker of fretted silver. To the right of the path chosen by Mario and Joanna, a tree crowned with a topknot of ivy sheltered a noisy tribe of starlings. It swayed gently under the birds' impetuous communings. Over the pink granite bridge swung a glossy private carriage drawn by a pair of bays, and Mario pulled Joanna aside so that she should not be spattered by the mud which lay thick on the road.

Having crossed the river the two climbed the farther hill. Here and there were seats on little semicircular terraces facing the University, and on one of these they sat down. Mario, as usual, spoke first.

"How like olives those are, except for the colour," he said, "are they not?" He was pointing to a group of small, distorted trees on the slope below them.

"I've never seen olive trees."

"No? But you shall, and soon. Yes, as soon as possible." Mario spoke meditatively, as if calculating, and his eyes did not leave the trees. The girl wondered at his prolonged interest in them.

"What kind of trees are they?" he asked her.

Joanna didn't know.

Now he looked at her. "Do you know anything?"

Joanna crimsoned. Truly, beside this man she felt her ignorance. But deeper than her shame was the sensual gratification of this inferiority.

"That one is a willow, I know," she said, pointing to a nearer tree. Its long pliant boughs trailed their ends on the grass all round it, hiding the central stem. "Isn't it like a cage?"

"A cage, yes," he agreed; and again he turned his eyes from the tree to Joanna's face.

"How would you like to live in a cage, a cage full of sunshine and beauty and delight, a cage of which the man you loved kept the key?"

"I don't think I should like it, thank you."

"Why not?"

"A cage is a prison, isn't it?"

"A prison!" Mario made a gesture of despair. "Oh, you English women with your phrases!"

"I'm not English, I'm Scotch."

"Well, you Scottish women with your theories! Tell me what are the things in the world of best worth to a woman? Are they not air, light, gaiety, love, ease, shelter from the brutalities of life, children, tenderness, adoration? Does this freedom you talk of secure these? Does it not in reality make them impossible? Tell me, you learned little girl of Glasgow, will freedom give you what you hunger for? Look at me, and tell me."

But Joanna stared persistently at the willow.

" Look at me," he repeated.

" Why should I look at you," she opposed him with low-voiced obstinacy, " if I want to go on looking at the tree ? " Her words sounded to her indescribably childish and silly, but she was near to tears.

" You are afraid to look at me," said Mario ; and the old taunt succeeded. Joanna turned her face to him. More beautiful she was to him then than any picture he had formed of her. He leaned nearer, gripping the back of the bench with one hand.

" I feel as if once, centuries ago, I had kept you in a cage, and you liked it," he said. " And so that I might have your portrait painted, without the painter falling in love with you, I dressed you as a young man. I shall take you to see that portrait in London ; and later when we go to Italy together, I shall get Maddalena, my sister, to make you a suit of black cloth with a linen chemise open at the neck, like the girl in the picture. Maddalena is clever at dress. She will teach you also how to clothe yourself as a woman ; for even in this you are ignorant. The coat you wear now is so hideous, I shudder at it. Yes, Maddalena shall teach you much. But I shall teach you more. Then, after many years, when at last your youth is gone and your beauty, you will be a fit companion for men. What do you say ? Will you stay and go to school there ? " Mario's voice rose as he waved an arm at the darkening University. " Or will you come away and learn from me ? There you will have books and bones. Here with me "—touching his breast—" you will have all that is of value, in either books or bones—you will have life. And very soon you must decide."

VI

Next morning Joanna woke very early, yet feeling unusually refreshed. She was conscious of an exquisite calm, and had a vision, crystal-clear and unshaken, of existence. All difficulties fell from her. She knew now as if it were written on her bedroom wall that she would be Mario's wife, and would go away with him to Italy. Already she had shed her life in Glasgow like a husk—had it happened in sleep ? Before her now lay the new life, and she set her face towards it freed. She was done with questioning. Everything was beautifully simple. Mario needed her : no one else did. It was wonderful to be needed by this dark, exigent man with the curious beauty that took her breath away. Everything could be left to him. She had only to hold out her hands—to give. Splendid, giving to anyone who wanted what you had with such blazing eagerness. She would think no more about Bob. He had failed her, or she had failed him. Which, she might never know. Thinking of Bob, she seemed to see his face drowned in tears. There was a fountain of tears in her for Bob, or for herself in connection with Bob. That must be sealed up. There were no tears in her for Mario. This was a thought that gave strength. Mario might frighten her. He would never be able to hurt her, as Bob had hurt her—as Bob was hurting her even now. It was through her dreams that Bob hurt her. About Mario she had no dreams. He was her escape into reality.

Resting there in bed, lapped by the silken warmth of her half-awakened body, she wondered why Mario, who wanted her so much more than ever Bob had wanted her, should estimate her so much lower. Bob had admired her drawing, her clothes, the way she did her hair. But Mario——

She recalled the first time she had taken him to her studio. How he had poured scorn on her drawing, reminding her in his denunciations of Nilsson, the Swedish master of design at the Art School, who was the only teacher for whom she had even attempted to work during this last term.

" You draw with your head alone," Mario had said. " One must draw with one's heart, one's blood." And in quick boredom he had turned from her work to the pair of old wine glasses from which, eight months before, Bob and she had drunk their betrothal champagne.

" These now," he had exclaimed, " these are truly beautiful. Look at them and see how the maker understood the working of glass with his heart as well as with his brain. And so in the glass you find the wickedness of his heart proclaimed as well as the goodness, a piece of pure, defiant art. In your drawing you suppress the evil that partly creates you, so there is no good there either, no beauty of life. How did you come by the glasses ? They are Irish, I should think ? "

Taking them from the mantelpiece, blowing off the studio dust, holding them delicately to the light, Mario had considered them with that intentness of his which was always a wonder to Joanna. He never looked at anything vaguely, as she, confused and absorbed by her own emotions, so constantly did.

He had raised his brows, as she told him how she had bought them of a dealer for a few shillings.

"But I won't tell him *why* I got them," she had said to herself. "That will be a secret always between them and me and Bob."

Yet immediately something that did not seem herself had made her tell him.

He had watched her face during the brief, hesitating recital, still holding the glasses delicately by their stems, one in either hand, between the forefinger and the thumb. And when she was done, he had raised his hands a very little, and opened his fingers. And the glasses—the lovely wine-glasses that were like river water full of the shimmer of wavelets and criss-cross reeds—had been shattered on the hearth-stone in ten million shivers.

He had offered no apology. "That then is the end of them," he had said. That was all.

Yes; it might be that she did not love this man, but she exulted in him. She exulted in his certitude, in his power of action. To her he appeared unhampered, and therefore god-like, adorable. And he so gloriously knew what he wanted. He wanted her—Joanna—out of all the world of women. Well, he was to have her. It was decided, and decided by some power quite outside of her will.

VII

From that moment the end was lost sight of in the many exigencies of the means. On the amazing central fact of her marriage Joanna did not let herself dwell, even in her most solitary hours. All her energies, and her awaking powers of management, were thrown into bringing about the wedding with the least possible delay.

Once she had pledged herself to Mario, there seemed no valid reason for delay, while there were many for haste. The sooner he returned to Italy, the better their prospects. But he would not suffer a parting. He was afraid of losing her. And Joanna was glad of his refusal; for she shared his fear, shared it strangely on his account. "If he goes away he'll never get me!" was her scarce articulate thought. So they both conspired in doing away with the inevitable obstacles.

And soon their haste, which to their small circle had at first seemed the height of unreason, assumed an air almost of common sense. It was a little sudden perhaps, but after all the circumstances were exceptional

As for Juley, in the turn things had taken she perceived the finger of God. Of late she had been conscious of Joanna's restless lassitude. But from any appeal for confidence the girl had at once recoiled farther than ever into herself. To pray and sorrow in private, then, was all the mother could do. And might not Mario be God's answer? One must have faith. Had Sholto been alive, all would have been different.

VIII

In Glasgow at the moment the Bannermans were awkwardly placed for a pastor, so after much talk it was decided that the wedding should take place in London. Mario went on first to arrange matters with the Italian Consul, who was a friend; and Joanna followed with her mother.

They so nearly missed the London train that it had begun to move before they were on board. Juley, worn out by the rush, sank down at once in the carriage; but Joanna stayed in the corridor, and hung out of the window to say good-bye to her brothers.

Linnet, rushing alongside, thrust something into her hand —something small wrapped in tissue paper.

"That's my present," he panted. "I hadn't any money, but I thought you'd be able to wear this. You'd better not tell mother. She might be vexed."

Joanna clutched the little packet, and nodded and smiled. She couldn't see for tears. The train ran faster and Linnet stopped. He waved his cap up and down in a queer, jerky way, as if shy of moving his arms in public. Farther down the platform stood Sholto, making wide gestures with two hand-kerchiefs. He had been learning signalling in his cadet corps at school.

Suddenly the sister felt like a deserter. How could she leave the boys! Why was she doing it? To get married? It seemed unnatural, monstrous. Sholto had worked hard to get his present finished in time. It was a poker-worked toilet set—brushes, hand-mirror, boxes and tray—all with the same lily-of-the-valley design. She leaned out waving. She waved and waved till the train, curving, cut the platform from sight. Then in the corridor she opened Linnet's present. He had given her his father's gold signet-ring. It had been his since his fifteenth birthday, and though he never wore it they all knew he treasured it. It bore the Bannerman crest—*pro patria* under a naked demi-man holding a banner. Joanna put it on under her glove.

IX

The night before the wedding, Georgie cried a good deal, for she was sure Joanna didn't properly love the man she was marrying, and marriage without love was the desecration of desecrations. Georgie came to sleep at the little temperance hotel in Bloomsbury where Juley had taken rooms, and she shared Joanna's bed. Joanna's replies to her questions confirmed her worst fears. Her sister was entering a loveless marriage.

But Georgie understood that it could not be stopped; and miserable as she was, it was Georgie who insisted on a white satin bow upon the coachman's whip.

They had hired a carriage with two horses—Georgie said they must have two—to take them to the Registrar's where Mario waited with his friend the Consul. The marriage was over in five minutes, and they all drove on to the station for lunch.

Joanna, in a blue travelling dress, the price of which she would not tell Georgie, and a little white, close-fitting hat, smote on her mother's heart. She looked so unprepared, so lamentably young. Yet to the last she had sheered away from all maternal warnings and counsel.

The farewell was scrappy and confused. Juley, at the last moment, remembering injunctions about Aunt Perdy to whom she was sending presents, almost forgot to kiss Joanna good-bye. Georgie blubbered, but bore up. Mario was angry because there were other people in the carriage. But at this Joanna felt a secret relief.

Not till they were on the Dover packet did she come alive to the strange adventure. She had not been out of England before. The Channel boat was different from any steamer on the Clyde. The waters of the Channel rippled and shone, as she had never seen other waters ripple and shine. Near her some people chatted in French. The sailors ran about. There was a smell of biscuits and brandy, of ropes, of tar, of engines, of the sea—the smell of foreign travel.

A handsome woman, very well dressed, with beautifully tinted hair, scarlet lips and blackened eyelids, looked Joanna down and up, and Joanna took her envy for criticism. Mario had gone to find deck chairs. He stood at some distance speaking to a sailor, his shoulders moving. Very foreign and animated, yet very much at home he seemed to her in these unaccustomed surroundings. Afraid, but thrilled through and through, his bride watched him. That man in the grey suit was her husband. He was a stranger to her : at this moment he appeared a complete stranger. Yet she had left her mother, her home, all that was familiar, to come away with him.

This then was life at last ! But it seemed less real, more dream-like than anything that had gone before. She was going to a strange land, was going among strangers, was going alone with that passionate stranger in the grey suit. The train of experience was alight. Greatly she feared it. But not for anything would she have escaped.

Soon Mario came, with the sailor carrying chairs. When he had made things comfortable in his deft, experienced way, he groped under the spread rug for Joanna's hand. The middle-aged woman with the very red lips looked on for a moment ; then she turned with a little smile, and leaning on the deck-rail, gazed toward the coast of France.

CHAPTER VII

I

THEY were to spend their honeymoon at Vallombrosa. For Mario the place had happy memories of childhood; for Joanna the lovely sounding name seemed to breathe the essence of a dream Italy. She imagined Vallombrosa as a wonderful, classic valley, shaded by great trees such as never grew at home, and it was grief to her that they could not go there by a through train from Calais. They would have to stay a night in Florence on the way.

Mario had not told his sister of their movements, so no one met them at the station. Joanna had not believed any journey could be so long and so tiring; but as they crossed the deserted piazza to their hotel, a porter running before them with their hand luggage, the midnight air refreshed her wonderfully. She was invigorated too, even in the darkness, by the strangeness of everything. Among these unfamiliar buildings, breathing this new air, walking under this foreign sky, the man with whom she had passed the last forty-eight hours in the cramped room of a railway carriage became suddenly an old and tried friend. She clung to his arm and reassured herself by stealing glances at his dim profile. Though he did not once turn his face to hers she knew he was pre-occupied utterly by thoughts of her.

At the hotel bureau some letters were handed to Mario, but he stuffed them into his pocket without looking at them. Then Joanna and he were taken up in a lift, and followed their luggage down a long passage. The bedroom had the highest ceiling Joanna had ever seen in a bedroom, and the loftiest windows, with curtains arranged in a different way from any curtains at home. But she was most of all struck by the two little high beds. These were pushed together, made up as one, and turned into a huge diaphanous tent by white net draperies which hung from high wooden poles. Instinctively

Joanna fancied some bridal symbol, and she would not have been surprised if the snowy hangings had been crowned with orange blossoms. But Mario, seeing her interest, explained mosquito-curtains to her; and as she curiously fingered the net, the porter smiled and said something to Mario. It was clearly the first time the young signora had been in Italy!

When they were left alone Mario glanced over his letters and handed one in a grey envelope to Joanna. "For you," he said, and throwing his own unopened on a table he went into the adjoining bathroom, where Joanna heard him turn on a water-tap.

At the sight of the handwriting on her letter, Joanna caught her breath. It was from Bob! Its presence here in Italy appeared a miracle till she saw that it had been forwarded from Collessie Street in Linnet's hand. It must have reached home immediately after her leaving, and so had outrun her on the journey south. What could Bob have to say? But what did it matter what he said? The envelope felt very thin. Suppose now, too late, Bob were to tell her that he loved her, that he had loved her all along? Why else should he have written?

Sitting half on, half against the bed, so that the poles at the corners creaked from the strain on the netting, Joanna read the short note Bob had written her. He wished her well—he had passed his examination—would shortly start for Africa—he was hers ever—Bob. And underneath the signature as a postscript he had set the words, "Have a good time." That was all.

Joanna, more shaken than she knew by the sight of Bob's handwriting, was relieved, and chagrined, in the same moment. She was tired out too from the journey, irritated by the dust which felt gritty against her skin all over her body, overwrought by the excitement of Mario's persistent wooing in the dark railway carriage. Throwing back her head, and puckering up her face like a child, she burst out crying. As the first loud desolate wail escaped her she felt tremendous surprise. "I've never cried like this before," she said within herself. "What can be happening to me?" And she went on crying aloud, finding wonderful relief and a kind of healing in the new unrestraint.

Hearing the noise above his own splashing, Mario came running in to her with a frightened face. His hands were wet, and he had taken off his coat and his collar, which made him into a stranger again. He questioned Joanna anxiously. What was wrong? She did not know; but between her astonished sobs she tried to tell him. She was afraid he would be angry. But instead he was kind. She handed him the letter to read, and having glanced through it, he let it fall on the carpet, comforting her with his cool, damp hands. And presently, before she had quite stopped crying, he took her to the mirror and made her laugh at the sight of her dirty, tear-stained cheeks. He pulled the pins out of her hat with his deft fingers, and covered her face with kisses.

"You see I love you, dirt and all!" he said, holding her, laughing at her, brushing the letter and her tears aside as mere childishness. Joanna's heart was warm with gratitude to him. This man knew how to treat her. And now with his wet pushed-back hair, and his strong bare neck, he looked boyish, different from the Mario she had known before. He had irresistible grace. No one had warned her of the beauty men conceal beneath their disfiguring clothes, their stiff collars.

II

Early next morning she was wakened by the chant of a goatherd passing with his flock under the hotel windows. Hearing it first in her dreams, this most fascinating of Florentine street-cries seemed to her a melody of unearthly sweetness. Then following, and mingling with it, came other strange cries and sounds floating from the foreign street through the closed shutters into the quiet high-walled room. It was dark in the room, but she became immediately aware that sunlight of a kind she had never yet seen was filling the outside world, beating strongly like waves against the fast-bolted shutters.

Everything was strange. But strangest of all was to see on the pillow beside hers the dark disordered head of the man who had married her. He was still asleep, his face turned away; and keeping quite still on her side with her knees drawn up and her palm under her cheek, Joanna thought of the past night. Wave after wave of purely physical recollections swept through her; but at the same time in her brain a cool spectator seemed to be sitting aloof and in judgment. This then was marriage! This droll device, this astonishing, grotesque experience was what the poets had sung since the beginning. To this all her quivering dreams had led, all Mario's wooing touches and his glances of fire! The reality made her feel a stranger in a strange world. Not a rebellious stranger. She was humbly anxious to conform to reality—eager to accept and get used to the new aspect of things. But she was before all things astounded.

Suddenly she felt she must gaze at her husband under the altered conditions he had created, and raising herself very cautiously on her elbow she leaned over and peered down at him in the half-light. He was sleeping like a child with imperceptible breathing, and he had the innocent look of a child on his unconscious face.

Joanna, by gentle degrees shifted her position till she was crouching over Mario, then suddenly he opened infantine eyes. She was caught, and she hung above him breathless, gazing ensnared, stirred to a new feeling by the changing in his eyes from babe to man. The next moment his hands had found her, and he drew her down, uttering a deep chuckling groan of content. "Mia moglie," he breathed triumphantly. "Mia moglie, mia moglie, moglie mia!"

III

Vallombrosa was as deserted as lovers could wish. The season had ended weeks ago. Hotels and pensions were forbiddingly closed as if for eternity and except for the peasants, and the bitter-faced young priest, there was not a soul about. Even the *Foresta* had its shutters barred, though the careful padrone walked through the house each day throwing them open to the sunshine for a few hours to keep the place aired. The humble little Villino Medici to which Mario and Joanna went was the only exception, and its proprietor was never tired of telling his guests that they were having the finest weather of the year hitherto. There was hot sunshine all day, and only the least hint of frost every evening.

Joanna had been entranced by their journey up in the funicular. This was the last thing she had expected—to go uphill to Vallombrosa! It was late afternoon and the yet unfallen gold of chestnuts and Italian oaks glowed with an intimate joyousness against the remote amethyst of the sky which grew deeper moment by moment. The few passengers—some soldiers and market-women, with whom at first Mario and his wife shared the train, alighted at stopping places on the lower part of the hill; so the two were soon left alone except for the conductor, who had twinkling eyes, an indigo chin and a huge grey moustache. He smiled indulgently on them, and allowed them to stand out on the little platform in front, while he turned his fat shoulders on them and read his *Corriere* as long as the light lasted.

They leaned forward on the rail, he watching her, she gazing with delight first on one side, then on another, of the stony winding track which hardly seemed to violate the hillside. The little engine behind them throbbed gallantly as it pushed them up and up. They did not speak much, but now and then Mario kissed Joanna's shoulder, keeping his lips there till she felt their warmth and their hunger through her thin blouse. It seemed years since the early morning when she had found something ludicrous and inadequate in the decree of nature. Now she thought of the coming night with awakening senses; and for the first time with deliberate intent to stir her husband's pulses she turned in the quivering light and looked at him. Joanna hardly recognized herself in this voluptuous charmer under Italian skies. But was it right? Did all wives feel and behave like this? She thought of her mother, of Mrs. Boyd, of Aunt Georgina, of the teaching and the traditions on which she had been nourished. Which was right—those traditions or this abandonment? It seemed impossible that both could be right, yet could anything be wrong which gave such release, such harmony with the golden world and the violet heavens? It harmed no one, and it swept away the uneasiness under which her youth had laboured for so long. She could laugh now in a voice she hardly knew, could cry easily, refreshingly, could express her emotion swiftly in gestures. She no longer jarred on herself. Joanna remembered a frequent saying of her mother's that the test of a thing's rightness was whether one could pray to God about it without shame. Well, she had never felt so full of worship Therefore it must be right—and yet——

With her husband's arm round her, she looked down between the gold and silver of some birch trees to the great plain below. The mist lay there like fallen columns, and the river, which Mario told her was the Arno, wound in and out shiny like a snail's track. A high old villa on a pointed hill massed itself grandly with its body-guard of cypresses against the sky. Some trees near had scarlet stems from which a few green leaves hung limply. As Joanna gazed, the sky, changing from violet to an intenser blue, seemed to tremble downwards on the waiting earth like a lover assured of his welcome yet incredulous of his good fortune. Again she turned her face to Mario, this time without a trace of consciousness or coquetry, and all the magic of the Italian night now dwelt for her in his eyes.

They had to drive from the station some miles in a little open carriage. There was no moon, and the road ran in darkness through the high, breathless pine forests. But lying back with their heads against the folded hood of the carriage they could watch the deep blue, winding river of the night sky flowing between the tree-tops with its foam of stars. So as to lean back comfortably Joanna took off her hat, and wound a white scarf round her head and neck. Mario said it made her look like a nun, and he knelt on the carriage floor at her feet to make love to her. His beseeching face seemed to her like a piece of escaped starlight on her knees.

IV

Next morning he took her through the woods to a little pillared shrine in which the dead leaves were drifted in heaps. On the way they passed many other shrines, and Joanna exclaimed at their number and at the feeling of happiness their presence gave to her. In Mario's shrine he and his sister Maddalena had often played as children, and as he sat there now with his wife, he talked gaily of his boyhood, which had been very happy.

Again and again, as he was speaking, Joanna felt all the old, accustomed moral values slipping away, and it came to her that she must put new ones in their places, without a soul from the old life to help her.

In a perfectly matter-of-fact way Mario told that his father had never married his mother—as was indeed reasonable, seeing that Count Rasponi was the head of a so famous family, and Maria Cecchi merely the daughter of a professor of mechanics at Turin. Besides, the whole affair had been simply a youthful escapade. As was proper, however, Maria's father had brought pressure to bear on the house of Rasponi, with the fitting result that Mario was legitimized and educated at his father's expense. Within a year of his birth his mother

had found a husband in her own class—a simple surgeon—and
of that marriage was Maddalena born.

Since reaching her teens, said Mario, his half-sister had
treated him constantly as though he, not she, had been the
younger. She had not married, and since the death of both
her parents he had lived with her. Warmly he praised her
qualities. "When you see her," he smiled, "you will see a
veritable Italian woman."

But Joanna was nervous of the ordeal awaiting her in
Florence, where a long visit to Maddalena had been promised.
And even when they had left the shrine, crossing a road and
descending a green slope all dappled with sunshine, she was
still anxiously forecasting the meeting between herself and
this unknown, perhaps hostile sister-in-law.

Nothing Mario could say brought reassurance. Yet a
moment later Maddalena was forgotten, and all else. For
Joanna, attracted irresistibly by a company of trees which
stood farther down in a hollow of the slope, had run forward,
and was trying how many falling leaves she could catch.

There were perhaps a dozen trees together, with stems as
white as milk and their leaves blowing silver against the blue
sky; and in their slender posturings and shadows interlaced,
they were like a group of Botticelli's women.

Mario stood and laughed as she raced to and fro after the
leaves. Every puff of the morning air loosened one or two;
sometimes in a stillness many showered at once. But they
evaded the grasp like wild things in their wavering course
downwards, and each time she lost one Joanna cried out with
disappointment.

"Each leaf you catch brings a happy year!" she called
out, bird-like and shrill, to Mario. And though he found her
excitement childish, and in some curious way unwelcome, he
presently joined in the game. Already Joanna had grown
clever at it. She was getting leaf after leaf, and she laughed
with joyous spitefulness because her husband did not catch
one.

Then they grew tired and sat down, and Joanna counted her
happy years. Sheep came and cropped the short grass near
them, and in another part of the dimpled field two little horses
never ceased waving their tails. The hours went winged.
Here life seemed quite simple. There was no past, no future,
only the simple, beautifully rounded present.

v

Three days later Mario said he must stay indoors that afternoon to write letters. He suggested that Joanna too should write, sitting at the table beside him. As yet she had only sent a post-card home each day, and had torn up several attempts at a letter to her mother.

But she felt incapable of setting words on paper, and said that she would wait for him outside.

A look of distress crossed Mario's face, but he let her go, telling her twice over exactly to which spot between the disused fish-ponds of the monastery he would follow her in a very short time. As they parted there was a moment of enmity between them, and Joanna knew that he had guessed at and hated her longing to be alone.

Yet as she went slowly down the hill, her solitude was very sweet to her. It was the first time she had been alone in any way that counted since her marriage. When Mario was with her she could only feel ; now she could think quietly, luxuriously. It was as if tight coils in her mind were unloosed. And this though she had been unaware lately of any strain in his company.

Sitting on a log between the ponds and the edge of the wood, she faced the neat quadrangles of water, and her thoughts flew to Collessie Street. What were they all doing ?

Without warning an overmastering affection for her mother swept through her.

"When I go back," she told herself passionately, " I'll be loving and most tender, and mother will be so happy at that. And the boys too. Why have I always been so cold, when I love them so very dearly ? I wonder they can like me at all. But they *will* love me when they find how changed I am. I should like them to love me tremendously."

Then sharply came the realization of foolishness in all such thoughts. The old life was over, and with it its chances of loving and winning love. There might be other chances later, never the same again. And now it seemed to Joanna that she could easily, oh, so easily, have been a loving daughter. It was simply that she had not thought of it at the time.

Again she found herself saying, " When I get back——" and again had to pull herself up. How was it that she could not make herself believe that she had finally broken with the life at home ? How was it that she could never for long rid herself of the irrational conviction that her life with Mario was an interlude which would soon pass ?

"When I get back"—only the night before she had unwittingly let the phrase fall in talk with Mario, and had stopped short, seeing the look in his eyes. He had demanded the meaning of her words, but she had no explanation. "You speak as if you were my mistress," he had said. "Remember you are my wife ; and as I am an Italian, you are my wife for as long as I live."

He had looked strangely angry, Joanna thought, considering that it was after all a natural slip. But now, as she sat waiting for him through this first long half-hour of separation, she knew she could figure no future in their marriage. Once, twice, three times she tried ; and the vain attempts made her so unhappy that she rose and went a little way into the wood.

"I have no imagination, that's it," she told herself for comfort ; "or perhaps all newly married women feel like that."

As she strayed in and out amid the thin skirting of trees, she knew, as if she saw him, how Mario was writing with a frown on his face, and hurriedly, that he might join her with the least possible delay. Before letting her go, he had told her she need never expect to walk out alone in Florence, not even for five minutes. But this she determined must be put down to his passing vexation. That he should have spoken it in earnest, she could not well conceive. Yet there had been in his face as he spoke a look of fixed, almost maniacal resolve, that she was shaken at the remembrance. She had once wondered if Bob were mad. Now she asked herself the same question of Mario. Were all men mad ? She felt lonely in the world, like some one from another star. Would she ever learn the ways of earth ?—ever feel herself at home here ? If she had even possessed memories of another world, there would be some solid standing in this. But as she was, she seemed to belong nowhere.

At that moment Mario stepped out of the villino looking in her direction. From her shelter of trees Joanna saw him, and saw him worried by her absence, but she would make no sign. Instead, to tease him still more, she hid behind one of the broader tree-trunks, and gathered her bright blue skirts close to her legs, so that there might be no reassuring flutter. As the afternoon was cool, she had borrowed one of her husband's knitted waistcoats with sleeves, which he wore when cycling; and with the little orange wool coat over her vivid gown, she looked like some gay-coloured, shy bird.

She couldn't help laughing to herself as she watched the unwillingness with which Mario turned in at the monastery gates with his letters. If they did not go at once they would miss the post. Besides, she knew that he had to buy stamps. But she saw him hesitate, and twice he looked over his shoulder before he could enter the little post office at the top of the courtyard.

He was gone but a few seconds; then pushing his letters hastily into the outside box, he ran across the wide paved space, and came running all the way down to the fish-ponds.

Joanna, still in hiding, smiled broadly and held her breath. Her heart was leaping deliciously. When he came quite close she meant to run into his arms. Now she could hear his quickened breathing, as he looked uncertainly on either side.

Then he called her name. "Giovanna! Giovanna!" he called. And she no longer smiled. At the note of unlooked-for panic in his voice, her blood stood still. All idea of the embrace she had planned, died in her. She stepped out from behind her tree, confronting him. His face was livid, insane, and he stumbled over a root as he ran towards her.

"Never do that again," he commanded in a strangling fury. "But you shall not again have the chance while I live, for not again shall you go out by yourself."

He stood close to her, and now that his fear was past, he was threatening her. Joanna shrank a step back, but he caught her wrists.

"What did it mean, last night, that you spoke as if we shall not for long be together? Eh? You tell me, what did it mean?"

Joanna shook her head; and she had to moisten her lips with her tongue before she could answer.

"I don't know."

"You don't know! Dio mio! Can I trust you? What are you? What kind of a woman? I don't know. I know nothing of you. You have treacherous eyes. Down in the field yesterday they were green as the grass. Now they are grey. They change. And your little tongue just now crept out between your lips like a viper. What is the meaning of it ? Why do you hide from me ? "

Joanna, though now she felt both afraid and in the wrong, stared proudly at her husband, then turned her eyes away with ostentatious carelessness. Anyhow he had no right to speak so to her, and she must be angry in self-defence. At the same time there was a secret, inebriating enjoyment for her in it all. In a new way she became conscious of her power as a woman.

" I did it for fun of course," she said. " Can't you understand a joke ? "

" You did it for fun ? A joke ! One day you would perhaps think it fun to be unfaithful to me ? It would be your little joke to deceive your husband ? Perhaps this is the kind of woman you really are ? Have you been unfaithful to me already ? Here among the trees. That dog of a priest——"

At Joanna's very heart something cried out that she was truly accused ; but to stifle and deny that voice all her powers leapt up like ruffians. Her brain repulsed his words as preposterous, her flesh sprang taut, so that with one sharp movement she wrenched her hands free, and from her lips came an exclamation as of one bitterly injured.

But in anger she knew at once she was no match for Mario, and the next moment she had rushed into another falseness.

" Mario," she said, looking at him very quietly, "I don't understand. You know I only hid for fun. It was silly of me, and I'm sorry it put you out ; but I did nothing wrong."

She spoke with false, lovely gentleness, deceiving herself as well as Mario, and immediately he was full of penitence.

" Forgive what I said. It meant nothing. But you make me suffer so terribly. You should not have hidden in that way. I cannot bear it. Never hide from me again. Let us say no more, either of us. Let us kiss and forgive."

He held out his arms with the expression Joanna most loved on his face—human and pleading, very winning to her ; and she ran into his embrace.

" What are you like ? " he whispered, when they had stood some moments wrapped together in that solitary place. " What are you like, Giovanna ? " and he drew back his head the better to see his wife's face. "To me your body is like steel and white swansdown. Your neck, your breasts, are soft as swansdown. Your straight, fine thighs are like steel. Your arms, so long and small, are like the necks of swans. I should like never to let you go. I wish you could be buckled to me, close, close like this for always. When you go from me I feel as if my vitals had been torn out—so empty —quite useless."

He held her still closer, bracing his body hard against hers, and suddenly he laughed.

"I love you for being so strong," he said. "Do you know you have muscles like a leopardess? I must teach you to fence with the sabres. I have a pair in Florence. We shall fence in the evenings when I come home, in our own room, and you shall wear the black suit Maddalena is to make for you. I believe, Giovanna, you could wrestle with me and make it difficult for me to throw you!"

At the challenge, Joanna who had been hanging limp and heavy in his arms, tightened her hold on him with an excited laugh. Though so near the Villino, their seclusion at this hour was perfect. Over her husband's shoulder, between the trees, away along the road she could just see a tiny black figure— the priest, on his way to Compline. She remembered his young, unhappy face, and for that moment it was not Mario that she held against her breast.

They began to wrestle.

Silently, save for little, gasping laughs when one for the minute got the better, they strove with one another. They swayed to and fro, staggering. Sometimes they would lean against a tree, panting, then started afresh.

Joanna fought her hardest at once, and Mario matched himself to her, always keeping something in reserve. As a school-girl might, Joanna really strained every nerve to prove the stronger. Till, at length, seeing the laughter in her face die under the grimness of supreme effort, Mario used his full strength suddenly, and threw her.

She had tried her best, and she rejoiced that he had beaten her. He had made her his anew, and she longed for him. For the first time she was truly his bride, he her bridegroom.

"Mario! Oh, Mario, look at the sky!" she breathed— "the colour of it."

As they lay there all slackly, resting on their backs on the sweet ground, recovering their breath, staring up and up between the tree-tops at the quiet sky, the monastery bell began to ring for Compline. The smell of fresh-hewn wood came to them, and the sharp fragrance of the pine needles. Now and then a cone rustled heavily from branch to branch, and thudded to the earth. Somewhere a cicada whirred, like a pigmy's loom weaving indefatigably some fairy-web. Another hidden being spoke in eager whisperings, as a pencil moving over paper speaks, faltering at times as if the poet flagged, but only to begin again with the speed of inspiration. Yet another tiny creature of the forest shrilled and shrilled with its insistent, thread-like voice.

The austere, Gothic woodland, regular as stone, measured and set in that place by anointed hands, was full of life. There was life in the aisles of air between the trees, life in the dark plumes, life in the stark shafts, life amid the defiant roots.

The sky palpitated from blue to violet, from violet to a still deeper blue ; and a star came down and glittered like a tear in the black meshes of the pines.

VI

From that evening till the end of their fortnight at Vallombrosa, Joanna lived wholly in the new world Mario had created for her. It was a glowing world, inhabited only by the man and the desired woman.

They were always out of doors, and the forest was a shield shutting them off from every beyond of thought. Joanna's bodily well-being was flawless, and they walked, sometimes long distances, Mario taking pride in her vigour and staying power.

She was no longer troubled by a conviction of impermanence, nor by the dread of what awaited her ; but Mario, though he never left her side, was often in torture. He felt she was escaping him always. When she gazed away from him at trees or stars in a long rapture he could hardly bear it. Even when she entranced him by her leaping response to his passion, he had the sense that she was keeping her ultimate self immune—that she was holding back, waiting for some other touch than his. But of all this he said nothing to her. He could not even formulate it clearly to himself. Only by some frantic quality in his embraces did his grievance find expression.

What they had was not love. But it had beauty, and it served.

VII

It was in Florence that she began to feel herself a prisoner. They had not been two days with Maddalena in the little brown villa at San Gervasio before Joanna knew how far Mario had been from joking when he had spoken of keeping her in a cage.

In Glasgow the seeming extravagance of his words had helped her to blind herself to their truth. By the fish-ponds at Vallombrosa she had chosen to take his outbreak as a lover's passing frenzy. Even in Florence at first she refused to believe that her husband, if he could, would have had her go veiled like an Eastern woman; that he would have kept her sequestered behind high walls while business claimed him; that this desire of his was no bridegroom's freak, but a necessity of his nature—as much a part of him as his pallor or the blackness of his hair.

And Maddalena shared his view. Maddalena was to keep the door of the cage.

It was true that walking in the streets of Florence was an entirely different experience from walking in the streets of Glasgow. Joanna had to admit that to herself even before Maddalena pointed it out. With her West of Scotland fairness of skin, so distinct from any Italian fairness, she was a clear mark for every bold Italian eye. Besides, at the moment, she carried upon her the lovely bloom which comes to some women when they are first possessed. People twisted their heads round to look and drew one another's attention to her; and she dreaded the stares because of Mario's distorted face. She found this rage of his hard to reconcile with his light treatment of Bob's letter.

One day, within a week of their arrival, they went together to change some English money at Cook's office in the Via Tornabuoni. The place was crowded. A young Italian, marking Joanna, nudged his companion, and they both fixed eyes on her, murmuring to each other. They were at some distance, but in spite of the crowd, Joanna knew by Mario's lowering brows that he had observed them. He even stepped towards them balefully as they passed out by the glass doors to the street.

"If only he wouldn't take any notice," she thought with anger. Then just before her, at the little window of the *Bureau de Change*, some question was asked with a marked Edinburgh accent. Talking to the clerk about a circular note stood a middle-aged Scotsman. He had grey hair and a kind, shrewd face, and by the side of Mario's frenzy his known demeanour lacerated her with home-sickness. What was she doing among these insolent and jealous Italians? She longed to ask help of this safe man with the so familiar speech. From the look of him she felt sure he must know her Aunt Georgina. But when he moved away without a glance in her direction, she merely took his place mutely, and picked up her silver and nickel pieces without counting them.

Not speaking, she and Mario walked back down the Via Tornabuoni. Mario was inwardly vowing that his wife should go no step by herself in town or country, no matter how she might plead. He wondered if even Maddalena could be trusted with her. Not only was he maddened by the staring, but he had seen, as they left Cook's, a look of contempt and rebellion on Joanna's face. Joanna, for her part was aghast at the situation, and knew not which to hate more—the impudent Florentines or Mario's unreasonable anger with what after all seemed a custom of his country. She was alarmed too by her pain of home-sickness at sight of the man from Edinburgh. Had she not always felt alien in Edinburgh? Even in Glasgow had she not fancied herself a changeling? And here was a new loneliness engulfing her. Was there no place in the world where she might feel at home?

Both miserable, they made their way slowly through the slow-moving crowds of the Via Ceretane which was already sunk from daylight; and with the flame of sunset behind them, they made for the Piazza del Duomo where their tram was.

Two days before, seeing the Duomo for the first time, Joanna had remained aloof. To Mario's disappointment she had been unimpressed by the chequered mass of its marble.

But now, looking up from the pool of nightfall where they walked, she held her breath.

There, lifted up to burn and rejoice, claiming the sun for its own, like the face of some heavy, splendid flower—some *dahlia gloriosa* with a thousand hearts—was the façade.

At the sight, Joanna's private trouble fell from her, and a new impersonal happiness she was learning to recognize surged in her again. Ah, what a coward she had been about the man from Edinburgh ! What could he do for her ? He could but take her back to all she had left and must go on leaving.

But Mario ! Mario was of a piece with the new life. Mario was descended from the men who had spun this blossom out of stone ; and he desired her for beauty he saw in her. She too, like the façade, had a heart for the sun. And he had discovered it. Let Mario use her for his happiness in the way he would. Let him kill her if that was his way. But in spirit at least she would never now go back.

His wife's enthusiasm, and the quick recovery of pleasure in her face, turned Mario's humour. During the race for the tram, which had already started, they were both mad with excitement. All the way home they wooed each other.

VIII

But the bars of the cage were still there, and as one result of their presence Joanna was sorely deprived of the bodily exercise which had always meant so much to her. Mario, having now started work, left the villa at seven, or even earlier each morning. He had not to be at his office till half-past eight, but liked always to spend an hour first in the Cascine experimenting with the new brakes or seats or pedals that he was continually inventing. He did not return until six—sometimes seven o'clock, when it was already dark.

Maddalena hated walking. Though only thirty-five, she was already very stout. And as the ordinary household shopping was done by the cook soon after dawn, Joanna was compelled to spend the greater part of her time either indoors or lounging in the garden.

She tried to sketch.

The little villa, with its ochre walls of stucco on which had been painted imitation cross-timbers of a faded chocolate colour, was not attractive. But the *stabilimento* behind, where the contadini and their beasts lived, offered some pleasant arrangements of wall and terrace, some tempting patterns of sunshine and deep shadow.

For hours at a time she tried to put on paper some of the charm she saw in the *podere*, and all the while she kept reproaching herself for not having worked more seriously at her drawing when she had the chance. She was always quite dissatisfied with her efforts, and generally ended by laying aside her pencil and falling into a dream.

One morning she had been for half an hour thus drawing and despairing. She sat on a cushion upon the low brick wall which surrounded the well, and though it was past the middle of December the garden was full of strong sunshine. On the terrace above the well grew a pomegranate tree. Its lower branches were still green, but it had shaken off its upper foliage, and the slender flakes of gold lay all around. Some were fallen in the well, and these swam on the black water, a flotilla of yellow canoes, wonderfully frail yet with jaunty prows. On the terrace below the well a fig-tree, quite denuded of its leaves, held aloft a few figs right on the tips of its topmost twigs. Joanna thought some giant's child might have stuck them there for fun. No one would ever get them off now.

As she sat there dreaming and idle, half against her own will, she began to survey her new existence.

That afternoon, when Maddalena had finished her siesta, they would go together into Florence to the shops. They would not even walk as far as the Querce, but would wait for the Fiesole tram at the bottom of the rough lane which led from the villa ; and while they waited, Maddalena would sit to rest on one of the green iron chairs in front of the trattoria where Mario kept his bicycle. During the journey to town Joanna would catch glimpses of Italy that were almost too tantalizing to bear—glimpses of a hidden court-yard, a little piazza with a spouting fountain, a shop-window, a narrow, tempting street, a secretive palace. This was her Italy—glimpses and dreams. She was hungry to see everything more closely and at leisure. But on plunged the tram with much pounding of bells and tooting of horns to the Duomo. And at the Duomo they would at once hire a vetturino to take them from one shop to another.

Each article had to be bought at a different shop, and as Maddalena was very particular, each purchase demanded time and deliberation, quite apart from the great final haggle over the price. Maddalena did beautiful Florentine needle-work, and all the materials had to be of the best. In one shop she bought the linen, and the salesman had to lift down roll after roll of the cool, fine, woven flax from his high shelves before his customer was satisfied. Even then she would look over every metre herself before consenting to beat down the price. No thick thread, nor flaw of uneven weaving escaped her black eyes, and she was held in great respect by the shop-people. Her needles and reels came from another shop—the only place in Florence, she told Joanna, where thread could be depended on. It was near the Or San Michele, and beside it was another for embroidery frames and hoops. Here to-day, a frame was to be bought for Joanna, who was being taught drawn-thread work. But the shop that took up most time of all was the tiny one on the Lung 'Arno, where squares and long insertions and medallions of hand-made fillet were to be had. Maddalena went there not so much to buy (for it was a trap for tourists) as to learn new patterns and stitches. And Joanna knew that they would spend nearly an hour there, looking over piles of delicately fashioned dragons, and ships in full sail, and wolves suckling Romulus and Remus, before Maddalena bought the one small piece she had come for. After that, most likely they would go to Gilli's for Maddalena's glass of marsala, and Joanna would refuse the sweet wine in spite of persuasion, greedily drinking instead some China tea that tasted of straw, and eating little cakes stuffed with chestnuts.

Maddalena, who, with her moustache, her dense body, her dark, slightly twisted face, and her deep voice, had something of the schoolmistress about her, was trying to instruct her brother's wife. She had taken to Joanna immediately, and Joanna felt warm to her. But to the Italian woman the girl from Scotland seemed almost as ill-educated as a savage. Maddalena could not, for example, get over her sister-in-law's ignorance of all languages save her own, and though she herself spoke English almost as well as her brother, she refused as a rule to speak it with Joanna. If Joanna didn't understand what had been said in Italian, it would be repeated in French. Often the girl wondered what she had been doing during her eight years at the excellent school in Glasgow. Her own ignorance appalled her.

Another source of amazement to Maddalena, was Joanna's general untidiness. She was never ill-humoured about it, only boundlessly astonished; for the gently bred Italian girl is unfailingly and scrupulously tidy. One day she caught

Joanna in the act which had so often grieved Juley. The girl
was kicking off her outdoor shoes without untying the laces,
and the older woman cried aloud in horror. She snatched up
the shoes, examined their scratched heels, almost in tears,
and a flood of deprecatory speech flowed from her.

"And where are your shoe-trees?" she demanded at
length.

Joanna confessed she had none.

"No shoe-trees! Mother of God!" Maddalena exclaimed
in her masculine voice, so harsh, yet so warm, and she cast
her eyes up till the whites gleamed in her olive face. Next
day she made Joanna buy enough trees for all her shoes.

She had laughed and cried over Joanna's trousseau, declaring it was "all bits."

"Not two chemises alike!" she marvelled. "And Dio
mio! the fineness of this nightgown! With us only demi-
mondaines want such things: why, it will be in ribbons in
no time. Ah, you see here! What did I say? Already
a tear under the arm. That is where they always go first.
The other side too! Santa Vergine! You English! Is this
what you name a darn?"

And there and then she had made Joanna unpick her hasty
mending with a special pair of fine scissors, and had showed
her how a darn should look.

It was impossible to take anything she might say in bad
part, and Joanna had learned more from her sister-in-law of
material efficiency in a few weeks than from her mother in
years of despairing correction. She had learned to admire
order for its own sake, which was at least a step towards its
achievement. With a good will she had set about embroidering
her initials—J.E.R.—on every one of her under-garments,
and Maddalena's ready praise of her clever, if untrained,
fingers, was very pleasant. In a short time she actually felt
uncomfortable if she didn't put her shoes on their trees the
moment she had taken them off.

But the life they led at the villa did not satisfy her. And
as she sat by the well this morning, her dissatisfaction began
to take form in her thoughts. She saw Maddalena's existence,
so complete, so productive of contentment, and having the
charm of success. And beside it she placed her mother's
ineffectual, uncomfortable struggle. And she could not
overcome the belief that her mother's way of life was the

better, that it was inexplicably finer, nobler, more winning.

The comparison roused her, and she turned on herself in terrified disgust.

"What am I? And what am I doing?" she asked herself; and her face burned with shame at the answers she had to give to these questions. She had accepted the rôle for which Mario had cast her. She had drugged her spirit, had lived for her husband's return in the evenings, had dreamed throughout the day of the night's coming embraces. Was this marriage? No, it could not be. Or if it were, there was something wrong about it—something at any rate that was wrong for her.

Not for nothing had Juley nurtured her babes on the belief that God has a spiritual purpose in the life of each one of his creatures, and a purpose for the fulfilment of which the creature is largely responsible. Joanna had tried more than once to express something of this to Mario; but he had condemned such ideas as pernicious and egoistic, and she understood perfectly what he meant. Yet there it was—hardly so much an idea for Juley's children as a fact, a thing bred in their bones by generations of prayer and faith and sacrifice. Mario might say what he liked: he might even be right; but here and now Joanna knew that she would never get wholly away from it.

As if to meet the new, if still vague independence rising in her, she sprang to her feet and walked along the terrace to the little garden gate which led to the steep lane called the Via Barbacane. Pausing there for a moment she looked swiftly about her. She could hear a contadino singing at the top of his voice behind the outhouses as he picked olives, and every now and then he made a rustling in the tree like a great bird, though he never faltered in his loud, heartbreaking song. Joanna stood so still, listening and looking, that on the warm hard earth of the path a lizard darted between her feet. But there was no human being to be seen; and drawing a long breath she slipped out of the garden and started running up the hillside.

It was very exciting to be out alone against Mario's orders, and the excitement added a glowing quality to the beauty the girl saw on either hand. The walled lane ran between *poderi* of ploughed land, and over the walls the olive trees stretched their branches, now thickly strung with harvest-ripe fruit. Here and there the muscular, grey wood had thrust its gnarled elbows through the stone-work, making it bulge dangerously, and in places dislodging it altogether. All the way up the hill on one side a hedge of monthly roses, full two yards high, ran along the wall's top. It was lusty and lovely—thickly covered still with its shell-like flowers, which showed more fragile than ever because of the hale scarlet and yellow hips which were maturing on the same stems as the new buds. And between the gaps of the hedge, and above it, was the blue, blue sky of the Tramontana.

Joanna, all her blood dancing, climbed as far as a little balustraded platform of stone which curved out to her left where the wall ended, in a graceful semicircle. A stone bench ran round it, and its playful builder had decorated it with pillars bearing fir cones on their capitals.

She knelt on the seat, leaned her elbows on the ledge, and looked down at the world lying in a bath of morning sunshine. Her eyes wandered from Florence to the grey hillsides that glittered when the air moved. She looked at the yellow villas, blind and basking. She remembered one—almost hidden from here among its cypresses—which Mario had pointed out as the home of a woman celebrated for her loves. *La Porziuncola*, it had been called, and Joanna had a vivid memory of the little sunken door in the wall, where it was said the lover was wont to enter. On one of their rare walks Mario had taken her past it.

But now, as she looked, *La Porziuncola*, the other shuttered villas, the restless, glittering spume of olives on the slopes, the quieter shining of Florence and her Arno, seemed to her but a part of the passing dream which was her marriage.

"It can't go on," she thought. "It won't last. It isn't real. It is playing at something—pretending, as children pretend when they play."

The very strength of the December sunshine struck her as incredible, and the hillsides were soulless, surely.

Yet it was no dream. The seat was hard, and its cold struck through to her knees. She really was disobeying Mario in being here. She really had a husband and gaoler, who at this moment was somewhere down there absorbed in his beloved machinery.

Joanna recalled the happy oblivion on his face whenever he was busy about his bicycle. That very morning Maddalena and she had gone down as far as the steps at the end of the lane to see him off. They had stood there hatless, trembling a little in the early freshness, but enjoying it, while he got his machine out of the *trattoria*. He had touched it here and there with loving hands to see that all was right, and had frowned at something which he said would soon want repairing. Then he had kissed Joanna's hand, started with unusual difficulty, and waved his hat without turning his head. The two women had waited, looking after him till he disappeared round a far corner and only the distant pulsing of the engine came back to them.

And scarcely three hours had passed since then. How many hours were there till his return ? Joanna counted on her fingers, and sighed. Yes, he was still her lover. She still looked eagerly for his coming, and in the pleasure of greeting him sought compensation for the empty hours of his absence.

But this evening, she determined she would tell him some of her morning thoughts, persisting till he came to understand her trouble. She would ask him to help her, would show that somehow their love was at stake. She remembered a phrase of her mother's in a talk they had had during her engagement. " It is easy enough to fall in love, my childie," Juley had said, " but to love wisely is sometimes very hard."

The mere thought, repudiated at first, that love was hard, came to Joanna now as a stimulating discovery. Of course it was hard. It needed courage to love. Acquiescence was not the way. And at once she pictured herself walking up the lane with Mario when he got home, persuading him to come with her as far as the stone seat, telling him how she had come there earlier, by herself.

This she must tell him, even if it made him angry. He must not hear of it first through Maddalena. And fearful that Maddalena might at that very moment be looking for her by the well to give her an embroidery lesson, Joanna rose and hastened back towards the house.

As she turned the last corner, coming quickly downhill, she saw that two men stood on the road just outside the garden gate.

Immediately she was struck by disquiet. There was some oddness in the way they were talking, turning constantly to look up towards the villa, yet not going in. One of them, a tall man with thick iron-grey hair, carried his hat in his hand,

and kept mopping his brow with a blue silk handkerchief. He seemed terribly worried with the sun full in his face. The other, who had his back to Joanna, was small, and spick and span.

The absurd idea darted through the girl's brain that Mario had sent these people from Florence to spy upon her. She could not believe them ordinary visitors. Now they were crossing the ditch by the little paved bridge from the lane; but again they hesitated uneasily before going on. They looked almost felonious, and the smaller carried a black bag.

Joanna wondered if she could possibly slip past by the upper terrace, and so get unseen to the house before them. By the time she reached the gate they had disappeared round a bend in the path. Perhaps she was too late! Breathlessly she scrambled across to the higher path, and flew round by the *podere*.

But as she came down the flight of rough stone steps close to the villa, she saw that she was caught.

Immediately below her, on her right, were the two men, both now holding their hats in their hands, and on her left, Maddalena, with a question in her face moved from the house to meet them.

Then Maddalena *had* been in the garden looking for her, thought Joanna. What should she do? She might still go back, and run round behind the house, entering by the other side. They had not noticed her. But she found she could not stir from the spot. She had to wait. She must see the meeting between the men and Maddalena, to whom clearly they were strangers.

Now they had met. The tall man started mopping his brow again: the little man was speaking.

Suddenly Maddalena's hand flew to her mouth. She uttered a loud scream. And Joanna, leaping down the stone steps, was too late to help. Her sister-in-law had slipped down quite neatly and softly and was lying all her length across the terrace.

*   *   *   *   *

Mario was dead, Joanna knew that before they could tell her.

He had been killed in the Cascine. His "auto-velocipede," the men said, had collided with a carriage. Death must have been instantaneous. His body was at the mortuary of the

Misericordia, whither the Brothers had carried it from the
scene of the accident. The smaller of the two men, who was
a doctor, begged Joanna not to go there. And he looked her
up and down searchingly with his wise eyes. The coffin could
be brought home later, if they wished it, he said. But better
have the funeral from the mortuary. Anyhow, God help
them not to look on the poor, shattered body. It had been
a terrible accident, terrible. But no suffering. That was
something. All must have been over in a second of time.
The poor signore had been riding his auto-velocipede at great
speed, and on the wrong side of the road, at one of those
sharp crossings near the race-course. The coachman of the
carriage must be exonerated in the matter. He was, poor
fellow, in a state of collapse. But he had not been to blame.
Undoubtedly the signore had been riding on the wrong side.

All the things from Mario's pockets were in the doctor's
bag. Word of the accident had first been taken to the office,
that address being the only one to be found on the body.
There the manager had done all that remained to be done.
The tall man was the manager from the office. Joanna
remembered afterwards how the loose flesh of his face hung
down under his cheeks and chin, like a hound's dew-laps,
and he had great pouches under his eyes.

IX

After the funeral, Joanna did not see the sun for a fortnight.
She never went out, not even to the garden.

She alone had followed the coffin to the grave, for Maddalena still lay in a darkened room. But she had not seen her
dead husband. The Brothers at the Misericordia supported
the doctor in this ; and thinking to treasure her last sight of
him alive, Joanna had not insisted. The bicycle, she had seen.
It was crushed and twisted, as might have been a penny
toy.

She did not weep. But when she was not tending Maddalena
she sat huddled up, her head on her hands, her eyes staring
into distance. And a deep vertical line came between her
brows.

At first, all the time, and again and again, she was irresistibly
trying to re-live the experience which had been Mario's in the
moment of meeting death. It was as if, before grieving for
her own loss, she must share this thing with him. She saw

the cross-roads, where she had once been with him, the hidden, noiseless carriage, the tearing bicycle, with Mario on it—part of it. There must have been one clear, frantic moment of knowledge. Then the smash. Joanna lived through it with every sinew and nerve in her body strung. They had brought not a word, not even a cry for her to hold on to. If only there had come the smallest message. Why had he been riding on the wrong side? It was not like him. Yet it was like him to be wiped out in a moment.

In spite of her obedience to the Brothers, when she tried now to call up the white, vivid face which had been so delightful to her, she could only see it agonized, infuriated, or piteously disfigured. Was it because she had disobeyed him that last day? Why else should he look so angry with her in death? Why else should he be riding on the wrong side? She tried to put the thought from her, but it recurred. Each night she prayed on her knees that she might dream of him smiling at her; but she slept hardly at all, and when she did she started awake with murder on her soul.

Letters came from home—a few shy lines from each of the boys, a long scrawl from Georgie—very affectionate, and begging her sister to use the words " passed on " instead of " died "—and from her mother almost daily letters, which by the many erasures Joanna knew had been written in forbidden hours. Juley had at once offered to come to Italy. But the girl forbade it, saying she would herself come home as soon as she could leave Maddalena in the company of an old friend who was coming from Sicily to be with her.

To return home seemed the only reasonable course. Joanna had come to feel a great tenderness for Maddalena. She was moved as well as surprised to find how the elder woman clung to her. For Mario's death had worked a curious change between the two women; and now it was the southerner who with every action betrayed her spiritual dependence on the northerner. But save for Maddalena there was no life for Joanna in Florence, and as the days crept past and past, she had to admit that life was still before her. In time Maddalena would once more take up the orderly threads of existence in her efficient hands, and the friend from Sicily would probably make her home at the villa. But Joanna

could not consent to live on her sister-in-law. Apart from
the remnant of Mario's savings—a bare fifty pounds—she
was left without money. No. She must go back to Glasgow
and learn how to live. There were listless hours, wasted
years to be made good. She felt rather like a child who
has played truant from school, and is led back to its task.

Joanna decided that she would break the return journey
at Viareggio, there to see Aunt Perdy and deliver Juley's
present. A visit had more than once been suggested, but till
now it had not been practicable.

At the station in Florence she hung round Maddalena's
neck. Though Maddalena's face was swollen above the
high, tight-fitting, black neckband, and her eyelids were
sodden and puffy, she seemed to have shed all her tears.
But amid the distractions of packing it was two days since
Joanna had cried, and now her eyes streamed. People looked
with open expressions of sympathy at the embracing women
dressed in deepest Continental mourning. At first Joanna
had tried to keep some moderation in her weeds, but seeing
at once that her sister-in-law would be hurt by any opposition
in the matter, she had become passive. It would be easy
to modify her dress when she reached home. Now she wore
a skirt bordered with a hem of crape half a yard deep, and
a bodice without an inch of white anywhere. And the black
veiling, which fell from the brim of her hat, reached almost
to her heels at the back. With her youth and her white
skin she was notable, and she felt like an adventuress. A
pang of surprised amusement shot through her when she
thought what Mario's feelings would have been at seeing her
thus conspicuous. It was as if, far down in the dark mourning waters a silver bubble of laughter were released and
struggling upwards. The inclination to laugh was intense,
inebriating. It seemed years since she had laughed. For
a wild moment she thought she must spout her soul out in an
eruption of the old schoolgirl madness of laughter. But the
moment passed ; and she only hugged Maddalena the tighter
because of it, and smiled at her the more tenderly.

When the train bore her out of the station and into the
sunshine of the unstricken world, a new, rare spring of happiness came welling up suddenly in her life. She had no definite
thought of its source. She merely knew that somehow,
undeservedly, she had escaped. The words passed through

her mind : " Our soul is escaped as a bird out of the snare of the fowlers ; the snare is broken and we are escaped." In spite of a voice of denial deep-buried in her, she saw herself in the image of a dove.

But it was with more than the wood-pigeon's wildness that she was now spreading her wings. In her body she still grieved for Mario ; but she was unbroken, and still hungry for life which was only beginning. Though she was going home, she was not going back—not going with the man from Edinburgh. Home was the next step forward ; that was all. And now that she knew how ill-equipped she was, she must work. How she must work ! As the train ran on through the singing fields, Joanna drank the sunshine with an overflowing heart. Like one who has done murder in self-defence, and is reprieved, she was full of honey-sweet defiance against death.

It was still early in the afternoon when she climbed down from the train at Viareggio.

For a moment she looked about her, lost. Had no one come to meet her after all ?

Then she knew, for her aunt, an outlandish figure, came flying towards her from the far end of the station, as if on fawn-coloured wings.

The wings, on a nearer view, turned out to be the cape-sleeves of a buff dolman which had been fashionable ten or twelve years before, and which Perdy always wore on her rare descents to the town. As she ran to meet her niece, this garment fled apart in front, showing the coarse full skirt of a contadina, and her zoccoli clacked sharply on the hard track, as her heels in their thick, red-cotton socks parted from the wooden soles with every step. On her head was a man's tweed cap, with the peak pulled well over her eyes. And under it her short hair showed, cut in a thick fringe.

Joanna immediately dropped her luggage and went blushing to meet her mother's sister. And after Maddalena's hundredth embrace Aunt Perdy's first was like a home-coming. Was it the voice, the intonation, the sweetish odour of her breath, or something in the feeling of her arms, wondered the girl, that made her at once so familiar ? In Aunt Perdy's face, with its strangely formed lips and burning eyes, Joanna could not see much likeness to her mother or to Georgie ; yet it was as if she were hugging and being hugged by both of them ;

and by Linnet and Sholto too. She felt herself taken to the family bosom.

Aunt Perdy, when she had kissed Joanna repeatedly on both cheeks, held her off by the shoulders, saying she must have " a good look " at her. But in a trice her steadfast gaze went from her niece's glowing face to the long widow's veil which floated behind.

" Fie, for shame, child ! " she exclaimed, stretching her hand over Joanna's shoulder and drawing the trail of crape towards her. " You—an Erskine—to wear such a thing ! As though we were of those that sorrow without hope. I'm amazed at you. Is that all my poor sister has taught her girls ?

Joanna tried to explain that she had not wished to hurt her sister-in-law's feelings. But Aunt Perdy would not listen.

"Weak, weak ! " she said, shaking her head. "But 'tis written on your face. The moment I met you, I saw it. You are too yielding. I used to be too yielding. Life has taught me better, though. You know what dear Browning says—

' That rage was right in the main, that acquiescence vain '

And remember that though we are told that Christ ' pleased not Himself,' we know very well that neither did He please others. But see, we'll say no more now. Luckily I always carry my shears with me."

Aunt Perdy groped under her wonderful dolman among the folds of her skirt, and presently brought to light a long pair of scissors which were fastened by several yards of tape to her waist. She then walked slowly round Joanna, commanding her to stand still while she cut off the draperies of widowhood.

"There, that's better ! " she said. She was delighted as a child with her work. " And now give auntie another hearty kiss ! "

Again she pressed Joanna to her breast, again held her off for inspection, exclaiming, as if she now saw her for the first time, " So this is Juley's little daughter ! "

By this time everybody in the station was staring at them : staring not rudely or furtively as people would have stared in England, but with unconcealed interest, and encouraging smiles for such a display of family emotion. (It is only in the matter of sex that the Italian is ill-mannered.) And while Joanna felt that she would have been welcomed quite as warmly without onlookers, she knew her aunt was stimulated by their audience. "This is an historical meeting," Perdy seemed to say, with a careless invitation to the public, "between a very remarkable woman and her niece Look on by all means. It does not matter to me ; nor to her, if she is indeed my niece ! "

To the gnarled, old peasant whom she had brought with her to carry the luggage, she announced Joanna as her Scottish niece, and the man nodded and smiled. He had to congratulate the Signora on having so beautiful a relation, with a face like the Blessed Virgin's, and all the way from Scotland too !

They left the station, and the peasant took them in a cart through the town, over the canal where men naked to the waist were lifting great blocks of marble out of barges, and across a stretch of perfectly flat country till they reached Torre del Lago

From here they were to climb on foot to Aunt Perdy's cottage ; and the man Tommaso drove off to put the pony up, leaving the women to wait by the roadside with the luggage till his return.

He would be gone about twenty minutes, Aunt Perdy said ; so she and Joanna carried their belongings between them, from the road to the shore of the lake which was only a short way off. It would be pleasanter to wait there.

Joanna was entranced by the pale, outspread sheet of water, so different from any of the lochs at home. A mirage, she thought, must look like this. Even before Aunt Perdy told her, she had known it must be quite shallow all over.

When they had been sitting there a few minutes a small, flat-bottomed boat ran softly in to shore, not far from them, swishing between the parted reeds ; and the two men in it stepped over the side, and hauled their craft easily some yards inland among the bushes.

Joanna and Aunt Perdy watched, and as the men left the boat and made for the road, Aunt Perdy's short-sighted eyes narrowed, straining in their direction.

"What *are* they carrying, Aunt Perdy ? " asked Joanna, a note of childish horror in her voice. "They look like big bunches of feathers—but they seem so heavy. Oh, but they *are* birds ! And I believe they are fluttering ! They are alive ! "

But already her companion was gone, and had descended upon the two peasants like a whirlwind.

"Slaves and cowards!" Aunt Perdy was saying in her peculiar but voluble Italian, when Joanna came up with them. "Ill-educated, without intelligence, pieces of brute-beasts!" (She spared them none of the phrases most wounding to Italians.) "Was it for this, Niccolo, that I nursed your wife night and day for a week when she was delivered of twins? And you, Francesco! You, whose sweet name-saint was the little brother of the birds! Are you not ashamed to fill your disgusting belly with the flesh off these little, happy bones?"

"I do not eat them, Signora," said Francesco sheepishly. "They are for the market. Times are hard. A man must live."

Aunt Perdy stamped her foot in its zoccolo.

"Idiot!" she retorted. "God have patience with you, for the saints never will! How much do you suppose you will get for them in Viareggio?"

"Two soldi apiece, Signora,"

"Let me buy them from him," pleaded Joanna, and she felt for her purse. She could not take her eyes off the birds —alive and hanging there in four great bunches. But firmly, almost roughly, her aunt caught back her hand.

"Hold your tongue, silly child!" she said. "Francesco, you cannot impose upon the Scottish Signora. You know perfectly that in the time it takes you to snare the rondinelli and carry them to the market, you could earn twice as much by digging my garden. It is only because you are lazy and cruel that you prefer to make a few soldi by taking life. And what happens to the money? Ah, yes, indeed! How many soldi return with you out of the little wine-shop in the Via Cavour? Eh, you, Niccolo? Your wife told me some pretty things when she was ill. And Francesco need not grin, for he is little better. You will set the birds free at once, or I promise you get no help from me the next time trouble comes."

Niccolo and Francesco accepted the situation. They had been at work snaring the lake swallows since before dawn; but now they merely looked once at one another and shrugged.

Aunt Perdy grasped a bunch of Niccolo's birds, but at first Joanna was afraid to touch the little creatures. She could not believe that they were not maimed. But Francesco showed her smilingly how each one had the tips of its wings twisted together, and then tied with thread, so that several dozen could be strung conveniently on a single string. All the Signorina had to do, was to cut the threads, and straighten the feathers afterwards. But she must hold the bird's body firmly all the while, or in struggling it might break a wing or a leg before it was ready to fly off. He gave her a penknife to work with. Aunt Perdy was snipping away, recklessly it seemed to Joanna, with her huge shears.

As she took the first little, palpitating body in her left hand, Joanna's heart throbbed with an almost painful elation.

She remembered Cousin Gerald and the chaffinches at Duntarvie, and how she had quivered when he had pointed his knife at her breast. Birds had always played a memorable part in her dreams, persisting there like a symbol. Sometimes she had dreamed she was holding her hands above her head, while hundreds of swallows passed through her widely spread fingers, brushing her skin deliciously with their feathers. At other times she was gazing up into a sky thick-strewn with stars, with stars like seeds as they fly from the hand of the sower ; when to her amazement and her great rapture, she perceived that they were not stars, but swallows—millions and millions of swallows, wheeling, and forming into innumerable companies for their autumnal flight. And the moon had turned their breasts into silver, and their wings into the glitter of diamonds.

These birds in her fingers now, were mostly a kind of lake swallow—black and white, fashioned for swiftness and a swooping flight. It seemed a wonder how they had ever been snared. They had vicious, yellow beaks with which they jabbed unceasingly at Joanna's flesh ; and their bright eyes, though really quite expressionless, seemed wide with terror.

But the consummate moment was when one could raise one's hand and watch the free bird fly. For an instant the swallow's cold, bewildered claws clung to the palm, scratching deep into the flesh. Then it was gone over the lake. Then it was no more than a swooping black speck among the others yonder.

As each took flight, Joanna's heart went with it. Had not she too been snared ? Snared indeed by her own desire ; but still more, by her own desire set free. And each bird as it went from her, was as a thank-offering for freedom.

One bird she kept to the last. It was different from the

others. Much larger. A heavy breasted grey bird, rather like a sea-gull, but with a finer beak, dead straight, and pointed as a rapier. It had lain in her hands, more passive than the swallows, as if dazed. And before she let it fly, she kissed it deep among its breast feathers. Might it perhaps be her messenger, and fly from her to Mario?

Anyhow her kiss was an unspoken message, breathing remorse, asking forgiveness, proclaiming triumph.

x

" No baby coming ? " asked Aunt Perdy, her eyes running over her niece's figure as they took off their coats indoors. Joanna shook her head.

" Ah, well, perhaps it is better so ; though this visit to auntie in her lonely nest would have been something to tell a child in the years to come, wouldn't it ? Your mother will be disappointed, I dare say. Juley was always mad about babies. But you will marry again, Joanna, and give her grandchildren, I can see that. Trust Aunt Perdy's eyes. Now come up the ladder, and you can take off your hat in the bedroom. Let me go first to show you. Bring your coat with you, and anything else. I leave nothing about down-stairs. Then we can talk till Aurora has the supper ready. Aurora ! " she called loudly, " Aurora ! Aurora ! Vieni ! "

Running feet sounded from the garden, and a big, handsome contadina of about eighteen, dashed into the cottage, smiling all over her face.

Aunt Perdy, as she had done with Tommaso, presented her niece grandiloquently for the servant's ready admiration. Then, instead of going upstairs, she went out to superintend the picking of the vegetables, and Joanna heard her giving her orders for supper in a torrent of Italian.

They had reached Aunt Perdy's remote dwelling after a hot forty minutes' climb, by a footpath so narrow that the three had to walk Indian file, Tommaso leading, with Joanna's luggage on his shoulder. The place was no more than a cottage, and that of the humblest kind. But it had been built on a shelf of the hill ; and standing at the door with Aunt Perdy's carefully tended vegetable patches on either hand, one grandly overlooked the whole province. Below lay the great plain like a cloak of many colours flung there outspread from the mountains to the sea. On the right the Apennines were its collar, sweeping in a rich curve upwards to the jewels and point-lace of the Carraras. On the left its embroidered fringes were laved by the Mediterranean from Bocca d'Arno all the way round the deeply indented coast-line to the long foreland of Spezia.

The cottage consisted of two rooms—an upper and a lower —separated by a flooring of pine which was unplastered below, and so roughly joined that there were gaps large enough to slip a finger through. The lower room was paved with square red tiles, and barely furnished with a deal table, a painted wooden bookcase, three cheap chairs, and a shabby but fine old armchair of woven cane—the only one with cushions. Some white enamel cups and saucers mixed with common stoneware stood along the shelves of a fixed dresser on one wall ; and the whole of another wall was filled by the fireplace, which gave dignity to everything with its huge sloping hood of stone.

Joanna, glancing at the bookcase when she was for a moment alone, saw Burns's Poems, *The Pilgrim's Progress Looking Backward, A Romance of two Worlds*, and *The Schonberg, Cotta Family*. There were also several works by Pulsford, Harris, and Laurence Oliphant, some more novels by Miss Corelli, and some by Ouida. In all, there were not more than two dozen books.

On the walls hung a number of old-fashioned daguerreotypes as well as one or two photographs made vulgar by enlargement. In one of these Joanna recognized at once the gentle, fanatic countenance of her Erskine grandfather, whose same adored portrait hung over her mother's bed at home. And above this Aunt Perdy had nailed a reproduction of Holman Hunt's " Light of the World," the only coloured picture in the room.

She had pointed to this the moment they entered the cottage.

" You see, I will have no imaginative pictures on my walls, except one," she said, " and that Jesus. All the others are photographs of the men who have made Aunt Perdy what she is There you see your darling grandpapa, my good angel who comes often from Heaven to commune with me in this lonely spot, and to tell me what are the words I must say to poor humanity as it struggles in the mire of ignorance. Over there is dear Pulsford. You know his *Morgen Rothe* ? What ! You have never read it ? Poor child, you have not

yet begun to live.   And here, here is my beloved Laurence
Oliphant—my appointed soul's mate, as I have come to
believe during this last fortnight, after much prayer and
meditation."

But the photograph which most interested Joanna was a
faded cabinet one which had been nailed up in an inconspicu-
ous corner by the bookcase.   It was so like Gerald that for
a moment she took it for his picture.   But on looking closer,
she saw that this young man had little whiskers and an old-
fashioned collar.   Then she knew it for a likeness of Gerald's
father, her Uncle Henry, a vague figure of whom her mother
seldom spoke.   He was dead, Joanna knew ; and she was
dimly aware that for years before his death he and Aunt
Perdy had lived apart.

As her Aunt returned, Joanna instinctively moved away
from the photograph.

"Yes, that is poor Henry," said Perdy, observing the
movement.   "I keep his picture there to remind myself
that I have forgiven him the great wrong he did me when he
put me into what he called a ' Nursing Home, and kept me
locked up there that he might indulge his fleshly lust with my
children's governess, whom he never had the courage to
marry.   No doubt you have had a garbled story from your
mother ?   There is not a word of truth in that.   But basta !
As I have said, I forgave Henry long ago—even before God
punished him by a lingering illness before calling him on
to another phase in his development.   I would gladly have
nursed him, if he would have allowed me.   But he refused
my offer, and did not even answer my letter of tender forgiveness.   In that horrible asylum all those on whom I laid my
hands were immediately cured.   Thus God causes the wrath
of men to praise Him, Joanna."

During this speech, Aunt Perdy had passed her arm round
her niece's waist, and at some points the girl could barely resist
her inclination to burst into a fit of laughter.

"Your stomach is shaking, child," remarked Aunt Perdy.
"You are laughing at me.   No.   You needn't apologize or
explain.   I see that, in spite of the sorrow God has sent, you
are still one of the herd.   I must have patience with you.
Some day perhaps you will understand.   Now follow me
upstairs."

Joanna climbed after her aunt up the steep ladder which

led through a square opening in the ceiling to the upper part of the house.

This was even simpler than the living-room, and contained neither cupboard nor fireplace. There were two iron bedsteads, a chest of drawers, an enamel basin and ewer, and a printed calico curtain in a corner concealing a few clothes. The floor was uncarpeted save for a worn strip between the beds. But here also everything was scrupulously clean.

Joanna was glad to relieve her increasing feeling of tension by at once opening her travelling case, and unpacking the presents she had brought from Glasgow. There were several pounds of tea, on which Aunt Perdy pounced joyfully, and she fingered with critical approval the roll of good wearing stuff her sister had sent—rough grey tweed with a herring-bone pattern. She was pleased too with the half-dozen pairs of Balbriggan stockings and the stout moirette petticoat. But what took her fancy most of all was a pair of half-worn brown velvet slippers, with cross-straps and high heels, belonging to Joanna. Before Joanna could beg her to keep them, she had put them on instead of her zoccoli, and even over the coarsely knitted socks they fitted her. In her delight she walked up and down the room, holding out her full skirts like a young girl and looking down with pleasure at her elegant feet.

" I can see you have not the Erskine feet," she said, glancing at Joanna's, " though they are well enough shaped and not large. But look at mine. Though I am over fifty, they are as they were when I was seventeen. And see ! "

Eagerly unfastening Joanna's slippers, and standing on the rough boards in her scarlet stocking soles, Aunt Perdy sprang right on to the tips of her pretty toes like a ballerina, and stayed there poised for perhaps ten seconds, her arms outstretched and her fine serious face thrown back in triumph.

It was true. She had marvellous feet, small, and with strongly curved insteps. On coming into the house she had laid aside her mannish cap and the dolman, and Joanna thought she looked stranger than ever. Her light brown hair, in which there were only a few threads of grey, was cut in a straight fringe starting far up on the crown and coming almost to her eyebrows. Her eyes could at any moment, and apparently at will, fill with fire ; and in spite of its many fine wrinkles and the absence of colour from the cheeks, her face was indomitably youthful. Both face and neck were of an even, yellowish tint. Her breast was full and deep. Only in a careless sagging of the stomach and thickening of the hips did she show her age.

,The next moment she was unrolling and measuring Juley's tweed to make sure there was enough for a new winter dress. The amount hardly satisfied her, and she began to examine Joanna's crape-edged skirt to see if it would do as a pattern.

"How queer the fashions are now," she exclaimed, keenly interested, but with some disgust in her voice. "Are they really wearing such skirts in Florence ? I think them ugly and immodest, fitting so closely round the hips. You have the Erskine figure, Joanna. Our women always had good, well-grown bodies. Turn round, and let me look at you. Yes, you are well set up, and have a good complexion like your mother, though she was never so pretty as you. But I had a fuller bosom at your age. A woman should be big-breasted, the Italian men say. And I think they are right."

"Mother has sometimes said I am like you," ventured Joanna, who hardly knew what to do with herself under her aunt's scrutiny.

"Like me ? Nonsense, child ! Your mouth a little perhaps. Let me see ? Yes, possibly a *very* little. But you have not, and never will have, my wonderful eyes. Have you ever seen eyes like mine ? I have never met any one who has. The young priest at Cammaiuola, our nearest village, whom I am helping and teaching, says my eyes seem always to be gazing straight into Heaven. Yours, Joanna, when they stop dreaming, will have the earthward gaze. I can see and feel it. No, don't argue with me. Aunt Perdy knows these things. You will love with an earthly love, and you will suffer, as all those born in March must suffer, shedding tears that are sweeter than the smiles of others. But it is not yet clear if you will ever attain to the Universal, the Soul-love, which is mine. Why is it I can go about alone here without fear, at any hour of the night or day—here among these mountains where there are so many brutal men ? It is because I have the perfect love which casteth out fear. If my bosom and my wonderful eyes were to fire a man's passion, so that it entered his heart to do me a wrong, I should take him tenderly in my arms and give him freely all the love he is capable of taking. (Men are thirsting for such love, Joanna, though they may not be aware of it : and few women there are who have it to give.) Then he will go on his way a happier man. And when the fumes of wine or lust have gone from his brain he will know that he has been embraced by one whose soul is already in Heaven looking on the brightness of the Lamb, though her ageing body still walks the earth."

As she spoke—almost chanting in her ecstasy—Aunt Perdy's face grew more and more radiant, her eyes more madly luminous, till Joanna could not bear to look at her.

Gladly the girl would have escaped ; and not from her aunt's rapture alone, but from the strong, terrifying response there was to that rapture in herself. She shrank from the deep exposure.

But as she could not escape, she held herself like stone, sitting there on the edge of the bed and staring at the herring bone tweed. And the elder woman found her stolid.

Neither silence nor interruption, however, could long stay the stream of Perdy's speech ; and it was still flowing steadily when later in the evening they sat downstairs eating their supper of artichokes fried among eggs in a great earthenware dish. Ordinary talk was impossible, and Joanna soon gave up the attempt. Perdy, even when she put a question, never allowed any one but herself to answer it. All she wanted was a listener. But so manifest was this need, that Joanna wondered how she ever managed to pass a day in solitude.

During supper a small lamp filled the room with deep shadow rather than with light, and in the glow of the charcoal fire Aurora, who cooked and waited on them, looked like a goddess. Joanna could hardly take her eyes from the servant's neck, which rose a thick and golden column from the great shoulders ; and when she turned from the stove to bring them a dish, she walked royally, swinging on her hips. While Aunt Perdy talked and talked, Joanna and Aurora kept smiling at one another with the warm and secret understanding of youth.

Still Joanna listened ; for when Perdy was not speaking of herself, she spoke of the Erskine family ; and on her lips the most trifling events assumed an epic quality. An old Dumfries-shire nurse of her childhood moved like a giantess amid her talk ; an ancient Huguenot lady known as " Grandy," with a title and a wonderful ebony wig, who had looked after

Perdy and her sisters for some years after their mother's death, stood out as another large and gracious figure; a dwarf who had run away from a travelling circus at Peebles to take refuge in the manse, and who had become the children's ill-tempered but loving slave till his death a year later, gave a note of grotesqueness. But all these dim figures, which recalled to Joanna a hundred half-heard tales of home, were no more than the background in Aunt Perdy's narrative to the stupendous figure of Papa. Papa was all and in all. And constantly Joanna found herself glancing up at the wall from which the ecstatic face of the old minister looked down at his daughter and his granddaughter.

It had been a grief to Robert Erskine that no son was born to him ; for his son was to have been called Hildebrand after his hero, and he was to have been a great man. But with characteristic vigour this father of four daughters had put his dream behind him, and had thrown all his zeal into the education of his girls. After four of Shakespeare's heroines he had named them—Miranda, Perdita, Juliet and Hermione— though at home they became known as Annie, Perdy, Juley and Minnie. And though Annie had died at twenty of a fever contracted during one of their educational trips in the Campagna, and Juley at seventeen was on the verge of a mental breakdown through over-study, his children's faces still glowed when they spoke of him.

"Never forget, Joanna," said Perdy, "that grandpapa was one of the world's great men. Your mother must at least have told you that. Even your Aunt Minnie, who is one of the silliest women imaginable, has done that much for her unfortunate children. Papa was not appreciated by his contemporaries any more than I am by mine. But in the end greatness must be recognized ; and my aim is to leave in my writings a picture of papa which shall be an inspiration to future generations. I, in myself, am nothing." (As she spoke, Perdy stretched out her arms in a magnificent gesture of humility.) "I cannot of myself write one word that will live. But as soon as I have sat down with an obedient heart at that little table by the window, and have taken my pen in my hand, papa comes to my elbow. And though, alas, I cannot see him, I hear his voice as I heard it in childhood— gentle yet stern —and he says to me, 'Perdita, my child, child of my loins most beloved, write the words I speak to

you now, and write no other words, for all other words are
of the Devil.' Once or twice—nay, many times, for I am
weak and sinful still, and in the flesh—the Devil has come to
tempt me upon my hill-top; and I have disobeyed darling
papa's command. I have written words of my own, or I have
made believe that papa was still at my elbow when he was no
longer there (for there are times when God has other work for
him to do). But when I do that, when I write my own poor
words, or the false words the Devil whispers, do you know
what happens, Joanna ? " On the very breath of the question
Aunt Perdy broke off, turning to Aurora. "Aurora, this
butter is rancid again. Where did you get it ? There is
no excuse at this time of year. Take it away, and tell Maria
that the Scottish Signora is displeased with her."

Having dispatched Aurora, Aunt Perdy bent her gaze once
more on Joanna, leaning forward with blazing eyes.

"Where was I, Joanna ? Ah, yes. When I disobey sweet
papa, this is what happens. I go to bed and to sleep. And
in my sleep a hand is laid on my shoulder, and a voice says,
'Blot the wicked words of self!' And still in my sleep I
get up, and after climbing down the ladder I remember no
more. But when I come down in the morning as usual, I
find that all the words that were words of self have been blotted
by my own hand."

When she had listened to the sound of her aunt's voice for
more than two hours, Joanna was near the end of her strength.
Supper was long over, Aurora had bidden them good night
and gone home; the charcoal no longer glowed in the wells of
the stove; the lamp flickered from lack of oil. Wearied out
with the last weeks of grief and sleeplessness, with the excitements of the day, with the toiling walk uphill, with the strangeness of everything, Joanna's head fell upon her breast.

"Dear auntie," she murmured, raising it with an effort,
" I am so terribly, terribly tired."

" I can see you are exhausted," replied Perdy, " and
exhaustion is a poison. No one ought ever to be exhausted.
It is stupidity, nothing else. It comes from not knowing
how to rest. That is what poor Henry never could see. He
was always wanting to sleep. Now I, since I have learned
how to rest—how to relax every nerve and muscle perfectly,
as I shall teach you presently—need hardly any sleep. The
great thing is to think of your body as a string of beads :

then you can give it the rest and refreshment it requires without sleeping for seven or eight hours like a hog."

Joanna made a final effort to listen. But after some time she only understood dimly that something was being read to her. Aunt Perdy's voice was like a river flowing through the room, flowing and flowing, and filling the room with waves of sound. And the sound came and went like the noise of a weir in the breeze. At one moment it seemed to Joanna that she was listening to her mother. Yes, that was her mother talking of "poor, poor human nature!" Then it was surely Georgie's voice, assertive, full of challenging assurance. Now her grandfather, whose voice in the flesh she had never heard, was addressing her from his place on the dark wall. Then again the tones seemed to be the echo of her own secret heart. It was the voice, not of a person but of a family.

But at length only phrases came to her, drifting like islands on a tide of sound—"The Father-Motherhood of God"—"The Central Sphere"—"The Divinity of Sex"—"The Man-Woman Creator." Then single words began to spin like motes in the beams of the guttering candle—"Duality"—"Soul"—"Man"—"Dove"—"Love"—"Love"—"Love." Then gradually she sank beyond the reach of words. And so she stayed, till drawn up by Aunt Perdy's ice-cold hands upon her wrists she knew she was being told with contemptuous kindness that it was time for bed.

END OF BOOK I.

BOOK II

" . . . Open a door of utterance."—Col. iv. **3.**

CHAPTER I

I

TO please me, to please your mother, Joanna—and it
is not very often nowadays that I ask either you or
Linnet to do anything to please me."

It was Juley that spoke.

Joanna, tormented by the vexation and pertinacity in her
mother's voice, looked up from her drawing-board and across
the dark parlour. She was sitting close up to the window
eagerly using the last of the daylight for her work ; but Juley
stood uncertainly by the door, grasping the knob with one
hand, while with the other she contrived awkwardly to hold
a small tray loaded with tea things.

To the daughter by the window the mother's face in the
interior was only a pale blur ; but she knew its expression
as surely as though she could see the distressed features.
And her blood rose in irritated protest.

She was working. She was trying to finish a lunette-shaped
design for to-morrow's class at the School of Art. Why
couldn't her mother let her alone ? It was all very well coup-
ling her name thus with Linnet's. But in practice Linnet was
left unmolested, and went his queer, separate way alone.
And it had been the same with Sholto till he had left home
a year ago. It seemed as if the boys were exempt from their
mother's spiritual passion. She even did her best to forward
them in the world, scraping together the money for Sholto to
start fair in the colonies when he should be ready to go, and
keeping unpunctual Linnet up to the mark in his attendance at Mr. Boyd's law office, where he was now apprenticed.

But what she considered the unspiritual ambitions of her
daughters she had never ceased to mourn, and as Georgie

145

was away, it was Joanna who chiefly suffered the strain of being yearned over.

"I say it again, Joanna, my child," continued Juley ; and though she tried to put sternness into her tones they remained simply vexed : "To please Mrs. Lovatt, or Mr. Nilsson, or Phemie Pringle, or any of the new friends you have made since you came home, there is no trouble you will not take, and take gladly. But if poor mother asks you to do something for her sake, it always goes against the grain. How is it ? You get lots of flattery, Joanna, outside your home, but I must speak the truth to you ; and this that I have said, however it may grieve us both, is the truth. Think how little it is I am asking of you—simply to give one short hour of next Friday to read and pray quietly with a few of God's dear good workers ! And remember, my daughter, you will not have mother with you always. She is growing older, and her constant prayer is that she may not be spared to old age, to be a burden to herself and others."

Joanna sprang to her feet. She was seething with a helpless sense of injustice. It was more than three years now since she had returned from Italy, a widow, to her mother's house, and scenes of this kind were familiar enough. But all of a sudden at this moment she found the situation intolerable. It was intolerable that her mother should stand there pleading with her, holding the tray so ungracefully, looking in her shabby dress more like a servant than the mistress of the house. In a confused fury, but controlling her movements, she crossed the room and took the tray roughly from Juley's hands.

"I'm sorry, mother," she said. "If you want it so much, I'll go to the meeting." But she was incapable of any accent of relenting tenderness.

"Thank you, Jo ! " The mother smiled now in timid triumph. "You really will come ? You promise mother not to let anything prevent you ? "

"Haven't I said I'll come ? " The girl's exasperation brought violent shoots of pain to the back of her eyeballs. "Surely," she thought, "mother might let it alone, now she has got her way ! " And before taking the tray to the pantry, she added, "But remember it is only to please *you*, not to please Miss Gedge."

Juley sighed deeply, as she went to light the gas and draw

down the parlour blinds. But she looked happier. For after all, Joanna had promised to come on Wednesday night; and Joanna was not to know that the meeting in the tiny vestry of St. Saviour's (the Low and very evangelical English Church to which Juley now went) had been specially arranged for her spiritual benefit by dear Eva Gedge. If Joanna had known, she would have been angry, and nothing would have made her yield. Was it perhaps a little unfair? As the mother swept the table carefully clear of crumbs, and strewed them outside on the window-sill for sparrows, an expression of shame did strive for a moment with the satisfied craft in her face. But it was only for a moment. The deceit, she reminded herself, if deceit there were, was for her precious child's eternal welfare. Besides, this little gathering of one or two together, with Joanna in their midst, was dear Eva's idea. And it was dear Eva's calling to deal with young people. Why else was she at the head of Elmbank Training College for deaconesses?

Joanna, in the pantry, rolled back her sleeves, turned on the hot water, and set herself the unnecessary task of washing up. The dishes might quite as well have been left for the housemaid whose day out it was. But if Juley saw them she was sure to slink in later and do them herself. It was a provoking piece of knowledge, and the daughter, as she rinsed the cups and saucers, stared tensely out between the bars of the pantry window at the familiar, darkening slope of the back-green. There at the top was the wall along which she had so often raced; and in the angle of the wall was a disused ashpit, which at eight years old it had been her dream to turn into a little house for herself and Cousin Gerald. True, she had taken no practical steps towards making it habitable, but the picture had so persisted in her mind that for many months she had not been able to pass a piece of coal in the street, or a stray potato, without picking it up. At once she had seen herself in her tiny house, bending over the fire, and cooking the loved one's supper, while he praised her for her thrift.

And there in another corner of the wall was the carpentry shed, which looked sad since Sholto's departure to a farm in the Lothians where he was learning stock-breeding. Joanna wished that Sholto could have stayed at home instead of Linnet. She and Linnet depressed each other; and the sister felt a kind of horror at seeing her own faults so clearly emphasized in her brother. She was ignorant of the real current of his life, and, in all but superficial ways, the two had come to avoid each other, seeking help outside in different directions.

Suddenly the tears started to Joanna's eyes, and her high-strung fury changed to simple dreariness. Through these childish memories called forth by the sight of the back-green, and these thoughts of the nearer past, she had completed a circle of emotion. Once more she was confronted by her immediate trouble, the trouble concerning her mother. And for a moment she tasted despair.

Almost three years, now, she had been at home ; and it had come to this. She had got no farther than this in fulfilling her dream of daughterhood by the fish-ponds of Vallombrosa. In practice she could not be the daughter of these dreams. Still less could she be the daughter her mother so passionately wanted. Why was it ? Many times she had asked herself that question, and now she stumbled against it again. She loved her mother : her mother loved her. The dream at Vallombrosa had at least had that much of truth And all the time in Florence she had known herself spiritually involved with her mother in some inexplicable way. Then why, when they were under the same roof, was there this unending conflict between them ? Whose fault was it ?

Chafed and puzzled as she was by this questioning, Joanna was well accustomed to it, and had her own way of escape, which she presently took. Just as before her marriage she had constantly taken refuge in a world of dreams, so now, shaken awake by the vivid, physical experience with Mario, she fled outwards to embrace the newly discovered actual. Well she knew her way out. Had she not trodden it these three years a thousand times ? So the unfallen tears soon dried in her eyes, and before the last cup was put away she was once more entirely absorbed in thoughts of the lunette she had to finish for Mr. Nilsson's class next day. Mr. Nilsson, her favourite master, what would he say about it ? Thank Heaven she had her work.

With the natural end of her mourning for Mario, Joanna had become in a perfectly fresh way conscious of the outside world. She had seemed to re-enter life like one new-born, and now for the first time was experiencing the vigour of her youth. A shadow and a burden were lifted, a film taken from her eyes. She was able now to interpret the sense of escape that had come to her in the train as she left Florence, and she understood more fully why her heart had almost broken with thankfulness by the lakeside as the rondinelli took their flight from her hand. She was not merely a woman reprieved, but a woman awakened.

Even now she could not at all times identify herself with this new, intoxicating, workaday world, which for so long she had disdained in favour of dreams. The other people who were in it, and part of it, must see through her, she often fancied, guessing her no true-born inhabitant. But she did not want to be an alien. She had given herself readily to its refreshingly tangible complexities, and quickly she made a place for herself in it, a place where her mother could not follow her.

Aquaintances she now had in flocks. People of course knew her story and rejoiced in it. Her looks were in keeping with romance. She was everywhere received with a mixture of sympathy and envy which was delicately flattering. She talked with shy eagerness, listened reverently, admired, and with encouragement, criticized. For her the most ordinary social event in this unknown world was highly coloured. She might well have been eighteen instead of twenty-four.

And alongside of this enlargement, without making any special effort, she had surprised herself by acquiring the habit of work. She was making real progress, and in a quiet way had become a figure at the School of Art. The masters were on friendly terms with her : the students discussed her clothes and her features. It was astonishing how much livelier her pencil had become, and she had a passionate appreciation of drapery. Her ambition was to earn her own living—some day to go to London.

But by Juley every step of this social and artistic advance was subtly opposed. It was a strange, unremitting conflict. The more the mother perceived the daughter's gifts, the more desperately she deplored any little worldly success the girl might have. There was unscrupulous warfare between them.

And with this result : that Joanna was spurred on her way far more steadily by the discouragement at home than by all the easily elicited praise outside. Both were useful ;

but even when it irked her most, the true stimulant lay in
the handicap her mother was to her, and obscurely she knew
this.

Poor Juley on her side had no such compensations. Besides,
she lacked the saving hardness of youth. She too was sorrowfully puzzled by the turn things had taken. Life had been so
very sweet to her for a little immediately after Joanna's
home-coming. She had rejoiced in what she described to
Eva Gedge as " the softening influence of sorrow," had welcomed the passing simplicity that grief brings. Bereaved
Joanna had been very loving and so gentle that to the
mother it seemed as if " a real change of heart " must have
taken place. The two had been more nearly united than ever
before.

But these first days—or were they only hours ?—had passed
all too quickly for Juley into a treasured memory. And now
she saw her dear child, dearer now than ever, drifting farther
from her and from grace : becoming, as the years passed,
more and more worldly and pleasure-loving.

If Juley faltered at times in this view, letting her natural
maternal pride have the upper hand, or excusing her daughter's youth, there was Eva Gedge, and Eva knew how to
apply the spur. Such an experience as Joanna had been
through, said Eva, *must* lead either to heart-whole dedication
or to a more callous resistance. And to know in which
direction Joanna was moving, had not one merely to look at
the friends she chose for herself ? This was an accusation
to which Juley had no answer but a sigh.

Eva's graceless part, indeed, was to foment whatever was
mean and sterile, and to drag down all that was fine and productive, in a contest which, let alone, had little of baseness
in it. Like Mabel, she was essentially a divider. Barren
of life herself, her deepest passion was to balk and defeat the
entering of others into life.

Not that she was herself aware of her rôle, nor that
others, seeing her warm show of interest in the face of Joanna's
cold politeness, would easily have guessed it. She was always
the first to smile, with Christian cordiality, when Juley tried
to bring daughter and friend to a better understanding.
And though it sorely irked her, she almost always refrained
from putting into words her constant disparagement of
Joanna's natural qualities. Often she wore a martyred air.

And truly enough there was martyrdom to her envious nature in Juley's mounting pride in the younger woman.

As for Joanna, she had become angry with a kind of scornful jealousy. She knew that Eva's influence was hateful. She knew that her mother, in the deep, human part of herself, was glad that she, Joanna, could no more love Eva than Eva could help envying her. Yet she was helpless. And whenever she had been the subject of a prayerful conference between them, she writhed anew under the reinforcement of authority in her mother's voice, and under the malign gleam that darted from the prominent, black eyes behind Eva's glasses.

So Joanna was steeled against them both. She knew not how often her mother, out of tender consideration for her, did violence to herself—keeping difficult silences, restraining sorrowful exclamations, suppressing unkind criticisms of her daughter's new friends. Nor did she know the depth of her mother's loneliness, which by a moment of lavish affection either she or Linnet could better have assuaged than Miss Gedge by many hours of spiritual conversation.

II

So far as Juley and Miss Gedge were concerned, Joanna had three friends—Mrs. Lovatt, Carl Nilsson, and Phemie Pringle; but each of these represented a growing host of undesirable acquaintances.

Mildred Lovatt, upon Joanna's return to Glasgow, had hastened to pay a call of mingled condolence and curiosity. It was known what part she had played in Miss Bannerman's romantic marriage; and the moment she had reconnoitred at Collessie Street, she was generously determined to welcome Joanna (but Joanna alone) to her special circle.

That it was a special circle every one admitted. Indeed if Mildred did not speak of it as a *salon*, that was only because there were undoubtedly people in Glasgow who might not take such a word seriously. As a *salon* she certainly thought of it; and even the scornful uninvited never denied that it included, in a fitful way, ten times the number of celebrities the lady could have achieved with thrice her income in London. Not only was she able to tap the University and the School of Art, which between them should represent the intellect of any city, but her drawing-room in Panmure Crescent had become a known resort for such distinguished visitors as came from London to lecture, act, paint, or make music on the banks of the Clyde.

And Joanna was young enough to find it thrilling that she should meet famous people in the intimacy of a friend's drawing-room. What matter if she rarely saw them oftener than once, and then did not get farther than a few remarks about the weather ? But she learned quickly to keep from mentioning her notabilities at home, except privately to Linnet. One evening, at the tea-table, having overflowed in eager chatter about some well-known actor, her words had died under Juley's sad and steadfast gaze. And the lips of Eva Gedge, who happened to be there, had suddenly gone rigid.

III

Miss Gedge herself, however, was less unsparing in her criticism of Mrs. Lovatt, than was Joanna's second friend, Carl Nilsson.

Four years earlier, when the middle-aged Swedish artist had come, preceded by a high reputation, to teach design at the Glasgow School, Mrs. Lovatt had piped her sweetest to him. But from the first he had refused to dance. He was a misfit at her parties. Then, as the months passed, and it became clear that there was to be periodic trouble between the temperaments of Nilsson and the Art Director, he was tactfully excluded from the Panmure Crescent *salon*. Seeing that the Director, Mr. Valentine Plummer, was the *salon's* principal pilaster, this could not be wondered at. Had Nilsson not been too valuable to the School, he would have been excluded there also. As it was, Mr. Plummer could only make things uncomfortable for him ; and Nilsson, knowing his position secure, retaliated in full measure. Nilsson of course had his own small circle of friends, but outside this he was regarded generally as rather quarrelsome and difficult.

To Joanna, the little man had been consistently friendly, and she knew him of more value than Mrs. Lovatt and all her kind. She had vaguely felt drawn to him—amused and attracted by his irritability—during the term before her marriage.

And now, with his sharp criticisms which she sensitively welcomed, and his adroit praises which never made her ashamed, he had become to her a real helper. He gave her a kind of attention she had not had before from any one.

Also it was at Nilsson's studio that she first met Phemie Pringle.

He was at work in the School on a fresco in which was a group of women, and asked Joanna to give him sittings for some details of his heads and hands (she had a " useful head," he told her). And during these sittings, away from the interruption of the School, their friendship had prospered. Carl seemed to enjoy talking to her about herself quite as much as she enjoyed listening. She was not a bit in love with him, but it excited her to hear from his own lips how she appeared to this man for whom she had the deepest respect. She felt she could learn immensely from him, and he gratified her Scottish passion for self-improvement.

On one particular afternoon he had entertained her as he worked by tracing the whole history of their acquaintance.

" I had my eye on you," he said, winking at Joanna in the odd way that Mildred Lovatt declared was so offensive. " Yes, since the first week I came to your damned School of Plumbers. ' She is nice—worth while,' I said to myself, ' but all shut away ; and so heavy and dull '—what you call it ?—ladylike—and, oh, my Lord God, so sentimental ! No aplomb, no dash, no poise—a formless lump of femaleness—impossible ! In that female amœba there might possibly be a potential woman ; again possibly not.' Your Britain is full of the not possibles. ' She had better get a lover, quick march,' I thought, ' or I give nothing for her chances.' But I confess to you now : I did not see how you were to get the lover. I watched you. You kept them a hundred miles away—all these young Glasgow students who were ready to flirt with you. Then, hey presto ! I hear one day you are married ! But I was pleased ! And to a foreigner, too ! Better and better ! And off to Italy in such a hurry ! That's the style ! Yes, I rubbed my hands when I heard. ' She is saved ! ' I said."

" And am I saved ? " asked Joanna, with her broad, halfmalicious smile. She might have been listening to a story about some one else, except that her heart felt like a fruit ripening on a south wall when the sun is strong.

" Not quite, perhaps. But one feels a beginning has been made. And now, Madame Joanna, if you would turn the head just a little—Na ! Too much ! I said *a little*—to the left. So, is good. For one moment, till the kettle shall boil for our tea."

She sat quite still for him, keeping her head in the position he wanted, and sunning herself in his talk. There was something so genuine in the man that his interest was very sweet. It was good that he should think her worth while.

But Joanna's too self-satisfied reverie was interrupted by the noise of quick steps in the passage which led from the street to the studio. Both quick, they were, and heavy-sounding like the steps of a child. And next moment the flap of the letter-box was vigorously rattled, and a high, gladsome voice called " Coo-ee ! " through the slit.

Nilsson threw aside his pencil, and a smile of extraordinary pleasure spread over his ruddy face. He was a short man, beginning to get stout, and though the hair on his head was all gone grey, his beard and moustache still held the colour of bright rust. To Joanna at this moment he looked suddenly boyish.

" Now you shall meet my Phemie ! " he exclaimed with delight. " She is the pearl of Glasgow. How glad I am that you should meet her ! "

As he skipped across to the door, Joanna's heart contracted in a spasm of mortification. What a fool she had been to imagine Nilsson especially interested in herself !

But with her first glance at the newcomer—a glance of keenest curiosity—some of her hastily discarded complacence was reinstalled. How could Nilsson be so delighted with this silly, common little over-dressed person who came marching blithely into the room ? Why, she spoke with a villainous South Side accent, and had a runaway chin !

" Miss Euphemia Pringle—Signora Rasponi ! " sang out Nilsson. And as he took the kettle off the gas-ring for tea, he kept a sidelong eye on the meeting between the two young women.

When she had put her own firm, square little hand into Joanna's, Phemie tilted back her face, and looked with eyes that brimmed with laughter from Joanna to her host.

" You never told me you were having a lady friend to tea ! " she rallied him. " It's a real shock to find I'm not the One and Only ! "

Though Joanna at this thought her more than ever common,

she could not help watching Nilsson's visitor with that fascinated envy we feel when suddenly confronted with an embodiment of all the qualities in which we ourselves are lacking.

Phemie laid down a silk-fringed hand-bag decorated with beads, settled herself in a chair that was rather too high for her short legs, and started fanning her bright cheeks with a sheet of drawing-paper. Her smallest movement was full of festivity.

"Yon's an awful-like stair of yours for a poor thing like me with a weak heart!" She spoke to Nilsson, but her smile was for Joanna. She sought the other girl's sympathy, not for her inane remark, but for all the gaiety there was in life; so that Joanna had to smile back in admission.

And although during tea Phemie said nothing more ambitious than this, yet Joanna quite lost the first impression of silliness. Phemie's eyes were too clear of self-absorption for silliness, and her silences were too intent. When any one else spoke she was poised in almost embarrassing attention.

Nilsson asked her if she would sing for them.

"I want you to try my new Steinway," he said. And he told how he had bought the piano at an auction sale in Renfield Street for five pounds.

"Is that a fact?" exclaimed Phemie, with a colloquial exaggeration that showed how impressed she was. "Yon was a fair bargain!"

She had risen quite readily on being asked to sing, and she took off her hat as she spoke, stabbing the pins into it carelessly and throwing it on a chair before she crossed to the piano.

It stood in the far corner of the studio—an out-of-date table-grand, really cumbersome, with its thick body and carved, straddling legs; and seated before it, Phemie looked very little and dainty. Now that her over-trimmed hat was off, she showed a delicate head with hair parted smoothly and coiled behind. The light, which came through a yellow blind beyond the piano, seemed to take pleasure in enveloping her.

She struck some chords, gently giving the worn instrument its chance, her listening face turning the while sideways towards the window. It was a beautiful movement of her long neck and sloping shoulders, a quite unconscious disengaging of herself from the others, so that she became aloof in her circle of yellow light—she and the huge, old black piano.

Then her breast rose, her throat swelled like a bird's, and there came quite softly like a fine-drawn thread of gold, the first high, sweet note of her song.

Nilsson lay back sighing in his chair, his eyes closed, and a look of utter contentment on his face. But Joanna leaned forward, her elbows on her knees, her eyes on the singer, thirsty for each lovely, careful note.

This girl, whom half an hour earlier she had summed up as common and silly, was an artist, no less! What a mistake she had made! Now she was eager to accept her humiliation. And above all, if only it might be, she longed to make Euphemia Pringle her friend.

IV

When the girls left Nilsson's together, they walked eastwards along Sauchiehall Street, looking at the milliners' windows and talking mostly about what they saw there. But under all they said there was a happy excitement. "We are going to be friends!" each kept thinking with delight. Now and again Joanna stole a look at Phemie, and with every look she found new pleasure in the valiant little profile. And Phemie was impressed and carried away by something in the other that she could not define to herself. "A real, wee *madam*!" was how she would describe Joanna to her sisters when she got home.

But she had a disclosure to make before she could be sure of this new friendship, and as they turned the crowded corner into Renfield Street she came out with it.

"Shall I take you in to the business?" she asked, watching the other's face keenly. "Mamma will likely be gone, but Annie and Florrie should still be there; and young Nora might be in, meeting them."

Joanna said she would like to be taken, and wanted to know what kind of a business it was.

"You're never telling me you don't know *Pringle's*?"

But Phemie's astonishment was forced, for she was on the defensive: "It's mamma's shop, and two of our girls help in it."

There was no doubt in either of them that it was a disclosure; and as they looked steadily into each other's eyes, Joanna was casting about for the way to put things right between them. She felt herself somehow to blame for the troublesome shop. She knew it well, as everybody in Glasgow did: *Pringle's*, the *Ladies' and Children's Outfitter*. But never before had she had a friend with a shop in the family. She could see Mildred Lovatt's smile.

"Of course I know it," she said, after a scarcely perceptible pause. "I'm wearing a chemise now that I got there. It's the best I ever had!"

"That's the worst of mamma's things," rejoined Phemie. "They wear everlastingly. I have one on too—for a wonder!"

They both laughed a little tremulously now that their anxiety was gone. It was all right. Things were going to be all right between them.

v

Thus it was, that Joanna came for the first time upon the reservoir of human life which gives to Glasgow its essential character. And she came upon it in its purity at *Sans Souci*, the villa on the South Side of the river, where the Pringle family vociferously lived.

It is curious how completely a household like the Bannermans' may lead an alien existence in a town. Juley, only coming to live in Glasgow on her marriage, had long kept the feelings of an exile; and something of this had been communicated to her children. On Sholto's side, the family associations had been with the citizens of the passing generation, and his public ties had died with him. Even in his lifetime Edinburgh had come to be regarded as the true Bannerman headquarters.

It followed that the children had chosen their few playmates most naturally from among the exotics. And this was especially true of Joanna, with the hysterical aloofness of her youth. She had grown up wonderfully ignorant of her native place. Her West-End school-fellows, with their clipped syllables and narrowed vowel sounds (fondly imitative of an " English " accent), had revealed but a fragment of its integral life, and that, as it were, under protest.

But in the world of *Sans Souci*, the mocking, hard-working, mercurial people were true citizens. Their streams of being flowed bright and uncontaminated from Glasgow's central pulse. And they knew it. They were more at home in Paris than in Edinburgh. Buchanan Street existed for them alone.

At first, thrown among so many young and pleasure-loving women, Joanna felt bewildered. But soon she was making good all the enjoyment denied to her shadowed and painful teens.

At *Sans Souci* there was a constant noise of talk and laughter. Married sons and daughters ran continually in and out. The unmarried ones lived in an atmosphere of sweethearting which pervaded the rooms and the garden. The family was sharply divided into blondes and brunettes, accounted for by the Italian strain. (For old Mr. Pringle, who wore a sombrero in the garden and had flashing eyes, lost no time in making it clear to Joanna that his distant forbears had been called, not Pringle, but Pellegrini.)

From the crowd of them—"our Florrie," "our Tom's wife," "our Polly's wee girl," "our Nora's 'latest'"—there principally emerged for Joanna, Annie, grave and handsome with a pile of honey-coloured hair, Nora, black-haired, skinny, and almost uncannily vivacious, and pale, strange-eyed Jimmie who was generally understood to be Phemie's young man.

All the doors of all the rooms were left open, and long conversations were carried on by people in different rooms, on different floors. The single servant, which mamma considered sufficient for the needs of any family, never stayed long. But her going inconvenienced nobody. Even when she had not yet gone, there would always be more people in the kitchen than in the drawing-room. Particularly when mamma was in the house was it an understood thing that no one should sit down for more than a minute at a time. To be settled in an armchair reading was violently contrary to mamma's fixed notions of young womanhood. It was not thus that she had built the business up.

And for mamma the business was life, was romance. She had built it up herself out of nothing, her husband finally taking his humble place in it as book-keeper (for Mrs. Pringle could not add a column of figures); and her nine children and these children's friends were shadowy to her, except in so far as they touched the well-being of the business. When Joanna was introduced, Mrs. Pringle had taken her hand in a strong clasp, very like Phemie's own. But there had been no scrutiny whatever in the innocent eyes that were set far apart in the broad, babyish face; and Joanna had felt sure she would not be recognized on a second meeting. Mere human beings were excluded from the absorbing pattern of this woman's existence.

Assuredly it would have been difficult to find anything in greater contrast to the quiet, sad-coloured life at Collessie Street, with its intense spiritual currents, than this household of *Sans Souci*.

CHAPTER II

I

"I'VE got Louis Pender (you know his work, of course) coming here unexpectedly for the week-end, and as there is a students' dance at the School to-morrow night, I thought we might go on there after dinner with our little party. Will you be one of us ? Do. We dine at a quarter to eight. Don't answer, but come."

On the morning of the day appointed for Miss Gedge's meeting, the post brought Joanna this invitation from Mrs. Lovatt, and she read it through in a growing distraction.

It seemed to her that she had never before wanted so much to accept an invitation as she did now ; and a malignant fate had fixed the affair at St. Saviour's for seven o'clock that same night ! She would know better another time than to let herself be nagged into giving her word.

But in the same moment Joanna took her resolution. Come what might, she would be at Mildred's at a quarter to eight ; and she would be there if possible without having broken the promise to her mother. How this was to be done, she did not yet know. She only knew that a way must be found.

True, this was the first time in her life that she had heard of Louis Pender. And under Nilsson's influence she was becoming less impressible by Mildred's celebrities. True, also, the little dancing she knew had been picked up during play-hours at school, and she had never been to a dance. But at this moment she could imagine nothing more desirable on earth than that she should meet this man with the pleasant name at dinner, and go to the dance afterwards. She wanted to dance, even should she not have the courage to accept a partner for anything but a reel or a set of lancers, in either of which she felt secure.

She looked again at the letter.

"Also, as an experiment," wrote Mrs. Lovatt in her slap-dash hand-writing, "I have asked that young Mr. Urquhart whom you may remember in our Italian class. In spite of his appalling shyness, I gather he remembers you. I discovered him to-day having tea at the Tullises'. It seems Professor T. thinks well of him as a budding anthropologist."

And there was a postscript, telling that Louis Pender was in Glasgow as the possible painter of some panels in the City Chambers, about which there had been some talk of late.

Yes : Joanna was determined to go that evening to Panmure Crescent ; but how was it to be done ?

Quite apart from the St. Saviour's complication, she well knew that the dinner could only have been achieved by great skill, and the dance by deceit or open rebellion. In all these things her mother's will was set hard against hers. And there was the particular promise besides !

There was no means she did not now consider, from flagrant lying to wild revolt ; from the plea of illness, to the attempted cajolery of Miss Gedge to alter the hour of prayer. But one by one each plan had to be rejected, and again nothing remained but the sheer determination.

Then, sudden and simple, like the unexpected appearance of the sun on a black day, came the solution.

In a fever of excitement she laid her plans. She was triumphant, amazed that she had not thought of this at once. It would involve no more deception than either she or Georgie had perforce practised a hundred times before where their mother was concerned.

At half-past five, she went to her bedroom, locked the door, and dressed for the dance. Her dress, which she now wore for the first time, had been made, amid the mingled jeers and acclamations of *Sans Souci* from a curious old piece of grenadine belonging to Juley's girlhood—black, with bright blue stripes and at intervals little yellow embroidered flowers. It had a low bodice, tiny sleeves, and a very full, short skirt. And when the girl had put on over it her day blouse and a dark skirt, covering all with a coat, no one would have guessed her secret. She pulled a pair of black stockings over her bright blue, silk ones, and she hid her slippers and a black lace fan in the inside pocket of her coat. It was done !

When Juley came down to the lobby, ready in time for once, she found her daughter waiting for her with red cheeks

and shining eyes. It gave her great delight that Joanna
took her arm affectionately in the street, and her hopes for
the meeting ran high.

II

Not until the proceedings at St. Saviour's were in full cry,
did Joanna know herself to be their quarry.

Long ago in self-defence she had perfected her faculty for
not listening, and on this occasion she had rendered herself
inaccessible the more easily as no answering speech was
required of her. Exulting in her hidden finery, and full of
anticipations for the coming evening, she had been for some
time wrapped quite securely away.

Indeed a more observant person than she, might well have
been misled by the innocent beginnings of the meeting. Not
more than a dozen people were present, including Juley,
Joanna and Miss Gedge. The others were Mr. Bridgewater,
the incumbent ; Miss Bostock, a deaconess ; and some of Miss
Gedge's students, who wore their dark blue uniforms.

After a short request by Mr. Bridgewater, that their coming
together here might not fail in its intent, a hymn had been
sung. A passage from the Bible followed. Then at a prearranged signal, all the women rose, turned themselves about ;
and fluttered to their knees. Whereupon the clergyman,
having done his part, tiptoed out and left them, softly closing
the vestry door behind him.

It was this odd departure of Mr. Bridgewater that first
roused Joanna to what was forward ; and when, after a few
strained moments, Eva Gedge led in prayer, she knew herself entrapped.

There was no mistaking the suggestions that were now laid
before the Lord—first by Eva ; then, after a pause of dreadful discomfort, by Miss Bostock ; then, at the end of a breathless term of suspense, by one of the younger women. These
last clearly suffered acute nervousness at having to address
their God in public. But this was an art they had
come to Miss Gedge to learn, so not one of them would
relinquish such an opportunity for practice.

And in scarcely veiled language, every one present was
praying for Joanna.

Joanna's first impulse, when she realized how matters

stood, was of sheer wrath. She wanted to leap up and fling out of the vestry full of praying women.

But she did not so act. She realized at once that such rudeness, while it would pain her mother, would give the highest satisfaction to Miss Gedge. Besides, what, after all, did it matter? These people could not harm her, could not prevent her from doing as she wished. She turned her head, furtively counting the bowed backs. By now, the last—the very last, surely—of the students was praying. She was a timid creature, and her shaking voice sounded sincere.

"We ask Thee," she was saying, "that our dear young sister, with the gifts Thou hast given her, may not be among those that perish, but may enter with all joy and everlasting delight into fulness of life, both here and hereafter!"

At the words, "fulness of life"—really so sweetly spoken by the trembling young woman,—Joanna was swept by a wholly unlooked-for wave of emotion. She could do no other than make the prayer her own. But in the succeeding silence she grew cold again. The same thought was in everyone's mind. Was not Juley going to pray?

In an icy panic, Joanna changed her own cry for life into the supplication that her mother might keep silence.

"O God, don't let Mother pray out loud, for Jesus' sake, Amen!" Again and again she repeated the same phrase with passionate fervour; and a huge load was lifted from her, when with a quiet rustle of skirts they all rose from their knees.

The meeting was over.

As they stood at first, silent, Joanna felt embarrassed. At her mother whose face was bathed in tears, she could not look: at Miss Gedge she would not.

So she gazed steadfastly at the shy girl who had last prayed.

"Thank you," she said at length, the first to speak. And she moved nearer to where the other stood. "I liked your prayer, and I hope it will be answered. It was good of you to come."

The student blushed as deeply as Joanna was blushing, but she shone as well, and a cloud came upon Eva Gedge's face.

Joanna enjoyed a moment of pure malice. She had triumphed. Then turning to her mother she spoke loudly enough for Eva to overhear.

"I shall have to go at once, Mother," she said. "I pro-

mised Mrs. Lovatt to call there this evening. It may be
fairly late before I'm back. You musn't wait up."

And she was gone before a word could be said in reply.

It was already twenty minutes to eight, but Mildred's
house was not far off, and Joanna could be fleet.

III

Even to herself Joanna did not admit how nervous she
became in the Lovatts' house. But from the moment the
front door closed between her and the street, there was always a tightening of all her nerves. As she passed through
the square entrance hall, so unlike any other known to her,
with its black-tiled floor, bright blue carpet, and white walls
hung with black-framed etchings, her very muscles would
stiffen a little in the involuntary effort which these decora-
tions seemed to demand. In the same way, the rooms,
though they were neither so large as the rooms in Collessie
Street, nor nearly so rich as Aunt Georgina's, imposed a
peculiar restraint. The way in which a few flowers stood up
from a shallow glass dish ; the black sofa bolsters tasselled
with gold ; the signed scribbles in pencil (generous as to margin) by Sargent or Burne-Jones, which leaned unfixed on a
moulding against the drawing-room wall ; and here and there,
resting on the same ledge for the convenience of handling,
a framed autograph letter—these were evidences of a world
in which Joanna did not yet move easily, a world where the
small talk, like the material furnishings, had its own shib-
boleths of seeming freedom and simplicity.

But on this evening Joanna had great hopes of escaping
the usual ordeal. The swift transition from St. Saviour's
to the house in Panmure Crescent, the emotional tension
of the prayer meeting, the bizarre concealment of her ball-
dress, acted upon her like some stimulating and skilfully
mixed potion.

Although not late, she was the last guest to arrive, and was
glad to have the bedroom to herself so that she could take off
her outer clothes unnoticed. The extra garments and the
race through the streets had made her hot, and it was a delicious refreshment to emerge in her thin evening gown. As
she shook out the voluminous skirt before Mildred's cheval
glass she seemed to herself as light as gossamer. She palpitated in response to the brightness in her own eyes, to the

wild colour in her cheeks, to the inebriating savour of life on her palate. And on the way down the blue-carpeted stair, she felt as if the vessel of her being were full to the lip with incandescent flame. From the moment she entered the drawing-room she knew she need fear nothing, for this evening at least.

To her bright, unseeing gaze the room seemed full of people standing up. Actually there were only six, counting herself. She shook hands with the Lovatts and with Mrs. Plummer, a woman distressingly thin, with masses of untidy black hair and a green velvet dress. Then turning in obedience to a sign from her hostess, she became conscious of a strange man, blasé yet dapper, with a straw-coloured moustache and rather prominent hazel eyes. He was staring at her through the strong lenses of his glasses with the painter's intentness. Indeed, but for that look, which she had sometimes seen in the eyes of Nilsson, Joanna would not have taken Louis Pender for an artist. Particularly by the side of Mr. Lovatt, the carpet manufacturer, with his stooping shoulders, velvet jacket and silky grey beard, his guest appeared a person entirely worldly. Of the three men present, he was the only one wearing a stiff shirt, and his dust-coloured hair was quite short and carefully brushed. It looked incongruous with the astonishing yellow moustache.

Yet in spite of this deference to convention there was something so resentful in the man's whole presence that the friendliness of his hand-clasp came to Joanna as a surprise. She looked inquiringly, involuntarily, straight into his eyes, and while she saw how their colour was accentuated by fair lashes, she had the curious sensation that her heart was holding its breath. When he heard Joanna's foreign name Pender's lids lifted slightly with interest.

So engrossed was she that it was an effort to attend to what Mrs. Lovatt was saying. But presently Joanna understood that she was to accept Mr. Urquhart's shyly proffered arm to the dining-room.

On the staircase she was so conscious of Pender who walked behind with Mrs. Lovatt, that she did not say a word to her companion. But on renewing the acquaintance it had surprised her to find how well she remembered him. This was the first time she had set eyes on him since the Italian class, from which she had not knowingly carried away any vivid impression of him : yet now his dark, silent face, and bashful body appeared almost intimately familiar.

At dinner he hesitated several times before achieving speech, and Joanna, instead of helping him, waited with indolent cruelty. She guessed at his shyness, but in her own hour of release showed no mercy. Besides she was watching Pender who sat opposite at the further corner of the table. There was a jauntiness in his movements which might have been taken for self-assertiveness. But somehow, Joanna knew better. Somehow, with a secret warmth of knowledge she saw him unsure, bitter, on the defensive.

"I only learned yesterday from Mrs. Lovatt that you were back in Glasgow."

Lawrence had spoken at last, and Joanna was caught by the pedantry of his phrasing. So shy he was, yet so precise ! And she smiled at him, dazzling him with all the new joy in her heart.

"And I *learn*," she replied, "that you are the coming anthropologist ! " As she spoke, he saw her gay smile change into a regular schoolgirl grin which put everything else out of his head. Not till this moment had he known how keenly he had looked forward to meeting her again. He still remembered the pain of unreasoning anger and emptiness with which he had heard of her marriage and departure to Italy.

How was it that she had been back for three whole years without his having once seen her ?

"Glasgow is a bigger place than one thinks after all," was what he succeeded presently in saying.

But Joanna only smiled a vague assent, and he saw that he had lost her. She was listening, not to him but to the talk between Pender and Mrs. Lovatt. She had gathered that Mrs. Tullis, the Professor's wife, was calling next day to meet Pender.

"As I shall stay down here until I know one way or the other," Pender was saying, "I may as well do a portrait of her if she'll sit to me. Yes, I was to have painted her two years ago, up in town. But Tullis got his Glasgow job and carried her off, so nothing came of it. It wasn't a commission of course. She was a friend of my wife's."

Then he was married !

Rousing herself Joanna turned again to Lawrence.

"You are a friend of the Tullises?" she asked him. But Mrs. Lovatt cut gaily across his unready reply.

"Yes, Mr. Urquhart, *you* tell us! Do *you* think Mrs. Tullis so pretty?" she demanded to his consternation, dragging the young man into the open.

At Mildred's question, Joanna looked instinctively at Pender's face; and she saw embarrassment like a cloud pass over it, leaving it the next moment quite devoid of expression.

While Lawrence sought his answer, Mrs. Plummer spoke for him.

"I think she is really *rather* beautiful!" said she, with her overweighted head on one side, and as if she gained a reflected glory by praising the good looks of another woman. "There's a something of the woods about her, don't you think, that's very lovely? *Farouche*, I think is the word."

"For myself," Mrs. Lovatt retorted, "I should rather have said vixenish than *farouche*, with that hair and those two little sharp white teeth in front. "Pretty Mrs. Fox," is my name for her. Come and meet her here to-morrow, Joanna, and tell me if you don't agree with me."

"Mildred always was jealous of red-headed women," whispered Mr. Lovatt in a stage aside to Joanna. And the others laughed and fell apart.

Joanna, who did not know the professor's wife by sight, had taken no part in the discussion. And she had been all the time aware of Pender's so different isolation, which yet seemed to bring him nearer to her. She felt a hatred rising in her against this Mrs. Tullis, against Mrs. Pender, against Mildred, perhaps against all women, because they were somehow responsible for the despicable uneasiness under Pender's practised surface.

She wondered if he would want to talk to her at all at the dance. Then she would discover him, perhaps.

With this thought, this longing, there flashed unbidden in her memory the vision of a little door in Italy, once pointed out by Mario. It was that door in the garden wall of a villa through which a famous woman was said to have welcomed her lover. Strange that Joanna should think of it now! Strange that it should have remained forgotten all these years to recur this evening like an unacknowledged, all unsatisfied desire!

IV

At the School the fun was in full swing when Mildred's party arrived. A waltz came to an end as they were taking off their wraps, and Joanna thought Mrs. Plummer would never stop re-arranging her hair, which stayed perfectly untidy in spite of prolonged fingering.

When at last they entered the dancing-room, the students were grouping themselves noisily for the foursome reel. Most of the dancers already stood facing one another, in two double lines which stretched from end to end of the long class-room; but still here and there some couples ran linked, laughing and sliding on the polished floor in a race for the few gaps left. Onlookers sat round on benches or on the floor. Many had kept on their overalls of holland or blue linen, and numbers of the girls were so young that their hair still hung over their shoulders. There was something easy-going, almost countrified about these dances. The sloping timbered ceiling, hung with a few lanterns of yellowish paper, made Joanna feel as if she were in a barn; and she thought that the easels and thrones stacked in each corner looked like farm implements.

And if it was a village festival, Mr. Valentine Plummer united in himself the parts of the Squire and the Parson. He came effusively to greet the newcomers, pressed them to join in at once, and shepherded them to the far end of the room. "There is always room at the top," he said, cracking his little parsonish joke. But neither the Lovatts nor Mrs. Plummer nor Pender could dance the reel.

Lawrence Urquhart glanced at Joanna.

"You, then, bella Signora!" exclaimed the Director jocosely. "Come. Shall it be said that a Scotswoman refused to take part in a reel?"

"Will you?" asked Lawrence.

But Joanna shook her head, excusing herself.

"Ah! but do, do dance it!"

Not Lawrence this time but Louis Pender had spoken. He stood close to Joanna, and begged like a lively child who fears the loss of a long-promised treat. And Joanna, blushing deeply with pleasure, laughed and yielded.

She gave her hand to Urquhart who was clenching his

black, mortified brows. Only to please this other was he accepted !

Although a couple was wanted almost where they stood, he set off with her to the far end of the room. It was some satisfaction to him that he was really dragging her there ; but he suffered too all the way from the hateful reluctance of her body. She was humiliated by his knowledge that she desired to dance before the other man. But by her backward drag on his arm she thrust him down so far below herself that her humiliation was a triumph compared with his.

Still he plodded on, his head forward and hanging a little. And they had barely got to their places when the band let fly with the tune.

To Joanna's great astonishment Urquhart danced well. It was the last thing she had expected of him ; but he sprang featly to music, and his body was delivered by the steady rhythm from all stiffness and self-consciousness. As he passed and re-passed her in the figure eight, taking first one of her hands and then the other ; as he placed his own hands on his slight hips or raised them high above his head ; as he swung his partners round, each time lifting them clean off the floor ; above all as he came to go through his complicated steps facing Joanna, gravely leaping on his small Highland feet ; the young man was wholly possessed. He had to the full that tranced and happy seriousness which is the spirit of a national dance.

From the outset he caught Joanna up into something of his own dignity, winning her surprised acknowledgment. Then, as the reel progressed, she began to lose all sense of identity. Every moment she became less herself, more a mere rhythmical expression of the soil from which they both had sprung. The memory dawned in her of some far back ancestress, of whom unheedingly she had heard her mother tell. Fresh, dim, sweet like dawn, she could see the Stirlingshire farmer's daughter carrying the milk-pails at sunrise and at sunset to the Castle on its hill. She could hear the swinging clink of the pails, could smell the spilt, clover-sweet milk, while the farmer's daughter gave her lips to the young, unknown Welsh soldier who kept the drawbridge. *She* was that lass, that meeting, without which her being would not have been. And soon she was not even these. Beneath the candid darkness of Lawrence Urquhart's face, soon she was no more than a field of barley that swings unseen in the wind before dawn.

But suddenly, though the music went on, and though her feet persisted in its rhythms, she was recalled into herself. Louis Pender, edging along by the wall, had come unknown to where she was dancing. And now that she had seen him, she knew nothing else but that he watched her through his glasses with his practised, unhappy eyes. She did not look at him, but his being there changed everything for her. It changed subtly the spirit of her dancing into a conscious revelation and a less conscious withholding. She became an appeal, a claim, a scarcely endurable excitement. She could not help herself.

The moment the music stopped she longed to get rid of her partner. He was inexpressive again, but that was not why she wanted to be quit of him. When they had sat silent in the corridor for a minute, and he had brought her a little red glass of lemonade, the next dance was announced. It was a schottische, and Joanna feared that Urquhart would ask for it. While she was wondering how to refuse, Carl Nilsson passed them. She had not known him there till then, and ran to him with relief, an impetuous greeting on her lips.

She introduced the two men, and Urquhart went up in her mind as she saw them clearly take to each other from the first. Carl was no dancer, he said, and had only looked in for a moment. He was even now making for home. Yet he stood talking to the younger man, which Joanna knew he would not have done out of mere politeness. Her own escape, however, was still first with her. And as soon as she could, she slipped away to where Mrs. Lovatt was sitting. She did not even notice that Carl and Lawrence had drawn two chairs for themselves into a quieter angle of the corridor.

V

She knew now that Pender would seek her out.

For hours she had been looking, unknowingly, for this moment. It had lain veiled in her throughout the dinner ; had become more and more immanent during the dark cab drive ; and had leapt into certainty as a tiger leaps from its lair, when she had caught sight of him watching the dance.

And now she had the impulse to fly. In spite of her experience she was too raw and unprepared—afraid too, terribly afraid. She rose, making in a panic for the corridor. She could hide downstairs.

But in the doorway she came face to face with Pender. His eyes filled with light.

"Here you are!" he said. And he stood smiling at her with extraordinary kindness, such as she had never seen on any face before. But as they stood looking at each other, a different sparkling triumphed over the light of kindness in his eyes, and there was excitement in the square, nervous hand that stroked his moustache.

The woman remained perfectly still in the doorway. She was stiff with shyness and delight, and could move neither backward into the room nor forward into the corridor. The man's physical nearness robbed her of initiative.

"Is there ever such a thing as a waltz at your Glasgow balls?" he asked with a touch of petulance that she liked. "I understand the next dance is a scot—— scot——, something that sounds like catching cold."

"A schottische?" Joanna laughed.

Up flew Pender's eyebrows, and without any other perceptible change, every line in his face and body became expressive of comic despair.

"I ask you, do you see me dancing it?"

He had the comedian's gift, and Joanna's laughter rang out readily. Yet it was above all when he was clowning for her entertainment that she felt the underlying discord and distress of the man. Her heart seemed to drip sweetly with pity for him, like a full honey-comb. It was as if her blood told her that there was virtue in her for his healing, his lavish consolation.

"Come and sit it out with me," he urged. "I've seen the very place for us downstairs. It's so hot and noisy up here. I hate it."

There were empty chairs on the landing, and Pender with Joanna on his arm hesitated a second before taking her downstairs. It was one of these little human waverings that are so pathetic on the eve of an already settled fate. There they stood poised, she in her gay dress, all billowing in the draught from the ball-room, her face turned like a flower, like a question, to the man's, abiding his decision; he, refusing his answer, taking counsel alone, weighing his little world that he hated yet feared, between his palms, and gnawing anxiously at his petulant under-lip.

"I suppose at dances in London there are nothing but waltzes now?" Joanna asked, when they had got half-way downstairs. But she did not even notice that her question remained unanswered. She was all exultation in the surety that he too had been waiting for this. Had he not looked for a place apart where they could sit together and talk?

When he led her along a darkened passage on the ground floor, she guessed they were going to the Antique Class-room; but the room they entered was worlds removed from the familiar place in which she had worked through many an hour of daylight. Its known contours were all disfigured by moonlight, and by the straggling rays of a street lamp which came mixed with moonlight through the long plaster-coated windows. The statues lurked strangely in corners. The place was not illumined; its darkness was made manifest, and its unsuspected secrets of darkness.

In silence Joanna perched on a high stool, and her companion pulled forward a small throne on castors, and sat upon it between her and the windows which all ran along one wall. Colour could not persist in this underworld, and Joanna's head and shoulders and breast, rising from her dress, might have been of marble but for the living shadows. Pender's face was in deep shade. She could only see the glint of his glasses, and his lightly clasped hands, caught by a shaft of light from the street as he leaned forward, elbows on knees. The music of the schottische came to them from far above, not as melody, but as a monotonous pulse of sound. They were together, hidden, remote, in a forsaken world revolving in melancholy but beautiful twilight.

"What a thing light is!" exclaimed Pender in low, struck tones. "As I see you now, I shouldn't know you for the same woman I saw ten minutes ago, dancing."

Joanna, in the reel, had seemed to him, for all her slightness of figure, like a young heifer in a clover field, essentially sturdy, full of unbroken, untouched vigour; and the combination of this with her face which he found over-refined in features, had inflamed him to a degree astonishing to himself. Now she was suddenly aloof as a moon-maiden, and his passion recoiled into himself. But he was surer than before of her attraction for him,—surer rather of the special quality of the attraction.

"Yes, everything is different," she agreed, her voice also quiet with wonder. "I am only beginning to see you now. It's so queer, isn't it, how every bit of colour is washed out? I can never help thinking that colour is really form, though I suppose we know it isn't."

The speech pleased Pender.

"Who really knows what colour is?" he said. "But I believe I get that feeling at times——." His grave, interested voice was charming to Joanna; and suddenly he leaned further forward, looking up at her, his face coming into the shaft of light, his eyes no longer appraising.

"Will you sit for me some day?" he asked, with such boyish, shy directness, that it was like taking off a mask or throwing open a door for her to enter.

"I'd like to," Joanna replied in simple delight: but even as she spoke her simplicity gave way to excitement, and she became rigid with it as she had been in the doorway upstairs.

"Good. That is settled." Pender spoke evenly, but the excitement was mounting in him also. "As soon as I can get some sort of a studio rigged up, I'll let you know,"—and though he had leaned back into the darkness again, Joanna could feel the unsheathed boldness of his eyes like weapons, there in the darkness like weapons ready to strike. And suddenly she remembered something of the hawk in his face—was it the eyes, the nose, or was it no matter of feature?

Two long ends of narrow, bright blue ribbon hung from Joanna's waist to the floor on the side where Pender was; and when he had spoken she saw his hand go out and take hold of these. She saw his hand slip gleaming, snake-like, through the discovering ray, passing swiftly from dark to dark, and though it was only her ribbon he touched, a quiver passed through her whole frame.

"You are going to paint Mrs. Tullis too?" Against her will Joanna asked this, but she must hear his voice when he spoke of this other woman.

Pender stopped his winding up of the ribbon, which had seemed as if lessening the distance between them, and answered rather stiffly:

"I may, if she has time to sit." Then he went on with his winding, gathering a larger and larger spool of the silk girdle between his finger and thumb.

"You like her?"

Under Joanna's persistence he moved abruptly, but with what meaning she could not tell.

"She's a very charming woman—or was—" he said, and he flicked the spool of ribbon from him so that it lay spilt again on the floor. "I've not seen her for some time. But don't you know her?"

"No. You say you like her?" Joanna hated herself, but could not refrain.

For this last minute they had talked in strained, unhappy voices, but Pender broke the tension between them with a little laugh.

"I couldn't say till I see her again whether I like her or not," he said, speaking now quite naturally. "I once liked her very much indeed; but one never knows how one will feel after six months, let alone two years and more. Don't you find it so?"

So he had told her! And though Joanna was taken aback by what she rightly felt to be the directness of his reply, she understood and was grateful. This man, she realized, had his loves, like the Italians of whom Mario and Maddalena had been used to speak casually. He was of those who took unfaithfulness in marriage as a matter of course. And there flickered again in the girl's mind, like a single phrase from a melody but once heard, the remembrance of that little, secret door, set deep in the wall of *La Porziuncola*.

"While I'm waiting about in Glasgow——" he was speaking again. "——I hear there's a cottage and studio I might get at a place called Carmunnock—said to be nice. Do you know that part? I couldn't stand being in Glasgow itself."

Joanna spoke a little about the country round Carmunnock, and the talk faded out.

They rose indefinitely and moved to the door.

On the lighted stairs each looked timidly at each to discover the new thing, the fine, frail intimacy that had sprung up between them in the darkness.

"Do you know what I wanted when I was watching you dance?" said he, smiling into her eyes. "I wanted to see you on the Downs, in the wind, with your face red from the sun, and your hair all blown about anyhow. Do you think I ever shall ? "

" I'm afraid there are no Downs at Carmunnock," she replied, smiling back with an unaccustomed touch of coquetry.

" That's a pity."

" But there are moors."

" A moor would serve," he allowed, showing his amusement.

" Will your wife be coming to Glasgow ? " Joanna presently asked, in a different, very steady voice. And at the question so flatly put, Louis gave her a glance in which resentment was struggling with his amusement.

" She may, or may not," he answered, in some confusion.

This woman's bluntness stimulated, and at the same time repelled him a little. She had had a husband, he told himself ; so she must know her whereabouts. Had she been the untouched creature she seemed, of course he would have let her be. There was danger in her certainly. But it was his danger. He supposed she could look out for herself.

Upstairs he asked her for the waltz which had just begun. She refused : he insisted. But it was a failure. And when he had gone half round the room with her, trying every few turns to make her reverse, he stopped and took her away.

" You were right : you are no waltzer, my child," he said, resignedly.

At his rudeness the tears sprang to Joanna's eyes. She was already sick with vexation at her failure.

" I was never allowed to have lessons," she said, biting her trembling lower lip. " This is the first dance I've ever been to."

Upon this he eyed her quickly.

" Well, well, never mind my rudeness," he said in hasty shame. " It's easy enough to learn. I didn't want to hurt you, but it was such a disappointment."

Though there was some penitence here, he was still childishly overcome by his impatience of being thwarted in a pleasure. He asked no further question, and Joanna felt he would not have been interested had she told him of the prayer meeting and her hidden ball-dress. Yet she knew he was somehow vitally interested in her. How was it, then ? She was at a loss, and groping for the key of his nature.

It was late when the waltz finished. Joanna realized that

she must go home. Mildred, who was passing on Valentine Plummer's arm, told them that Urquhart had gone some time ago. And when she added that he was working at nights for a fellowship, Joanna felt a stab to her vanity. She would have been gratified to think that he had left early on her account. She was relieved however that he had not seen her in the waltz with Pender.

The rain was slashing outside, but she had only to cross the road to be at home. And so great now was her longing for solitude, that she could hardly endure the walk downstairs in Pender's company, nor his insistence in seeing her to her very door.

"You will get drenched," she remonstrated, looking at his bare head in the slanting rain; and with a hurried handshake she ran up the steps of her mother's house and let herself in.

But when the door was shut between them, she bent down to look back at him through the old devil's beard in the glass She looked, as long ago she had once looked at her dead father.

Louis was turning away, slowly in spite of the rain.

CHAPTER III

I

ON Saturday afternoon, according to Mildred's invitation, Joanna went to Panmure Crescent

The house, as she entered it, had none of its usual effect upon her, and she passed through the blue and black hall quite absorbed. With what face would he meet her?

But only her hostess and Lawrence Urquhart were in the drawing-room.

"Fancy! Mr. Pender has had to go back to town: isn't it *too* sad?" said Mildred, as she shook hands.

Joanna, standing there in the middle of the room, felt as if she had been dealt a violent and treacherous blow. It was a wonder to her that she remained erect. But even so, a moment passed before she could admit to herself that anything had happened. "Town" to any Glasgow person means Buchanan Street: and though Joanna perfectly grasped the meaning of the word on Mildred's lips, she seized on this poor excuse for confusion as a momentary anaesthetic. Only thus could she survive the first shock without betrayal.

Then as the drug wore off she faced the news with gathering strength. He had gone away to London. She was not to see him to-day. She might not ever see him again. She only knew by their shattering how many pictures of meeting she had woven since the parting of the night before. With a costly effort she collected herself now and shook Urquhart's outstretched hand.

"It's hard lines on us,"—Mrs. Lovatt was talking as she poured out tea—"and I expect Mrs. Tullis will feel sold if she comes: but it was good news for Pender. He got the telegram at lunch-time and just caught the two o'clock train. Some dealer from Paris wants to see him about a one man show there. I could hardly believe it, when he told me this would be the first, either in Paris *or* London. It seems too prepos-

177

terous. But he says the money or the luck has always been wanting. That Pender should still be so hard up is a standing wonder to me. When I *think* of his things——! There's only one Pender. Don't you agree?"

"I take it," said Urquhart, "that he hasn't practised the great art of self-advertisement."

(Joanna moved impatiently in her chair. "*I take it!*" What a stilted way he had of speaking!)

"That's it exactly!" responded Mildred with animation. "And not only that, but he has never troubled to hide his contempt for those who do practise it. They say he is the most unpopular artist among artists in London. There's no doubt that something in his personality has stood in the way of his getting on. But it's a sin all the same. To think of the prices his stuff will fetch the minute he's dead! And I've no doubt the dealers are beginning to realize this. The brutes!"

"Would you guess," she continued, handing a cup to Joanna, "that he was getting on for fifty? Forty-seven, he must be, at the very least. Would you think so?"

"I can never guess ages," replied Joanna, as she had to reply, "but I shouldn't have thought him so old."

To her fifty was age, was worlds removed from herself. Her father, she knew, had been barely fifty when he died, and she had always thought of him as an old man.

Yet in connection with Louis Pender, the word fifty, remained meaningless. So far as she was concerned it had no bearing on him.

"Physically he may look younger, perhaps," said Urquhart with calm unexpectedness, "but I, myself, should have put him down as older."

Under the questioning looks of both the women, he was quite aware that he had blundered, but he persisted.

"I mean," he said, "he looks to me so sick and tired of everything."

"I think he looks very much younger than his age," said Joanna displeased.

"So do I, I must say," agreed Mildred, "though of course I know what you mean, Mr. Urquhart. He looks rather disillusioned. His marriage—ah well!" And she sighed, lifting her brows a little.

Presently she noticed that Joanna's eyes had strayed ques-

tioningly to a pile of art magazines surmounted by a case
tied with tapes, which lay on the sofa opposite beside Lawrence
Urquhart.

" Don't tell me that I never showed you my Penders ! "
she exclaimed. " Is it possible ? Mr. Urquhart has just
been looking at them. Pass the case, will you, Mr. Urquhart ? Or will you sit on the sofa, Joanna ? "

Hungering for a sight of Pender's work, Joanna crossed to
where Urquhart was, and sat down by him. As he handed
her the uppermost picture, her eyes were so dizzied with excitement that she could scarcely see ; but instinctively, with
protective deceit, she held it from her in the approved attitude of the student.

Then gradually as her blood subsided and her eyes served
her again, she became conscious of disappointment.

Could it be possible that he was only a fan painter ? Certainly this that she held in her hand was the design for a fan !

To spare her the weight the drawings would have been upon
her knees, Lawrence passed them to her one by one, and she
resented his handling of them. More and more burningly
she resented his presence, Mildred's presence, Mildred's running commentary of explanation and praise. If only she
might be alone with Pender's work !

" That now, that you are looking at ! " cried Mildred
pointing a forefinger. " It's early work of course, and one
can see that he was under the spell of Veronese. But even
then it seems to me he had nothing to learn from Veronese
himself in the matter of colour. Just see the red of that dress
by the pillar in the fore-ground, with the blue, night sky
behind these high-arched windows. Doesn't it *sing ? And*
the composition ! All these figures on a small fan : yet the
whole is as broad and mellow as a fresco on the wall of a
palace. The sense of space is marvellous."

Under this fire of enthusiasm Joanna felt her every nerve
frayed. But at the very point when she believed her endurance was at an end, the drawing-room door opened and Mrs.
Tullis was announced.

As soon as she had touched pretty Mrs. Tullis's hard hand,
and heard her little hard laugh which sounded too often,
Joanna blamed and despised her.

The woman had finish. And that Joanna admired jealously. She had a kittenish charm too, though it was harden-

ing a little, growing a thought brittle. Enviable looks she had, lovely hair and eyes. And under all there was a hard, excitable sexuality, for which against her will Joanna was sensible of a certain respect. She believed Mrs. Tullis worlds more attractive to a man like Pender—or for that matter to any man—than she herself could ever hope to be. She felt crude by the side of Mrs. Tullis. Yet in that same instant she denied Mrs. Tullis's claim to any attraction or beauty whatsoever. Nay, even while she sat trembling with primitive jealousy, she was possessed of the proud and dangerous knowledge of her own intrinsic superiority. She could not have named it, could not even examine into it. But there lay in her a gift for Pender which he could never receive or have received from this other woman. And in this she triumphed.

Within ten minutes, not merely jealousy, but ordinary interest had faded ; and Joanna began to look once more at the drawings, now all collected in spite of Urquhart, on her lap.

And by degrees, as the voices of Mrs. Tullis and her hostess sounded alternately, now speaking of Pender's enforced, hasty return to London, now questioning Urquhart politely as to the exact subject of his thesis for a forthcoming fellowship, she found herself entering into the fantasy of the artist.

At first she had been taken aback by the occasional weakness and even faultiness of his drawing. Now, with her sight sharpened by decisive emotion, she realized only that she was entering the country of his desire, and that it was a country which she had longed all her life to visit.

It was a world of elegance passionately felt, of gallantry founded on a perfection of melancholy. Its beauty was full of farewells, at times resigned, at times defiant, but always exquisite. And before one could enter this world one had to learn the idiom of its creator. This was the more difficult, because, unlike so many moderns, Pender had imposed on himself severe conventions. It seemed he had to work in fetters. Joanna discovered that he was least sure of himself when confronted by an actual sitter or a real landscape. With any attempt at realism the soul was apt to go out of his work.

When Mrs. Tullis left, Joanna hardly marked her going.

II

During the next week she worked little and carelessly, dividing her time between Panmure Crescent and *Sans Souci*.

She found herself avoiding Carl Nilsson's inquiring eye on the few occasions when she attended his class, and was thankful that he never persisted to the point of speech.

She grew skilful at inventing pretexts for seeing Mildred, and if in their talk Pender's name was not spoken, she returned home feeling empty. She brooded over each scrap of knowledge, piecing them together. Very soon she was in possession of all that Mildred could give her.

It appealed to her imagination that by the strangest of chances Pender had been born in Glasgow.

His father a Hungarian actor with a self-cultivated talent for scene-painting, and his mother, an English parson's daughter, who, eloping with the elder Louis, had made a quite noteworthy career for herself on the stage, had been staying in theatrical lodgings in Glasgow when their only child was born. Later they had ceased their roving life, establishing themselves at Ealing ; and until she became an old woman, Madame Pender—as she called herself in her widowhood—had maintained some reputation as a teacher of elocution in that suburb.

From the first, young Louis had showed a gift for drawing, and his mother had let him follow his bent at the Art School. He had quarrelled with his teachers, been disliked by his fellow-students, and failed to win all save one of the scholarships on which his parent's heart was set. But even so there was never any doubt of his ability. And now at middle age, after many rebuffs and much bad fortune, he had in his own peculiar way arrived.

Concerning his marriage, Joanna could not bring herself to question her friend directly. But there was no need. For here, with some head-shaking, Mildred was at her most communicative.

He had married young, she said,—a handsome girl of more distinguished social connections than his own. And his wife's money, though it had unfortunately been lost within a few years of their marriage, had helped at a critical time in his career. It was common talk that for many years past he had foraged for love (though always with a certain discretion) outside matrimony ; and surprise was sometimes expressed that an open break had never occurred. Now it was no longer expected. People understood that the couple were held together by worldly interest and by their twin sons, born in the first year of marriage, old enough now for one to be in the army and the other just entering the Indian Civil Service.

III

At *Sans Souci*, apart from Phemie herself, it was the music which had become the great attraction for Joanna.

Though Phemie was the only one who had been trained save in the most haphazard way, the whole family was gifted with music, and the sisters, besides having good natural voices, possessed an extraordinary sense of style.

Joanna never tired of listening on the evenings when five or six of the girls crowded round Phemie at the piano, to " try over bits,"—sometimes out of an operetta, at other times from the St. Matthew or the St. John Passion Music ; for they all belonged to the Bach Choir and practised hard for the Easter performance in the Cathedral.

Then how serious, fresh and beautiful the Pringle girls looked. But always, after a time, Nora the youngest grew tired of not laughing : and she would introduce some absurd words or, with all the terrific complacency of a *prima donna,* some flowery musical phrase of her own ; until at last the chiding gravity of the others was upset. Once " our Nora " started there was no stopping her, and from making subtly comic grimaces, she would grow wilder and wilder in her clowning till every one was in paroxysms, and there could be no more Bach that night.

Nora it was who discovered in some magazine the mar-vellous "bloom-bath" alleged to be the secret of Mrs. Langtry's beauty. And one afternoon when Joanna should have been at the Art School, she and Nora and Phemie in their petti-coats, with shrieks of laughter and pain nearly steamed the skin off their faces. There was always some " ploy " for-ward with the Pringles, and Joanna, who in these ways had never been young before, entered into everything like a schoolgirl.

It was some time before she realized that the Pringle girls deeply hated the disorder and publicity of their home-life : that although outwardly they combined with zest to keep it going, each concealed a passionate longing for escape.

Phemie especially fretted for the day when she and her Jimmie would be able to afford marriage. And the existence the two had planned for themselves, was in every respect opposed to existence at *Sans Souci*. A dignified and beautiful quiet was its essential.

" No ornaments hardly, as they only make work," Phemie was discoursing one night as she showed Joanna the piled-up treasures of her " bottom-drawer." " But lots of really lovely linen, all kept with lavender in among it. O ! I do love the feel of good linen in my hands, don't you, Joanna ? "

And lifting out a folded linen sheet, elaborately hem-stitched, Phemie sniffed its fragrance appreciatively with her little nose.

" And all the furniture real antique,—Jimmie has collected quite a lot—not ' arty,' you know Joanna, but just old and *good*,—and chintz covered with roses in the drawing-room,—and all Jimmie's books, and a Bechstein grand,—and the bed-room all white with pink roses on the wall-paper—roses I do love and adore. And at nights Jimmie and I will sit before the fire in perfect arm-chairs reading—and of course I'll change every evening into a tea-gown—the most exquisite ever !—pink of the palest—and *fearfully* simple ! "

As she spoke, Phemie was rummaging in the drawer (she could keep no drawer tidy—not even this sacred bottom one) ; and presently finding what she sought, she drew forth a night-gown of gossamer.

" What do you think of this pattern, my darling ? *That's* none of Mamma's goods, as you may perchance guess ; our Nora got it from an American girl. Feel the stuff ! "

Joanna laid admiring fingers on the lawn and lace, and put her cheek luxuriously against its softness. She thought of Maddalena, and seemed to hear her bass voice denouncing the beautifully flimsy garment. And surely Maddalena would have died of horror could she have seen Phemie dressing any afternoon to meet her Jimmie in town ! Every drawer and door in the bedroom stood open ; and from a tousled trunk under the bed, Phemie would select a flower, a feather, a tip of fur, or bow of ribbon, which, straightening impatiently before the mirror, she would pin upon a hat from which last day's trimmings had been hastily torn. Sometimes the result was happy, oftener it was not. But always, as she turned her bird-like head this way and that, to see the effect of the decoration, Joanna was delighted by her friend's odd, endearing beauty.

" You see," continued Phemie, breaking into Joanna's

thoughts of Maddalena, " I suppose a woman is a kind of fairy to a man.   Isn't that so, my darling ? "

IV

One Thursday, calling at Panmure Crescent on the pretext of returning a borrowed book, Joanna found Lawrence Urquhart there again.   She was vexed at this.   It was three weeks now since Pender's going, and she had come hoping for word of his return.   But she could not bring herself to speak of him before Urquhart.

" I'm glad you have come to-day, Joanna," was Mildred's greeting.   " I have news for you."

" I think it will please you," she continued, nodding mysteriously.   " Just wait a moment.   The letter is downstairs."   And she left the room.

A pulse beat in Joanna's throat.   Surely, at last he must have written.   Or was there news from the Town Council ? If his designs had been accepted he should soon be back in Glasgow.   More than ever now she wished Urquhart absent. Why should he dog her footsteps in this way ?

But he seemed unconscious of her resentment, and the moment Mildred had gone, he began to talk with less than his usual hesitation.

He had just discovered, he told her, that his Mother, who as a girl had "sat under" Joanna's grandfather at St. Jude's, had been in those days a constant playmate of the Bannerman children.   Her particular friend, it seemed, had been a daughter called " Gina."

" That must have been Aunt Georgina," assented Joanna, " though it is difficult to think she was ever little, and even if she was, I can hardly believe that anyone would dare to call her ' Gina ! ' "

" Come one afternoon to our house and talk to my mother about her," invited Lawrence.   " She will love it if you will. She asked me to tell you so."

Joanna promised that she would call upon Mrs. Urquhart, and an afternoon was fixed for the following week.   Even while she told herself that in common courtesy she could do no less, she found herself interested suddenly in the young man's dark irregularity of feature.   Certainly his face could light up in an unexpected way.

Mildred now returned holding an open letter.

"Here it is," she said. "Now listen, and tell me if this isn't what you have been longing for? No, you musn't go, Mr. Urquhart. It's nothing private. No, indeed it isn't. Do stay and give us your opinion."

Lawrence, who had risen, sat down again with a glance at Joanna's averted profile, and the letter was read out.

It offered Joanna her first chance of earning money.

A friend of the Lovatts, the manager of a leading Glasgow drapery firm, was making a new departure. He wanted something fresh in the way of catalogues, frontispieces, and advertisements generally. Designs were to be submitted. Here was the chance for young talent. Did the Lovatts know of any?

"If you think I'm good enough," said Joanna more than doubtfully when Mildred had finished. It was indeed what she had longed for—the first step towards that independent life in London which was her dream. Yet the actual suggestion filled her chiefly with a terrified sense of incompetence. It seemed absurd that work of hers whould be thought fit for reproduction and payment. How she must have imposed on people that such an idea should be for a moment considered! Now they would find her out.

Yet she knew she would try.

"Why of course you are good enough," Mildred encouraged her. "And I hope for *one* design you'll send that nice thing you were working on the other day—women dancing— I was so struck with it! I don't wonder Val Plummer says you have a feeling for drapery."

"What is more, Nilsson says the same," put in Lawrence, glowing with satisfaction, and Joanna was reminded by his remark that in the three weeks since the dance the two, introduced by her, had become good friends.

So it was arranged, and Joanna found that she had agreed to send in six designs by a given time. After all, she told herself, if she failed she could kill herself!

In spite of her disappointment about Pender, of whom no word had been spoken, she trod home that afternoon on air.

v

According to her promise, Joanna set out for the Urquharts on the following Thursday afternoon: but she grudged the time. Her designs were going to take even longer than she had expected, and she was aghast at the unfinished and feeble appearance of work which unchallenged had pleased her a month before.

The widow, whose only child Lawrence was, lived in a small top flat near the Boyds in North Kelvinside. On her way there, therefore, Joanna had to cross the high bridge which for her would always be associated with Bob Ranken, and then she had to pass the steps where four years ago she and Bob had parted.

When she came to the bridge, to her surprise a slight trembling seized her. Far behind and done with was that experience, yet the peculiar misery of it still remained quick, and as it were ambushed to spring out hurtfully upon her at the touch of memory. Why was it? Why was it that there was no such quality of torture—of canker almost—in her memories, so much more tragic, of Mario?

For a moment she leaned on the parapet where she and Bob had once stood, calling themselves lovers: and in that moment, more clearly than by spoken word, the truth of that past emotion was made known to her.

How she had lied to herself and to Bob! How sick she had been with self-love! Why, she had merely invented him as a lover to meet her need; had cared only for her own invention, never a scrap for the living man she had used therefor. Now she was open-eyed and ashamed. Bob had been more honest than she. He had at least been struggling amid the bewilderment of his blood towards a truthful attitude. If only he could have pierced clean through all her pretences, they might have emerged together, achieving real contact. As it was, she was thankful for the bitter and humiliating knowledge that had come to her at length, and she was grateful to Bob for his part in it. Now that she *knew*, the venom was gone from the memory. For her there would be no decking of altars to sweet first love. The dead branch could be ruthlessly lopped off.

And she did not regret. Even her falseness, she did not regret. No!

She gazed down on the full, brown February flood. The last pieces of ice were breaking from the banks, and being jostled in mid-current among torn branches of trees. Although a spring thaw had set in, many of the rhododendron bushes were still covered with hoar-frost. On some bushes the folded leaves hung down like the lop ears of a hare;

on others they were cocked up in tufts like the feathers of a field-marshal's hat. Everywhere the evergreen bushes flourished, hardy and rank, and between them rushed the swollen, headlong water.

Ah! How remorselessly the stream swept away all the debris of winter it could reach! As Joanna watched it in fascination she was one with it, and she rejoiced. Her life— was it not as that flood? Was it not muddy, littered, unlike the life she would have imagined or chosen? But it *was* a life. It moved. It possessed the impulse, the impetus, the inner fount of desire—not of mere detached wishes that succeed each other capriciously, but of desire that springs from some undiscoverable source, and is imperious as the waters in spring-time. If only she had the courage to obey her true desire always, would she not be purged ultimately of all her falseness? This at least was her scarcely articulate faith.

At the Urquharts, a charwoman, disguised against her will as a housemaid, admitted Joanna and led the way stealthily down a long, dark and stuffy passage. Even in the darkness the solid tastelessness of the dwelling was made known, and there were many traces of that kind of careful spirit (as different from simple thriftiness as from poverty) which cannot endure to let outward show correspond with reduced circumstances.

At the far end of the passage they came to the dining-room, and as she entered, Joanna's sense of oppression was increased by the sight of a large table, spread (solely, as it seemed, in her honour) with so many specimens of tea-bread that it looked like an exhibition of bakery. She could not have told why, but the plated tea-baskets at the corners, the great abundance of rock-cakes, the tall, forbidding tea-pot on its beaded mat, and the chairs of horse-hair and very ruddy mahogany which had been pushed up to the damask, did undoubtedly combine rather in the cold effort to defy criticism than in any spontaneous hospitality.

But as Mrs. Urquhart crossed the room to greet her, Joanna was fully enlightened. Here was the source of suffocation in the house. Here in this woman with the large, pale, comely face, the beautiful snow-white hair, of an astonishing thickness (at one time no doubt, black like her son's), and the great, cashmere bosom, surmounted by a heavy, gold brooch like a snake coiled and knotted. In her large, comely white-ness, Mrs. Urquhart seemed to Joanna to absorb light and oxygen as might some powerfully succulent plant. Any-thing staying beside her for long, must surely yield up its share and languish. Though one of the two windows was open at the top, Joanna could have cried out for air as her hostess bore down upon her.

Not that Lawrence's mother was not smiling, even gushing in her manner. In talking she frequently leaned her body towards Joanna's with an enveloping movement clearly meant to convey an impression of quite remarkable warmth. Each time this happened it is true that Joanna found herself draw-ing back with instinctive hostility : but whenever she had done so, she was somehow made to feel herself in the wrong.

"What! I give such a hearty welcome to my son's guest, and this is all the thanks I get!" Mrs. Urquhart seemed to say.

Aloud, she was making the ordinary, polite enquiries after Mrs. Bannerman's well-being. But here again, her words and the impression she conveyed were two very different things ; and Joanna, though she struggled against it, understood at once that in the speaker's estimation, her mother was a highly ridiculous and eccentric person.

"I had a great admiration," continued Mrs. Urquhart,— "a very great admiration for your dear father, Mrs. —— you must excuse me, I have never grasped your married name."

Joanna informed her, and flushing rather from annoyance than from shyness, begged to be addressed by her Christian name. Her request came automatically, simply because it was expected of her, and even as it crossed her lips she knew she was being bullied by this heavy, white woman. She was sure that the excuse about her surname was untrue. Yet was it not all friendliness on Mrs. Urquhart's part ?

"Yes, I admired Father," repeated the elder woman, ex-uding a geniality which was falsified by the little, calculating, fixed eyes. "I worked with him many a day at the Foundry Boys and the Children's Dinner Table ; and when my boy told me you were coming to tea, I was glad to welcome you for Father's sake. No man in Glasgow, I have always said, was more respected. And so handsome too : and a smile for every one. Lawrence had an idea that you had his features.

but I cannot say I see it. No : to my way of thinking you favour your mother."

Joanna having nothing else to say felt she must thank her hostess at this point for having so kindly invited her.

"Not at all," was the rejoinder. "Lawrence will tell you I make all his friends welcome as far as my means permit. I was always one to let the boy choose his own companions, and I encourage him to bring them to the house. It cannot be said of me, as of *some* mothers, that I grudge any innocent pleasure to the young folks. If only Lawrence appreciated this. But you would wonder at how many of his evenings he spends with friends Mother never sees."

As some response to this was expected, Joanna supposed at random that Lawrence had to see such friends in connection with his work.

"He seems to be a worker," she said with an attempt to brighten things up. She resented being forced thus into the position of Lawrence's defender : but it was true that she credited him with tenacity.

"I'm glad to hear it."

The mother spoke these words in such a curious tone that Joanna looked full at her. But she looked away again in distaste of what she saw.

"I suppose he has told you," Mrs. Urquhart pursued, "that his present fellowship ends within the year ? "

Joanna wished angrily that Lawrence would come and interrupt this stifling conversation. Why was he not there ? Was there a purpose in his absence ? But while she longed to disclaim any knowledge whatever of his affairs, she found herself speaking against her will of the thesis she knew Lawrence was just then writing on some anthropological subject in competition for the Hume Fellowship.

"Ah ! I'm glad he confides in you, Mrs.—Joanna," said Mrs. Urquhart. " Of course he will have told you of the trip to the continent he is bent on taking shortly with this Mr. Nilsson ? "

"With Carl Nilsson ? Really ! " Joanna exclaimed, now with genuine pleasure. "How I envy your son ! I'm sure no one could be a more perfect travelling companion than Carl. I'm so glad. It was I who introduced them to each other, you know."

It would not be true to say there was no ring of defiance in

Joanna's enthusiasm; and the sense of conflict between the two women increased.

"I haven't a word to say against Mr. Nilsson." Mrs. Urquhart spoke in cold reproof. "I have never met the man. I merely hope he realizes that the boy's work has to come first. *You,* my dear, will understand me when I say it is pure mother love makes me so anxious. *Nothing* must distract Lawrence's attention from his work at present. You have seen already that I grudge him no reasonable pleasure."

During this speech, and more of the same kind that followed, Joanna felt like a fly which is trussed up more and more completely in the scarcely perceptible trammels of a spider. Great was her relief when a sound in the passage outside told of Lawrence's arrival.

Mrs. Urquhart, who had heard also, rose and moved to make the tea with an agility surprising in one so stout.

"I always feel," she concluded, just before her son came in, "that a female friend, a little *older* than himself, can have such a very *steadying* effect on a young man."

During tea, Lawrence spoke and ate little but he looked more than once from Joanna to his mother, and from his mother back again to Joanna. More than once his mother reproached him for his inattentiveness in the matter of handing cakes. But she herself made up for this by constantly pressing food upon her guest. She was affronted when Joanna refused a second kind of jam.

"Both preserves are home-made," declared the hostess, "as I ought to know, seeing I made them myself. But perhaps there is some other kind you would prefer? There is apricot in the sideboard."

Sooner than this, Joanna yielded and helped herself, but the food seemed to choke her.

To the invitation, sent by Juley, that she would come one day to Collessie Street, Mrs. Urquhart shook her head.

"I'm none too strong," she said, "with my heart, as Lawrence will tell you; and could never climb that terrible hill of yours. But maybe Mother could manage round here one of these days?"

Joanna replied that her mother was no caller, either.

"But we are flitting in May," she added. "We shall be near here then. Yes," she went on in answer to a look from

Lawrence, " our house in Collessie Street is too big for us
now. My brother Sholto is away, and before long I hope to
get work in London. So——"

" You're never going to leave your mother alone again ? "
interrupted Mrs. Urquhart, while Lawrence searched Joanna's face silently, so that she wished she had not spoken.

" Not alone, Mrs. Urquhart," she replied in a tone of forced
lightness. " There's Linnet, my other brother, at home.
Besides I don't think Mother will want always to stay in
Glasgow. My sister is in London. Why should we not all
be there together after a few years ? "

This last idea, of a family life in London, was a protective
invention of the moment. It was far enough in truth from
Joanna's latest ambition. Yet, affected as she was by Lawrence's questioning eyes so steadily set upon her, it became
when once uttered a possibility to be considered.

" All the same, what right," she asked herself angrily,
" has he to look at me like that ? " And with cheeks
aflame, she continued to talk rapidly about the new house.

" It is in La France Quadrant," she exclaimed,—" just
opposite,—one of the main-door flats. I believe you could
see it from here." And rising abruptly she went to the window. She was glad to turn away her face.

Lawrence followed, and they both stood looking across the
bushy gully of the Kelvin.

" Yes. There ! Not far from the lower bridge,"—Joanna
showed him, pointing, as if her life depended on it, with the
tip of her fore-finger pressed against the pane,—" almost opposite the flint mill. Do you see the yellow blinds, three,
four,—*five* windows beyond the lane ? That's it ! "

Before she left she asked Lawrence if he would come to
Collessie Street on Sunday afternoon. Both her brothers
would be there, she said. Sholto was arriving from his farm
on Saturday, to stay at home till his ship sailed for Australia
a fortnight hence.

She invited him hoping that he might refuse ; but Lawrence, looking simply glad, accepted at once.

VI

That Friday a telegram was handed to Juley at breakfast.
Telegrams did not make her nervous, but always before

reading one she would close her eyes and utter within herself a brief prayer for strength, in case it should be God's will to try her.

She did so now, Linnet and Joanna waiting impatiently.

But immediately she had read, she took off her spectacles and her face was irradiated by a tender, beaming smile.

"Dear, warm-hearted Georgie!" she exclaimed, bright-eyed.

She read Georgie's message aloud.

"Must join you dear people and say goodbye darling Sholto arrive tomorrow morning love Georgie."

For a moment Joanna's heart sank. How was she to get on with her designs amid the upheaval of Georgie's visit and Sholto's prolonged leave-taking? There was always something at home to keep one from working. Yet she too was pleased at the thought of the family re-union. She would have been disappointed had a second telegram come from Georgie annulling the first.

That morning, instead of drawing, she busied herself in her bedroom making it attractive for her sister. She cleared some drawers and a space in the wardrobe, and spent more than an hour polishing the long neglected Venetian-glass toilet bottles with gilt filigree tops, which had been Maddalena's wedding present. And in the afternoon she flung herself with ardour into the making of several pairs of twilled silk pyjamas she had cut out many weeks ago as her share of Sholto's new outfit.

Feverish and half frenzied in her determination to finish them then and there, or at the least to have one pair ready and laid out on his bed against Sholto's arrival, she was still sitting over the sewing-machine at two in the morning.

"Joanna, dear, do go to bed now!" remonstrated her mother, coming to the parlour door for the third time since midnight. "I'm sure you are keeping the neighbours awake. That poor machine must need oiling, I think."

It was true: the old treadle machine which Juley as a bride had received from Aunt Georgina, and had felt as a reproach (for she was no seamstress), was making a clatter in the quiet, small hours, like the clatter of a stony field under the harrow.

But Joanna, though for some time past she had been finding the noise hardly endurable, spoke without stopping her work

or even looking round. She merely slackened a very little.
"Don't worry about me, Mother." she exclaimed frac-
tiously above the rattle of the old Singer. "If you'd only
get to bed yourself it would please Sholto and Georgie far
better than anything else you could do. You know it would.
But of course you'll go on sitting up and distressing us all.
It's different for me. I can sit up for once. I don't want
to be machining when they are here. I can finish the buttonholes and things while we are talking, but I must do the
stitching now. It won't take much longer."

The last few words were uttered almost in a shout, as the
girl set tearing off again like mad upon a long trouser seam ;
and the night was filled with the racket.

For a moment Juley stood irresolute in the doorway.
Then knowing by experience that Joanna's obstinacy matched
her own, she went back sadly and without another word to
her writing. She was still fully-dressed though heavy-eyed
and weary. For hours she had been struggling against
sleep at her desk, in the forlorn hope that, contrary to all
knowledge, she might thus get clear and have a mind at
leisure for her son on the morrow.

But within ten minutes she re-appeared in the parlour
with a happier face. She had brought some eatables upon
a little tray. These she set down on the edge of the machine
table, smiling ingratiatingly at Joanna. And Joanna looked
up and smiled too and stopped working. The night became at once blessedly quiet. There were two glasses of milk,
some gingerbread, a few raisins on a saucer, and a small tin
box containing a special kind of flaked chocolate which Juley
always kept in a corner of her desk.

Mother and daughter ate almost in silence, but happy
together now with a delicious, secret communion and acknowledgment.

Even so, Juley (in most things generous) could not help
being stingy towards Joanna over the raisins and the chocolate. They were always kept apart for herself alone and were
sacred to her desk and her midnight labours.

In the morning Georgie's train arrived so punctually and
she took such an unusually fast cab, that she was home almost
half an hour before they had counted on seeing her.

Joanna, in her chemise when she heard the sound of wheels,
and with her hair still in a dishevelled plait, flew downstairs

without sparing the time even to throw on a dressing-gown. On the landing, half-way, she ran into Linnet.

He had only that moment rolled out of bed, and was crumpled all over, hardly awake yet. His fair dank hair which no longer had any tendency to curl, lay in ruffled swathes about his head, and Joanna was shocked by the dullness of his eyes with their blinking, puffed lids. How little she had looked at Linnet lately! What was he doing with himself? Where did his life lie? He seemed to have so little part in the life at home. But at this moment Georgie's arrival took precedence of all these questions, and the brother and sister having exchanged a hurried, nervous glance, started a race down the remaining flight of stairs. Pell-mell and laughing they went, taking two steps at a time, and they arrived together panting just as Georgie threw down her luggage on the lobby floor.

After the first impulsive hugs, the three stood chatting, overwhelmed by a sudden shyness and uncertainty.

Joanna took an overcoat of Linnet's from the hat-stand and pulled it on over her chemise, snuggling into it with a shiver for the early morning air was fresh.

"No! Sholto hadn't come yet. . . . His train was due in about half an hour.—Wouldn't Georgie like a bath? . . . Had she slept at all on the journey?—Surely that was a new hat she was wearing?—But since when had she taken to veils?—Carl Nilsson said veils were so bad for the eyes, especially veils with spots like that.—But how well Georgie was looking, wasn't she?—No, no! Not fatter!—Thinner on the whole!" And Georgie declared that Joanna with her pig-tail and the loose, short-skirted, tweed coat, looked just as she used to look at school.

"But, Linnet, my dear boy, you look *awful!*" exclaimed Georgie turning to her brother and pushing the spotted veil farther off her eyes. "What's wrong with him, Joanna?" (Georgie had that wounding habit of involving a third person, a sort of dumb partner, in her adverse criticisms.)

"Haven't shaved, that's all," mumbled Linnet, putting his hand up to his face defensively. "Think I'll go and have a wash now." And he moved away from them and towards the stair-case.

"I hope you don't look like that every morning when you get up. Does he, Joey?" Georgie called out after him in high good-humour. But just as she was about to hurl another elder-sisterly gibe, advising Linnet to eschew all shades of mauve in his night attire, a wail of distress came from the landing above.

All three young people turned up their faces.

It was their mother. She leaned, in her thick, iron-grey dressing-gown, over the bannister opposite her bedroom door, and was covering the top of her head with both her hands. By her voice they knew she was almost weeping.

"That isn't Georgie!" she cried reproachfully. "No, Georgie, I won't have you coming up yet. You are too early! Your train isn't due yet by my watch, and I put it right last night. Now that you are here of course it can't be helped : but you must wait till poor Mother puts her fichu on. You children don't think!"

Having delivered herself Juley disappeared into her bedroom and shut the door behind her.

Georgie burst out laughing.

"There's no place like home!" she averred delightedly. "Everything is always the same. Why do I expect it to be different each time I come back? But what was that Mother said about a fichu, Joanna?"

The younger sister explained. Juley's hair had lately become very thin upon the top. It was difficult to dress, so she had taken to appearing at breakfast with a white net fichu draped over her head, and fastened with a brooch under her chin. Wearing this fichu (which not only concealed her defect in a becoming manner but postponed indefinitely the daily purgatory before the mirror) Juley had seen herself greeting Georgie in the lobby with outstretched arms, and she was utterly disappointed at the failure of her welcome.

"No, don't come in!" she called out, though she was half laughing at herself now, as Georgie opened the bedroom door. But it was no use, and the next moment her warm arms were round her child.

Breakfast was happy and noisy, and Joanna, taking part, but always a little outside, thought that surely there had never been such a pleasant family party. She longed only for Sholto to join them. How entirely different from any other family they were! Was there not an atmosphere, a charm, impossible to explain? She loved most of all her mother's puzzled face when any of them made a joke she could not follow.

The fichu was duly admired by Georgie.

"It makes you look foreign, Mother," she said, "like a picture I have seen somewhere." And she was right. The simple drapery, unspoiled by lace, accentuated the breadth of Juley's abruptly sloping forehead, and with her rather prominent, worn eyelids and her eyes of sad, but unquenchable enthusiasm, she might well have been one of Dürer's sacred women.

Then the dining-room door opened quietly and Sholto appeared. (Janet, the old cook, had run to let him in before he could ring the bell, and she stood behind him now, smiling proudly at them all.)

"Hul-lo, you people!" he exclaimed, in his jolly, rather slow, young man's voice; and Joanna felt warm and shy all over. It was only a few months since they had seen him last, but the sister easily forgot while he was away that her little brother was a grown man now.

As he stooped to kiss his mother she stroked his cheek with earnest tenderness.

"Well, son?" she said.

But the others were all over him, chattering like so many daws.

"Doesn't he look a farmer, just?"

"Look at the colour of his face!"

"Sholto, your neck is like a bull's!"

"Another white pudding for Master Sholto, please, Janet," ordered Juley, smiling, and trying to make herself heard above the din. "Bairns, bairns, Mother's ears are splitting!"

But they paid no heed to her, and as in the old days she mustered her flock and was heartily proud of them. There they were, her "hens of gold," and in spite of all Eva Gedge might say and might say truly, the sight of them pleased her.

So she sat looking from one to another, not following nor anxious to follow any of their talk.

Linnet, shaved and dressed, was a different being. His long, narrow face showed pale certainly beside his brother's, but he was the handsomer of the two; and those somewhat exhausted features of his, with the very broad shoulders, long limbs and slender body so like his father's, made a fine gentleman of him. Sholto, half a head shorter, was stocky with great thighs and calves. His features seemed still unfinished. But he had frank, slow-moving eyes and was loveable. He and Linnet chaffed each other with awkward, but observant affection.

As Joanna watched them, the thought of Lawrence Urquhart cropped up in her mind. Why had she asked him to call to-morrow ? She now had the idea that her brothers for some reason would look down on him. They would even reckon the advantage they had in being Academy boys while Lawrence had only attended the High School. Georgie too was always an unsparing critic of her sister's friends. She had once said that she could not—" was very sorry, but simply *could* not"—get over Phemie Pringle's commonness.

Yet there it was, Phemie was an artist and great of soul where Georgie was the vainest of amateurs. And Lawrence ? Comparing him in her secret mind with her brothers, Joanna felt him to be of finer grain, more compact and passionate, with more purpose hidden in him.

But when it came, as it happened, his visit counted to Joanna chiefly because of the piece of news of which he was the bearer.

Louis Pender, Lawrence was able to tell her, was coming back to Glasgow in a fortnight. He was coming on the very day Sholto's boat was to sail. The Committee, after sharp disagreement had accepted two of his designs, holding over the others provisionally.

It was indeed curious how intensely and secretly this knowledge infused itself amid the disturbing atmosphere of Sholto's farewell. It lurked for Joanna in every preparation for her brother's departure and her agitation sought relief in a feverish, practical energy.

For this at the moment there was plenty of scope. There were, for one thing, the nerve-racking shopping expeditions with Sholto and Juley, both impossible shoppers. Sholto so hated any shop he entered that he always endeavoured to escape without buying what he had come for. It could be got to-morrow, he would say ; or probably even better in Australia when he arrived. But Juley, proceeding with a slowness of mind and body that was an affliction to her children, regarded each separate purchase as a campaign in itself. She looked for advice of every shopman, explaining all the circumstances to him, with much reminiscence where she was an old customer : and in every department she found that her son needed far more than she had at first thought necessary. She strongly condemned what she called " scamping ways of doing things," and in most of the shops she considered it would be as well to replenish Linnet's wardrobe at the same time. It was a real pleasure to a salesman if he could confront Juley with an improvement or a new invention. She could be carried away by an ingenious patent stud.

Georgie, on the other hand, whatever the purchase, had always seen something very much better and more convenient, not to say cheaper, in London, and she did not fail to make these reproachful facts known to the Glasgow shopkeepers. This enraged Sholto, and he depended on Joanna to make things easier for him. After that first happy breakfast hour, he and Georgie had argued fiercely about everything (particularly about politics and religion), and one day upon Joanna's suddenly taking Sholto's side in the discussion Georgie had burst into tears. It was in the middle of dinner, and Georgie had rushed from the room calling out that nobody loved her now at home, and that she would be glad to get back to London again. At this Sholto had sworn, Linnet had bolted his pudding and gone off to one of his eternal appointments, and Juley had sent Joanna to comfort her sister and bring her back to table. Soon all their nerves were on edge.

Amid all this Joanna found it so hard to go on with her designs that she almost gave up the idea of sending them in. But the thought of Pender acted here as a spur. She believed that to be worthy of meeting him again she must live up to the loftiest standards of duty, and this drove her to the desperate measure of early rising. Sometimes too she was able for an hour at a time to take refuge in Nilsson's studio ; and her lofty standard, it must be confessed, did not prevent her acceptance of all the help he offered. In one case, without the least pang of conscience, she allowed him to alter a drawing substantially, and in the end her work was handed in well up to time, just two days before Sholto's sailing.

On that Saturday they were a wretched little party down at the docks, waiting about four hours with Sholto already on the deck of the liner which seemed rooted to the wharf. It appeared fantastic to believe that Sholto was really going to that place called Australia. Who had been the first to suggest such a preposterous thing ? But he was on board. It was done. Lots of other people went, and their friends and mothers were seeing them off calmly enough. They must just pretend to be like the others. It was an alleviation that Georgie was not there. (After all she had returned to London four days earlier.)

They all longed for the liner to move, but nothing happened, and nobody could give them any definite information, except that passengers must remain on the ship and friends on the wharf.

Presently Linnet remembered quite suddenly that though it was Saturday he had to call for something at the office, and with a foolish wave of his hat towards the liner he went away. But Juley and Joanna stayed on and on, hanging about. Sometimes they walked up and down, sometimes they rested on barrels or on coils of rope till they were chilled again by the March evening. It was horribly sad, and quite useless to wait. But to have left now would have been like shirking one's watch beside a dead body. It began to grow dark. Lights were hoisted on the masts of the ships, and here and there on the wharf.

At last a man carrying a lantern came up to them and told that the start had been postponed till next morning early. But all passengers, he said, must stay on the ship. He promised to deliver the farewell notes they now wrote to Sholto. When that was done they left the wharf. They were dropping with fatigue.

Entering the first eating-house they could find in the dingy street which led from the docks, they were brought a great black pot of tea, piles of ready-buttered bread, and a dish of thick, briny bacon with eggs. Though the fare was rough it was cleanly served, and Juley ate and drank greedily. As she grew older and more prone to exhaustion, food seemed to act more and more quickly upon her as a stimulant. Often now she would climb the steps at home, so weary from shopping and the steep hill that she had to sink down on one of the lobby chairs with all her parcels still in her arms. But if there was food ready for her she would devour it and feel immediately revived. At the same time, she always ate under protest. She was growing stouter, becoming heavy about the hips, like her elder sister Perdy, but she had not Perdy's agility. She deplored her heaviness and tried to deny herself starchy food. But if there was one thing Juley loved, it was a potato. Early in the meal she would utterly refuse to partake of that vegetable. Then she would declare for "just half a one, for a treat, and not to waste the gravy": and after that, when she thought no one was looking, she would help herself to a small quantity time after time. To make up for this "sinful self-indulgence" she would dose herself between whiles with patent medicines. She had a dread of internal trouble, especially of such kind as would involve any operation, but it was illness, not death that she feared. She was quite ready, she said, when this heavy, fleshly tabernacle should be worn out, to go. She did not wish to grow old and a burden. In speaking of Heaven she had still the face of a young girl.

But while Juley restored herself there behind the wharf, recovering energy with each mouthful in the sordid little shop, Joanna could hardly touch anything. With mechanical persistence she kept trying to imagine the moving away of Sholto's ship at dawn, and could not. She could only see it rooted there by the wharf for ever and ever. It was like a nightmare. She could not believe in Australia nor in the ship's power to sail there, nor in Sholto's continued existence. Really she was delirious with exhaustion.

But she was not unhappy. Beneath the senseless whirring of her fatigue there was the knowledge of Pender's coming. It had been there hidden all day, unexamined, yet making life endurable. And now it rose and rose, till all her consciousness was suffused with it. Again and again she looked at the watch on her wrist, the little gold watch with its Milanese plaited strap which Mario had given her. "By now," she thought, "his train has passed Carlisle." "Perhaps he is drinking tea in the restaurant car." (As she pictured him she could see exactly, though she had never in his presence consciously noticed it, the peculiar way in which his square fingers grasped the handle of a cup, and the strong curve of his wrist as the sleeve slipped back a little.) "By now he must be very near Glasgow." "He must be gathering up his things." "Now, if he has come at all, he has certainly arrived." "Even if the train is later than it ever is, he must be here." "Will Mildred meet him, as he is going at first to stay with her?" "Or will he leave the station alone in a cab ? " " How long will he stay at Panmure Crescent before going to the studio-cottage Mildred is so proud of having found for him at Carmunnock ? "

But what did any of these things matter ? Nothing ! It only mattered that after so many weeks he was already here. That at this very moment he was in Glasgow. That he was breathing the same air that she breathed. That some day soon she would see his square-fingered hands, and feel his strange, prominent eyes upon her.

CHAPTER IV

I

EXACTLY four weeks later, at much the same hour of the day (although, the Spring being further advanced, the sky had not yet begun to make its preparations for sunset), anyone walking across the summit of Garnethill would have noticed a man who waited at the street's highest point. Further, anyone of the smallest experience would have known that this man waited there for a woman. In his thick, buttoned-up, dark grey overcoat, he stood in the middle of the roadway, disdaining criticism and both pavements, and now and then with a movement half nervous and half defiant he adjusted his soft, light grey hat to an even jauntier angle. He wore gloves and carried a stick. His very outline against the sky was suggestive of gallantry.

Since his return to Glasgow Louis Pender and Joanna had met frequently. They had met at Panmure Crescent; she had come with Mildred to see the Carmunnock studio where he was now living; the Plummers had brought her to the City Chambers to look at the scaffolding and other preparations for his work there. But each of these meetings had been in the company of others. Not since the night of the dance had the two spoken alone together for more than a few scanty seconds; and not till the day before this May afternoon had Louis found an opportunity to suggest the kind of meeting for which he was now waiting. It had been in obedience to circumstance the merest tentative suggestion of an appointment on his part, and without ratification on hers, so as he stood there on the hill he was agitated by a pleasant, boyish nervousness. Experience, however, bade him hope, as also did his shrewd reading of Joanna's character. He had lost no time in learning her story from Mildred, and judged rightly that she had reckless blood.

But would she come? It was not in Pender's nature to be

fatuous in these matters, and he held, in spite of a fair share of conquests, a really low estimate of his own attractiveness. When six o'clock struck, and there was no sign of the young woman for whose appearance he owned to a surprising hunger, he mildly cursed himself for a middle-aged fool. Another quarter of an hour he would wait, he decided, and no longer. And with a superstitious notion that his too eager looking might foil its own end, he turned his back on the direction from which the nymph might most reasonably be expected to come.

At least, thought he then—being forty-seven and having survived many excitements and disappointments—he might enjoy the extraordinary, mounting beauty of the evening about him. Perhaps after all it was only in cities of the North that one got such a voluptuous contrast and harmony as now presented itself to his gaze ? Above the stony, clear austerity of the town curved the sky. It curved, holding its fill of light, ebullient, like a bubble of serenest blue ; and forming that bubble's tumultuous outer rim were the piled-up, yellow, flamboyant clouds whose huge tops seemed on a level with Pender's admiring eyes.

A month ago he would not have believed it possible to find himself so charmed in this dismal hole of a place called Glasgow. But neither would he a month ago have credited himself with any interest in a woman so strong as he now felt. It had surprised him during his stay in London that Joanna's image had persisted. Perhaps it had still more surprised him on his return to find no waning in her appeal. It was odd, he mused, that he should run across this girl just when he fancied himself done with amorous interludes. Odd, too, that she should be so different in type from the women he had gone after hitherto. He had always admired short-featured women with square jaws, and strongly marked cheek-bones, women who carried their own shadows about with them. And here was one who was at the mercy of every variation of light. He was not even sure that he admired her. She certainly troubled him.

But anyhow, confound her, she wasn't coming ! It was a quarter-past six. He was tired of studying the buoyant outlines of those yellow clouds. He would wait only five minutes more. A woman came punctually to a first appointment or not at all.

And while Louis waited there, a stone's throw from the Bannermans' house, Joanna had been looking despairingly for him at the far end of the hill, low down and out of sight, some hundred yards away.

It was her nature to think that *she* must always be the one who had the more trouble to take, the longer way to travel : so she had stayed there a full ten minutes before it struck her that he might possibly have meant the corner nearest her home. "The corner of Dunbar Street," he had said ambiguously.

Now she became certain that he had been at the other corner all the while and that she would find him gone.

She ran all the way up the long hill. She had no hope.

But there he was ! There on the topmost point of the grey stone ridge. He was standing with his back to her, still as a stone man against the sky. Only the ends of his loose tweed coat flapped a little in the air.

The instant she saw him Joanna stopped running. She must recover her breath. So she went on at a walking pace, and it was an astonishment to her that she was still able to advance, to place one foot regularly before another on the granite setts of the hill. For the sight of him there, waiting with such patience for her so long after the time appointed, had a violent effect upon her knees.

Then before she had walked a dozen more steps towards him Louis turned his head and saw her, and the next moment they had met. They looked into each other's eyes with a first swift searching, as their hands clasped firmly.

"You have come," said he. "I had almost given you up."

While she explained her mistake and he blamed himself, neither listening to the other's words, they turned towards the now setting sun and with the strong glow of it full in their faces began to walk downhill.

Until the first breathlessness of their meeting had subsided they could only make superficial conversation. Louis pointed out to his companion that with the sun so low now in the sky, all the colour in the world lay behind them to the East, and he had to make her turn round several times before he could convince her. But really, while they argued with vehement lightness, each was groping under every tone and move-

ment and all the flurry of sensual excitement for the truth of
the other.

The region through which they were now walking was for
Joanna full of childish memories, which in a curious way added
to her excitement. They had passed the dark Synagogue
with its dome, the Salvation Army Shelter, which had once
been a little farm-house and still stood in its blackened garden,
and the smart new Cancer Hospital built of garish, red stone.
And on the other side ran fine, dismal, old family dwellings with
porticoes and high, square-paned windows which now sheltered
obscure mantle-makers, cheap teachers of elocution, and theatrical landladies. It was one of these houses which had been
old Horatio Bannerman's manse in the early days.

But Louis looked about him with a little shudder of distaste.

" How very depressing all this is ! " he said.

When Joanna could not help championing it, he looked at
her with a warm amused smile, which faded however when
she asked him rather timidly about his own childhood.

" I can't remember," he replied emptily. " It's queer
how little I can remember. I don't think it particularly
interested me being a child."

That Joanna could not understand.

" I remember everything—*everything !* " she told him,
wondering.

" Well, for one thing you aren't so far from your childhood as I am," Louis replied, speaking in a certain light tone
which gave his companion a peculiar sense of unhappiness.
" That makes a difference, you know. Wait till you are my
age."

" No, no ! I'll remember till I'm dead." It was almost as
if she warded off a blow.

" Not the disagreeable things, surely ? Or were you always
happy as a child ? " he asked, looking at her. He was not
interested in their talk, nor in what she was about to say :
but he liked to see her face thus serious. She looked now, he
thought, like an early Gothic Madonna, rather faultily carved
perhaps, but with inspiration.

" No, I wasn't." Joanna looked at him in return. " But
I like to remember, even the unhappy things. They seem
part of it all, part of me. I couldn't bear to forget. It
would be like losing bits of myself."

"Oh, come! That's morbid, I consider. I prefer to be like the sundial and 'reckon none but sunny hours,' or whatever the exact words may be. Anything unhappy or dull or painful I make haste to forget. I assure you it is an excellent habit."

Joanna shook her head. All that he had said was hurtful, full of death to her, but it was impossible for her to explain either to him or to herself why it was so.

"I'm not like that," was all she could say. She spoke, however, with a stoutness that was pleasing to him. He was curiously moved by this woman's egoism, grateful for her absurd seriousness.

"Then we are different, you and I," he said gently, and he smiled full at her, charming her suddenly, winning her with what she felt to be a rare tenderness.

"But," he went on, in a different voice and with a light in his eyes that was purely predatory, "I'll tell you something I shall never forget to my dying day. And that is the first moment I set eyes on you that evening at the Lovatts."

Joanna, in bliss, remained silent.

"Neither shall I forget," Louis resumed, "seeing you dance the reel up at the School. These, you see, are the kind of things I remember and want to remember. Do you know what I was doing up on the hill there while I was waiting for you?"

"No."

"Try to guess."

"Perhaps remembering other times you had waited for a woman?" she said.

Louis laughed with enjoyment.

"No, Mrs. Clever, and I wasn't. I was trying to draw the lines of your face from memory against the sky as if it were a canvas."

Again Joanna had nothing to say.

"If you don't like me to tell you such things, Signora Rasponi," he continued, "mind you tell me to stop."

He had got her to look at him again, and again she spoke with that stoutness of hers that so pleased and tickled him.

"I like it," she said.

Louis was really amused by her, refreshed, and at the same time he could not quite make her out.

When they had got to the bottom of the steep hill and were walking on the level, still westwards, he began to talk to her about his work.

" I ought to be ashamed of myself,"—he spoke with impatience, almost disgust—" at being so pleased over this twopenny-halfpenny commission. Why, by this time of day, people ought to be begging and praying me all over the place to paint their walls. But they don't, you know ! And here am I, as bucked as if I were a pavement artist at being rather reluctantly asked to add my daub to the other daubs in that ghastly, chocolate-coloured building you Glasgow people are so proud of. You'll admit, I hope, that it is a beastly pile ? "

" It is ugly, I suppose," Joanna conceded. Yet she remembered the rich and splendid vision it had been to her as a child when her father had taken them all to receptions up its alabaster staircase.

" I've no doubt, however," added her companion, " that it will be uglier still when I have contributed my own particular piece of ugliness to it."

His self-aspersion was wounding as an insult. Why did he give her ground to stand upon and then take it back from under her feet ? Had he himself no foothold ? He seemed continually to lead her along a sure path, only to leave her with a flippant gesture at the edge of a precipice.

" I am no longer pleased with my drawing for the panel," he went on restlessly. " The lunette is well enough. But the panel, I now see, is rubbish or nearly so. I am altering it. The Committee will have to like the change or lump it."

" I thought it so lovely," said Joanna.

"Very nice of you : but unhappily your kind thoughts, my child, don't affect the design," said Louis. " No. The thing isn't good and it has got to be altered or not done at all. But for God's sake let us talk of something else. Tell me—" he asked, pointing to a new, still unoccupied block of flats they were now passing—" why do you build so much up here with that red stone ? I don't like it, do you ? It always stays so raw looking—on a wet day almost bleeding. But let's have a look at the inside of this, shall we ? See, the doors are not on yet. Come. Do let us ! "

Eager as a child, Louis led the way across a bridge of planks left by the workmen at the entrance. The building was finished all but the fittings, and now awaited the glaziers and paper-hangers.

Joanna followed him up the stairs which were littered with shavings and rubble. His swift transitions of mood affected her painfully, but she became calmer as they mounted from floor to floor and examined the rooms of the various dwellings-to-be.

"I think we'll make this the drawing-room. Or do you think the nursery, my dear ? " Louis asked her, play-acting.

Joanna, being no actress, could not respond in the same vein, but she stood laughing at him, happy again, and watching him, with a curious, maternal tenderness as she listened to his easy flow of nonsense,

Suddenly he broke off and came nearer to her.

"By God, I wish it were all true," he said very seriously. "You look so lovely in this light standing there smiling at me with your eyes shining. I wish I could live with you. Would you like to live with me ? Say you would, just to please me."

Joanna remained quite still.

"You must not say such things to me."

"Why not ? "

"For one thing, there's your wife."

"There's my wife, yes. Shall I tell you about her ? "

Joanna's eyes widened as he stared into them defiantly. And her heart leapt. She had felt from the first that Pender's wife did not essentially matter. Now she was sure of it.

"If you like," she said, and waited.

"Well, I think you may understand. Anyhow this is how things are," he said. "I married when I was twenty-three. Alice was a little older, not much. The boys were born the first year. They are twins you know and their mother pretty nearly died with them. When she got better she couldn't bear me to come near her. That kind of physical terror is common enough, as perhaps you know, but at the time it was a fearful blow to me. We went on of course, thinking it would pass, even in time thinking it had passed. But it hadn't, and somehow the bottom was knocked out of things. I can't quite explain, but it was. Perhaps we were wrong from the start. To do my wife justice she recognized it as well as I did, and set to work to make the best of it in her own way just as I did in mine. Only our ways were different. You can guess perhaps what happened. Even under good conditions I won't say I should have made a faithful husband. As it was you'll admit I had at least an excuse. You'll say I should have left her. At one time I was very near to it. But I didn't, and I can't honestly say I've regretted it. You must remember she wanted me—*needed* me, she said—in the other ways. Then there were always the boys. Somehow I shouldn't like to go back on them ; or shall we say I haven't yet found anything that seemed to make it worth while doing so ? So you see ! ''

During this recital Joanna had withdrawn her eyes from his, but she could feel his bold, nervous stare while she looked past him and out at the street through the unglazed windows. The lamps were being lighted one by one in the dusk. She did not to the full realize the disbelief in himself which was the essential thread running through this man's confession : she merely felt sad for him and for herself.

" Do you blame me ? " he asked, longing for her reproach.

"Yes. I mean, no. How can I blame you ? " Neither at this moment had Joanna any belief. She and he were under the same spell of helplessness, as if drugged.

" Well then ? "

" Doesn't your wife mind ? " she asked, knowing it an idle question.

" She can't have it both ways, can she ? Come. After all. And I've got to be considered too."

" Was it Mrs. Tullis you nearly went away with ? "

" Yes. It was."

" I'm glad you didn't."

" So am I. By Heaven I'm glad."

It was almost dark as Louis and Joanna walked in silence up the long semi-circular slope to the Park. By unspoken consent they had taken the longer way to avoid passing Panmure Crescent. And soon they were crossing a wide deserted circus of houses, making for the highest gates of all.

" Walk a little in front of me," said Louis, falling behind.

" How I like to watch you move," he told her from there, as he followed her slowly through the gates. " I walk behind and worship. I should love above all things to see you walking so, but quite naked in the summer dusk. Just so, between these iron gates."

He spoke with such simplicity that Joanna could only rejoice in his frank worship. He gave glamour into her keeping. Gladly would she have walked naked for his delight in the soft darkness.

Presently, when they reached the great treble flight of grey granite steps leading down into the Park, Joanna sat on the stone balustrade and Louis stood beside her with one foot on the low escarpment. He took off his hat welcoming the little breeze that stirred up to them from the river. There was no moon, and beyond the lighted lamps on the terrace the sky showed richly blue. In front the faint regular lines of the wide stairway descended into a blue haze : behind was the sweeping curve of pavement and railing flanked by tall houses with fretted roofs.

Suddenly Louis bent closer to Joanna, kissing her without a word on the point of her shoulder, and to her dismay she broke down utterly.

In consternation then he sat by her side to comfort her.

"I'm sorry. Oh, I'm sorry, my child, if I've offended or hurt you. Truly I am. But what was I to do ? You mustn't cry so. No, no, really you mustn't. What have I done ? Now do stop. Upon my soul if you don't cheer up I shall be crying myself directly. You know, you take things altogether too seriously. Don't let us be too serious. Tell me now, am I to apologize or what ? I'll do anything you say. Is this your way of showing virtuous indignation ? Come—tell me ! "

"You know it isn't," said Joanna wiping her eyes but unable to help smiling at him as he bent forward.

"What then ? "

"I don't know. I suppose I love you."

Louis quite taken aback did not speak at once. Then gazing up at her sideways he gave her one of his wonderful affectionate looks.

"I'm afraid, Joanna, that you are a fearful goose," he said, using her Christian name for the first time.

"I'm afraid I am, Louis."

As they looked into each other's eyes she wished he would take her.

"Never mind ; this light is very becoming to you, my dear," said Louis, holding back, he did not know why. "In fact you look perfectly lovely to me at this moment. And see these steps, and that stony terrace curving away back so finely. You might go anywhere, I tell you—Italy, Greece, anywhere you like : I don't care—you could find nothing more beautiful. And at this moment you seem to me the most beautiful woman in the world. So why be sad ? Do let us, ah ! do let us be happy. I so want to be light-hearted."

But he did not kiss her again that night, not even at parting.

II

From that day, however, they met constantly, nor did they ever part without arranging a further meeting. Both were quite careless of outside comment. They were absorbed in the unending debate and conflict between them. Soon they became lovers in all but the final abandonment, and this was never out of their thoughts.

Joanna was not happy : neither was she unhappy. She was again undergoing a change—a divestment of which the meaning could not become clear for her until the process was completed. Swaddled from before birth in religious emotionalism, in romance and spiritual exaltation, it was natural that she should cling to these suffocating wrappings. Should cling, that is, with the conscious mental part of her, so that as far as she was conscious she was false. It had to be so. She had virtue on the other hand in the unconscious but actual acceptance of the changes that were her fate. And the proof that her virtue was stronger than her falseness lay in the fact that no man she attracted could act falsely toward her. Punish them she might, but she drew the truth from them.

Thus, though it seemed monstrous to her at times that all the weight of the decision should lie as it did upon her, that Louis should only talk and wait and walk unburdened, still she knew it must be so. Just because it was she that chose to regard their love as something final, she must be the one to decide.

Meanwhile Louis took what he could of her, fitfully. He continued to woo her with the touches and kisses without which she would now have found existence barren. But there were days when he made as if he would put her away from him with words of warning and farewell. Again he would declare himself as fundamentally lightminded, telling her with radiant amusement of his earlier affairs, urging her to throw aside the foolish gravity of her nature and upbringing, and with him to regard love as the most charming and recreative of pastimes.

Not for any length of time could Joanna retain this view. But it had a strong appeal for her, the more that it discovered clearly in her the longing to compete on their own ground with the unknown, fascinating women of whom Louis told her. Once she had held all such women to be inconsiderable. But she had seen them afresh through her lover's eyes. She must match her powers against theirs, must commit herself to the test instead of scorning it, to prove her greater worth if it existed. She still believed she could outdo them in weaving a spell for Louis, and passionately she coveted his acknowledgment of this. In every mood, serious or light, she felt sure that she could keep his respect. Unhappiness she expected, but never the unhappiness of his scorn. And like her Aunt Perdy she could summon an elation for pure disaster.

So everything pushed her towards Louis, everything, that is, within herself. But in him there was that which long kept her from yielding. It was something immoveable in him, against which she hurled herself without understanding. Always she waited for some change in him that never came. But he remained staunch to himself and so in the long run to her.

"Surely there are two things," she said to him one day, "there's love, and there's the other thing ? "

Louis turned his head to look at her, and smiled as if valuing her earnestness even while he laughed at it. It was a Sunday, and she had brought luncheon in a basket to the deserted City Chambers where the canvas, begun in Pender's studio, had been temporarily put in its destined place. He insisted upon continuing the painting there, after the manner of the Italian fresco painters. "It is to hang here," he declared, "not on the line at the Royal Academy or in Mrs. Lovatt's drawing-room ; and it is here that it must look well, if it looks well anywhere." So after a gay picnic in his little workroom hidden away on the top floor, they had climbed out upon the sunshiny leads to talk.

"To my mind," he replied, " there is no essential difference between the two. Or perhaps it is simply that I'm only capable of what you so tactfully call ' the other thing.' Anyhow I won't deceive you about myself. I want you frightfully, as I think you must know by this time. And I want you in

a way that it seems to me just now—mind, that's all I say—
in a way that it certainly seems to me just now I have never
wanted any woman before. The queer thing is I feel quite
unworthy of you, my dear, pretty child (actually, you look
pretty this afternoon, neither beautiful nor plain, but pretty!)
It seems far, far too good to be true that you should for a
single moment want me as I now want you. Yet for all that
I don't suppose I'm offering you what you with your notions
would call love. Mind, I believe if I were free, in spite of all
experience and caution, I would be asking you to marry me.
I know, you see—that's the worst of it—that you are too good
for anything else. You know that too, Joanna. You know
I respect you like anything, and always shall. Yet upon my
soul I'm not prepared, as things are at present, to bolt with
you to America or wherever it is people go who give up all
for love, as they say. Not that you would fly with me, I
daresay, if I asked you. Don't think I'm taking things fatu-
ously for granted. I'm not. But there, you know what I
mean, my dear heart."

"You mean you are too worldly-minded," said Joanna with
pain and contempt in her voice.

"Perhaps. Call it what you like. It may be that I am
not a good enough artist, or it may be that my nature is
peculiar. Anyhow, to do my work I need a certain kind of
stimulus, which I can only get in conventional society. Heaven
knows I've no illusions about it. And as often as not it
bores me to the point of nausea. But I always come back to
the knowledge that I need it."

In the silence that followed this speech a distant church
bell began to toll and a clock nearer at hand gave out the
hour.

"Mercy! It will be dark in no time!" cried Louis starting up. "I must get back to work. Will you come up on
the scaffolding with me? I want you to see the lunette
from there too."

"You know," he said boyishly on the way downstairs,
"I always want to hear what you think. That's the strange
truth, Joanna dear. There are times I feel I could work the
ends off my fingers for you."

As she climbed after him up the ladder, and stood by him
on the narrow, frail platform listening to his vehement exposition, Joanna tasted happiness. If only for the moment, he

was pleased with his work, and this endeared him to her without wounding her. As he set to painting he whistled gaily under his breath. And in two minutes he had completely forgotten her. But never had she felt closer to him than then. She could have stayed for ever, it seemed to her, unnoticed and joyful by his side. Indeed it was some time before turning quickly for a brush he saw her happy face. Hardly pausing, he realized her then and smiled and kissed her. He was speedy and warm : Joanna adored him.

" Get some tea, and call me in half an hour, " he bade her, " the light won't last longer."

She was swift to obey him ; and as she brewed tea for them both upstairs in the little studio all pleasantly littered with traces of him, her bliss was so acute that she felt her elements must dissolve and fly apart. So long as Louis believed in himself she was content. Even to be the toy and the refreshment of one who knew himself a creator of beauty was enough.

But one day, later on, when she tried to tell something of this to him, Louis protested.

" Don't be a fool ! " he exclaimed. " You are talking bosh. You know it's bosh ! "

There was nothing unpleasing to Joanna in his roughness, especially as she could detect the pleasure concealed beneath it, and she remained unmoved. She was sitting to him that morning in his Carmunnock cottage for the third time, but he was dissatisfied so far with all his sketches of her.

" It is the truth, Louis," she retorted gravely.

" Now, look here, my child," he said in his gravest tone and laying his pencil aside. " You are working yourself up about me, and you mustn't do it. I don't mean that you don't believe every word you say at the moment. I believe I understand you through and through. In some ways, allowing for different circumstances, we are not so very unlike, you and I. We are the kind of people for whom there does not seem much provision made in a modern world. In Greece I suppose we should have had our festivals and run about the hills in a leopard skin apiece, which would have been enormously becoming to you I've no doubt, though I shudder to think of my own figure in the costume. If you could only see your eyes, Joanna, when I am kissing you ! With you love is simple intoxication ; but an intoxication absolutely necessary to your well-being. And why not ? One of the things I like in you is that you are frank about it at heart. But don't take yourself too seriously. Listen to the wisdom of middle age and you will spare yourself much pain. What will happen is that one of these days you will find yourself wondering what you can have been thinking about. Look at me! I ask you to look at me, Joanna! What is there in me for a woman like you to care about? No, I assure you that much of your feeling for me is quite transitory. More's the pity for me! But you will not be able to say I haven't warned you. No reproaches, my dear, I beg of you, when the time comes!"

"You mean you are afraid you will get tired of me?" asked Joanna painfully. And as Louis made no answer, only smiling at her strangely, she went on. "You have got tired of so many women."

"O! Come!" he exclaimed grimacing a little. "I'm not the rake you make out. One thing is certain: I have not tired of so many as have tired of me. But seriously—now I am talking quite seriously—there have not been more than five or six women whom you could say had counted at all in my whole life. Don't you call that a very modest record? Remember I shall soon be fifty. I consider my allowance has been small, very small indeed. Five into fifty," he wound up frivolously, "why, it only comes out at one every ten years!"

"Tell me, Louis," persisted Joanna. "Do you think you would get tired of me?"

"How can I tell? Perhaps. Yes, perhaps. Who knows? If I were twenty I should say certainly not—swear it by all my gods. But I am forty-seven. What am I to say but the truth—*perhaps?* It is possible. I can't answer for myself, that's all. My dear, I want to be straight with you from the start. I feel that is your due."

There was a silence. Joanna felt hopeless, exasperated, puzzled. It was not so he had spoken the day before, when he had courted her with boyish ardour. And though she knew him equally sincere in both moods, it was the mood of disbelief that most deeply impressed her. There was something light and hard to-day under his mocking tenderness, like the claws concealed within the pads of the cat.

But an idea came that expanded her shrinking heart with a brave rush of joy. And the words proceeded out of her mouth, live things, independent of her volition.

"I'll tell you what, Louis. You will never get tired of me. One of these days you will fall in love with me, and you'll never be able to stop."

The bold statement sent a delirious shiver of terror through her, but she sat looking calmly at Louis without a smile. A shade of fear flashed through the inquisitive, fascinated eyes he turned on her, meeting her glance full.

"But I'm in love with you as it is," he muttered. (It was true that he had never been more subjugated than at that moment, had never felt so strongly the curious moral spell she had for him).

But she shook her head, smiling now as he became grave. Now she was no longer the wounded mouse in the cat's keeping. She had towered in one moment above her persecutor, demanding and obtaining worship.

"I say you will," she repeated. "I am not afraid!"

"That settles it then," said Louis. And after a moment, he added—"I must say you seem to know all about it!"

Instead of answering, Joanna rose and moved towards the window near which he was sitting. Louis followed her with his eyes. There were certainly times when she was full of magic for him and this was one of them.

"I wonder if it will rain before I get home?" she was saying, as she looked out at the gathering blackness of cloud against which the trees, now almost in full leaf were intense, mounting flames of green.

"That's right!" Louis retorted with forced lightness. "Let's talk about the weather. I'll forget that I'm madly in love with you. It's an excellent idea. Or politics? Politics is always safe. What do you think? Will there be a general election soon? But tell me first: have you fallen in love with anyone since we said good-bye last night? You seem to me, one way and another, to meet a fair number of young men. There's that young fellow with the dark, devoted eyes—Urquhart. He would make you a good husband now. Why don't you take him? I'm sure you have only to mention it to him."

At the unlooked-for mention of Urquhart's name, Joanna turned her head in curiosity. Why should Louis, like Mildred Lovatt, insist that Lawrence was in love with her? And her brothers too! After Lawrence's unremarkable call at Collessie Street two months before, since when she had not met him, they had teased her about him. But she herself was by no means certain. He was too persistently friendly. And lately, during his absence on the continent with Nilsson, her unsought friendship with him had taken on a new and more permanent aspect. Out of the joy of his heart Lawrence had written to her from Holland, from Switzerland, from Italy. And she had found herself rather to her own surprise responding with unaffected warmth and freedom. How well she could sympathize with the raptures of that first escape from the walls and the sounds and sights of home!

"Do you think," Joanna asked Louis, still looking questioningly, at him—"Do you think that was he by the steps the other night?"

"I neither know, my dear child, nor do I care," replied Louis. "But as this is the third time you have asked me that same question, I take it that *you* do care."

No. Joanna protested that she didn't care either. It was only that she was curious to know.

What had happened was this. While Joanna had stood waiting in the late afternoon near the granite steps of the park where Louis was to join her, she had noticed at some distance a figure very like Lawrence Urquhart's also apparently waiting, and she had felt that her doings were watched. Then Louis had come and the figure had disappeared. Could it have been Lawrence? He was certainly due to be back in Glasgow, but she had not heard of his return.

"I'll tell you what it is," continued Louis. "You are a bad, dangerous woman, a devourer of men, Joanna. That's what you are. With all your talk about love and 'the other thing' forsooth! And your delicate madonnaish airs! You simply want us all to be mad for you. That's the long and the short of it. Now isn't it?"

But he had quite forgotten Lawrence now; and as his tongue tripped on between his smiling lips, irresponsibly, Louis, with all his mind and body was really only waiting for the moment when Joanna would have to pass him again on her way from the window. When that moment came he clasped her waist, and Joanna responded, throwing her arms gladly round his neck.

"We are just a pair of innocent babes, you and I," he declared, "infants—that's what we are. You can take it from me. But the whole wretched world is a conspiracy to call us guilty. That's all that's wrong."

"I should like to defy the world. I feel able," said Joanna, with elation.

"As you please, my noble goose! But I cannot join you. I know the old monster too well. It's no use. We should only get smashed. No. There's only one way permitted to us, and you know it. And speaking for myself, I think it absurd that we should not take it. Shall we not take it? Ah! Do be weak, and let's take it!"

"But I want to be strong. I don't mind paying," said Joanna.

"No. Be weak! Please be weak," he urged.

She made no further protest, but lost herself in his embrace which was more passionate than ever before.

III

Next morning on first waking she felt such misery that for some moments she mistook it for physical illness. But with gathering consciousness she knew her body quite free from pain. Her trouble then was not physical. What was it? With a sudden access of suffering that made her flesh shrink, she remembered yesterday's parting embrace. It overwhelmed her that she could so yield to a man not yet in fact her lover. What was to become of her?

Yet last night there had been no sense of wrong-doing. It was as if certain moral standards she had thought long since discarded, had re-asserted themselves treacherously while she slept.

For a long half-hour, Joanna lay trying with tense nerves to see wherein she was a sinner. In such an attempt it was inevitable that the religious teaching of her childhood should have a part. Indeed the very attempt showed how far she still was under the spell of that teaching. For her there was no escape save by following it out remorselessly in action. In Juley's evangel common morality must ever give place to the larger spiritual issue and so in the end to a dominant egoism. As " between their own souls and God " she had always declared her children's errors. Therefore, while Joanna, like King David, was prepared to cry " Against Thee, Thee only, have I sinned!" her conscience on Mrs. Pender's account troubled her as little as did the laws of Moses. Such

were mere worldly concerns to be paid for, if put on one side,
by mere worldly suffering. Sin, if sin there were, lay elsewhere.

Yet searching now by this misleading, but not ignoble
light, the only sin Joanna could discover lay in her lover's
insufficiency. If only Louis could have committed himself
with her to the risks and sacrifices involved, she would have
been untroubled. But he lacked either the certainty or the
courage of his love, and this infirmity of spirit in him imposed
sin upon her also. No man sinneth to himself! Herein
then lay the wrong for them both.

She was ready to acknowledge this and to accept her share
of it. But having done so, her mind was immediately filled
with schemes for its removal. Where was the use of perceiving a sin unless it could be obviated ? Louis must come
by the assurance he lacked. Only so could her conscience and
his be appeased. Then it mattered not what the world did
to them.

But here again Joanna was driven back time after time
upon her original, deep-set belief, her instinct (so perfectly
in harmony with her physical passion) that Louis could be
wholly won only by the giving of herself in faith. There could
be no pledge, no assurance from him beforehand. And this
was the reason why the choice remained with her.

But if that was so, sin could be exorcised only by sinning,
not by renunciation. Was this the truth ?

Unable to think further, Joanna rose at length and dressed.
It was Saturday, and there was nothing to do. Often on a
Saturday she went walking in the country with Louis. But
this week there were friends with him from London and she
would not see him until Tuesday. How was she to pass the
day ?

At breakfast her mother begged her reproachfully to go to
La France Quadrant with a measuring tape and note-book.
The removal was now fixed for a fortnight hence, and Joanna's
self-imposed task of measuring beforehand for furniture and
carpets had already been shirked more than once. But this
morning, grateful for the enforced activity, she set out at
once.

The hours slipped away quickly as she went from one empty,
tree-shaded room to another in the new house overlooking
the flint mill. The mechanical yet exacting work was sooth-

ing to her state of mind ; and by the time she re-emerged from
the Quadrant, a little dazed by the steady physical effort she
had been making, one o'clock sounded to her surprise across
from the University tower.

She was too late then for the midday meal at home. And
there, directly opposite were the shining plate-glass windows
of Sangster the baker. The smell of hot bread rose from
the pavement gratings and made her mouth water : the
trays of glistening, sweet cakes, and the rows of mahogany-
coloured " cookies," still undetached and gleaming with
their high varnish of egg, gave her a peculiar sensation in
her jaws which was almost pain. She could not pass the
place

On leaving the white, spring sunshine of the street and
entering the dark inner shop, she did not at once see very
clearly. But a young man seated near the door drew her
attention by one of those slight but uncontrollable movements
that never go unremarked. The next moment her sun-dazzled
eyes had recognized Lawrence Urquhart.

So he was back !

He at once made room for her at his table so that she
had no choice but to sit by him. He was drinking coffee
and had been reading from a big brown book which was
propped against the sugar basin. This he moved aside,
shutting it carelessly without troubling to notice the page
or to replace the marker which lay beside it.

After the first greeting with its little spontaneous rush of
pleasure for the unforeseen encounter, shyness came upon
them both. He said he had been back these three days, and
then she was sure it was he who had witnessed the meeting
between herself and Louis by the granite steps. But when he
went on to tell her that his mother had fallen ill while out of
town so that he was travelling up and down daily and had not
yet spent a night in Glasgow since his return, Joanna became
again uncertain. It annoyed her that she should be sensitive
now for the first time to his opinion. What did it matter
whether he had seen her or not ?

To cover their awkwardness they tried to talk of Nilsson,
of the places Lawrence had visited, of the first payment for
her designs which Joanna had received some days ago accom-
panied by an order for more work. But very soon the conversation failed again, and Joanna ate more quickly and

drank her coffee without wasting a moment in her desire to be off.

"It seems a sin," he said presently, stretching out his hand for a cake he did not want—"Don't you think it seems a sin to stay in town on an afternoon like this?"

Joanna had to admit that it was a lovely spring day.

"Couldn't we go for a walk?" he asked then, speaking as if the idea had that moment struck him. And seeing that she was going to refuse him without considering he went on:

"I know such a good walk, quite short, by the canal all the way. The hawthorn is going to be a wonder this year, and there's a place for tea near one of the locks. I wonder do you know it?"

As he grew more urgent Joanna became colder, more detached from him. He had not finished speaking, before she wondered, slighting him in secret, whether this walk of his might prove one which later she could show to Louis. Louis was always accusing her of ignorance of her own country-side.

But as her companion searched her face, something in his good eyes, penetrated her suddenly, unexpectedly, deeply. Not that she would acknowledge it. On the contrary in that very moment she busied her mind more and more consciously, more and more in pure wickedness, on Louis's behalf, and it was as if she dealt deliberate wounds to the eyes that faced her across the little table. But all the same she had become possessed of the triumphant knowledge of how those same eyes, at present so steady and anxious, would lighten, would transform themselves under her kisses.

Meanwhile she heard herself giving perfunctory consent to Lawrence's suggestions for the afternoon, and with a show of polite interest which masked even from herself her shocking excitement, she listened to his enthusiastic description of a "kind of little farm place" above the lock where the woman gave one home-made jam and fresh-baked girdle-scones for tea. After all (Joanna excused her acquiescence to herself, unconscionably) it would be better than staying all afternoon at home. To-morrow—Sunday—would be bad enough, and she had Monday as well to get through before seeing Louis. The sudden thought followed that on Tuesday Louis would learn of her walk with Lawrence. This was enlivening;

and involuntarily she smiled at her companion as if prepared
now for enjoyment. He found it hard to subdue the delight
caused in him by that smile of malicious sweetness.

But when they were got well on their way, and were strolling
side by side—a pair of young lovers to the casual eye—
along the canal bank which was festive with newly formed
leaves and the hard, ball-like beginnings of blossom, she re-
pented that she had come. How lacking in savour was
this compared with even her least happy hours with Louis !
What was Louis doing now at this very moment ? What
sort of people were those London friends of his ? As the longing to be with Louis increased like a fever, her self-distaste
for having consented to the present situation was also aug-
mented ; and as both emotions intensified each other, her
spite against Lawrence crouched yet lower and stiffened for
the spring.

She was not made gentler by the fact that Lawrence was
talking more than he usually did in her company. He was
talking with positive gaiety ; now of the habits of the mayflies
which drifted in derelict heaps on the surface of the canal,
now of a prospective lectureship in Mythology and Folklore
for which in time he hoped to be a candidate, now of the
Black Cat at Bruges where Nilsson had introduced him to the
great, half mad, Irish sculptor, Conolly.   Again, with a curious
kind of tremulous, very youthful unction which Joanna particularly resented, partly because it was so Scotch in him,
partly because she guessed it a cloak for emotion, he under-
took to describe at length a solitary walk he had made from
Zurich across the Alps into Italy.

And as with so many ordinarily silent people, speech, when
it came to him was all absorbing. Lawrence's companion
well knew that he went untroubled by her presence for this
hour at least, and as he persisted glowing and unobservant,
she withdrew herself in a more and more violent aloofness.   As
the tigress withdraws upon herself under the dark thicket
before she leaps with gathered strength upon some unwitting
beast that gambols outside in the sunshine, so Joanna with
her bright hair blowing, and her fresh, virginal cheeks, was
essentially at this moment a thing hunched-up with the
desire to inflict pain. How dared Lawrence stretch
himself, unconscious as an animal in the spring sunshine, finding happiness in himself, in all about him, even in her unre-

sponsive companionship, while she walked by his side in tor-
ment ? How dared he ?

In her fury of malevolence she had the impulse to push him
with all her might into the dark water of the canal. Then
how she would rush to Louis, abandoned and laughing ! How
she would throw herself into his arms !

But later, as they sat drinking tea and eating floury girdle-
scones in the cottage which was on a little hillock above the
lockhouse, her anger against Lawrence changed its form
insidiously. And now if Lawrence was more than ever in
her power, Joanna was no less the victim of a ruthless
force.

With leaping excitement she looked across at his con-
tented face. He was grown handsomer, as she had already
noticed, from his holiday and happy exposure to the sun ;
and as she looked she knew finally and clearly that she must
see his features transfigured as she alone could transfigure
them. She must have him no longer content but entirely
at her mercy.

Abruptly she rose and moved from the table to the window.
These last few minutes had brought a silence between them.
She had seen a puzzled look cross her friend's face, and with
all the weight of imposed and inherited inhibitions she was
struggling against her deepest impulse.

"It was good of you to bring me to this pretty place,"
she said. It was the first banality that came to her, but in
each tone of her voice the triumph of impulse sounded.

In reply Lawrence got up and came to her, knocking against
a chair on his way across the room. He was shaken through
and through by her altered manner and voice, by the strange
glance she had given him before she turned away, by the subtle
but overwhelming appeal of her movement and of her whole
body there by the window.

He stood behind her waiting. He was near enough for her
to feel his breathing on the nape of her neck. But still he
waited in terrible hesitation. From the first he had kept
his feeling for this woman apart, had refused to connect it
with that passionate dreaming which he regarded as the bane
of his life, and he could not now believe what his senses were
telling him loudly enough.

"Not at all," he replied feebly. (He would try even at the
last gasp to put the incredible thing from him and avoid

everlasting catastrophe). "On the contrary, it was so friendly of you to come—more friendly even than I dared to hope from your letters."

But now Joanna turned her face to him, and he was lost. All her features seemed to him to utter a cry for help. The eyes were the eyes of a woman drowning and already half submerged. But more than in the eyes the urgency was centred in the mouth with its sad, young contours. He could see the strong teeth which for some reason in their slight irregularity had more power than any other single characteristic of hers to haunt and disturb him.

And what was her appeal? Was it for comfort? For refuge? For love? He did not know. He only knew that whatever it was, she must be answered. And with the whole world darkening about him he put out his hand and took hers.

"I think you would be the best of friends," said she, uncertainly, and she trembled. They both stood trembling together, full of fear, all the world an abyss beneath them. Only in the remote distance Joanna seemed to perceive the faint, luminous beginnings of a rainbow that arched over a world of grey chaos. There, there it was! Dim, but shining, the gateway of escape from Louis.

"Do you really mean that?" asked Lawrence, almost voiceless, and his eyes never moved for an instant from the lips he so awfully loved. Joanna, with a sudden departure of strength from her knees, had sunk down facing him upon the chintz-covered window seat. Through the widely-thrown open lattice they could feel the cool airs of the spring sundown, and below was the white-washed lock house, so cold and compact and pretty in the mounting shadow, and the closed lock gates through the joints of which the heavy, thwarted water hissed threateningly.

"I do mean it," Joanna answered, looking at his hands, and though she was fighting hard for steadiness, her voice went wavering pathetically like a lost child's. "I wish I could know you were my friend. I think I need you——"

Not one other word could she speak. But there was no need, for the next moment Lawrence's black head was against her knees, against the knees that even now he dared not picture as a woman's. He had dropped crouching on the floor before her, burying his face in her skirts, and his arms clasped her with trembling determination.

" You know I am yours," he said, " to do as you wish with, at any time, in any way."

" Do you mean you love me ? " Over Joanna's chaotic grey world the rainbow gateway of escape arched more and more radiantly. Here was what Louis could never give her, what at the eleventh hour would save her from Louis.

But when Lawrence first raised his head and looked up at her she was filled with sheer terror seeing what she had done. So, she thought in dismay, must dying men look.

" You must always have known I loved you," he replied.

IV

When she was alone again and at home Joanna tried hard to shut out all that had happened but a single fact. Lawrence had offered her a way of escape from Louis. She had called and he had answered, and so there was plighted troth between them. No matter that from the moment of his single embrace she had retreated as subtly as surely from him : no matter that now in solitude she was becoming for the first time in her adult life aware of sheer wickedness gushing up in her as a spring essential to her nature :—there should be no going back. With each hour that passed, the desire increased to inflict suffering. What lay behind this desire and beyond its fulfilment she refused to contemplate.

At first she was determined to write to Louis cutting herself off entirely and at once. But when Sunday morning came she could not do this. Instead she sent him a note telling him that she had engaged herself to marry Lawrence Urquhart and that she would explain everything face to face if he cared to meet her on the coming Tuesday, as had already been arranged between them.

From the moment of posting this, all her force contracted into a single spark of expectancy. To see his face—that was her one need. As for Lawrence, there would be time later on to think of him. She was not to see him again till Wednesday His mother's illness had helped Joanna to make this arrangement.

V

In Collessie Street there was a deathly atmosphere of Sabbath. Linnet had gone out : Juley was closeted in prayer

with Eva Gedge : one of the neighbours played hymns lingeringly on an American organ.—Joanna felt she must run out
of the house or go mad.

But where to run to ?   The streets were worse than indoors.
Though it was afternoon they resounded with gratuitous
church bells.   They were tolerable at such times only for swift
passage.   And to whom could she pass through them ?
Mildred was gone to London for Easter : Carl Nilsson was in
Germany : the Pringles, like most other people, were out of
town.

It crossed Joanna's mind, however, with a spurt of hope,
that it was just possible Phemie might be alone at *Sans Souci*.
On the Saturday, there had been, she remembered, an orches-
tral concert at which Phemie's favourite soprano had been
singing.   Surely for such an occasion she would have returned
to town.   It was at least worth trying for.

So Joanna swung away to the South Side of the town,
perched and clinging to her hat on a wildly rocking tram-car.
(The electric cars rushed and swayed on a Sabbath with special
defiance as if repudiating the jog-trot observance of the horse-
cars they had not long supplanted.)   And she told herself
how glad Phemie would be, upon hearing of her engagement
to Lawrence.   Though little had been said between them of
Louis, she knew that her friend regarded that whole situation
as hopeless—or in her own vernacular as " simply no earthly."
And now, with the wind in her face and the gay motion of the
car as it tossed her up hill and down, Phemie's friend was
ready to admit the verdict.   It might not be true to say that
she had envied the straightforward devotion of young Jimmie,
in which Phemie throve and put forth blossoms like a healthy
plant.   But it was none the less a satisfaction that she could
take her place as it were, in the same sunny, unadventurous
plot.   After all, was there not a sweetness in plain, common
sense ?

But when she reached the villa all the blinds were drawn
down and there was no sign of life.

It was a disappointment.   She felt repulsed, quite flat
suddenly.   Only now did she realize how desperately she had
been counting on Phemie's approval.

Hoping against hope she entered the garden and walked up
the path to the front door.   To her joy the outer door at least
was unbarred.   She rang the bell eagerly, but waited in vain

for any answering sign from within. Again after a minute she rang, this time without expectancy. And again nothing happened except that another tram-car went rocking past outside on the road and the people on the top looked down on her efforts, mockingly, as it seemed to her.

Then, just as she was turning to go, one of the blinds in the bow-window of the dining-room moved a very little and she distinguished Phemie's face peering out below it.

"Phemie!" she cried, running up the steps as the face instantly disappeared again on recognizing her. "Phemie! Phemie!"

Within the house to her relief there was an answering cry, and she heard the familiar, characteristic sound of Phemie's feet thudding childishly across the stone hall.

But the moment she had set eyes on Phemie's face her own affairs sank into insignificance. It was so altered, that usually gay visage, with long-continued weeping, and the small, charming features were set in such lines of fear, that seeing it Joanna feared for her friend's wits.

At first they could do nothing but hug each other, Phemie returning Joanna's embrace convulsively. Then they went together into the sunless, calico-covered dining-room.

"Phemie, what is wrong?" exclaimed Joanna. "Tell me, what is it, my darling? Or shall I go away? Would you rather I went away?"

"No, no!" Phemie begged, clutching her like a despairing child. "Don't go. Don't leave me. I'm *that* glad to see you! I thought I was going out of my mind till you came. See, sit here. I'll make tea. Or no, let's go to the kitchen: this room is like death itself. O! Lord, what a comfort to have you. Wait, I'll tell you. I'll just put the kettle on first."

In the kitchen Joanna sat on the edge of the table watching her friend's impetuous movements (surely no one else had so to fly about to make a cup of tea!) and turning over in her mind all the calamities that could have happened. The fact that Phemie could think of tea was no proof that her trouble was a small one. If the Last Trump had sounded, Phemie would have contrived to get tea before answering the summons. Besides in spite of her lively movements there was still all the while that deep, painful frown between her brows. Joanna could not doubt that something serious had happened

"I'm going to New Zealand," announced Phemie when she had pushed away her thrice-emptied cup, and she threw back her face down which the tears were now rapidly coursing, —"going to-night,—and I'm *Terrified!* It's Jimmie," she continued. "He's in Liverpool now. No one knows but his father and me. And I'm to join him to-night. The day after to-morrow we sail. If we didn't he would have to go to prison. It's a fearful thing. Yes, wait,—I'll try to tell you —it really wasn't Jimmie's fault. At least heaps of men do the same, he says, every day, only they don't get found out just at the wrong time, and later on people only think how clever they were. But anyhow with him it was all for my sake—so that we could get married sooner—we were both sick tired of waiting—no one knows—lately it has been awful— if it's anyone's fault, it's Papa's and Mamma's. They could have helped us long ago instead of waiting to leave us money when they die. But they wouldn't. Parents are awfully wicked, I think, don't you? But oh, I don't want to go away. I mean I *didn't*. And you know Papa was giving us the villa next year, and we had nearly all the furniture for it. Now Jimmie's father will take that to pay part of the debt!"

Gradually, as she grew calmer, Phemie was able to give Joanna a preciser account of the catastrophe. Jimmie had been speculating with business money, and borrowed money at that. Phemie herself did not know the exact nature or extent of the crime. She only knew that he had done something big enough and bad enough to be sent to prison for; and that he had risked this only for love of her. Otherwise his record was clean. It was because of this that his father, and his creditors for the sake of his father, were willing to hush things up. But the condition of hushing up was that he should leave the country at once. And if there was one thing Phemie was sure of, it was that once the facts came to her parents' ears, she would never—never on this earth—be allowed to follow her disgraced lover. It was now, she felt, or never. And Jimmie needed her and she needed him, and she had promised, and their passages were booked steerage, and they were to be married by special licence before sailing on Tuesday, and here was her ticket to Liverpool which Jimmie had given her yesterday—in her stocking for safety. But it would be a lie to say that the prospect did not fill her with absolute terror.

To her the voyage was a horror, the new country a place of rawness and struggle, desperate struggle for one's bare subsistence. The Pringle family was too newly removed from real poverty for its daughter not to have this dread ; and more and more exquisite as it receded seemed the South Side villa with its antiques, its deep armchairs, its rose-patterned chintzes.

To Joanna, out of whose blood generations of easy if frugal living had bred all fear of destitution, this was the least part of Phemie's trouble. How joyfully thought she, would she have followed a dishonoured and penniless Louis to any part of the world if he had but summoned her.

And it was by this envy more than by sympathy that she presently succeeded in cheering her friend to some degree. At first Phemie was astounded by the mere possibility of envy of her lot, but it did not fail in its effect. Indeed before an hour was passed she found herself able to laugh with tremulous amusement. After tea they had gone upstairs to finish the packing which Joanna's arrival had interrupted. And Joanna had set about making an inventory of the once precious bottom-drawer possessions which had mostly to be left behind. No doubt Annie, whose own wedding was not far off, would buy the things and send her sister the money. Annie could be counted on for that. As they spoke of this, Joanna's own secret trembled on her lips, but she could not bring herself to utter it.

Phemie's train was at seven, and as the afternoon drew on she grew nervous again. Without Joanna, she declared she simply did not know how ever she should have managed. It was Joanna who strapped the luggage, her own fingers trembled so and Joanna went for the cab while she sat shaking all over on the edge of the bed. But half dead with fear as she was, Phemie had no doubts. Nothing could have dissuaded her. She was Jimmie's, and this awful thing had to be gone through. So far, except for one or two moments under Joanna's influence during the packing, she had enjoyed none of the savour of adventure. It was too real as she saw it, too stark for that. But Jimmie would be on the platform at Liverpool waiting for her : and once with him she would be all right. She clung blindly to that.

Joanna would have made the journey with her, but Phemie refused with sudden firmness. " I must learn to do things by myself now," she said, trembling but resolute," otherwise I shan't be much good to Jimmie out there."

So they said good bye. Phemie hung out of the carriage window fluttering her sopping handkerchief, and Joanna weeping also, torn between tenderness, the pain of parting, and sharpest envy, stood waving on the platform till the train was out of sight.

There was nothing to do now but to go drearily home.

VI

That night she was restless and her sleep full of uneasy dreaming. She dreamed that Jimmie was her lover and had laid his head in her lap. But when he looked up, his face was the face of Lawrence Urquhart, and Joanna felt ashamed before him, knowing that she had that day promised to go with Louis to New Zealand.

On the Monday morning she had work to do but could not settle to anything.

By this time, she kept thinking, Louis must have got her letter. What did he think ? She grew more and more miserably certain that he would not come the next day, that she would never see him again. Then she wouldn't, she vowed vindictively, see Lawrence either. She would join Phemie and her Jimmie at Liverpool and get them to take her abroad with them. For some indefinable reason she could not endure the idea of seeing Lawrence again unless she had first seen Louis. She felt wild, defiant, false to every one. Let them think of her and treat her as they liked ! She would escape from them all. She would go to some place where she could live in utter solitude. But first she wanted to hurt them all, to revenge herself on them.

She could not stay still indoors, and soon after breakfast went out and walked in the streets staring at shop-windows. A lust came upon her for the acquirement of new clothes. This she did not attempt to withstand. True she had no money. All she had had in her purse the day before (two pounds, which was the remains of the first payment for her designs) had been slipped as a surprise wedding present in among the folds of Phemie's honeymoon night-gown. But this did not stop her. She knew that as Miss Bannerman, if not under her married name, she could get credit anywhere in town. So she bought herself a coat that had taken her fancy. It was of powder blue cloth, belted like a highwayman's. And to go with it she discovered a gallant hat. Leaving her old coat and hat to be sent up later, she paraded home in these new clothes. She knew not how she was to wait till the morrow.

She was inspecting her new finery afresh after the midday meal, in front of the long mirror in her bedroom, when Janet the old cook knocked at the door and cried out querulously that there was a visitor for Miss Joanna downstairs.

Before opening, Joanna bundled her purchases guiltily into the wardrobe. Who could have called? It was not yet three o'clock!

The cook stood panting outside on the landing. She exuded reproach, holding her hand with a world of meaning to the left side of her large, starchy print bosom. Mary the housemaid had been ill and was having a fortnight's holiday before the ordeal of the flitting. (The Bannermans kept but two servants these days.) And as it was Janet herself who had elected to carry on single-handed in the interim, sooner than have " a strange girl about," Janet had acquired the right to be cross and sorry for herself from morning till night, but most particularly in the afternoon when anyone was ill-advised enough to ring the front door bell before three o'clock.

" There's a gentleman downstairs," she said, speaking quite faintly now that she was observed. " He asked for you— he gave his name—but I've nae heid for names, and if I had, thae stairs would have knocked it out o' me."

" No'm. Not a young gentleman," she replied in answer to a question from Joanna, and she fetched a yet more painful sigh, " at ony rate no' what you'd ca' young."

As Joanna crossed the landing to the top of the stairs she shook so that she was afraid she would not be able to walk down.

It must be Louis! He had come. It was only Monday, so his friends from London were still with him. But he had not been able to stay away after getting her news. He had even broken through his hitherto firm objection to calling at Collessie Street. This was the first time he had entered the house, and he had done it unasked.

She began the descent of the stairs.

At first she had to move slowly, mechanically : she was so

perfectly the victim of the beating of her own heart. Her heart was a flail, an appalling, demented flail, assaulting her. All other sensation was cancelled. Under its persecution she barely clutched consciousness, barely kept her body upright and progressive by clinging with her right hand to the steep, downward-sloping banister.

But by the time she reached the second flight she went free from that dominion. It was gone completely, as if it had never been. And now instead, her heart felt small, felt tiny, felt buoyant like a boat or a bird that is serenely lifted on a quiet, immense, triumphant surge. She had never been so exempt. It was something like the fearless, sudden clarity which had come in childhood when she climbed high up on a dangerous place or ran barefoot from stone to stone with perilous gathering momentum down the Duntarvie burn.

Save that now it was a dual and therefore a rarer, maturer ecstasy. She was poised and keen, a hawk in mid-air, a speck of perfect bliss upheld in perfection of readiness for the predatory swoop. Yet in that same instant she also lived in every pulse for that other consummation of her nature in which her breast would be transfixed by talons stronger than her own.

And therein—shining in this moment of dual revelation—her new knowledge lay clear. Why, she asked herself in amazement, had she all her life taken for granted that she was innately gentle, candid, good, when in reality she was quite as innately fierce, treacherous, wicked ? She had been taught, of course, that all human virtues were sadly tinctured as by some tragic accident with their "natural" opposites,—qualities wild and dark ; but that in the struggle towards perfection such qualities—remnants of the jungle from which Christ redeemed us—must be expelled increasingly from our lives. In their total expulsion perfection would lie, and Heaven be achieved. And this famous and stimulating doctrine had never been seriously questioned by her. She had not been able to accept Georgie's gratifying theory that all evil was but perverted good. But now, descending the familiar staircase, as by lightning, Joanna saw a different truth. It was a truth of which she had many times before had glimpses. With Gerald, with Mario, even with Bob—always when her essential female being had come into conflict with the male, obscure hints of it had sought admission to her understanding. But not until now had it really emerged as something complete, authoritative like the writing on the wall.

Joanna's discovery was that " evil " (in the Christian sense of the word) quite as much as " good " had made her alive, that " evil " quite as much as " good " had made her an individual, a human being, a divine creation herself capable of creative life.

Further she perceived that this admission altered everything. It was as if before her eyes the Creator had once more divided chaos with a word into darkness and light. No longer did her "good " show dimmed and confused by her evil, nor her evil faintly transfused by her good. Her good was now dazzling and apart, a pure element of light : her evil was utter and separate, a pure element of darkness. They were the two sides of a coin. The dove was on one side ; on the other side the hawk. To obliterate either was to invalidate the coinage, to defame the mint from which it had issue. And the two could be mingled only in the discreditable act of destruction.

To her it was a vision, no less. She knew she would never be quite the same after it as she had been before.

Smiling, half-blinded as if by bursting sun-rays, though the house was dark enough and it was a dull day out of doors, Joanna opened the door of the room where Louis was waiting for her. She became aware at once—by some other than her ocular sense, it seemed to her—that he was grave as she had never seen him, and intensely anxious ; and her smile broadened. She wanted to shout with laughter till the hidden stars shook in their places. He had made her suffer. Now it was his turn.

They stood facing each other without any formal greeting.

" Was that true that you wrote me ? " he asked.

When she heard his voice Joanna's vengeance passed. With his first syllable that part of her consummation was complete and she rendered up the ascendancy to him. As he watched her in cold fury she ceased to be the kestrel poised : she became instead the small bird that flutters close to the ground for its life. After all there was a justice in things : she admitted that rejoicing.

` " Is it true ? " Louis repeated.

" Yes," she said. She dared not look at him.

" Well, of course you are free to do as you please,"—he
struck out at her with venom, " and I suppose I'm hardly in
the position to criticize. All I can say is that such a trick is
the last thing I expected of you. Till I got your letter this
morning, I didn't know how well I had thought of you. No
one in this world but yourself could have convinced me that
all the time you had been carrying on with another man.
Engaged to be married! Pah! I'm ashamed of you and
still more ashamed of myself. Don't you think it was going
a bit out of your way to stab an old fool in the back like that ?
But what's the use of talking ? I'm sure I don't know why
I came here to see you. After all, as I've already said, your
life is your own to do as you like with, and I've no doubt you
have got some kind of satisfaction out of fooling me. You
have certainly succeeded."

Joanna, who had been very white in the face at the beginning of this speech, was red before it was finished. She
sat down heavily on the sofa and now her eyes never left
Louis. But he would not look at her now. Such pain as this
she had not expected.

" Louis," she said, " say what you like to me, but that about
fooling you, about carrying on with Lawrence isn't true, and
you certainly are a fool if you believe it. He never made
love to me till Saturday, or perhaps I made love to him.
Something drove me to it. *You* drove me to it. But till
then I hadn't the faintest idea. "

Louis had to believe this.

" I give it up then," he said with an assumption of still
greater indifference though before he spoke he had covertly
scrutinized the quivering girl. " You are all the more incomprehensible to me."

" What's the meaning of it all," he continued more
warmly. " Can you tell me ? I promise I'll listen as
patiently as I can, and try to understand. Here's a woman.
On Friday she swears she loves me, throws herself at my head,
in fact ! On Saturday she promises to marry some one
else. There must, I suppose, be some reason ? Is it that
marriage is so greatly to be coveted ? I thought you agreed
with me about that. Didn't you tell me one day of your own
accord——? "

" I never stopped loving you ! " interrupted Joanna passionately, and she pressed the palm of one hand against her

throat. "You know it well enough. And I don't want to get married. At least not yet and not to Lawrence."

"If that's so, then you must be mad, that's all," returned Louis; "and I think you are, too"; But a change had come over his face, and for a second his fingers went slyly to his bright moustache, an action that always made Joanna's blood mount like wine.

She held her hands tightly together in her lap.

"Don't you see," she pleaded, "it's because *you* don't love me enough I can't be——I don't——what can I say?——I musn't let you go on making love to me when you really care so little. For you as well as myself; I can't, can I? Don't you feel in your heart that I'm right not to? Tell me honestly what you think I should do, and I'll do it."

Louis looked at her for some moments in silence.

"It seems to me," he said at length, "that there's no more to be said. You know best what it is you want: and if you don't think I love you enough you are the one to judge. I can't offer to marry you. Frankly, if I could, I believe I would—if *that's* any good to you. But it isn't, I know. Nothing I can say or do is any good to you. Don't you think I've gone over that a hundred times in my mind? And just because I feel as I do towards you I'm the last person to advise you. I see you sitting there looking like I don't know what—I never quite know what you make me think of—and I feel I'd rather you were dead than in another man's arms. There you are! And what use is that to you? I believe you really want to get married. Besides, in any case you have decided that I don't love you enough."

"So, Signora Rasponi," he continued with one of his flourishes, when he had waited in vain for some retort from Joanna, "it only remains to wish you every happiness in the lot to which it has pleased heaven to call you."

"Really, my dear," he finished, becoming suddenly tired and simple, "perhaps you are quite right. I honestly hope so. Anyhow I wish you all the luck. I can't say more, can I? I only want you to do the best for yourself. And now good bye." He picked up his hat and stick and held out his hand.

Joanna did not move. She had ached to rend open this man's heart, to wrest from him the secret truth of his being. And she had failed. He had kept himself almost wholly inviolate. But in the attempt she had discovered anew that she needed him. He must stay. She could not let him go. All her energy now centred on this, that he must not go. Perhaps for the first time since childhood she was in deadly earnest. The insistent, warping histrionics of girlhood were gone. She was a simple, desperate woman trying to hold a man for her need.

"Can't you understand?" she demanded miserably. "I've made a fool of myself, not of you. I've made a stupid, dreadful mistake. You know I love only you. But I hoped—— Don't you see?——"

"*No!*" she exclaimed, raising her voice loudly in anger. "No. No. No!"—and she struck upon her knees with her clenched hands while the tears of utter humiliation rushed scalding from her eyes—"it's impossible, quite impossible that you should ever understand, Idiot that I was! I see that now."

Louis laid aside his hat and stick again with one of the curious, deliberate movements which with him marked excitement. And he sat himself down by Joanna on the sofa.

"Idiot you are!" he agreed. "But truly, Joanna, do you want me?"

"I do, Louis, you know I do. But do you want me?"

"By God! I do. O! my dear child. What a ghastly pang when I thought I'd lost you."

He sighed deeply, boyishly. It was a great danger that was overpast; and now that she was once more against his breast and returning his kisses, it seemed as if their love, always sweet, was wonderfully enhanced. This was all they thought of. They easily refused to envisage the part played by Lawrence Urquhart in their new-found happiness. Surely they had been born for this thing, and the attempt to escape it was worse than idle? The result, whether for happiness or sorrow must be left in the hands of nature who had driven them into each other's arms. Any penalty paid by themselves or by others was better than the denial of so strong an impulse.

At last they drew apart, and Louis said he must go. But Joanna sprang up radiant, with shining eyes and dishevelled hair.

"Wait for me one minute. I'll walk to the station with you!"

She rushed upstairs, threw on the new coat and hat, and rejoined him within two minutes. Her lover noted with a

pang that she looked a mere schoolgirl. Her cheeks were
blazing.

"What! New clothes?" he exclaimed in a peculiar tone.
"You like them?"

"Very much. They are the best I've seen you in. But
you are a mad-woman, you know. I'm not at all sure that
young Urquhart isn't well quit of you."

VII

In the evening Joanna wrote to Lawrence. It was a longer
letter than the one she had sent to Louis, and was written with
labour and self-loathing. She tried to persuade herself that
Lawrence would not suffer more than she had suffered with
Bob. Sometimes one was made to suffer; sometimes one
made others suffer: that was life. Besides, Lawrence,
loving her as he did, would necessarily have suffered even if
she had not given him this false promise of happiness. She
had only accelerated, not created his misfortune. So she
reasoned, while she filled her letter with ready-made phrases of
penitence. She was "dreadfully sorry and ashamed," her
conduct had been "unforgivable."

It was hardly possible for her to say the truth to him,
for the truth would have run something like this:—
"Because you have a fitful, incomprehensible attraction for
me, and because I trust you more than anyone I know, also
because I wanted to feel I had power over you, I have used you
shamefully. I have made you tell me that you loved me, not
only to make sure of that, but to force the hand of the man
I am myself in love with. On the whole I have succeeded, and
now, though I am surprised at myself and perhaps ashamed,
I am not repentant. All I wish is never to see you again.
Your pain might trouble me, and I want to be free from
remorse and reproach to follow my desire. If you will keep
out of my way I shall try to feel friendly towards you."

This, however, though not the letter Joanna wrote, was not
so very unlike the letter that Lawrence was to read at the
other end. Throughout all the trite, laborious phrases put
down upon the paper the reality made itself felt clearly enough.

That same night Juley took to her bed with a bad gastric
attack which had been threatening her for some time, and
the doctor was sent for. It was not immediately serious, he

said when he had questioned her, but she must have special care if it was not to become so. Above all, for the next few weeks she should have absolute rest.

But while the doctor was speaking, there spread over Juley's face a crafty and obstinate expression well known to her children. As soon as he was gone she declared that she felt better and that it was a pity he had been sent for at all. And next morning, do what they would, she got up. She could rest, she said, " after the Flitting," which on account of incoming tenants to Collessie Street, could not well be put off to a later date. Meanwhile it was urgent that she should set to, and start clearing those many " places " of hers which were choked with the accumulations of nearly thirty years.

This clearing business was an obsession and a shame to Juley, and a matter in which she was fiercely secretive. And sacred above all from the prying eyes of her children and servants did she hold the famous middle part of her huge bedroom wardrobe with its many shelves and drawers. When the children were small they had regarded as a treat of treats that they should be in the room on the rare occasion of a clearing of this receptacle by their mother. It was always kept locked and the key in Juley's key-basket. Even when Joanna became a woman she had felt it something of an honour to be handed the key and asked to fetch something out of the front part. And now, by the doctor's explicit orders, the entire wardrobe with all the other places to be cleared, was delivered into her hands.

There was no doubt that Juley would have defied the doctor (even with Eva Gedge and her children to back him) had not Linnet conceived the happy idea of sending for Mrs. Boyd. And to everybody's relief Mrs. Boyd came.

Either because of her pleasant and equable disposition, which Juley so wistfully admired, or because long ago in her girlhood she was known to have cherished a romantic passion for the elder Sholto, Maggie Boyd had a more dependable influence over Juley than anyone else, and it was certainly clever of Linnet to have thought of her. Since the Bannermans had left St. Jude's they had seen very little of their father's old friend; but for this very reason she would have all the more weight now.

It was Joanna who went for her, and no sooner had the little old lady taken in the situation than she put on her bonnet and cloak and came back to Collessie Street, bringing her daughter, Mamie, with her.

She would have no nonsense, she announced, calmly leading Juley in her grey dressing-gown away from a bewildered survey of the crowded box room under the stairs and back to the bedroom. Juley was to come straight to High Kelvin Place this very day, to be nursed and kept in order. Joanna and Mamie between them would be responsible for the flitting.

"Two great strapping girls," she insisted, indicating the two rather slender young women who sat either side on the edge of Juley's bed. "If you leave everything to the young people, my dear, you will soon be led to see that your illness was providential. And there's Janet too! A regular host in herself. Don't tell me! I had no idea you were such a faithless Christian, Juley Bannerman!"

Very soon it was decided. Juley protested. She even cried a little. But she was smiling through her tears. Really she loved to be exhorted, accused of lack of faith, treated as a child, except by her own household. And though it still distressed her to think of her wardrobe and the disgrace of her cupboards, she was actually got off in a cab by the afternoon, all wrapped up in shawls and childishly excited at the prospect of being ill at High Kelvin Place.

Rather to Joanna's surprise, two days had passed without word or sign from Lawrence. But on Wednesday morning the post brought a letter addressed in his hand. It was black-edged.

With a premonition of distress she opened it and read :—

"Dear Joanna,

"They say troubles never come singly. Certainly that has been my experience these last few days. When I got home here on Saturday evening I found my mother had taken a turn for the worse and she died on Monday. It was her heart that gave out. Then this morning your letter reached me. I am still too confused and stunned to grasp all that it means, and fortunately as I must suppose, my whole attention is still required for practical matters in connection with my mother's death. You say I am to forget what passed between us on Saturday, as it was all a mistake on your part. Bitter as this is to me I can understand it well enough. What I cannot understand is how I ever for a moment believed it was anything but a dream. But why is it better that I should not see you again ? I do not want, nor do I mean to make any appeal *ad misericordiam*, if that is what you are afraid of. But in the circumstances surely it is for me to decide whether or not I am to see you again on the former friendly footing ? You cannot know what it is to me to see you or you would not ask this. If, as you say, you are the one in fault, how is it in your right to dictate in the matter of my small remaining claim ? You say you would rather have suffered yourself than make me suffer. If this is true then let your penance be the continuance of our friendship. Perhaps I need that just now more than the other.

"Forgive me if I seem rude, and believe me,

Ever your friend,

"LAWRENCE URQUHART."

As she read this letter, anger struggled with acknow-ledgment in Joanna. Somehow she was thwarted by it, belittled and punished and put down, while the writer rose suddenly to a new place in her thoughts. She had to admit his right to make her feel not so much wicked as wanton and petty : but it angered her that fate had tendered him the unexpected courage to use this right. If his mother had not died at that moment Joanna tried to tell herself he would have sent a very different message. What, she wondered with deep interest, had his mother's death meant to him ? Anyhow, she begrudged the event that had strengthened him by dealing the two blows simultaneously. Could it be then that she had coveted the sole power of dealing him pain ?

In reply she wrote a formal letter of sympathy, and told him that she would be busy moving house for the next few weeks.

VIII

Through the next ten days she worked with Mamie Boyd and Janet, but harder than both of them put together. She worked harder than at any time before in her life, and far more efficiently. For the time, she put her draw-ings and all else aside ; and from early each morning till past midnight, with hurried intervals for meals, hurled herself at the set task.

She had met Louis but once since their readjustment, and then only for a few minutes in the street. He too, as if in harmony with her, had taken to working harder and longer than before.

But their one meeting had been significant, full of understanding and tremulous concord. Desire had hovered and beckoned behind the flimsy mask of his attention as Joanna told Louis how she was placed in sole charge of all the arrangements at home : and while she was speaking his dumb appeal received its answer without need of words. He was smiling, she very grave as he read the steadfast promise in her eyes.

And both Mamie, who was her elder by five years, and Janet, who had been privileged to scold her not so long ago, obeyed her without question. They carried out her plans, which were surprisingly ingenious and practical, as if she were a proved general. In every one of her actions Louis was in some way involved, but now she would not think about him. Her imagination, was a falcon, hooded and chained till the appointed moment, but all her executive faculties were sharpened. She seemed to have eyes all round her head, to dwell upon a high watch-tower, to be able to think collectively of a dozen things at one time.

The state of the hidden places at Collessie Street was a fresh revelation to her of her mother's cumbered life, and she became every hour more reckless in the work of simplification. She was sure that nine-tenths of the stuff they had housed all these years would be neither used nor missed by any member of the family. Fuller and fuller grew the old ash-pit in the back green. But Joanna had an inbred hatred of waste ; and she would trudge up and down the long stairs fifty times a day with her arms full, while Mamie made her heaps into bundles and despatched them to this poor person or that charity. And at night, dazed with fatigue and satisfaction, she would stumble up to bed. When she lay down at first her thighs and the muscles of her back ached so acutely that she groaned aloud, but within five minutes she would be sleeping like a stone.

In the sacrilege of the wardrobe she would allow no one else to share.

As the great, curving, mirrored door swung heavily back upon its hinges Joanna was a child again ; and the enclosure with its trays and drawers, and its middle place lined with faded blue box-pleating, appeared to her as the very ark of romance. But at the quick of her excitement was something which had nothing to do with memory or with childhood except in so far as it signified the departure from both. This, not the hour of her marriage with Mario, was the time of severance, the final breaking of the umbilical cord. Very slowly had she drawn apart from her mother. Even while she had thought herself detached she had really been held and harried. But now she was removing her entire being in an act of irreparable rebellion. And this was the symbol : this laying of her new, alien hands upon her mother's treasures.

For here were all the little souvenirs of Juley's lifetime, most of them valueless in themselves, but so precious to her that her children were accustomed to hold them in reverence.

Among the many packets of letters and faded photographs neatly docketed and banded with elastic that snapped at a touch, Joanna found stray pages from an old Erskine journal The delicately penned entries were very affectionate, " Our sweet baby Perdy cut her second tooth on Thursday of this week. Old Nursie calls her our ' hen of gold,' "—was one that caught Joanna's eye. From further back in the same drawer came an inlaid cedar box. This was stuffed with tiny locks and plaits of hair, each having been lovingly labelled, —" Our little Miranda's hair at two and a half years. Sept. 1846."—" Darling Papa's hair, at the time of his death. Jan. 3, 1870."—" A piece of my hair cut off during an attack of brain fever in Rome, 1860 "—" Mamma's hair as an infant."—" Baby Robert's hair."—Who, wondered Joanna, was baby Robert ? And here was one of her own locks as a baby, fair, like gold silk, and Georgie's only a little darker, and Sholto's quite dark like greenish bronze, and Linnet's like white floss. How many tresses there were !

She drew out her mother's. It was unlike the other tight little sheaves of hair, being fine and long—full half a yard long —and the sheen of youth was upon it still. (Eighteen, Juley had been, when her father's passion for education had brought serious illness upon her.) Joanna carried it lying silkily across her extended hands to the window, let the light play on it, kissed it, with sudden, sorrowful passion inhaled its pleasant, aromatic odour. And there before the dressing-table mirror which had so often reflected her mother's painful toilets, she laid it against her own light brown head. As she had thought, it was of the very same texture and colour as her own hair.

Having restored it tenderly to its place, her next interest was her mother's square old jewel-case. A wedding present this; big and solid, covered with black Russia leather and lined with bridal satin. In spite of her knowledge of the contents Joanna felt a stirring of the old childish excitement on opening it and lifting out the trays. Once Juley had had a diamond ring and some pearl ornaments, presents from her bridegroom, but she had lost these long ago ; and now there remained only some pebble and silver brooches, a cameo or two, a bunch of worn seals, a set of beautiful but clumsy amethysts which were an Erskine heirloom, an ivory carved fan with some of the sticks broken, a silver vinaigrette that still smelt faintly invigorating, the children's broken strings of coral—the girl went over all these, fingering them with a fresh curiosity, but there was nothing here she did not know by heart.

Right at the bottom of the deepest drawer however she was to come upon some almost forgotten possessions.

Here was some bed linen too fine for the household chest : here, pinned within a towel was the Bannerman christening-robe with its intricate, wonderful embroidery of thistles all down the front. And beside it were a bunch of rare laces tied with tape and an infant's scarlet slipper.

But the real find was a shawl which Joanna had never seen before. Had she set eyes on it, even in her earliest childhood, she was sure she could not have forgotten it. Folded up, it had taken very little space in the drawer, for it was woven all of silk thread, and its deep fringe was of ivory coloured silk. But the pulses of its finder quickened as she shook the foreign thing out into a great gay square. It more than covered Juley's double bed with its rich, mellowed whiteness, and there were flowers and leaves all over it—big blotches of scarlet and yellow and blue flowers, and little blue-green leaves that interlaced, and tendrils that were purplish, almost black, between.

When she had looked her fill at it Joanna folded it again and put it on the top of a separate pile which had been growing steadily at one particular corner of the bed.

IX

On Friday, the day before the vans were expected, Joanna told the astonished but grateful Janet that she might sleep till Monday at a sister's house. She would only be asked to come for some hours to Collessie Street the next day. Linnet had already found a bed with friends, and the Boyds were taking it for granted that Joanna would come to them.

On the Saturday morning she was very early astir. The transcendent assurance of the preceding days still possessed her, and she felt finely strung, alert, complete mistress of herself and of those about her, a perfectly adjusted instrument.

Up and down stairs she followed the burdened, staggering men, carried out many of the things herself, was there ready with a cloth when a few drops of rain fell upon the drawing-room cabinet as it stood on the pavement.

She was hovering on the pavement, inspecting the half-packed vans and thinking how poor and undignified even the most cherished pieces of furniture appeared under the open sky, when Louis came up behind her, and touched her and spoke.

He was hungry and thirsty for a sight of her, he said; and his eyes bore out his words as they rested by turns on her flushed face, her little head which she had bound from the dust with a green and yellow handkerchief, her old brown skirt half covered by a black apron. Might he come and see her to-night? Where would she be? Would she be alone? When and where would she ever be alone? There was something in his face as he pressed her (she did not take it for shame) that made him look a little brutal; but his brutality was something she could exorcise. She would be waiting for him in the evening at the new house. Alone? Yes, if it could be. But he must go away now. When he had gone she fled indoors and stood for a minute in one of the empty rooms, very still and white, with her hands clasped.

Later, when all was done and she and Janet were drinking a last cup of tea in the stripped parlour, using the window-sill as a table, Mamie Boyd arrived.

"How fresh you do look!" she exclaimed as she kissed Joanna; "more as if you had been having a holiday than a flitting! But you must be feeling quite worn out all the same. I'll wait with you as long as there's anything to do. Mother says I'm not on any account to come home without you."

While Mamie entered into a long explanation of why she

had not been able to turn up earlier, Joanna was in an un-reasoning terror. Would the Boyds somehow coerce her into coming to them ? The image was absurd but she could see herself being dragged by force past the door of the new house and over the bridge to High Kelvin Place.

By what excuses she managed presently to shake Mamie off she could never afterwards remember. She did it however without giving any definite promise, and almost pushed her too hospitable friend down the front steps. Soon afterwards Janet also departed, having made the feeblest of protests.

Left to herself Joanna went slowly from room to room of the empty house in a mute farewell. Here, under this roof she had spent her childhood and adolescence, and in leaving it she knew she was leaving her first youth behind. She had loved this home as well as hated it and was prepared for some emotion of melancholy on the occasion of departure. But no such sentiment would rise in her. Her spirit had already taken flight forward to a riper phase of life, and she was glad of it, and only glad. Without a single pang she took leave of the despoiled, sad walls.

x

At La France Quadrant, when the unloaded vans had driven off with the men asprawl and joking inside, Joanna was able at last to shut the door upon staring humanity which had all day been so interested in her and her belongings. It was a relief.

She sat down on a packing-case in the still crowded hall. The new electric wiring had not yet been connected, and in the dusk of the spring evening the round stone pillars on either side of her might have been tree-trunks. The confused shad-ows from the laburnum outside were thrown on the glass panel and fanlight of the front door. She listened intently. The house was utterly still, and from outside she could hear no sound but the faint, determined rushing of the stream far down where it passed by the flint mill. She was cut off now from the rest of the world, remote and alone, waiting in a dense forest : and she felt a little afraid.

But once she had left the hall, going to the back of the house she began to be busy as a bird is busy with its nest. Already in one of the rooms each piece of furniture was in its place, the windows were curtained, and even some rugs had been unrolled upon the bare floor. Now Joanna fetched fuel from the kitchen, for the evening was cool, almost frosty, and when the fire had burned up she drew the curtains and began to unpack by candlelight.

For the last forty-eight hours she had been planning for this. Every least thing had been thought of beforehand. She was of those who ever desire material fitness and she had discovered the same desire in Louis also. It was one of the many bonds between their natures. In a suit-case she had put together the few family possessions which had seemed to her worthy of her lover's eye, and it did not take her long to dispose these. The result was far enough from the perfect beauty she longed for, but as she looked round upon her work she had a strong feeling of pleasure. In the flickering light of fire and candles it was a room prepared for the beloved and therefore lovely. For the first time Joanna was alive to the clear sincerity of design in the high silver candlesticks which had been a presentation to Horatio Bannerman from the St. Jude's congregation on the twenty-fifth anniversary of his ministry—and the foreign shawl, spread as a coverlet upon the wide mahogany couch gave a glamour.

Then, putting on her hat, and fingering the latch-key in her pocket to be quite sure she had it safe, she went out to the shops.

More than once during her errands there she asked herself what she was doing. She had no remembrance of having planned this. It was as though she were blindly carrying out the orders of another. But in one place there was a clock which pointed to half-past seven, and straight on that panic seized her. Louis, if he got no further message, was to be with her soon after eight, to sup with her. This sudden knowledge, as it seemed, sent her hastening toward home again. The parcels she had bought kept slipping precariously through her trembling fingers.

" I can still change my mind," she told herself as she plodded back in an agony to the house,—" or something may have prevented him so that he won't come—in any case I have only to tell him to go," and a wild aloof amusement shot through her at the thought that she might simply not open the door if he came.

But on her return to the Quadrant where the house was the last in a short, blind row, she saw that some one stood there.

Her heart thudded sickly. In spite of the uncertain light, she recognized the figure of Mrs. Boyd, Mrs. Boyd !

She had only to walk on, to call out, and she was saved ! But she neither spoke nor went forward. Instead she retreated with bird-like swiftness into a lane immediately upon her right, and there waited and watched, thanking the dim stars that the arrival had been during her absence from the house. Had she been in she must have been caught.

Meanwhile the old lady, after gazing reproachfully at the dark windows from the pavement, reascended the steps and rang the door-bell with vigour. Joanna heard it screech in its socket, once, twice ; and between whiles she heard the visitor's knuckles rapping sharply upon the glass pane of the door. Almost five minutes passed, and the girl in hiding, though her reason told her it was merely a question of waiting, was half dead with fear.

At last Mrs. Boyd gave it up and walked slowly away, passing the nearer end of Joanna's lane, and now and then looking back as if she still expected the house to give some sign. And Joanna pressed her body closer against the wall and kept quite still.

No sooner had she drawn a breath freely, than heavy footsteps coming up the lane from the far side struck a fresh terror into her. It was a policeman. He looked curiously at her as he passed, only seeing her face as a pale triangle beneath her hat, and under his official glance she clutched her purchases as if they were stolen goods. Her fingers were stiff with the dragging strings, and the wet stalks of a bunch of anemones had soaked through her gloves.

By this time, however, she knew that Mrs. Boyd must be well round the corner, so she made bold to leave the lane. The policeman on burly guard at the mouth of it followed her movements furtively and she could hardly endure it. She had to drop her parcels on the outside mat as she fumbled with chilled hands for the latch-key. But at last she was in, and at once she sank down in security.

Vanished now was her mirage of serenity, gone her exhilaration. She felt stripped, dislocated, defenceless. And it was Louis who had brought her to this ! She hated and blamed him bitterly.

But immediately upon her blame rose the clear, unsummoned memory of his face as she had first seen it. His face swam up at her out of the fog of reproachful thought, and under his teasing smile she read as never before his sadness and dissatisfaction.

Thought followed thought then that softened and calmed her. Having put her anemones in water she remembered that she had eaten scarcely anything since the morning. She must have food at once and a change of clothes, must wash the dust and weariness from her skin.

Before going out she had put on a kettle which now boiled noisily. The firelit room was peaceful, and she devoured some sandwiches with relish.

She was standing in the bathroom with her dress off, drying her neck and arms all fresh from the steaming water when the front door bell rang. She stared reassuringly up at herself in the little fixed mirror over the basin, for her heart seemed to have stopped. She heard the sound of her own blood winnowing in her ears, saw her eyes dilated and shining. And in that instant she knew she had come from marriage immune; she was giving herself as a sealed and virgin fountain into the hands of Louis. He, a man, might never know it, but it was true, and she was glad.

Flying back as she was, in her white petticoat and little white, sleeveless under-bodice, to the firelit room, she snatched the shawl off the couch and wrapped herself in it hurriedly. The bell in the basement pealed a second time. That it should sound a third time was not to be borne. A gay figure, she sped across the dark hall. Noiseless she went on stocking foot, trailing the long white fringes of the shawl behind her.

Yes, it was he! He had taken off his hat. As Joanna darted forward between the pillars which were like the trunks of beech-trees, she could see his shadow on the glass of the door. Against the thread-like, waving tangle of the laburnum, his head showed like a satyr's, eager and suffering. His suffering pierced her breast like a joyous spear.

She opened to him, and in a close, speechless embrace they leaned against the inner side of the door till the catch went home. Louis knew without asking that they were alone together in the house.

But Joanna, drawing back for a moment, saw that in his face which she would never quite forget or forgive, a look of shame. In spite of all he had said to her, he was ashamed.

There it was in his face warring with his delight, and by this dastard shame of his she herself for the moment was betrayed, was besmirched. True, it was only for a moment. In the radiance of her welcome and her giving the deadly thing passed from him. He became free, simple, exultant as herself. Still she had seen it; and all night it lurked like a foul wolf outside the room she had prepared, the firelit, secret room where the lovers were creatures of pure magic to each other.

Later, when she lay at rest in his hands, Joanna, still awake, was lapped strangely about by thoughts of death. Now death showed as beautiful to her as life, life as terrible as death. And she seemed to hold the secret of existence between her hollowed palms. It was a secret at once so stupendous and so simple that she wondered she had been so long of finding it out.

But soon her thoughts became confused, incongruous. The glowing coals crumbled downwards on the hearth with a quiet, grating sound. The ceiling leapt to an arch of guarding flame. Flames like sentinels sprang into being around the walls. They kept all shameful wolves away with their brandished swords. Whatever was to come after, she and Louis could sleep unscathed here. This innermost chamber, the very kernel of fire was their safe hiding place.

CHAPTER V

I

WHAT followed was a path into the unknown, and a path unexpectedly solitary.

It surprised, at first it frightened her that she was to get so little help from Louis. Without a doubt his presumed greater knowledge of life had been one of the powerful elements attracting her to him. With his advantages of age, experience, circumstances, he seemed to her to move surely in that fabulous world of mammon for which she had so hungered as a child and had not yet attained. For her he personified not only that for which the little green door in the wall of La Porziuncola had stood as the symbol, but also the finely decked luncheon table of Aunt Georgina. And between these two extremes of illicit adventure and conventional elegance (utterly dependent as they are one upon the other) lay the whole wondrous realm which is Society, which is æstheticism, which is history, which is the multi-coloured, solid-seeming fruit of human civilization. For a complexity of reasons, provincial and individual, the girl had always felt herself deprived of this traditional world. Now in Louis she was to possess it.

Yet they had not been lovers a week before she knew this same Louis powerless to direct their love's course. It was like being at sea with a companion whose sole idea of seamanship was to let drift. She could not easily grasp what was the truth, that to Louis also, because of her being as she was, their situation was essentially without precedent. Still less did she understand—albeit she was compelled to act upon it—the curious fact that Louis was clutching like a drowning man at her spiritual certitude. It was essentially the same movement as that made thirty years earlier by Sholto her father towards Juley her mother.

But if Louis in himself was Joanna's fascinating symbol

for the greatly coveted world of mammon down the ages, there was that in the contingencies of their coming together which answered with equal strength to the opposite need of her nature. He was not merely the fruit, he was forbidden : therefore in partaking she gratified her lust for rebellion and for sacrifice, for rejection of and by the world. This it was which had stirred in her long ago when she kissed the blind woman. But now the two opposing passions, the high barbarian pride of life and the deep Christian pride of humiliation, were mounting together to fulfilment. All the long contact with her lover was coloured by them. It was the first that held sway over her imagination. It was the second that vitally governed her actions. The second too insinuated itself like some exquisite drug into every sensual abandonment (not for nothing is it that the most desperate of sinners are the quickest to comprehend Christ's message).

And thus from the beginning she was careless of discovery. She wished if possible to spare her mother, and to this end, as also for convenience, could lie and scheme without scruple. But really she was indifferent to outside opinion, and it was probably this indifference that was answerable for the unfailing success of her schemes and her lies. Confidences apart, if one is at no pains to keep the truth from people they will scarcely ever suspect it.

True, there was something in Carl Nilsson's looks that betrayed him as a possible exception. But of this Joanna was glad. She often longed to speak to him of her life and her strange solitude ; but his own discretion kept her mouth shut. Phemie she would have told, had Phemie been in Glasgow ; but the information could not be committed to writing, and there was no one else in whom she wanted to confide.

In the absence of human counsellors she instinctively tried prayer. For a time it would often happen that while the mother was kneeling by her bedside, the daughter knelt also by hers, only a thin wall of lath and plaster dividing them as they sought along the same road for guidance and strength. And without doubt strength was given her—of a kind. Invariably she rose from her prayers happier, more serene, with reinforced endurance. But it was a sacrificial, deathly endurance, full of the exaltation of humility, exuding tenderness, pity and forgiveness towards Louis. And though it lifted and puffed up her spirit, somehow Joanna knew it was not good. She knew that such praying was a subtle indulgence and intoxication that she were better to abstain from. Some day she might learn another way of prayer. Meanwhile she thought she had gained a greater understanding of her mother's daily failure.

Probing for help in other directions, the girl now applied herself for the first time in her life with real eagerness to the world of books. Not till now had she apprehended the vital relation between that world and the world of actuality. And as it came home to her like a startling discovery she took to searching out in novels and biographies the cases that had anything in common with hers.

Unluckily the men and women in print were either so much nobler than Louis and she, or so much more depraved, or their circumstances were so entirely different, that their experience gave little help. She awoke in the process, however, to what had scarcely existed for her before—human character as distinguished from elementary emotions. It was one of Pender's fads that he could compose with greater freedom as well as more concentration if some one read aloud while he worked ; and Joanna, delighted by every new use he found for her, grew apt in the choice of books for that purpose. He liked her voice, was soothed by it, and often for long stretches she would hardly know how far any of the sense was reaching him through his primary absorption. But she was always re-assured in time by some sceptical or approving interjection. Best of all she was pleased when she could lead him on to the eager discussion of some point of conduct. They quarrelled most deeply over tragedy.

" People are like that," was his shrugging comment on the catastrophe in *Anna Karenina :* and he only smiled and went on painting when Joanna, with a whitening face, insisted that Anna could have saved the situation.

That was in the Carmunnock studio, now their securest meeting place. It was for their hours together there that Joanna particularly lived. Louis had taken it on a yearly tenancy ; for though he went often to London and abroad, staying away for months on end, Glasgow had for the time become his working head-quarters. The first panel and lunette in the City Chambers were finished some while ago, it was true, and it seemed doubtful whether he would be asked to do others there ; but to his amused pleasure a brewer with a castle on Loch Lomond had commissioned him (having seen the panel) to decorate the ancestral billiard-room. Between whiles he painted some portraits of Glasgow people (including Mrs. Tullis, of whom Joanna was secretly jealous, quite without cause) and in these portraits he experimented for the first time in realism. Whenever he wanted her, Joanna sat to him.

She lived for their hours together, but she lived—at any rate during that first year—in trepidation.

"My dear one! How nice you look to-day! "—If that were his greeting all was well. Louis would then be a god to her and a revelation. She loved the way he would speak of the wonders of the body.—"Every inch of you full of pores and ducts and odds and ends of things to make you live," as he put it. And he made her see what a marvel of balance it was that one could stand upright. "I think myself, you know," he had told her one day, looking at her very boyishly, "that a man has no right to go near a woman unless he feels, for the moment at least, that she's a goddess. I certainly feel so for you. On my word, Joanna, every time we meet it is a fresh adventure and you show me a new charm."

But it was not always like this with them. Joanna had learned to search his face swiftly as they met, and she kept the ears of a newt for his first utterance. She soon came to know and dread the comprehensive, slightly incredulous glance with which he could sum her up afresh. An unfortunate hat at such times could make him, it almost seemed, revise his whole opinion of her. And Joanna was not always happy in her hats. Once, in desperation at the prospect of a spoiled afternoon which she had read in his cool eyes, she had tossed the offending thing of straw and flowers high into a tree in the park where they had just met. But instead of sticking there, it had tumbled from branch to branch and down into the dust at their feet. And to her inexpressible mortification Louis, taking no pains to hide his annoyance, had made her put it on again.

And later on that same day he had ground her mercilessly between the mill-stones of his self-distrust and his rancour against life.

"Though I loathe things as they are," he confessed, "I don't really know what I want—what kind of a life."

Already that afternoon he had spat contempt at his work and harped on his middle-agedness with a peculiar disgust that sent despair like a shudder through Joanna's very flesh. Now, as his deep-set bitterness welled up in him, he struck out at her and at himself with equal savagery.

"I suppose I'm a coward," he girded. "Well, what's to be done about it ? If it's a hero you want, better have nothing more to do with me. It isn't too late. I've really done you no harm, have I ? My advice to you is—leave the old ship in time. Take a lesson from the rats, my dear. The worst of it is you are not of the rat tribe. You'd stick to me, I do believe. Why are you so good ? I don't think I want you to be so good. It only makes things worse for me."

By experience Joanna knew that whatever she might say would be wrong in reply to this outburst ; so she kept silent. It was in these tormented hours that she loved Louis most poignantly. But she was like a mother quite alone with a sick, deliriously fractious child when there is no doctor within miles. She would have done or given anything to restore him, would have forgone her sex if that had been possible (and sometimes she had the strange feeling that he desired this of her) ; but she could not tell his malady, and so was helpless.

When they had parted thus, she would wander in a limbo of blind and suffering endurance till their next meeting. Where was it, she questioned herself, that she failed him ? And again, how could she do aught but fail him so long as he would not take her wholly, wholly give himself ? Engirdled by the flames at La France Quadrant they had rushed together to assuage their immediate, mutual need, and she had fancied herself at last possessed. But with the dawn of the next day she had known that Louis no more than Bob, no more than Mario, had made her his. Nor had he committed himself to her. (This, though their love had emerged only the sweeter and the freer from that first embrace.) Dimly she realized that such a union as she desired beyond all desires was what her mother had in vain craved from her father through all the years of a marriage physically fruitful. Was it something that only women desire ? Did men fear and avoid the consummation of spirit it was bound to bring ? Or was it, whispered the sceptic in her, a lovely delusion ? There were, one must believe, certain false dreams—will o' the wisps—

which could lead the spirit disastrously astray. Was this such a dream?

But no! The absolute denial at least must be set aside. For there was Phemie's achievement with the unlikely Jimmie. Joanna could not tell how the knowledge had come to her that Phemie and Jimmie possessed the valid promise of what she herself desired. But there it was. She was sure of it. Could it be simply that it was a possession not given to such as herself, or to such as her mother?

All these wistful questionings, however, were apt to be dissipated by the next meeting, when Louis would be gay, loving, apparently at peace with the world. It seemed to Joanna then that if she were to suffer for ever, it would be light payment for the treasure he poured out to her. Then his superior age, his sex, his mind, were things for her to worship, not to wrestle with. She loved it that his judgments made her own seem petty and at fault, that he was kinder to human nature, more tolerant than she.

Also his richness of talent filled her with admiration. He had the tricks of music and of mimicry—could play by ear upon the piano with a sure delicate touch, could make his beloved rock with laughter by his beautifully sensitive imitation of a penguin in a hurry.

Or he would improvise a super-solemn dialogue on ART between Mrs. Lovatt and Val Plummer. His power of observation alone was a miracle to Joanna. During their very first meeting, he had shocked her by his oblivions. Now she became fully awake to her own dream-wrapt egoism. To please him—and in emulation too—she had begun to notice, to discover as if with new eyes the little, significant things of daily life. Also a sense of humour, long dormant, was pricking up in her like green blades in spring.

Was not this in itself a kind of consummation? It was certainly growth. And it brought with it so strong a sense of well-being that Joanna, sunning her unfolding petals, easily doubted the conclusions of sadder hours. Indeed the joy of a purely intellectual flowering is savoured all the more keenly because of the dark, unregarded fruits of death which are quietly ripening alongside.

II

Joanna and Linnet had formed one of those fluctuating friendships which may blossom at any time between two of the same family, especially when conditions in that family are becoming more and more impossible, and complete disintegration is at hand. The feeling between them had budded on that morning of Georgie's arrival, in the moment of dismay when Joanna had seen Linnet come out rumpled and lacklustre from his bedroom. Then during the hours of waiting on the quay, when they had shared the burden of their mother, the two had sent out signals to each other, signals of claim and distress, as might two sailors marooned upon neighbouring islands.

For a while, however, nothing had come of it. Joanna was far too much absorbed in her love, and her energies were too completely engaged in withstanding her lover's strange, recurrent exhaustions, to have anything to spare for her brother.

Yet it was through Louis that in due time the fleeting friendship was brought to flower.

They had been lovers a year, and Joanna was suffering from one of Louis's long absences, when she began with all the vigour of her awakened faculties, to handle a situation which till now had found her quite at its mercy. Of late something different from endurance (either of the stoical or the Christian variety) had stiffened itself in her. She knew that if she could not bring about a change between Louis and herself misery must ensue for both. And all that was most robust in her nature rose in a sudden demand for happiness, for happiness and fair play.

At the moment she was certainly miserable. It was the seventh time that Louis by his going had left her to an empty existence in Glasgow. That was what it had come to. Existence without him was a mere shell, a semblance, a waiting. Yet it appeared from his letters, that he all the while was contriving to lead a full enough, real enough life away from her. He spoke torturingly of his boys and their doings, of pleasant hours passed with friends, of successful parties in the newly decorated studio at Campden Hill. True, he wrote that things were only endurable because of her being there

in the background, that they would be intolerable were
it not for the thought of their next meeting. And Joanna
was happy in knowing that he meant what he said. But it
was not enough. Besides, if she in return were to write of
her hideous loneliness, he would be sure to reply in the distressed and powerless tone which she most dreaded. His
only suggestion—made for the hundredth time—would be
that she should come to London to live, as there he thought
things would be easier for them both. As if she herself were
not working towards London incessantly! But it would take
time as he knew. He knew she had promised her mother
to stay at home for at least another year until some satisfactory household arrangement could be come by. Meanwhile
she needed other comfort than that they should take things
as they came, remain cheerful in absence, make the best of
hours together.

It wasn't fair! Joanna had accepted it, borne with it,
even hugged it for twelve months and more. But it wasn't
fair! With a single irrevocable movement her characteristic sense of balance righted her.

And upon that conviction followed a definite withdrawal of
her tenderest self from Louis. If he would not have love
then let it be war. It was curious how her instinctive pro-
cedure tallied outwardly with his unwelcome advice. She
set about the separate, defiant enrichment of her own life.

And this was where Linnet, among other things, came in.

For in that separate, defiant enrichment of hers to which
Louis had driven her, Joanna grasped at any emotional
activity that offered.

She had known that Linnet had a lot of friends whom he
never brought home, though it was with them he spent his
spare time and all his holidays. She had known this, but it
had not concerned her. Now, as she hardened self-defen-
sively towards Louis, her shoot of tenderness for Linnet was
enlarged. For the first time she really listened, encouraging his confidence, and in so doing became in some measure
involved. It was clear that her brother and she and Louis
all suffered from the same *manie de la grandeur*. The form
only was different with Linnet.

All his friends were newly-rich. The girls were solidly
material in their worldliness and inclined to be fast. The
young men drank champagne with their luncheon at the

" North British," made a point of being seen about with the musical comedy star of the moment from London, and had always some " gemble " or other on hand at the Stock Exchange. They lived in suburban villas and had other villas at the coast. They kept motors and racing yachts. To Joanna their lives appeared ugly and on the whole vapid ; but to her new powers of observation nothing human came amiss. In some curious way too the mere fact of their wealth served her with Louis. Never meeting them, he learned of their doings only through Joanna's talk and letters, and he was childishly impressed and perturbed by the growing incident of her life apart from himself.

But what interested her to the point of horror was the transformed Linnet she now saw. It was evident that the Howdens, the Rintouls, the Bells and the rest (there were not above six families in this particular set) could not quite accept young Bannerman ("Linty " as they called him) as one of themselves. True, he dressed like them, like them wore his hat well back on his head, and shared in all their pursuits. But he was never able to invite them to his house, and always in his background there was the consciousness of a mother eccentric in ways prohibitive to the Bells, the Rintouls, and the Howdens. So it had come that Linnet, himself excruciatingly subject to his disabilities, had taken the only way open to his nature. He had traded on the family eccentricity, and in the circle he desired to enter, had constituted himself as clown. He had only to meet one of his gay friends, Joanna noticed, to be electrified into an almost frightening animation. Her heart ached for him as she watched him wave his arms about, and listened to his outrageous speeches. But what touched her to something deeper than pity was the unconscious isolation and contempt that lay beneath his fooling. He had succeeded in his aim. His friends rewarded his queer physical abandonment with laughter and a special kind of affection that apparently gratified him. He was both popular and privileged But his sister discerned in him something of the wistful, increative solitude which she had obscurely felt in her popular father. " A queer fish " his friends called him, and it was so he liked to think of himself. But as yet he had no being save in the shoal, and thus, not belonging there, had less being than they.

On his tentative introduction of Joanna, Linnet took a

slightly altered place in his friends' estimation and consequently in his own.

She was "uncommon looking," said the girls, and one of the Howden boys went so far as to fall in love with her for a whole fortnight. She tried to believe herself amused by this new phase of life, threw herself into it, and had the momentary satisfaction of rousing Pender's possessive instincts. But it could not last long. Before many weeks had passed she knew that Linnet was the only one among her new acquaintances to claim her sympathy, and the mushroom growth of her intimacy with the Howdens, the Bells and the Rintouls died rapidly away.

After all there were other things and far less tiresome that would answer the same end.

There was her work. She had discovered that Louis took an odd pride in her capacity to earn any money whatsoever. Accordingly she set herself to earn more, and soon with her fashion plates, and an evening class for teachers which she took twice a week at the School of Art she was making from £5 to £10 a month. This had the added advantage of bringing London nearer. Not that she had started saving as yet for that end. To Juley's grief all her daughter's money went, with an increasing extravagance of ideas, on self adornment. Nothing at this time was too good for Joanna, and she became noticeably elegant in her dress. Poor Juley had long and desperate confabulations with Eva Gedge over the child's growing worldly-mindedness.

III

A happier thing came when Carl Nilsson one day suggested that Joanna should go riding with him. In her immediate, joyful agreement she certainly had Louis again in mind, but she had also in mind her beloved rough-coated pony of the Duntarvie days. The idea in itself, that is, was congenial. Here was something far better worth spending one's money upon than anything to be had in the shops. And extravagance in clothing one's body appeared suddenly as a bore and a vulgarity to be dropped with Linnet's friends.

And after a few lessons in the great brown-befogged riding school which smelt of tan and ammonia, and echoed like a bath with raised voices and the thud of hoofs, Joanna became a good enough horse-woman. As she hastened to the mounting place her heart would flutter in her breast with delight. Her shining face on horseback often made Nilsson look at her with his sidelong, inquisitive gaze that was yet all friendliness, but when she asked him what was wrong he would only smile, praise her seat, and watch her cheeks brighten still more.

Henceforward she had few happier hours than those in which Carl and she went riding into the country together. Sometimes they would not start till Carl had done his morning's work, and on these days they would soberly jog out fifteen miles or so, probably in the direction of Killearn, alighting there at an inn for a dish of steak and onions better than any other steak and onions in the world. At other times they would wait until the later afternoon and go simply for a gallop in the fields about Milngavie. But Joanna liked it best on a Saturday : for then they could start very early, posting through the dark and misty autumn dawns, and pushing their way up through sopping little woods to high ground that they might canter forward to meet the rising sun. And it was after these rides that they went in just as they were, glowing and bespattered with mud and dew, to Sangsters for what Carl called " a hunter's breakfast "—porridge with cream, kidneys and bacon, toast and " baps " and " special " coffee, with a bottle of Graves to stand by. They were really merry these hunters' breakfasts. Though a table was kept apart for the riders, they always took possession of the place (half empty at that hour) with their rollicking spirits, and the waitresses seemed to participate. Carl had a ringing laugh that made the other late breakfasters or early lunchers turn their heads.

So it was that tales went round, and one day Eva Gedge reported the affair to Juley in such a manner that Juley unwillingly felt it laid upon her to remonstrate with Joanna. We ought, said she, to " avoid the appearance of evil." She herself " knew her children too well to listen for a moment to foolish gossip," but " dear Joanna must remember that she was still young and a widow, and it had pleased God to give her good looks beyond the average." At this most rare parental allusion to outward appearances Joanna stared. But she only kissed her mother with reassuring affection and went on her way.

The stables from which they hired their horses had been private at one time to a family mansion. This still stood at some distance, (the stables being on the outskirts of the grounds at a far corner) empty these several years and now waiting, blackly and squarely forlorn, for its demolition. But for some reason its surrounding gardens had been kept carefully tended : and especially before the early morning rides, when the grass and bushes were still grey with dew, Joanna keenly enjoyed the short cut which might be made by passing diagonally across the sloping lawns and shrubberies.

It was on one of these mornings that a new element was added to her pleasure in riding.

There had been a hoar frost the night before, whitening the grass, the trees, the high walls and railings, and Joanna crossing by herself to the stables with her skirt held up, left a trail of dark footprints behind her. There were no other tracks, so she knew she was the first to arrive. She could hear the groom chirruping beyond the stable wall, and the noise of nervous hoofs on the cobbles as he saddled the hacks— sounds that usually made her quicken her pace with an eager springing forward of her whole body. But on this morning she continued to walk slowly and without looking about her. She was absorbed entirely in the news received the night before, that Louis was on his way back to Glasgow. He was returning after a longer absence than usual, returning from Paris. She would see him the next day. His letter, full of devotion and hunger for her, was between her breasts at this moment, pressed close there by her buttoned-up riding-coat. And her heart was contracted with desperate longing and fear and joy.

But somebody was shouting her name. It was Carl, lower down in the garden behind her. She smiled automatically and turned round with a friendly gesture of greeting. This however was arrested midway, and her uplifted hand in its leather glove clutching a little riding-switch, dropped quickly to her side again.

For Carl was not alone. Lawrence Urquhart was with him—and dressed for riding.

Joanna was angered. As the two men came toward her, crisping with their boots through the short, brittle grass, she blamed first Lawrence, then Carl, and she met them with a blank face. Lawrence might, thought she, have kept away. He must know how impossible it was to carry out in practice his suggested friendship. The strain and futility of their few meetings during the past year (it was now eighteen months since his mother's death) should have convinced him of that. And since the last meeting, so long a time had elapsed that she had fancied him sensible to the situation. But here he was again. And now the rides would be spoiled!

As for Carl he was still more to blame than Lawrence. Carl, knowing, as she was sure he did, about Louis, had deliberately invited Lawrence to join them. It was wicked of Carl: no wonder he did not care to meet her gaze as he explained volubly that Urquhart had been having some lessons and only needed company to complete his enjoyment in the sport.

And to this tale Lawrence assented with a simplicity which astonished Joanna almost out of her anger. He had kept his dark eyes on her face while Carl spoke, smiling with a lively but baffling candour of pleasure. There was a perfect understanding between these two male beings that was like a conspiracy against her; and she resented it all the more that they were both so incomprehensible to her.

Incomprehensible they remained. But they had not ridden far with her before she recovered her good humour and forgave them—more than forgave them. After all—sang her quickened blood when they had got their beasts out of town and she was giving her companions a pounding lead round the gallop at the water works—after all they both knew how things were, and if they still liked to be in her company it was of their own choice. Before starting upon another breakneck round, she stole a look at Lawrence. He was only a tolerable rider, but on horseback as in the dance he escaped from his nervousness and was enjoying the exercise with a curious kind of still excitement. Though he used no enthusiastic expressions of pleasure Joanna knew that he had entered with her and with Carl into the spirit of the morning. A dark radiance emanated from him.

Soon a ride was not complete without him.

IV

To Louis Joanna made the most of these rides, and it pleased her to find that he was both envious (himself no horse-

man, and too old, he said, to learn) and jealous of her company
So now by severance was she learning to bind him to her. The
deep appeal for uncalculating union had failed : the sensual
appeal was erratic : now she was discovering a new emulative
relation in which the balance of power was re-established in
her favour. Once, laughing, Louis had told her of a Frenchman who, when asked if he believed in platonic friendship
between man and woman, replied—" Mais oui ! Après ! "
And undoubtedly as time went on, more and more of their
hours together were hours of sheer friendliness, especially on
the part of Louis. The suffering of these friendly hours fell
to Joanna, but she braced herself to bear it as something
inevitable. She could bear anything, thought she, seeing
Louis at peace. And he was often curiously peaceful in such
hours.

With the paintings he did of her he remained dissatisfied,
and he would not finish any. But he was constantly begging
her to sit.

" It is so strange," he exclaimed one day, " I always get
you better when I draw you from memory. Look at this ! "
And he showed Joanna a brilliant little figure drawing he
had done quite without notes when he was in Paris.

" There is your very self," he declared, satisfied for once,
" your movement—see that bold, beautiful action of the thigh.
—That is you—more you than the eyes in your head. And I
hope you admire the articulation of the knees, the fineness,
see there !—as it also is yours my pretty one,—more yours than
the nose on your face. Not that the face is so bad in the
drawing either, mind you. I've got you there too I think.
But of course the figure's the thing here. That's as I saw you
the day we took bread and cheese down to Loch Katrine :
do you remember ? And I dared you to bathe ! I'll not
forget how you looked, Joanna, running out to the water from
under those little hazel trees. I do believe I'll go on to my
dying day drawing you as you looked to me then."

Yet Louis did not offer her the drawing, and he took no
notice when she said she would love to have it.

She puzzled over this. At home, unknown to him, she
had a letter-case crammed with the treasured pen or pencil
sketches with which her lover habitually illustrated his talk—
scrawls done hastily on the backs of envelopes, on fly-leaves
torn out of books, on any scrap of paper that came handy.

But a serious drawing he had never given her, and there was no other material gift she could have wished to have from him. She had indeed been always deeply pleased, if also a little piqued, at his oblivion on the subject of presents. `She had liked it that in their goings about he would let her pay her share of things. For somehow she had known that he was not mean. She also knew that in spite of the sums he was now earning,— sums that seemed enormous to her when he mentioned them,— he was often really short of money. His personal habits were of the simplest, yet he was continually harassed by debt, of which he had a puritanical hatred. He had told her frankly that his London household was maintained in a manner beyond his means.

But all this was no reason why he should refuse her the drawing she so wanted, and she now begged for it, rather timidly.

Louis looked at her and moved his eyes away again.

" My wife hates me to part with any of my stuff," he said. " She has some kind of notion that it is her due, that if I were to die she would be provided for by having everything that wasn't sold in the usual way. As we live, you see, I can't save a halfpenny. She is queer about it perhaps but there it is. One way and another I owe her a good deal, and as I've been pretty filthy to her on the whole, I feel I must defer to her in this."

A chasm gaped in the little silence that followed. With his first words Joanna had suffered a hideous sinking of spirit. The very tones of his voice seemed echoing in response to some unsuspected hollowness in the world. She had a picture of her lover stamping with shamefaced bravado upon a vault in which his own dead body lay. Involuntarily she shut her eyes for a second. But she gave no other sign or word. She never again asked him for a drawing.

There were times when she felt she possessed him most in absence. When he was away he was in all she did, and she had increasing certitude that he felt his life vitalized by her. Never a letter-writer before, he had acquired, unasked, the habit of writing to her constantly and at length. He wrote from London, from Paris, from New York, from Moscow— flowing letters like his speech, and interspersed with drawings of people and things that had caught his fancy. (As his wife hated travelling he generally made his journeys alone)

His hand-writing came to affect Joanna like his bodily presence, made her tremble through her being when her eye lighted upon it. And in return she filled her letters to him with spontaneous but not wholly artless glamour. She knew so well these days how to pique and interest him that it cost her no effort, was indeed a keen excitement and enjoyment.

And their meetings became more like their letters—less stormy, less dependent on passion—except that in his presence Joanna played her part heavily burdened. Yet she believed it was a part worth playing. She had always one tale to tell, another tale to hear, and Louis revelled light-heartedly in the exchange. He often questioned whether they would have got one tithe of the fun and charm out of their experiences had these been matrimonially shared. The deadliest dinner party, he declared, became diverting when he had to describe it to her ; and the most common place events of her life, when she recounted them to him, were bathed in the light that never was by sea or land.

This then was their solution for the time. From their two years as lovers they emerged as two distinct and separate streams of existence. Momentarily they might and did flow as one. But they were never so much in unison as when they flowed apart, each sweeping outwards round a rich individual curve, each rushing in an opposite direction but ever onwards and ever with gathering impetus towards the next brief mingling.

v

Meanwhile life in La France Quadrant became every day more difficult. The business of housekeeping, even for so small a family, was too much now for Juley. She went weighed down with it, and people in the streets looked askance at her unslept face and dragging gait. She had her being in a cruel trough of muddle, released only when sleep overcame her, or when she could pray aloud with a companion, and so keep sleep at bay while she cried for succour. But she was vigorous still. She could not live in the house and see herself superseded by a daughter. At the utmost she would apportion only certain vague duties to Joanna ; and even here she was continually changing and fault-finding. At odd times, exasperating to one with work of her own to consider, she would make desperate appeals for daughterly help. Yet if Joanna tried unobtrusively to take some of the burden off her weary, indomitable shoulders, she was apt to resent it. A "companion" she would not hear of. "Treating me like a child or an idiot in my own house!" she exclaimed at the bare suggestion, and she would repeat the saying common with her "better to wear out, than rust out."

Both the remaining children knew that a change in their way of living would have to be made, and made soon. But what change? And how bring it about? In the frequent debates between them and their mother each was prompted by a secret, personal desire, and these desires were in conflict. Linnet longed to be in rooms of his own: Joanna was heading for London: Juley did not know what she wanted. Pierced as she was by the knowledge that her children wished to be gone from her, she yet clung to the familiar. She fought against any acknowledgment that it was failing her at every point.

But in March came the tidings that Georgie was engaged to a young man of whom she had made mention continually for two years past—a London doctor named Max Wyler— and at La France Quadrant the announcement was hailed with a special excitement. Apart from its ordinary interest it introduced a new and unexpected element into the family situation. At the least it would bring about an immediate and, as it were, official family conclave. For Georgie was coming home at once to be married (Max, she wrote, strongly disapproved of long engagements); and with her and her beloved (a Eugenist, she said he was) coming fresh to the problem, it was felt that some solution was imminent.

And at about the same time, cousin Mabel proposed a long visit. Mabel had been married for several years now in India, but on this her first visit home, was without her husband. Why should not Mabel also, knowing them all as she had done since childhood, have a voice in the Bannerman council?

Mabel did. She arrived looking as pretty and as shifty as ever (the East had hardly affected her peach-bloom complexion), and she was full of stories that proved how besottedly her husband was in love with her. Careful she was, too, to ask what had become of Bob Ranken. Subtly she smiled when she heard that he prospered and that Joanna still had an occasional letter from him.

And from the first Mabel was loud in her applause of the

fine new family plans which Georgie and her Max had evolved
between them, plans which were based on the separately
confidential letters Georgie had lately received from Joanna,
Linnet and her mother. (An astute man, this Max. Jewish,
by the irony of fate ; beautifully considerate and understanding with Juley ; giving her a new lease of life by permitting
her to regard him in the light of a possible convert ; charming
her with his persuasive tongue, his oriental, startling intelligent
eyes ; and exercising to the full upon her that magnetism
which only his enemies designated as the making of a clever
charlatan. Clearly, even to his enemies, a future lay ahead of
this tall and willowy young Hebrew with the curly black beard.
And how his Georgie adored him !)

Unfolded, his plans were these.

Joanna was to have her wish and go to London : (absurd
that she should neglect the chances of work now offering
there !) But she was to go, not merely, not even primarily
on her own account. She was to be a forerunner. With
Georgie married in London the mother too would surely have
to make her home there before long. She must of course
take her own time. And while Joanna was finding her feet, and
at the same time keeping her eyes open for a suitable house—
say in Hampstead (Georgie and he were to be in the Garden
Suburb)—no doubt Mrs. Bannerman would be glad to see
Linnet comfortably settled in Glasgow where his lot was cast.
For the present, a holiday from housekeeping was essential.
What was to prevent Mrs. Bannerman from spending the coming six months with her friend Eva ? Had it not been her
lifelong desire to devote herself to mission work ? Her children were now men and women. God had given her energy
and leisure. Many years of usefulness doubtless lay before
her. In London of all places, later on, when her strength
was restored, she could make her choice of congenial work.

How simple it all seemed after all ! Delightful. And so
full both of common sense and piety ! Mabel was almost
melting in her admiration of each point ; Joanna and Linnet
rejoiced silently in their different degrees ; Georgie looked
unspeakably proud and possessive of the new genius who had
deigned to confer himself on her family. Juley alone was
doubtful and had qualms. But even she had to agree in a
measure. Might not her doubts spring from lack of faith ?
She thought of the children her own eldest born was sure to

bear to this man—black-eyed, curly-haired babes with the blood of Abraham in their tender bodies. And deep within her soul the old hopes stirred afresh.

Georgie's wedding was a bourgeois but very happy affair in the drawing-room. A suitable minister had at first been something of a difficulty. Unfortunately Juley at the moment was in that particular stage of progression between two churches which debarred her from asking a favour of the pastor of either ; and it had of course to be explained that the new son-in-law was not more than tolerant at present of the Christian religion. A young missionary, however, who had just arrived at home on a holiday from Constantinople, was prevailed upon to officiate, and after that all went smoothly.

Max certainly behaved beautifully. At the way he kissed Juley's hand after the simple ceremony, Mrs. Boyd shed tears of joy : and seeing this, the bridegroom proceeded gallantly to kiss hers also, bending his long, elegant waist before her as if she were a queen. Even the laconic Linnet who gave Georgie away, had to admit that his brother-in-law was " a very decent chap, and clever, by God ! "

And some at least of the schemes suggested by Max in March were being carried out in practice three months later.

By June it was actually decided that Joanna should go to London. The other changes would follow ; though not— to Linnet's mortification—at once. His mother, after many prayerful but not wholly satisfactory colloquies with Eva, had decided to stay on with him until such time as a temporary and very humble niche should be created for her by her friend's kindness in the Lady Missionaries Training College. Linnet, she said sadly, would have long enough by himself later on. Besides for the next month or two Mabel was to be at La France Quadrant. Mabel had a year to spend in England, and she wished to devote a good part of that time to dear Aunt Juley. And Mabel had succeeded where others had failed, in coaxing Juley to hand over all the housekeeping for a few weeks at least.

VI

Before she left Joanna called on Carl Nilsson to say good bye.

Louis for some months past had been in London, and with

Phemie gone, Carl was the only person in Glasgow to whom she could really speak.

The little, grizzled artist looked rather sharply at her as, with a sense of dejection, she sat down on her own special chair in the studio (the same chair on which Phemie had perched on the afternoon of their first meeting). But for some minutes they only spoke of Phemie. On first reaching New Zealand things had gone hard with her. And she had been ill. But that she was happy, deeply fulfilled in her marriage, both her friends were assured by the tone of her letters.

And Urquhart ? Had Joanna had word lately of Urquhart at all ? asked Carl presently.

" He was passed over you know," he told her, " for the Folklore Lectureship—about two months ago. Yes, an outsider got it. Had she not heard ? "

But Joanna had heard nothing. It was three months or more, Carl must remember, since their last ride in his company. Didn't Carl recall it ? His horse had gone lame, and Lawrence and she had had to leave him behind at Milngavie ? She had never ridden since that day. She had been saving all her money for London (" As if *that* were the reason ! " said Carl's eyes), and she had heard and seen nothing of Lawrence since that day. She was sorry about his disappointment.

" And well may you be sorry, Signora Madonna ! " agreed Carl, looking as if he would gladly shake her. " I'm sorry too to have lost my pleasantest companion in Glasgow. Many a night has he sat where you sit now, talking with me till four in the morning. Many the good bottle we have emptied too, rearranging the world."

" Where—what—has he gone to London then ? " faltered Joanna with misgiving.

" No," Carl returned shortly, rising from his place. " No. You needn't be afraid. He's in Oxford, not in London *yet* ! He has gone to " scrub " as he calls it, for Manson, the anthropologist who soon brings out the last volume of *Arcana Promethea*—you have heard of the *Arcana* perhaps ?—a truly encyclopedic work on the evolution of culture For Urquhart I'm glad enough, though sorry for myself. It is work to suit him. He was in the marsh here—the *sluff* you call it ?—stuck and stagnant. There, he may find his rock-bottom. But Joanna—O ! my poor, stupid Joanna ! And all for a man that's as dead as dead ! Pfui ! "

At the onslaught, so unexpected and severe, Joanna flushed painfully and avoided her friend's shrewd gaze. In her heart there could be no misunderstanding of his words. The dead man he had spoken of was not Mario, not her dead husband. His words too had forced her to recall a confused but vexing memory. She was compelled to re-live that last ride which, owing to a mischance, had been taken alone in Lawrence's company. She saw again the muddy country lanes, darkness, the humid air of evening, and they framed the bitterness of a young man wounded in his manhood. She winced again under his reproaches. From below the hoofs of their horses, the thick, glistening mud had flown up at them, blackening the belly of Lawrence's tall, whitish hack ; and above them the dripping trees had bent over the road like the wires of a steel trap. How she had longed to escape from him and forget. And she had escaped, was going to forget ! But it was hateful that Lawrence had sat in this very chair and had talked about her to Carl. She wished never to see or think of Lawrence again. She was sorry, of course, that he had failed to get his lectureship. But she was glad, glad now without a single regret, that she was going to London. There would be no Carl there to reproach her. No Lawrence to love and accuse her. There would only be Louis. She would go her own way. No one should stop her

END OF BOOK II

BOOK III

CHAPTER I

I

JOANNA reached London on a Friday late in June.

She was met at Euston Station by Georgie, and carried enthusiastically off to her sister's beautifully hygienic home in the Garden Suburb. Without and within the house was all green and white. It suggested some very pleasant kind of institute rather than a personal dwelling place. Nevertheless its mistress had caused the name *Duntarvie* to be painted in clear letters upon the gate. Joanna duly admired everything.

But sincere as was this admiration of Joanna's, it was in no degree of the covetous sort ; and at breakfast on Saturday the elder sister was provoked to a considerable exasperation by the quiet obstinacy displayed by the younger on the subject of lodgings. It was not, she complained, as if Joanna could give any definite idea of what she did want. Why then should she be so positive in her refusal even to look at the rooms her brother-in-law had kindly bespoken for her, rooms green and white like Georgie's own, and so nice and near in a New Era boarding house opened only a week ago by one of Max's enterprising friends ? Joanna sat accused of prejudice by both Max and Georgie. But in vain. For she admitted it, and she did not see the New Era rooms.

And after luncheon she gave Georgie the slip, and within an hour, as if by instinct found herself in the region of Mayfair.

There she strolled about, ravished by glimpses of the Green Park and deeply pleased with all she saw. Here was the old order, beautiful and old-established, (a little dead perhaps at

271

the core—Georgie would certainly have called it rotten)
yet still by Joanna unpossessed. And what a finely grained,
modest surface it presented ! Here surely was the London
of Louis. Its appearance was extraordinarily touching to
her. Here she could have walked, thought she, all the afternoon and evening, seeing her lover on every hand : could have
walked for the sheer enjoyment of looking and finding him.
For that she should find in this Mayfair rooms for herself
seemed scarcely a possibility. Louis had warned her, laughing, that she would most likely have to be content with Maida
Vale or Kilburn or West Hampstead. And he ought to know.
He himself lived at Campden Hill. Mayfair indeed !

It was at this very moment that Joanna drew level with
a break in the low line of shops which now ran opposite.
The break was caused by a square, rather wide archway which
gave vent between the shops while leaving the dwelling-houses
above intact. That is to say it carried a room directly over
it. Joanna stopped and stared intently. It was a room surely
enough. It had an old jutting window which was bare of
curtains. And in that window all Joanna's dreams of a lodging in London were immediately crystallized.

She crosssed the road with a wildly beating heart.

She was still in Mayfair, but had slipped in her wanderings
into one of those little colonies of working people which are a
distinguishing feature of fashionable London. The more
prohibitive the quarter, the more certain one may be of finding
such a dependence tucked away in it ; and very often, as
in this case, it will happen that the dependence retains a living
dignity and a gaiety which have some time since departed
from the greater houses of the neighbourhood.

Here there was a smell of mews, and sounds of various
busyness came forth from the court to which Joanna's archway
gave entrance. Beneath the flat-faced old brick houses the
shops looked neat and prosperous, and shone with an attractive
light-hearted sort of respectability. On the left hand corner
of the archway an open fruit stall spread itself like a down-
turned fan that had been painted in bright, triangular sections,
green and red and yellow. On the right hand corner was an
undertaker's. Next door was a saddler's.

But it was upon the undertaker's that Joanna concentrated
her attention. For in this window, positively as if created
by her strong desire, a card was displayed. It advertised—

TWO UNFURNISHED ROOMS TO LET.

Apply 5 Chapel Court.

Several times over Joanna read this notice, and now all her longing was to discover whether one of the two rooms might be that above the archway. But so fearful was she of disappointment that she remained a full minute nerving herself for it. She stared at the card, at the discreetly elegant urn of polished stone against which the card was propped, at the three words—*Funerals, Cremations, Embalmings*—which, engraved in gilt upon some oak panelling, formed a chaste back-ground for the urn. Clearly a superior sort of undertaker's, this. Here were no brittle but imperishable wreaths under glass shades, no vaunting that *Pinking* and *Kilting* were done on the premises, no china scrolls bearing in black lettering the motto—"Lost, but not forgotten." *Reformed Funerals* was the reticent announcement across its plate-glass front ; and the dark grey urn, veined with a yet darker grey, was the only decoration.

Her courage in hand, Joanna entered Chapel Court and looked round it. How Louis would approve of this ! Some children played across the cheerful paved slope which was raised on one side above the level of the few little shops so that one would have to go down two or three steps to enter them. They were very small shops, like toy ones—a little news-vendor's, a little barber's, a little public house called *The Bird in Hand*. A washing fluttered from a sort of roof-garden where somebody had every reason to be proud of the petunias, perhaps still more of the nasturtiums. And the room over the archway had a window looking into the court as well. If only—if only she might show it as her own to Louis on Monday !

For till Monday she was not to see him. He was out of town till then. And it was a relief. On the threshold of her new life in London such a trembling had taken her. Louis in Glasgow she knew. But would Louis in London be the same man ? Would he find her the same woman ? Much, she felt, depended on their first meeting. Suppose it were unfortunate, one of their failures ? Suppose in London he no longer liked the look of her ? Coming along the streets that afternoon she had been studying the women with an almost painful concentration of inquiry. They had a look, a something that she lacked, and she felt sure her lover admired that something. If only she were certain, quite certain of what he felt for her!

As she searched for number five in the court, she recalled carefully the last talk between them.

" Do you love me ? " she had asked, and in the pause that followed, would gladly have withdrawn her question. But it was uttered now. No help for it! And she had waited miserably, furious with herself and with him.

" I believe I do, worse luck for me," he had said at length, giving her a quick, troubled glance. " But you needn't ask what I feel for you, Joanna. You must know perfectly well."

It was not the answer she hungered for, but she was thankful he had not simply replied with an impatient " Of course I do ! " And there had been a ring of rueful truth in his " worse luck for me."

But now she had found the door she wanted, a neat, moss-green door tucked away up three crooked steps in a corner. She knocked, waited, and at length heard the heavy, careful feet of a child coming down the stair inside. It must be a very steep stair thought she.

The next moment the door was cautiously opened and a very little boy, wearing a notably clean holland tunic, stood in the narrow aperture looking up at her.

Joanna looked down at him with eyes almost as grave as his own, and as she looked she hoped very much that he would like her. His curious seriousness, and indeed his whole small person was attractive to her. And this though there seemed to be something indefinably wrong with his proportions. He was not deformed, but his head looked too large for his rather dwindled limbs, a fault which was accentuated by the unusual thickness of his brown hair. And there was a look of premature intelligence in his grey, starry eyes, seldom to be seen in the eyes of a child who is not crippled.

" I saw the card in the window," said Joanna. " Is anyone at home ? " It took the little fellow a few moments to collect himself. He had a slight hesitation in speech, but the words when they came (saving that he could only pronounce *th* as *v*) were exquisitely enunciated.

" My Farver is out," he said, " and my muvver is out, My sister and I are at home. Muvver said she would be back very soon indeed. She is just *darting* to the chemist's."

Joanna smiled. Perhaps, thought she, his mother is a bird! The child himself, with his small figure squeezed between the barely-opened door and the jamb, looked not unlike a nestling whose wings are still absurd where flight is concerned.

" Do you think I could come in and wait till Mother comes back ? " she asked.

" I *fink* so, certainly," was the boy's well considered reply, and when he had spoken he widened the aperture where he stood and displayed a narrow, ladder-like stair covered with polished blue linoleum spotless as his tunic.

Joanna entered marvelling at his self-possession. He could not, she judged from his size, be more than six years old.

" I'm eight," he replied, however, to her question on this point—" and my sister is twelve. But I am small for eight," he added stoically, " and she is very long indeed for twelve."

Joanna asked him his name. It was Rodney Bannister Moon, he told her, which she thought a very nice, pretty name. And his sister—what was she called ?

" She's called Miss Moon," said he.

The visitor, feeling a rebuke in the perfect, bright gravity of this reply, asked no more questions. But as her host stumped manfully on his short legs up the stairs in front of her, he volunteered some further, and as it were pleasanter information.

" She's an invalid," he announced with great cheerfulness. " Would you like to see her ? She's been moving her head so nicely to-day, and when she opens her mouf I'm allowed to put a little sugar in. Just a *weeny, teeny* grain of course, or else it might choke her."

A door on the landing above stood open, and Joanna as she followed the boy wondering, had a glimpse of the little sitting-room to which he was leading her. It was a room (saving that the rug before the fireplace was littered with fine, curi-ously shaped pieces of metal) tidy to a scrupulous degree. And more than tidy indeed. For there were Dürer prints, hung with discrimination upon the plain, lavender walls, and an old diamond-paned bookcase stood opposite to the door, and in a corner, also visible from the staircase, was a Heppel-white music-stand with a violin-case beside it.

But once she had entered Joanna saw only a single object,

and it was none of these. It was a thing that lay flat on its back in a wicker spinal carriage near the window. It was an unhappiness from which, when one perceived it, it seemed wrong not to avert one's eyes. Yet one had to look. So this was Miss Moon !

Joanna looked, and looked again. She was thankful to have seen, with time for recovering herself, before the mother's arrival. And she was steadied by the unconcern of Miss Moon's brother.

" She had a fit this morning," he was saying, making polite conversation from where he was squatted on the rug, and without looking up from his interrupted work of piecing together the parts of a meccano. "When she has a fit, white stuff comes out of her mouf. But my Farver says it isn't the sugar really. My Farver says it is froff, like what a horse gets on its bit sometimes. You see "—he explained, summing up—" she's *afflicted*, that's what it is."

Joanna who had sat down in a little rocking-chair, looked again at the stricken one by the window, and she looked this time differently. The boy's way of regarding his sister as a wonderful sort of live doll had curiously cleared and altered her vision. Her first horror was gone, and looking simply, a child herself for the moment, she saw that the still face was beautiful. The close-cropped skull, its sharp temples so transparent and blue-veined, was shaped for splendour, and noble brows guarded the vacant, long-lashed eyes. In the piteous mouth alone was any trace of suffering visible. The clear eyes and forehead, the dilated nostrils, fragile as porcelain, had no recollection of the pain by which they had been purged into what they were. Miss Moon was like some seashell, delicately empty, cast high upon the beach, which it has taken the whole cruel ocean to blow into shape, to flute and carve and lave to a foam-like whiteness. Her long—surprisingly long—body (could it be that she was only twelve ?) was covered by a Jaeger rug, and no movement showed anywhere saving when the tapering, filigree fingers twitched, tinily convulsive, on the woolly, fawn-coloured stuff.

At the sound of a latch-key downstairs, Joanna rose instinctively from the rocking-chair. At being found here like this she felt somehow guilty.

"That's my Muvver," quoth Rodney undisturbed in his playing—if the word " play " could be applied to anything so intent as his occupation. And the next moment his mother entered.

At first in the rather dim light of the room—for a thunder-storm was gathering outside and the sky had darkened within the last ten minutes to a threatening degree—Joanna took Trissie Moon to be a woman little older than herself, that is to say some years under thirty. She was noticeably neat in figure, girlishly quick in movement, and her face with its dusky hair looped curtain-wise over the ears, seemed very youthful in the shadow of a mushroom-shaped hat.

" Have you been waiting some time ? I'm so sorry ! " she exclaimed with an exaggerated, slightly jarring brightness. (She was your hostess apologizing for lateness to an invited guest.) " That Knaggs man, you know, will talk and talk. All I wanted was to get Roddie's bottle re-filled ; but he would ask about Edwin, and were we going away at all this summer though we couldn't go last, nor for that matter the summer before. For he has a brother-in-law, he says, who could give us very moderate rooms at Dymchurch, a man called Stabb who plays the 'cello : and he thought Edwin and this man Stabb, if only they could find a third, might get up some trios of an evening. It would certainly please Edwin. I'll tell him about it to-night. But I doubt if it could be managed.—And all this time you have been waiting ! " she broke off—" Well, I hope Sonny has done the honours."

As the mother caressed her child's head with one hand (he ducking away from her impatiently) she took off her hat with the other, pressing her wrist against her brow a moment as if to placate a permanent ache there. And Joanna saw then how superficial had been that first impression of youthful-ness.

Mrs. Moon's face with its small, almost infantine features, had been cruelly used by trouble and the years. Under the greyish skin there was a bruised look—the dull yellow and purplish marks of irreparable fatigue ; and the tiny ruptured blood-vessels of effort beyond recovery, alone gave other colour to her cheeks. Her eyes were strangely dilated, still more strangely smiling, as if to deny with their final glance that her life was as a cord perilously stretched—near, ever so near to breaking point. On she talked with a rattling inconsequent gaiety of Mr. Knaggs the chemist, of Roddy, of Edwin (whom she took for granted Joanna knew to be

Mr. Moon and no other), of summer holidays in the long past, in the highly debateable future.

Very soon her listener had to abandon any attempt at following the ins and outs of a tale, for the understanding of which an essential was some familiarity with the people and events so freely referred to by the teller. Instead she used her energy to fight down the sensation she had of watching a sleep-walker who strayed along the precarious edge of a cliff. In time, however, by putting in a question now and then she did gather that the rooms of her quest were empty through the perfidy of somebody or other. Edwin, the unpractical, declared Mrs. Moon with a wild little laugh, had only lately abandoned his notion of turning the one upstairs into a music-room, the one over the archway into——

At this point, Joanna overjoyed, succeeded in making an interruption. Was the room over the archway then really one of the two that were to be let ? And if so, might she see it ?

Full at once of apologies, Mrs. Moon showed her the rooms in question and wanted to conduct her all over the house.

But a glimpse was enough.

Small the rooms were, but what did that matter ? They were attractive in shape, and had clear distempered walls, upstairs grey, over the arch, white. And they were cheap. While her landlady resumed her nebulous family history, determined to be impressive yet still more anxious to remain obscure, Joanna busied herself by furnishing her new quarters in thought. Upstairs she would sleep. Over the arch would be her studio. To every one of Mrs. Moon's ambiguous suggestions about charwomen, latch-keys and the like, she replied that that would do very well. Nor would she wait to see Mr. Moon whose return from a professional engagement was expected at any moment. Rather by the piecing together of evidence than from any definite statement, she had discovered that Edwin was employed in some important capacity by the undertaker downstairs.

As she crossed the road again on her return, Joanna looked back at the archway and at her window above it. No dwelling in her experience—not the house at Collessie Street, not the brown villa at San Gervasio, not the whitewashed farm of Duntarvie itself—had been so dear to her as this was going to be, this place in London of her own finding.

And on Monday she would bring Louis. He should see!
Kilburn, he had said: Maida Vale: West Hampstead!
It was in Mayfair she would live, and nowhere else. As her
pleased eye passed to the window of the shop below, her lover's
face as she would see it two days hence, rose vividly before
her. "So convenient too!"—she could hear him speaking,
could see the whimsical, affectionate twist of his lips.—"So
very convenient: you can be buried whenever you like!"
No longer had she the slightest fear of the coming meeting.
Everything would be all right now. And she stood there in
the middle of the road in Mayfair, and laughed with satisfaction.

II

In Joanna's life hitherto, no period had contained so prolonged a rapture of enjoyment as the six months that followed
her entering into possession of the room above the archway.

Louis in London was better than Louis in Glasgow in fifty
ways. His spirits were both higher and more equable; he
was kinder, yet at the same time far more passionate. And if
he was also busier, telling her seriously each time they parted
that his punctual appearance at their next tryst might be
prevented by circumstances unforeseeable, this was largely
balanced by two facts. One was the geographical fact of his
nearness: the other the physical fact of her own entire freedom. There was a telephone downstairs in the undertaker's
office at Chapel Court, by which means he would be able
to warn her of any ordinary changes in his plans, and by
this same means at certain hours of the day Joanna knew she
could have speech of him at his club.

But so far in these five months Louis had never once failed
her, and she had begun to doubt the possibility of such a thing
happening. Neither had he been away from London longer
than a couple of days at a time, saving for two weeks during
August, the two empty weeks which Joanna spent quite
happily in Scotland with her mother and Linnet.

From the very first a fresh element of delight had entered
their meetings. On the Monday after her arrival she had
flown confidently to the place appointed between them, and
that evening had returned to Georgie, radiant as from a corona-
tion. Louis had betrayed extravagant gladness at seeing

her, had been lost in admiration of Chapel Court and everything therein, had generously given her the credit not merely
for finding it, but for a dozen charms he was the first to see
there, had himself re-discovered the beauty of the Green Park
in his delighted showing of it to her. To her joy she had gone
up instead of down in her lover's eyes by comparison with the
London women whose rivalry she had feared. And in her
eyes his face in the new environment had acquired a fresh,
peculiar quality of intimacy which was inexpressibly dear.
By his glances, and by many small, involuntary movements of
guardianship as he piloted her about the streets and watched
over her impressions, he seemed to acknowledge a responsibility she had not once thrust upon him. It warmed and
established her to feel his real care for her happiness : it
touched him to chivalry to see how simply that happiness
was attained. He laughed at her childish jubilation over the
furnishing of *Number Five*. Yet of the two it may be questioned whether he were not the greater child. He regarded
both her and her house as his most exquisite playthings.

And all these joys, this delicious newness of enjoyment
after nearly three years of love, were heightened by a season of
surpassing beauty. A fine, very hot summer was succeeded
by an even lovelier autumn, and every sunset seemed to
participate in Joanna's elation.

On the June morning when she went forth alone to buy her
first chairs and tables, it would not have surprised her had
her half consumed body been drawn up swiftly through space
till it was lost in the life-giving, life-taking heart of the sun.
A man passing along the gutter of Tottenham Court Road
had boards hanging from his shoulders.

THE LORD HIMSELF !—Joanna read thereon—
SHALL DESCEND FROM HEAVEN WITH A
SHOUT !

—and instinctively, expectantly she had looked skyward.
There would need a god, no less, appearing in radiant omnipo-
tence, to comprehend such ecstasy as hers.

And surely that god would wear the transfigured face of
Louis himself ! Louis had been better than his word. He
had given her the world. London was hers like a jewel.
And how easily she wore it ! She was already at home, without shyness, in the Moon household : with a few introductions

given by Carl and by Mildred, she had soon found she might enter almost any studio she pleased : by means of her cousin Irene she could if she chose, make the passage to more conventional society. And at the back of all these manifestations of worldly fulfilment stood Louis. But for Louis not one of the paths opened by circumstance would have profited her. Because of Louis she tripped along them with the light feet of success. And because of Louis she needed none of these paths at all. For worldly possession also is a spiritual achievement.

III

It was four o'clock on a cold but fine afternoon in November when Joanna set out to pay her first call upon Cousin Irene.

She had asked Georgie more than once to come with her, but Georgie had refused with bridal self-importance. She would think, said she, of leaving cards on Irene when Irene had been to see her. She, not Irene, was the new married wife. Besides only let Joanna think for a moment of how Max compared in any scale of public importance with Irene's husband. ("Rising M.P. indeed!" exclaimed Georgie in hearty scorn. "That he may have been when Irene married him. I told Max that was what they called him in the *Scotsman*. But Max says he has done no more rising since than a piece of unleavened bread.") For Joanna to go was quite different—Georgie allowed that. Indeed she took to urging her younger sister to call and report. Irene's children, whose pictures she had seen in the illustrated papers were apparently very pretty. But all girls ! And at this observation Georgie had smiled mysteriously. It would appear that she herself had a foreknowledge of being the mother of sons.

So Joanna, upon a day just five months after her arrival, had arrayed herself in her London clothes and betaken herself to Bryanston Square where Irene's house was. It was now some time since she had acquired, partly by the help of Louis, still more by instinct, the outline of a fashionable young woman. And with that had come what she had so envied her cousin long ago—a free, self-contained assurance of manner. Yet on an occasion of this kind she could not escape a half-amused consciousness of masquerading.

She felt something of this now as she sailed gallantly up the very middle of her cousin's flight of steps and rang the bell. Surely the servant opening the door would see through her disguise! Or if the servant should be deceived, Irene with a glance would strip her naked and expose her in her ineradicable wildness.

While she stood there, loosening her dark furs and glancing over her shoulder at the square, two men passed along the pavement. One was young, the other middle-aged with a fine worldly face and great pouches of well-survived dissipation beneath his keen eyes. Both looked up at her, and from head to heel she was sensible of their approval. As she watched their course to the corner a few yards off, glad that their courtesy forbade a backward glance, she knew as if she had heard their speech that when the elder turned his head to the younger it was to praise her. Then, masquerader or no, she was accepted by this London at its best!

But even more than to her own success, Joanna at that moment had been alive to the attractiveness of the two men simply as male creatures. And here, strange as it may seem, was an experience unknown to her before her coming to London. Till then she had been penetrable only by an individual fascination. But now, in her awakened state so long deferred, all the tortured, sighing boys, all the cynical men of experience, all the world-weary elders might have taken her. It was by their ignorance alone that she went safe among them. Or perhaps by the fact that in Louis she possessed them all.

Just as the two men went round the corner—the younger only then permitting himself a swift half turn of the head in Joanna's direction—Irene's glossy double doors, which till this moment had confronted the visitor forbiddingly, were flung wide with a great show of hospitality by two smiling, be-streamered maid-servants.

"Just like Aunt Georgina's!" thought Joanna smiling, but not without a shiver of the old terror, as she passed in between them. She recollected a remark made recently by her cousin Mabel, that the house in Bryanston Square was but a reproduction brought up to date of the parental home in Edinburgh. It had been a crank of cranky old Lord Westermuir's that two women, and not the butler, should attend the front door of a town house: and many a time poor Juley, gathering her brood about her skirts for the ordeal, had likened herself to that pilgrim whose way ran betwixt two lions.

In the drawing-room Irene was combining the parts of hostess and Mamma before an audience of two women friends, and she afforded the vaguest of fashionable introductions to her cousin. Joanna found her less fluffy than of old and more substantial. The attractive frothiness had disappeared in favour of body, as it will with a glass of ale which has been let stand a while. Indeed with her fair hair, and her dress of smooth yellowish satin, Irene might well have conveyed the suggestion of pale, full-bodied ale, had not Joanna from the first moment been constrained to ransack her small zoological memory for an analogy still more apt. A camel! That was it! Cousin Irene was like a camel. But she was like such an elegant, well-tended and most lofty full-grown camel, that Joanna, even while she laughed in secret, was impressed and rendered slightly nervous.

The three children in their white embroideries and crisp ribbons had but that minute emerged from the nursery for inspection, and the sunny-haired cherub of a baby sat in Mamma's silken lap and played with Mamma's long amber necklace. They were sweet-looking little girls enough. But for the life of her Joanna could not see them as other than elegant, well-tended little camels—just three camels like Mamma, saving that for the moment they were blessed with youth. And her thoughts reverted with passionate preference to that other group of children she had come to love in Chapel Court. There was poor beautiful Edvina whose soul was gone elsewhere, there was Roddy with his intent jewel-like eyes, and there was little Ollie Garland, a neighbour's child, round-faced and timorous, who came almost daily to play in Number Five while her mother sought a precarious foothold in Fleet Street. What had these three that was wanting in Irene's glossy babies? Wherein lay the essential difference? That it was not merely external she felt sure. Convinced as Joanna was of her own correctness in all outward appearance, she felt exposed beneath the glances of Irene's friends. And even the children—or was this her fancy only?—seemed to watch her closely and defensively, as they would have watched some being of another species. As for Irene herself, one could hardly be insensible to the curiosity, the hostility, the calculation of her travelling eyes.

There it was: Joanna and her kind were different, and always would be different from Irene and Irene's kind, and as she replied formally to Irene's perfunctory family inquiries, this difference became even more manifest. Joanna now possessed the world as Irene would never possess it, but for that very reason she could never be of a part with its essence.

But happening to introduce Pender's name into the flagging conversation, and seeing the quickening of interest in the faces of Irene and her guests (Cousin Mabel had also said that if Irene might not regard any given London celebrity as a friend, that celebrity must be at least "the friend of a friend") Joanna's first conception of her difference contracted into a pettier defiance.

Could it be that something in her looks had betrayed her secret? Of a certainty she had not till this moment realized how increasingly during the past six months she had been forced into thinking of her love as an intrigue. With the flaming up of passion between herself and Louis in the new environment, had come the increased necessity for secrecy. Here he was among his friends. If Joanna wished to keep their happiness she must guard it jealously, must measure its safety continually by the world's standards. It had been easy to blind herself to these exigencies by the very ardour with which Louis had imposed them. Never had he showed himself so fearful of losing her: and was not that enough? But now, as Irene went on to ask why Georgie had never called, and, with a drawl accentuated to conceal a more genuine curiosity, put questions about Georgie's husband (clearly known by repute both to her and to her guests) Joanna had a swift horrified glimpse of herself rather as the world's prey than as its possessor. Was this the price demanded? A chasm of misery and shame seemed to open beneath her feet.

As soon as she could, she rose and made her escape. Irene had announced her intention of calling upon Georgie within a few days; had accorded an invitation for one of her forthcoming "evenings" to Joanna. The visit was over.

IV

Once in the open air she was happy again. It was as if she were rushing from Irene's doorstep to meet again her own palpitating and lovely existence, left there waiting outside in the street.

Though winter had followed early upon autumn, a beautiful day was expiring with the lighting of the lamps, and the young, living woman drew the blue and gold freshness of the West end square into her lungs with an access of vigour which in itself was delight.

She was going to meet Louis in Piccadilly. They would walk awhile, and then return together to Chapel Court where supper was prepared. For a wonder he had not only the late afternoon but all the evening free. And Joanna had strung Chinese lanterns across her archway room for welcome and delight. Again and again during the day she had lived beforehand through that moment when the door would be shut on the outside world. Into that first embrace would go the emotion of her solitary morning's work, her strong attraction by the two passing men, her scorn of Irene, her tenderness for Ollie and Roddy, her voluptuous breathing of the elixir of London. Louis should have them all.

A clock struck half-past four, and though her tryst was for a quarter past five, Joanna fell into a panic at the strokes of the bell and hailed a taxi-cab, asking the man to take her to the nearer end of Bond Street.

After five months in London she was still strangely ignorant of directions. Mention Regent Street to her and she would see a wide current of sparkling shallows down which she had often gone in a gay drifting from pavement to pavement drawn now to one side, now to the other, by the lure of the' shops on either hand. Speak of Trafalgar Square, and there would rise a great tilted expanse of stone—stone palaces full of treasures surrounding it—dazzling white clouds above it—a man walking past the iron railings of a church with a basketful of tulips on his head—yellow and scarlet tulips that had bright blue paper wound about their stems——Louis had kissed her in Trafalgar Square—suddenly, unexpectedly, had kissed her in broad daylight—amid the sound of fountains, blown spray, the calling of high, children's voices——. But put Joanna in Regent Street, and ask her to point the way to Trafalgar Square : and she could not have done it.

Set down however by her taxi-cab at the northern corner of Bond Street she felt herself fairly safe afoot for Piccadilly (unless indeed—always with her a possibility—the streets during the past night should have been dissolved and crystallized anew). And her reason insisted further that she had

fully thrice the time the walk needed. So with her mind
tolerably at rest she took her way at leisure among the other
leisurely, well-groomed men and women.

She went gazing with discretion, now at the people who
fascinated her by their sophisticated faces and movements,
now at the jewelled windows of the shops, now at the pure
and quivering sky that arched itself like an iridescent bubble
over many-masted London.

And once, not so long ago, she had hated this same London!
On the brief visit before her marriage, and upon her return
as a widow, during the few days spent with Georgie, it had
oppressed her almost to death. But now Louis had given it
to her like a plaything, and she carried always in her breast
a secret talisman of passion.

It was hers, all hers—the mounting sky, the decorous
people, the precious stuffs, the gold and silver and rubies
brought together from the ends of the earth. Only a trifling
accident of circumstance prevented her from laying immediate
hands upon those of her treasures which she most fancied at
the moment. Her essential knowledge of possession was no
whit disturbed by the unimportant fact that behind any of
these shining panes she would be asked to pay money before
she might carry her own goods away. Not all the riches of
Solomon will buy such a sense of possession.

Besides, in money also Joanna felt herself rich. She had
come to London with a hundred pounds—part her own savings, part a gift from her mother, and for the present she was
being allowed as well seven pounds a month. Soon she would
be able to write home and declare herself independent of this.
From the first, by her keeping in touch with her Glasgow
employer, the draper, irregular sums had come her way ; and
lately through one of Carl's London introductions, a new and
steadier means of earning had presented itself. This involved
the sketching of dresses at the theatre, a pursuit bringing with
it considerable excitement. For Joanna at the theatre was
still easily carried away by the glittering show of the world
there spread so cunningly before her. It was the theatre
rather than the play that affected her. And so it was with the
more experienced Louis. Did they go together, it was to
musical comedy. Joanna had no choice, and Louis, with only
occasional lapses into boredom, liked the music, the prettiness,
the absurdity, the deliverance from contact with reality

there to be found. Also he would point out how much more grateful to the eye were the audiences attending this kind of piece.

Afterwards they would quarrel happily over the catchy tunes. "No! You go wrong there! This is how it went!" Louis would cry, clapping his hand over Joanna's mouth. "Ta-ra-ra-tiddy-iddy-iddy-um-ta-tum!" And she would dispute it, until at length they got it right between them with a warm, unbounded sense of friendship.

There! Just as Joanna came within sight of the Piccadilly traffic, a piano-organ struck up one of the airs she and Louis had first heard together four months ago at the Gaiety. Since then how many recollections must that same refrain, repetitive as the call of a bird, have stored within itself for a thousand scattered lovers! To Joanna it recalled every least incident of their return from the theatre that breathless midsummer night when the stars had been like a million golden bees swarming in the dark hive of the sky.

And now, drawing nearer and nearer to the end of Bond Street, walking more and more slowly, vibrating with greater and greater violence to the surety that Louis, if not already there, was hastening towards the place, Joanna felt afraid. The passers-by must see her, thought she, moving among them like a blazing torch dangerous to their safety. And seeing her so, would they not contrive to put her out of being? She had the real fear that they would. But even if they did not, must she not of herself be consumed, must she not unhindered shoot upwards, a mere dissolving flame?

IV

But when she saw the face with which her lover was hurrying towards her, her heart dropped like a shot bird.

"I'm so sorry, my dear; so frightfully sorry—" he began to speak at once and with rapidity almost before they had met—"I can't tell you how sorry I am, how disappointed: but our evening has fallen through. What's her name— Marietta, my new daughter-in-law, has turned up. It was at the last moment and quite unexpected. How I got here at all I hardly know. But I remembered the telephone was no use to-day as you were going out early, and I hated to fail you altogether."

Side by side they turned, instinctively shunning the bustle

of Piccadilly, and they had walked some way up Dover Street
before Joanna could speak in reply. All her being, so exult-
antly exposed till a moment ago, now laboured under the
reverse it had suffered. It would take her a little while to
recover.

"You know, my dearest heart," pleaded Louis anxiously,
his eyes on her unhappy face. "If you are to be so upset
when this happens, we shall have to make an end. You must
know it can't be helped at times. Come: cheer up! I can
tell you it is as bad for me as for you. Worse perhaps. I
was living all day to-day for the evening. That dear little
room of yours. You know I was. You know there isn't a
place on earth where I'm half so happy, so peaceful? You
do know?" he urged, touching her arm appealingly as she remained silent. "Don't you? Say you do!"

"Yes."

"Well, then?"

But while they drank tea in a shop—Louis having decided
that he might risk just ten minutes longer with her—he fell
to talking quite gaily of his son's wife.

"She's a nice, charming girl," he declared. "I must
say it. With the most splendid yellow hair you ever saw in
your life." And he kissed the tips of his fingers to the air
in worship of Marietta's tresses. "Rather a fine person in
herself, too, I shouldn't be surprised," he added more soberly.
And he went on to hope that Marietta would sit for him. But
he suspected she was already in the way to make him a grandfather.

"Me! A grandfather, Joanna! Think of it! I'll have to
reform my character, shan't I? Yet how preposterous that
anyone should regard *you* as a siren who is leading my grey
hairs to perdition!"

Perhaps Louis however was not so sure after all. Anyhow
within two minutes he was bewailing that he and Joanna were
lovers.

"I so often long," he confessed, "to have you up to the
house and show you off to my friends. There's to-night. I
know you would like Marietta and she you. We could have
all sorts of pleasant times. And I'd be so proud of you. But
things as they are, spoil all that. Do you remember my
bringing old Perrin out to Chapel Court to see you? And
how horribly self-conscious we all were?"

Joanna assented but without speaking. Somehow, though Perrin had been as friendly and courteous as possible, she could not bear to be reminded of his visit.

"You are too good for this kind of thing, Joanna. That's the trouble," said Louis, gloomy and worried. And he looked at his watch.

(What a strange echo was there of something Bob had said long, long ago!) Joanna lifting eyes full of pain to his face, mutely opened her lips once, twice before the words came.

"Is any woman too good to be loved?" she asked at last.

He gave her a startled glance and his mouth, formed a word of sincere response, but he checked himself and veered off impatiently.

"What's the use of talking?" he protested. "With you and me it had to be like this, and that's all about it. Besides, hasn't it been worth it? If it were all to end to-day, hasn't it been worth it again and again? For me it has. I shall never go back on that. But for you?"

"For me too," answered Joanna looking at him sadly. And even though her lips shook, she repeated the affirmation steadily, like a knell.—"For me too."

"I'll tell you what!" said he, leaning forwards towards her with energy. "I'll tell you what, Joanna! All the rest of life is either a labour or a bore. That's what it comes to. And it may be as well to keep love quite separate. 'Better face facts,' a man said to me once, 'and never mix up love and marriage.' And there is some truth in it, don't you think so? Come!" he continued, rallying her affectionately. "Dear, pretty one, you mustn't look so sorrowful. Tell me—I have only two minutes more—tell me where you were calling this afternoon? Was it on friends of your sister? Garden Suburb people with sandals and djibbahs?"

Doing violence to herself, Joanna gave Louis quite a lively account of the visit in Bryanston Square. He laughed at her descriptions of camels great and little, and showed interest when she mentioned the name of Lady Pilkington as one of Irene's guests.

"Pilkington? Why that must be the explorer man's wife?" he interrupted. "Perrin is always talking of bringing them round. He pointed them out one night in the theatre. Is she good-looking? She made no impression whatever on me.

But what a fine ugly brute the man is ! I'd be glad of a chance to paint that queer, almost devilish, triangular mug of his ! "

Louis pondered for a moment.

"I'll tell you a secret, my girl," he continued warmly. "And you alone, mind ! Of late I've got a fresh glimpse of things. If only I could somehow beat out to it, I believe I should see my new way clear."

For Louis to speak in this way of his work was rare. And when he went on with diffident excitement to describe to her the beginnings of a new picture, Joanna was far more stirred than by words of love. Was this at last the budding between them that she had longed for ? If so Louis was hers, she his, even though the solid world should sunder them. She need have no fear.

She was unhappy again, however, when the conversation returned to Irene, and with a heat astonishing to herself, she was presently championing the people of the Garden Suburb by comparison with the Irenes and the Pilkingtons. The discussion indeed was rapidly assuming the features of a familiar quarrel between them.

"I know what you mean," said Joanna antagonistically, when Louis with hardening eyes had re-stated his inveterate preference for the world of fashion, "I know Georgie's friends are rather 'awful.' But they really are interested in ideas, and the Irenes aren't. Isn't that a great thing ? "

Louis looked elaborately bored.

"It may be," he conceded in fretful hostility, "though I think it's open to question whether these dire-looking people who take themselves so seriously are really the ones to help things on. Whether or no, I can't help my own liking for more conformable society. Can I ? "

To this Joanna agreed, but unhappily. For there had been that in his voice which proclaimed a discord in himself. And, as many a time before, she had the torturing vision of him as a man torn in twain.

But now, their ten minutes being long exceeded, he must go his ways and she hers.

"Pay no attention to my moods," he begged at parting. "Remember that, anyhow so far as you are concerned, they mean nothing. Things are difficult for me ; that's all. For you too, my dear. Don't I know ? You need never tell me. I know everything. I appreciate everything more than you can ever guess. It is never out of my mind what you do for me, what you are to me. So, Joanna, bear up if you can. You are the good thing in my life. Don't leave go of me. Without you I should be in the mire."

Next moment he was gone in his taxi-cab leaving her alone.

v

She walked back to Chapel Court, and all the way she was trying to draw the sustenance she terribly needed from her lover's parting words and demeanour. Her efforts met with some success : especially when she dwelt upon the last look he had given her, a look of solicitude that was at once sincere and helpless. But she no longer flitted through the streets like a flame. She went weighed down, unconscious of all about her, quenched, closed in upon herself, slow-moving as a deep-sea diver.

Since her coming to London, there had been only one incident to match with this. It had happened months ago, and had since been made light of in memory. But under present stress it came back to her with vengeful clearness.

Rather early one morning she had been alone in town, and was crossing a part of Oxford Street almost clear of traffic at that moment, when an open taxi-cab drove quickly past. In it was Louis, with another man towards whom his face was turned in laughing expostulation. Though Joanna was already near the middle of the roadway he did not see her. And next moment he was gone.

It was nothing of course. Joanna knew that as well as anyone could. She was well aware that Louis must inevitably drive about with friends in taxicabs, just as he walked, talked and ate with men and women she never saw, men and women who, taken together, were as nothing in his life compared with herself. She fully realized also that it was by mere accident she had now for the first time seen him entirely out of contact with herself. To-morrow he would be sure to tell her all about his companion, his destination at that early hour, even the subject of his expostulation. And they would laugh together over her spasm of jealous emotion.

But it *was* the first time. And there Joanna had stood, in the middle of the roadway, quite bereft, and staring after the taxi-cab as if in its swift passage it had snatched her very soul from her. Another driver had to shout at her in a fury.

He had only just saved himself from knocking her over.

Yes, in the face of all reason it had been a bitter experience. The sense her lover had conveyed of inhabiting a world from which she was excluded, his animation, his complete unconsciousness of her presence, the impossibility of thrusting her presence upon him by a gesture—these had been bitterness. And in these he had played but an involuntary part. In this new failure he was both conscious and acquiescent.

With deathly apprehension Joanna beheld a future full of similar failures,—involuntary failure alternating with failure that was voluntary. It was not to be borne.

But why was it not to be borne?

As the minutes passed, the girl's reasoned endurance and her stubborn will reasserted themselves, not for the first time. It was folly to say it could not be borne when she had already borne it more or less knowingly for a space of years. Did the mere seeing with one's eyes of something already known, make unbearable what was bearable before? Where was her courage? Had she not prepared herself for this many and many a time? Had Louis not warned her fairly? Had she not accepted the circumstances in which such trials of love were to be looked for? Had she not even desired such circumstances? Yet here she was shaken by the first trial.

So yet again did Joanna gather up all the deathly courage that was hers, and recover a deathly buoyancy. Yet again with her lover's appeal ringing afresh in her ears did she draw herself up to her full stature of proud humility. Let the next testing come when and how it might, she would be unshaken. She would show Louis a composed and cheerful countenance. Had he not so far humbled himself as to ask a favour of her? So long as he could do that: so long as she was his angel, his friend and his love, was there anything she could not endure?

As she crossed the road to Chapel Court she braced herself to look calmly upon her joyous decoration of the little studio. She would take down the gay, unlighted lanterns and put them away for a happier occasion without repining; would divide among the children the fruits and dainties she had provided for a love feast; and having herself eaten a sober meal, she would work until bed-time. She would not even allow herself the distraction of a book.

With a strong, puritan revulsion of disfavour did she now look back upon the inebriation of her afternoon. Sobriety showed as the condition to be striven for. A " godly, righteous and *sober* life " ! How wonderful, that an expression, until now quite devoid of personal significance, should spring up suddenly in living, most desirable beauty ! Henceforward she was determined to withstand that inherited tendency of hers to barren ecstasies.

Greatly restored by this discovery, Joanna immediately quickened her pace. It was as if no time must be lost in putting it into practice. And at the same moment that her feet stepped to a livelier measure, came a thought which caused a broad, amused smile to overspread her features. How amazingly ignorant, thought she, were those persons that would condemn her relations with Louis on grounds of laxity or self-indulgence ! What other situation between man and woman could demand so constant a self-discipline, such sacrifice, such effort, such a putting aside of all slackness and sloth ? Assuredly the reality was very different from anything she herself, standing by the little garden door of *La Porziuncola*, had imagined. Yet she was glad it was different ; glad to have it so ; glad of love's hardness.

No longer smiling, but grave and resolute, she was about to pass under the archway when Edwin Moon came out of the shop and made to speak with her. In a frock-coat and top-hat, he seemed smaller and more bent than usual. He was carrying his black attaché-case.

"A lovely evening, isn't it ? " he asked, looking submissively at the heavens. He had stopped, so Joanna was compelled to stop also. Clearly there was something further in his mind to say to her.

A little embarrassed, but patient with him by experience, Joanna waited. From the first she had felt a liking for the little, vague man with his shabby gait and his oddly dispassionate face. And lately her liking had developed into a kind of championship. She could not get out of her mind the sound of Trissie Moon's voice as she had heard it (overheard it rather) late one night in the summer. It had wakened her, that voice of Trissie's floating in at the widely opened window of her bedroom to the accompaniment of a flowing tap in the yard below, where husband and wife were together engaged upon a midnight cleansing of the kitchen.

" The longer I live with you the more you drive me mad ! "

This was the only complete phrase which had emerged clearly from the low, stinging tirade, pertinacious as the water that beat steadily upon the stones of the yard. Twice only could the involuntary listener detect the man's meek murmur in protest or self-defence. But the pushing, contumelious voice of the woman had gone on till it was checked by its own hoarseness. Then only it had faltered. Then only, after reviving time and again, but ever with lessening strength, had it fallen into a derisive implacable silence.

Since that night Joanna had sided in secret with the husband. And this though it was the wife who went constantly out of her way to be helpful. Especially in the matter of arranging Joanna's rooms Trissie Moon had spared no pains. Joanna indeed had never known anyone to compare with her in all that concerned a house. Her taste was wonderfully sure—it did not surprise her lodger to learn one day by chance that she had been a promising art student before her marriage —and her practical knowledge never failed. But gratitude and admiration notwithstanding, Joanna had acquired the habit of avoiding her presence when she could. It was not that she disliked Trissie. She had to admit a real, even a painful liking for her. But it had come as a relief, when a month ago, Trissie, declaring herself sick to death of household drudgery, and giving as an excuse that she must find extra money for Roddy's massage, had rushed into the management of a local laundry which was changing hands. Since then even the growing discomfort of the Moon household, under the neglect of its mistress and the efforts of spasmodic charwomen, seemed preferable to Trissie's strained smile and unceasing stream of talk.

But Mr. Moon was still speaking with diffident persistence, and as his manner was, circuitously approaching his point.

" I always say," he told Joanna mildly, " that the *pet* days of the year come in November and in March——the very late autumn, the very early spring.——There's a something in the air then—jocund ?—fecund ?—which is it ? So I find at least. But I rarely get anyone to agree with me. People say they feel ill in March and melancholy in November. I remember when we lived in Hampshire, we used to ride in the forest in November. There was nothing melancholy about that.——I had a strawberry mare equally good to ride or drive

——she was called Bathsheba after one of Hardy's heroines ——that of course is the Hardy country——for a time he was one of my—— " Edwin Moon's voice trailed off, and his pale, blue, ambiguous gaze travelled into space.

His companion was eager in expressing her entire agreement with regard to the pet days of the year. But this being decided between them, she was still waiting for what he really wanted to say.

" Is it an embalming this evening ? " Seeking for some chat to fill in the silence, Joanna pointed to the attaché-case in which she knew he carried his instruments. She had now known for some time in which capacities her landlord was engaged by the undertaker downstairs, and that he was no more than an ill-paid, if also indispensable, hireling in that profitable business. She also knew that as a rule he did not wear his top-hat if he had no more to do than to measure the client's body.

" Yes," he replied, brightening. " But not for us : for Maple's. Maples are sending a gentleman back to South Africa at the end of the week. And when the Equator has to be dealt with, they can trust no one in town with the job but myself. Most of the trade, as I daresay you know, is with the United States. And there are quite half a dozen embalmers in London who can deal safely as far as New York, and might even guarantee the overland journey to the West Coast. But the Equator—that's the real test."

Though he was a broken man and knew it, Mr. Moon could not keep the light of professional arrogance from dwelling at this moment in his eyes.

What had gone to the breaking of him, and by what slow or swift stages he had declined to his present way of life, Joanna did not know. Unwillingly—well-nigh under pro-test—she had gathered from Trissie's wild talk that once they had had money and professional standing (it looked as if Edwin had been a country doctor with means) ; that there had come a catastrophe involving disgrace ; that after an interval of some dark nature, they had gone to live in America where Roddy had been born. But she had always shrunk from gratifying her own natural curiosity by means of poor Trissie's incontinence, and had pried no farther than she could help into the undoubted mystery that surrounded the pair.

" What I wanted to ask you—Trissie is sure to be late home

again to-night—I wonder, would you be so very kind ?—if it wouldn't really be troubling you too much——? " At last Mr. Moon was getting to the pith of his request.

" You want me to keep an eye on the children ? " exclaimed Joanna, grasping his meaning with considerable relief. " Of course I will ! "

" It is kind of you to offer : very kind," he breathed," peering at her gratefully. " After that Swedish woman's pummelling to-day, Roddy ought to get to bed early. I'd see to it myself if it weren't for this." And he disparagingly indicated the attaché-case.

" I'll bathe him and give him his supper the minute I get in," promised Joanna with ready energy. " Is Ollie with us to-night ? " she asked as she moved off.

" I'm afraid she is. Yes. Mrs. Garland has a theatre, and asked us if we could keep Ollie late," admitted Mr. Moon. " It's unfortunate. Do you think you can manage both ? It seems too bad to ask it of you."

" You know I enjoy it," Joanna assured him smiling. It was not the first time, nor yet the tenth that similar requests had been made and similar apologies offered. True, it had generally been Trissie who had asked her lodger's help in various ways with the children (with the exception of Edvina's washing and bedding which was performed at five o'clock each day by a trained nurse who came for that purpose only) ; but Mr Moon must have known of it.

Upon entering the house, Joanna stepped upon several letters which lay dimly white upon the linoleum just within the front door where they had fallen from the postman's hand. By the light from a lamp in the court outside she could barely decipher their directions. Only one was for herself—a bulky one in her mother's unmistakable hand-writing. *Urgent* was marked clearly upon the left-hand top corner of the envelope. But in this there was nothing disturbing. For, as Juley had a strong sense of human frailty which made no exception of the postal service, her correspondents were well accustomed to find either of the words *Urgent* or *Immediate*, and frequently the word *Private* as well, upon the outside of her communications.

Joanna thought she would read this letter in her bedroom where she had been going to take off her coat and hat before joining the children. But having already laid her hand on the knob of the door leading to her separate staircase, she involuntarily paused to listen.

It was not usually so quiet as this in the house when Ollie was there. Though Ollie and Roddy seldom shared their games they were decidedly vocal in company. And if both voices were not to be heard placidly pursuing independent monologues, Ollie's at least would be lifted, loud and utterly absorbed, in unending song.

But on this evening not a sound came from upstairs. And Joanna, wondering and suddenly anxious, pushed her unopened letter into her pocket and went straight up through the dim little house to the Moons' sitting-room.

The moment she had opened the door, the queer silence was explained.

The walls of the lamp-lighted room, the mantel-piece, the furniture, even Edvina's empty carriage, were stuck all over with oddly shaped bits of paper. Roddy on the floor was laboriously writing with the very wet stump of a pencil upon similar bits of paper. His cheeks were bright scarlet with the efforts he was making and the excitement of what was already achieved. Ollie, plump-legged, round-faced and shorthaired, stood on tip-toe before the glazed book-case, and was busy plastering Roddy's work as high as ever she could reach upon the panes, having first wetted each printed or illustrated scrap with her tongue.

Both children looked round at the intruder with delighted but somewhat anxious eyes. Ollie particularly was on tenterhooks, and the corners of her smiling lips were ready to drop at a word.

" Why, whatever have you been up to, you two ? " Joanna exclaimed. And she examined more closely into the children's handiwork.

" Such a lovely game, being dead ! " declared Roddy's matter-of-fact voice. But Ollie hovered in uncertainty. She was wavering now on the brink of dismay, and did not take her bright, misgiving eyes off Joanna's face.

What they had got hold of, as Joanna now saw, was one of the monumental mason's catalogues from the office downstairs. All the slips of paper were tombstones. There were plain marble crosses and wormy Celtic ones ; there were broken pillars, massive sarcophagi, slabs and kerbs ; there were mourning angels, shattered vases and draped urns. The children had cut them out, growing less and less neat as they had progressed helter-skelter through the catalogue, and had filled each in with a name they knew.

Joanna studied one tombstone after another.

RODDY DIED, she read. Then *EDVINA DIED, OLLIE DIED, MOTHER DIED, FATHER DIED*. (All were in Roddie's bold but erratic printing, Ollie being a backward scholar). And beside what she took to be an attempt at her own name—*MISSES REST PONY DIED*, stuck by the side of the fireplace upon a very imposing piece of scrollworked sculpture, there was pinned up one of the undertaker's printed order forms. Here Roddy, unable to subdue his caligraphy to the spaces left blank for customers, had answered several questions at once with a single *YES* or *NO,* or by some secret hieroglyph of his own.

Thus, opposite—" Measurement of Body,"—he had put **X**

opposite—" Shell Cov'd
       Lead Coffin
       Mahogany Coffin }—he had put *YES*
       Outside Casket "

opposite—" Is Hand Bier required of us ?
Is our Hearse to go through by rail ?
Are Bearers to go through by rail ? }—he had
Valuations for probate ?   put *NO.*
Monumental Masonry ?
Terms of payment ? "

And wherever he had felt doubtful, or had been presented with a nice large space, he had firmly planted his own name — RODDY . . . RODDY . . . RODDY.

Joanna shuddered. She told herself it was absurd to feel anything but amusement, yet she could not help that shudder. For the very reason perhaps that she could well enter into the children's excitement at having all by themselves discovered so novel a game, she was quite overcome ; and for a few moments she dared not turn round from her inspection of the book-case, lest her unreasoned dread should be communicated to Ollie who stood just behind. Perfectly she knew how Ollie was standing there, twisting the corner of her pinafore between her fingers, awaiting the verdict. Roddy, she need not trouble about. Roddy was shielded impenetrably by the walls of the citadel in which he dwelt apart, exempt. Nothing from the outside world could come near him, much less wound him. But Ollie! From the first, Joanna had understood in little Ollie something of her own passionate wistfulness of desire towards the world. Ollie wanted the world. And she wanted it perfect, ever so perfect in gaiety and loveliness. So Ollie could not bear one hint of reproach or unhappiness.

At last, feeling she was mistress again of her countenance, Joanna turned, and immediately she had to meet the little girl's look of apprehension.

"I think that's rather a silly game," she said with studied lightness. She smiled and held out her hand. "Let's tidy the room all up, shall we?"

But Ollie threw back her head, and set up a loud and bitter wailing.

There is something so ultimate in the despairing crying of certain children that the solid ground of sufficiency seems to crumble beneath the feet of those that hear it. To all laughter and contentment it gives the lie : upon all theories of childish happiness, even upon the very possibility of any well founded happiness upon earth, it casts a deep shadow of doubt. It seems to recall all former mirth and to cancel it, or to show at least how closely the tears are at all times lying beneath. It seems to warn the hearer that in future joy no confidence must be placed.

"Ollie! Darling Ollie!" implored Joanna half distraught. And she folded the little shaken, sobbing figure to her breast. She had dropped to the floor upon her knees before Ollie, and there she rocked her backwards and forwards, giving and taking all the solace of the blood, but unable to console the spirit of one who, like herself, could hardly endure the inevitable approach of dissolution. The tears fell from her own eyes, and all the sadness of the afternoon, itself a foretaste of death, welled up in her afresh. Even while she gained ground with the child, soothing and cheering her by degrees, her own sadness welled up and overflowed.

"Come! Dear, darling, pretty Ollie! My pet! My sweetheart! My wee lamb! My hen of gold!" she besought. "Let us make Edvina's supper. You shall help. You shall stir the pan for me. And Roddy and you can both have splashy baths to-night. And if you like you may sleep in my bed till Mother comes for you. There ! And I'll read you *Beswarragel* again—the whole of it, though it's so long. There ! ''

And at last, after much coaxing and cuddling, Ollie's sobs subsided. They subsided and she was once more a happy little girl. She was just a happy little girl again, saving that every now and then she gave a curious reminiscent gulp, saving that she glanced very often up at Joanna with eyes suspiciously bright, saving that when she laughed, her laughter sounded perilously gay and boisterous.

It took Joanna a full hour and a half to finish with the children. Both in their different ways were greatly excited, and she had cause to rue some of her desperate promises, especially that one of the splashy bath before the fire.

Ollie in the tub, shaking her head wildly and screwing up her eyes under a wet fallen fringe of hair, rocked in the water and beat upon it unremittingly with her palms, until such moment as Roddy, standing by should shout the magic words " Peace ! Be still ! '' when she became immediately motionless. And when Roddy was in the bath the process was reversed. But in each case the periods of storm were prolonged out of all proportion to the periods of calm, and Joanna came near to losing patience.

"You know what Father said, Roddy," she pleaded. "That on the night after your massage you must be early in bed, or it won't do you any good. You know it is making your legs bigger and stronger already. Don't you want to be big and strong ? ''

As she urged him she was thinking how like the Moons it was that they should pinch themselves, as they undoubtedly were doing—not to speak of Trissie's working herself to threads at the laundry—so that expensive attention should be lavished upon Roddy's delicate limbs while they allowed him night after night to sit up till all hours, and gave him his supper at any time between five o'clock and eleven. The wonder was that the child should show any benefit from this one-sided treatment. But he certainly did ; and now with his clothes off he looked much like any other rather thin little boy.

"I like my massage," Roddy was remarking meditatively in response to Joanna's rally. "Miss Olssen's fingers are just like jewels on my back." But this observation, charming as it was, made him no faster in his deliberate washing of his person. And Joanna knew by experience that he would resent with all his manhood any offer of hers to do the soaping or sponging for him.

At last, however, she had got both the small, young naked bodies dried : Roddy's stringy and hard, yet so helplessly tender ; Ollie's, petal-soft, yet firm as a stephanotis bud. And she thought how defenceless, how touchingly exposed the man-child seemed by the side of the finished, compact budlikeness of the girl baby.

" Tell me Ollie——" she asked while she brushed the child's damp, short hair back from her forehead—fine, dead-straight hair it was, cut boyishly indeed, but so female to the touch, so different from Roddy's mane. "——Tell me, would you rather be a girl or a boy ? "

" I'd rather be a girl," laughed Ollie at once, but quite inattentively. She was trying all the while to twitch the jacket of Roddy's pyjama suit away from him before he could struggle into it.

" Keep still, Ollie, do ! Why would you rather be a girl ? " persisted Joanna. She was surprised a little by the child's readiness, and therefore doubtful if there had been any meaning behind her answer.

This time Ollie had to think for just a moment. She stood perfectly still under the brush.

Then—" Because I like boys best," she gravely replied.

But when Joanna could not help smiling, Ollie, in a little panic was no longer sure what she had said, or whether it was right or wrong.

She looked at Joanna sideways, questioning.

VI

When the children were asleep, the bath emptied, all remaining traces of tombstones removed, and a tea-tray put ready for the exhausted Trissie's arrival, it was nearly ten o'clock. Only now did Joanna remember her mother's letter. She opened it at once.

" MY BELOVED CHILD (it ran),—

" Much has happened of late which I have not felt able to mention in my ordinary letters to you. Mother had to meditate and pray before coming to such an important decision, and in her *great solitude* she had none to help her but our Heavenly Father who is ever so long-suffering towards the feeblest of his children. O! my own, darling daughter, may you never fail to seek that *Source* in times of trial when the Evil One lieth in wait, for other help is there none. You will not be surprised when I tell you, dear, that the *Matter* in which I have been seeking *Guidance*, is whether my future abode is to be in Glasgow or in London. You remember how we all talked of this at the time of dear Georgie's wedding?

"When you left, as I have already told you in my letters, Mabel was very kind and attentive. Indeed I knew not what I should have done without her. But now that she is gone, I feel I can tell you without seeming ungrateful that she was far, far from being one of my own precious girls. I do not think she intends it, but Mabel with her gift of sympathy has a way of making me say things of my nearest and dearest which I very much regret afterwards.

"Not long after Mabel left us, I saw that Linnet, impatient and restless, would really be better living by himself, at least for a time. Eva Gedge, whom I consulted, did not agree with me in this. She thought it my Christian duty to remain with Linnet. But God had shown me otherwise, as He did when I let you go, dear, to London. And I told this to Eva, at the same time offering myself for a few months' trial, as her co-worker in whatever way she thought best. I offered, if she liked, to take over Evening Prayers at the Training College, and to have special Bible Readings (dealing especially with prophecies of the Second Coming) for the students. For gifted as Eva is, and intellectually far above my reach—how often, Joanna, has Mother to pray against envy of the gifts of others! —I could not but see that there was a conventionality, even a seeming coldness about her prayers and exposition of the Holy Word. In all prayerful love I had thought this to show that her real sphere was organization. And as Eva has always tried to help me by pointing out any shortcomings of mine, I ventured with none but the most sisterly feelings to draw her attention to what I am sure is the truth. But you will hardly believe me when I tell you how completely her manner has changed towards me from that very moment. Christ's Kingdom is indeed still far off so long as His Chosen ones have so little of His spirit! It was a most painful, most bitter experience, and has made any further idea of my living under her roof (even if she were willing) quite impossible.

" This happened about three weeks ago, but wishing to say nothing unjust I did not tell you of it at once. Now, after much wavering I think I see my way clear. As soon as suitable rooms can be got for Linnet I must come to London. And I must do what you have all so often begged—I now see rightly—I must hand over all the housekeeping to you, if you still feel able for it, and confine myself to certain duties which will lighten your responsibilities. Your frequent affectionate letters and Georgie's have been a great strength to me in some dark hours, and I feel a growing longing to be with you in that great and wonderful city where so much is being done (do I not read of it continually in my weekly magazines ?) to hasten the Coming of His Kingdom which is all my prayer and desire. It will of course take some time to get Linnet comfortably settled here. But we shall go as we are *Led*, one step at a time. Meanwhile it might be as well—don't you think ?—to be on the look-out for a suitable, quite small house in the neighbourhood of Hampstead Heath ? I should wish, of course, not to be far from Georgie. If possible I'd rather not have a flat, never having fancied one (though I'm told the London people prefer them, and I know they are very different from our Glasgow closes). You need not be told how happy Mother is with a bit of garden to tend. But this may be too much to hope for——"

Joanna read this long letter—and there was much more of it—through to the end with a loving but heavy heart. Though it told her little that was unexpected, she knew now how surely she had come to count upon her mother's protracted unwillingness to leave Glasgow. The loss of this surety was a blow at her freedom and her new-found happiness. But she felt for Juley, and she was not free from self-reproach. She tried hard to persuade herself that, given entirely new conditions, she and her mother might be able to find a new and happier existence under the same roof.

Anyhow there was but one thing to be done, cost what it might later. She wrote a welcoming, affectionate letter home without delay.

CHAPTER II

I

BUT nine months passed : nine months, including Christmas and Easter holidays spent as usual by Joanna in Scotland ; and Juley seemed no nearer to the carrying out of her decision. Whether there was anything in the various practical excuses for delay periodically alleged by Juley in further letters and talks ; whether she did not as yet, after all, feel perfectly sure of Heavenly guidance ; or whether she was simply not equal to the uprooting, Joanna did not know. At intervals she continued to urge her mother's coming, but now that the summer holiday was again at hand, and nothing in the situation changed, she had begun once more to accept her freedom as a permanent condition.

Neither had Louis afforded her any further, or at least any definite occasion of testing, such as she had prepared herself for on that November evening. On the morning after his daughter-in-law's unexpected arrival he had set aside all family claims, and had gone with Joanna down into Surrey for a long blissful day's walking. They had climbed up, down, and about Leith Hill, and had discovered a solitary inn, with a wide triangular common to itself. And Louis had been at once more winning and more serious with her than ever before. Since then she had perfectly accommodated herself—or so she thought—to the inevitable difficulties of their situation. She had anyhow grown used to them ; and against them in the balance she could place a steady progress in her work. This much was certain — under the combined discipline and excitement of her life her technical accomplishment increased.

It was a brazen, stifling Sunday afternoon in August, the day before Bank Holiday. Louis had left town the morning before. Joanna did not start for Glasgow until the Tuesday morning. As usual, with London bereft of her lover, she found a blankness in the air. Everything seemed empty and echoing. But it was not wholly unpleasant. She liked to miss him. They had parted firmly, almost happily. Her mind was already set forward upon her holiday, badly needed, and beyond her holiday upon the next coming together. Moreover, without any doubt there was a sense of relief in the knowledge that she was free, to herself alone, for that day and the next : that she could come and go from the house without any fear of missing some call or telephone message from Louis. While he was in town, it was a fear that never quite left her.

In spirit, therefore, Joanna inhabited a kind of limbo to which she had long since become accustomed on these thresholds of holiday. But in the flesh, this afternoon at three o'clock, she sat with the Moons on their roof-garden.

At the moment, her head on one side, and only the absorbed curve of her lips showing beneath the drooping brim of her hat, she was making a birthday present for Ollie Garland. Some days before, she had black-lacquered a small wooden work-box, and now that the surface had hardened, she was painting a bright, impossible bird on the lid and little gay-coloured flowers on the sides.

" I do hope Ollie will like it ! " she exclaimed happily, not speaking to anyone in particular.

" What sort of a bird is it supposed to be ? " asked Trissie Moon, lifting her heated face and pushing back a fallen loop of her hair with her forearm. In the other earthy hand she clutched a trowel, and had been working this last hour at her nasturtiums with penal energy.

When Trissie was gardening one had to wonder what it was that she was so fiercely punishing in herself, or for what it was in another that she thus made expiation. Or was it merely some spite against life which she was confusedly wreaking upon the earth ? Her eyes, with the bruised shadows beneath them, were burning. Her pallid forehead glistened with sweat. Her mouth was set in lines of pain.

She was the only one on the roof-garden not at peace. Mr. Moon sat reading on a canvas chair. Edvina was asleep in her carriage, with a dark parasol stuck through the wicker work to keep the glare of the sky from her upturned face.

And Roddy, squatting on the leads, was placidly involved in a net-work of railway lines.

Joanna gave a little laugh in reply to Trissie's peremptory demand.

" I'm not sure," she admitted. " I'm making it up as I go. I thought a phœnix perhaps ? "

Edwin Moon looked over his spectacles and his *British Medical Journal* at the box in question.

" I don't think it's a phœnix. No," he observed unemphatically. And in the colourless tone of your true scholar, he proceeded to describe that mythological bird.

Joanna gave him an interested glance. Rarely would her landlord himself initiate any learned conversation. But while others talked loosely of this or that, it was astonishing how often apt or curious information was furnished in his mild voice.

" What about a bird of paradise, then ? " asked Joanna. " I think I'd like it to be a bird of paradise."

Mr. Moon seemed to give this his approval.

" And the less like the real thing the better," he suggested with the ghost of a twinkle in his quenched blue eyes.

" You know of course," he went on, " that there is a legendary bird of paradise as well as the one they kill for women's hats ? Give little Ollie the myth."

But Joanna knew nothing of the legend.

" Yes," Mr. Moon told her, as he picked up his *Journal* again. " According to the old zoologists this kind of bird was irresistibly attracted by the nutmegs strewn on the floors of certain island forests. And it came down in flocks and devoured the spice till it was drunk. While it was drunk its legs were eaten off by ants. So that afterwards it had to live always in the air. Having no legs it couldn't alight even to sleep, and was seen continually on the wing. Hence— bird of paradise."

Joanna had stopped her painting to listen.

" What a sad bird ! " she exclaimed. " I shan't tell Ollie that story." But to her own secret heart she added, " That bird is like me ! "

With her fine, sable-hair brush she put a scarlet feather—a high, delicate loop of scarlet—into her bird's tail. Then she put a sheer sweeping blue one. Then one that cascaded pure lemon yellow. And she held the box away, drawing back her head the better to appreciate her work. How well these clear colours were shrilled out upon the black! She had never succeeded with lacquer half so well before.

"Now I have the trick," she declared, "I'd love to do your tray for you, Trissie; and that old pencil-case of Roddy's. I feel I could paint every bit of wood in the house."

A gentle consciousness of pleasure came to her there on the roof-garden, and she loved her quiet companions. These Moons were her friends! What other friends had she made in London these fourteen months? In Georgie's world she was not at home; she was joyless in Irene's; and despite common interests she had made no intimates in the Chelsea studios. In all these quarters she had persevered chiefly because she was afraid, because she *dared* not lose superficial touch with her fellows, because she feared that the strangeness of her life might react in some monstrous external strangeness. But here with the Moons she was able to feel simply human, free and at her ease. She believed that both Trissie and Edwin had long ago guessed her secret, and that they understood. They were themselves sorrowful, outcast people, and therefore must surely be kind.

Joanna's meditation was interrupted at this point by an exclamation of annoyance which came from Trissie. For some time past, neglecting her gardening business, she had been peering through the trellis, apparently observing with apprehension the uncertain movements of a stranger in the court below.

"It *is* a visitor for us," she announced in despair. And as she spoke the knocker sounded upon the front door. "Who can it be? You must go, Edwin. My hands aren't fit to be seen. It's probably some one for you."

"I don't expect anyone, anyhow," said Joanna peacefully, and filling her brush with bright orange pigment, she proceeded to block in a nasturtium upon a blank side of Ollie's box.

Mr. Moon, having gone obediently downstairs, returned the next minute, "Some one to see Mrs. Rasponi," he informed them. "I've taken him up." And he sat down again to his reading.

As Joanna in a little confusion laid aside her paints, murmuring the while that she wondered who on earth it could be, a gleam of pure malice flashed from Trissie's eyes.

"It isn't Mr. Pender," she volunteered in a low, acrimonious voice. And she dug her trowel passionately into a tub of fresh mould. "It's a young man . . . dark . . . seemed not to know his way."

Like a fury she began tying up the long, helpless trails of her creepers with pieces of bast, tweaked viciously from a sheaf which she was holding between her compressed lips. But Joanna was too much absorbed in her own speculations to be more than dimly aware of the other woman's malevolence. And she passed unscathed into the house.

II

As she entered the archway room, her visitor—it was Lawrence Urquhart—turned quickly from the window to meet her. He looked more self-possessed than she remembered him, and so well, that when they had shaken hands, for want of anything better to say, she remarked upon it.

He admitted that he was quite well. How was she?

Joanna was quite well too. But as she assured him of this, she did not meet his eyes; and when he admired her room, she set rather hastily about displaying her possessions. That was her Italian mirror: these her mauve and gold lustre tea-cups picked up at Dorking: here was her Empire coffee-pot,—wasn't it a beauty?—and there by the window was the brass-clamped sea-chest she had got for a few shillings one wet day in an open-air market.

It was their first meeting since the last unhappy ride together more than a year ago, but in the interval Joanna had once accidentally had a glimpse of Lawrence unknown to him. It had been on a night when she was leaving a theatre with Louis. Lawrence with a friend—another young man—had been in the crowd, and the unexpected sight of his unconscious face had affected her so oddly that she had not pointed him out to Louis. Why was it, she had asked herself, that seeing Lawrence's features anew after absence, was like being confronted suddenly by some vital memory of childhood? He was only an acquaintance of her adult years. Why then should his eyes recall so strongly the very look of the pools in the burn at Duntarvie?"

But Lawrence was not yet living in London. He told her this as if it were the apology for his visit. He was here only for the Bank Holiday to make quite sure of a certain berth in

Fleet Street. . . . Yes, he was leaving Oxford . . . No
more work for him there after September. . . . And Joanna
must know what a sad, untidy, waste-papery sort of place
London was, of a Sunday afternoon. He agreed with
her that Glasgow was fifty times worse in the same circumstances. Still one felt even more left to oneself in London. At least he did. So he had taken a walk through the
Green Park ; and being then so near, had thought to look her
up—Carl had given him the address—but he had hardly
expected to find her in town.

He told her that outside this two days' run to London, he
was not having a holiday this year.

She had begun to pour tea from the Empire coffee-pot into
one of the mauve and gilt cups, but now she paused with questioning eyes upon him. All the time she had been wondering
obscurely wherein he was changed. It seemed that Oxford
had done for him what she believed London had done for
her. How had it come about in his case ?

" You look to me as if you had just returned from a holiday," she said with just a thread of vexation in her voice.
" I never saw you look better." And she went on with her
tea-making.

" It's more than I can say of you," he replied quietly.

Taken off her guard, Joanna looked up quickly and had to
meet his scrutiny. To her dismay she felt the blood rise hot
in her face.

" I expect I need my holiday," she said, handing the cup
to him less deftly than was her wont. He had moved from
his seat to take it, and now stood close by her, looking down
at her.

" But you needn't be so disagreeable about it," she added
harshly, fighting him off.

Though she was glad then to see him turn away in distress,
it was she that presently harked back to the subject.

" What makes you say I look such a fright ?" she could
not resist questioning him.

Lawrence protested that he had said no such thing.

" It sounded like that."

" No. You look. . . ." The young man frowned and
hesitated. But now Joanna had seen from his eyes that he
found her beautiful.

" Yes ? Go on," she insisted.

"Last night at the Coliseum, I saw a juggler," he began. He was keeping a dozen plates in the air at once. But it was his face I watched. He wasn't exactly anxious. He knew his job brilliantly. Still it was taking him all his time and every ounce of his strength to do it and keep a calm front."

Joanna waited. But it seemed that Lawrence was finished.

"And I look like him ? " she asked, keeping tight hold of herself. She was seething with anger.

"As I see you," persisted Lawrence bravely.

"I'm very sorry ! " She sat biting her lower lip which would miserably tremble. Then a single heavy tear slid out of one eye and ran with surprising momentum down her cheek and on to her lap.

She kept perfectly still. As it was the far-away cheek from Lawrence, and as she was sitting with her back to the light, she hoped he would not notice. But almost immediately a second tear, scalding and vexatious pushed itself over the lower lid of the other eye.

She sprang up and made for the window.

"Why . . . are you . . . so . . . horrid ? " she just managed to articulate. And then all in one gasping breath, . . . "Can't you see I'm tired ? I've been over-working. I need a holiday."

If now she expected a penitent, prostrate Lawrence, she was mistaken. He sat stark still in his place and did not say a word.

She recovered all the more quickly for his immobility, and turned herself about again with a face suffused.

"I wonder . . . " She could almost smile though her voice was still full of treacherous quavers. . . . "I wonder why I always behave like an idiot when I'm with you ? "

"Because I'm an idiot myself," was Lawrence's sour rejoinder. And though they both knew better, this helped to restore their calm.

"Listen . . . " she began presently as she helped herself to more tea. " . . . I saw you in the theatre one night. And——" she added with tremulous mischief——"you were not by yourself."

To her gratification Lawrence looked at her quite startled. "When was that ? "

"One Saturday night in summer."

" Let me see now," he considered warily. " Which theatre ? "

" Daly's."

" Ah ! Daly's ? " She could feel him hiding his relief. He remembered now. He had come up with a man . . . Martin, his name was . . . a very entertaining fellow . . . not unlike Carl Nilsson in some ways . . . he would like Joanna to have met Martin. And what had she thought of the piece ? Why had she not spoken to them he asked ?

Joanna explained some of the circumstances. It had been, she said, in the vestibule crush, struggling for cabs on a night suddenly turned to rain as he might remember. And then something forced her to add—" I was with Louis Pender ! "

But on this Lawrence made no comment.

Soon they spoke of other things. She put some vague questions about Oxford, and was struck by his detached and critical attitude. Here surely was another sign of change in him ? In Glasgow he had been in some awe of the very name.

" I've learned one thing there, anyhow," he told her. " I've learned to shudder at the thought of what I should have become with a tolerably successful academic career. I was shifted out of *that*, and a good job too ! "

Though he did not actually add in words—" I owe it to you,"—Joanna felt herself both implicated and exonerated. She asked him what his new choice was to be.

" Not journalism surely ? " she hazarded.

Lawrence replied—looking at her, and perceiving a certain repugnance in her face—that journalism it was, for the time at least. He had got a newspaper job of sorts—jumped at it indeed—because that would bring him to London, and because he could go on reading for the Bar at the same time. What it was all to come to, he himself did not yet know. He only knew that he wanted to be " in the stream of things."

" And professors aren't ? " asked Joanna.

" Not in the way I mean," he replied. " They are all fenced in and sheltered. A few of them keep up the pretence that this isn't so. But it is. It has got to be.

So they talked on for a while, sticking cautiously to generalities, till Lawrence sprang up, as if he had quite suddenly recollected an engagement elsewhere. As he said good bye he asked Joanna if she would go with him next day for a glimpse of Hampstead Heath. He had always wanted to see it on a Bank Holiday.

After a moment's hesitation she agreed. She always hated the blank day before a journey and Louis was out of town. "We might have another ride together, this time on wooden steeds," suggested Lawrence.

III

But the walk on Monday was no pleasure to Joanna. Though she had been well disposed toward Lawrence at parting and in her after-thoughts of him, the next meeting found her weary and hostile. She would like to have shut her ears to whatever he said, and the blaring, glaring, untidy Heath had none of the charm she had found there at the Whitsuntide holiday when Louis had been her companion. The vile, raucous voices were an affront, and the ugly laughter. She loathed the reeking faces and the horse-play. She refused after all to ride on the merry-go-round, refused to have tea anywhere but at home. It was all hateful to her.

Some relief came with the escape back to her rooms, though Chapel Court itself was noisy enough. She had thought to shake Lawrence off at the street door and go up alone. Surely he must feel as she did, what a failure the afternoon had been ? Then why had he not the sense to leave her ? But no ! He stuck like a burr, and seemed oblivious to the languor of her invitation.

Still things were better in the quiet interior, and there would be some comfort in tea sipped behind the closed shutters. Here over the archway one was safe. And the cool, untouched breeze crept in at the sides of the curtains.

Leaving Lawrence on their entrance, Joanna ran to her bedroom and threw off her hot and dusty outer clothes. Her thin dresses were already packed, so she had nothing to put on saving one of the holland smocks she wore for working. But no garment she had was more becoming to her, a fact which had more than once been pointed out by Louis. Assuredly in the cool, pleated linen, when she had laved her face, and doubled up her hair anew, she felt a different creature.

The young man gave a little start of joy as she came into the sitting-room. But his only spoken comment was that she looked " nice and cool."

For a while they talked of the heat. Then—" You know

what I said yesterday . . . ? " questioned Lawrence abruptly,
. . " that about having no more use for the back-waters ? "
Yes. Joanna remembered.

" It was you helped me to it," he said quietly, only his
breathing playing him false." . . . I wanted to tell you that.
You helped so tremendously. You have always stood for
the real world which I would have hidden from if I could."

Joanna wondered in all honesty how this could be. " I've
always been in such a dream myself," she declared, ". . . till
quite lately."

" Perhaps . . . "—he winced a little—— ". . . I don't
know about lately. But that first evening at Mrs. Lovatt's
house at dinner. You seemed a different person from the one
in old Cellebrini's class. You had got away, really away . . .
didn't belong any more to Glasgow. You hadn't been just
travelling or sight-seeing like the others. How I admired
the way you had escaped . . . it was something I needed so
badly and had so little courage for. Couldn't we start being
friends from now ? " he ended abruptly.

" We might. . . . " she allowed. But she hesitated.

" You seem to grudge it," his voice was sharp. " If you
knew how I need . . . what happiness it would mean to
me. . . . "

" That's exactly it," Joanna interrupted him quickly. " I
do believe we might be friends if only it weren't a thing you
thought you needed to make you happy. Don't you see ? "

" No. I don't think I do see." He was taken aback.

" I mean, surely happiness has to be in ourselves if it is to
be any use at all ? I've thought such a lot about this lately,"
said she with growing eagerness. " If your happiness is in
the hands of other people, or of any circumstances whatever,
it is really only misery. If you were happy in yourself now,
it would be all right. We could be friends and get pleasure
out of it. Otherwise I don't see the good."

Lawrence pondered this resentfully. There was too much
truth in what Joanna had said for him to scout it on the instant. Had he not all his life gone seeking happiness outside
himself ? It came to him now almost with the force of a discovery. And yet it was a lie—what a lie it was!—that
this woman he loved now so plausibly asked him to share.
He himself had lied when he had said her friendship would
make him happy. He did not expect happiness from it. He

needed what he could get of her. That was all . . . didn't even *want* it . . . *needed* it. And he cared not what he had to pay for it in wretchedness.

And just because he needed it, she wasn't playing fair. No, she wasn't. But he would have to share her lie. For he feared above all things to lose his chance of seeing her again.

"Then if I come to see you when I'm settled in London," he managed to say, with a peculiar smile, as he was leaving, "it will be because I'm happy in myself. I think you may count on seeing me."

All the evening Joanna was alone. Having finished her packing she started putting her rooms in order.

She existed submerged beneath the incessant holiday clamour. The revellers were returning to their homes, and by nine o'clock the trampling and shouting in the street had become a steady torture. The only respite came when a band of boys and girls passed along the pavement singing the music-hall song of the moment. They sang with the irreproachable ecstatic rhythm of the Cockney, their voices twanging out defiantly in parts.

Then in the court below, a piano-organ struck up, and people began to dance in front of the *Bird-in-Hand*. It was a taking tune, full of negro syncopations; and Joanna leaned her forehead against the pane of her back window and looked down at the dancers. A fat girl in crushed white muslin, with clumsy feet, wriggled her body monotonously to the music, and there was a fixed, mesmeric smile on her gleaming face. Opposite to her a decrepit man hopped in time, while a baby clutched one of his knees, and granny, careworn and fit to drop, rocked back and forth in toothless laughter at her old man's antics.

"In the stream of things!" Why should one want to be in the stream of things? questioned Joanna in her upper darkness. Yet it was true that it was terrible to be shut out in undesired solitude. A sudden hatred of this London, so noisily vacant without Louis, this London with its choice between a festering stream of things, and an insane and sterile solitude, rose in her heart like a corroding poison. And what of that invincible inward happiness of which she had so complacently discoursed to Lawrence but a short while ago? Ah, it was easy to talk! All she knew now was that her whole life stayed suspended till her next meeting with Louis.

September had come again, gusty and golden, and Joanna had not yet been put to that test she had almost a year before imagined herself as meeting with a perfection of equanimity.

She was in good spirits, standing before her mirror and trying on an absurd little blue hat. She pinned its feather—its feather that so beautifully matched her jade necklace—first at the front like a hussar ; then at back like a sportsman ; then at one side like a coquette. And she wondered if Phemie too was pinning on a feather at the other side of the world. Though she was only going to a private view of Arts and Crafts, where she was hardly likely to see Louis, she had dressed with special care.

Her summer holiday had refreshed her, and had been unexpectedly happy. She and Linnet and their mother had enjoyed themselves very peacefully in one of the remoter West Coast villages, and the weather had continued so fine that she had left them there for another week or two by the sea. That her mother and she would be setting up house together in London (Georgie expected a baby early in October) was finally decided. But it no longer seemed a calamity. It was simply a situation, and a situation, Joanna now boasted, could always be mastered with good will and management.

Certainly things for the moment were going well with her. Her holiday had been good, but it was still better to be back in London. Her theatre work was now well established, yet remained enough of a novelty to be an excitement. Louis had praised her last two drawings, and praise from him was sweet. Even sweeter had been the extraordinary solicitude he had shown on the night of her return a week before. Her train had been an hour late, but Louis was waiting on the platform—a thing she had scarcely allowed herself to hope for during the crowded and exhausting journey. He would have walked the station all night, he vowed, if need be. And, the Moons being away in the country (for the first time these three years, Trissie had written grimly), he had himself undertaken her comfort, not only at the station but in the empty house afterwards. He had coaxed her to eat and drink, had shaken out her travelling clothes, had insisted with unfamiliar tenderness on airing her sheets and taking off her shoes. More than by the expected passion of their first meeting after weeks of separation, had she been stirred and made glad by his new care of her.

She decided upon keeping the little green feather at one side.

Though there was not a tree in Chapel Court, its corners were heaped with leaves this yellow September afternoon, and the wind kept blowing them about the paving stones and against the walls of the houses. When front doors were opened it even blew them upstairs and into the top rooms ; and now and again a solitary, crumpled leaf, tossed high in the air, would fly in at a window.

One came sailing in at the top of Joanna's window now, just as she had set the feather to her liking. It sailed in, as if doubtfully, then floated downward and wavered against her breast.

"Another happy year ! " she murmured joyously as she caught it. There was no longer any grief in the memory of that company of milk-white trees of Vallombrosa under which she had fled about with Mario, trying to catch the falling leaves.

So exhilarated was she, and so vivid were all her sensations during the walk of twenty minutes to the gallery, that on getting there she found the specimens of Art and Craft dull by comparison.

Really—as often happens with a certain kind of solitary exhilaration when it is transferred from a vague to a definite setting—a peculiar reaction had taken place. Joanna herself was not immediately aware of it. She merely condemned the exhibits as astonishingly tame, and turned instead to look at the people. Very likely, she told herself, she might see some one she knew ; and with a little unacknowledged sinking of her heart she admitted it would be pleasant at the moment to have company.

Having already made a vain tour of all the rooms with this in mind, she now returned to the first room and began to watch the new arrivals as they came in from the street through the principal swing doors. Above these doors was a clock. It pointed, as Joanna absently noticed, to a quarter-past five.

All at once, as if some stony word had been uttered in her ear, her body became tense. She had seen Louis enter the room. And with him was his wife. Joanna had never seen his wife before, but she could not be mistaken. That smiling woman swathed in smoke grey for whom he had held open the door, was she. Joanna knew it, though now, as she saw, there were two other women with him. A tall old man and a young man followed.

The party, self-absorbed and moving leisurely, proceeded through the first room. Clearly the object of their visit did not lie here. And now Joanna was conscious only of disappointment. Louis had not seen her! How she had prayed, while awful things were happening in her breast, her throat, her limbs, that he would not see her. But now he was almost at the further door, and she could not bear it. Her feet carried her rapidly up the long, crowded room after him.

There they were, in the next room now. She stood in the doorway, looking. Why, of course it was the Mortlake tiles they had come to see! Some dozen of them were showing in that case . . . rare old Persian ones . . . " a sight more worth while than most pictures!" Louis had said of them once, cocking up his eyebrows in sincerest admiration. . . . And that tall, old man was Sir John Mortlake. . . . Had she not a drawing of his leonine head at home on the back of a receipt?

It was a small room, and as the Pender party had just met more friends, they seemed to fill it up. Louis was introducing some one to the smoke-grey woman. His voice and manner seemed to imply that the gallery existed for him and his friends. "You know my wife? . . ."

Each time his voice sounded shutters of darkness kept descending across Joanna's line of vision. But it was as if in addition to her ordinary sight she possessed some microscopic inner eye which was exempt from emotion; and with this she continued to register facts.

That young man, it said, was not Francis, his father's favourite: that was Oliver, the soldier son. And the pretty, fair girl was his wife, Marietta.

Yet, when it came to Mrs. Pender, the tinily working mechanism would only chronicle a dress. Nothing but a dress! A very beautiful dress it was . . . remarkable even among the many unusual toilettes surrounding it . . . other women had to turn and look at it with admiration. . . .' But what of the face above these subtle folds and draperies? Do what she would, Joanna could not see it. She was anxious to see it, and by looking once or twice aside, tried to refres, her vision for seeing it. But no! The nodding, smiling

ineloquent face of the woman baffled her each time. **And**
though she gazed till she was almost in a stupor with gazing,
she could see only a smiling *nothing* under a hat.

" She's nothing ! " cried the girl in her heart with fierce
satisfaction. " She's nothing . . . like Irene. How can **he**
laugh and talk like that ? Why does he bear it ? "

Undoubtedly Louis appeared very sprightly. Was **this**
his Society manner ? Joanna shivered. She remembered
his half amused strutting on the night she first met him. He
was never like that with her now, she thanked Heaven !

But this was what he could not give up for her. A nausea
crept over her.

Still she couldn't turn and leave the place. She could not
go till she had seen his face in recognition.

At that moment Louis turned with a roving eye and saw
her. He made no visible movement. For perhaps three
seconds he stood staring straight at her, maintaining the same
apparently easy posture, yet Joanna knew him rigid in every
sinew.

Then he shifted his hat very slightly on his head, and turned
away. There had not come the faintest change on his face.
It was less an acknowledgment than a denial. It would rob
her of identity.

Joanna went out. She passed down the long room steadily,
pushed herself through the swing doors, and after walking
blindly for some minutes found herself in Regent Street. Here
she paused for a moment as if overtaken in spite of her haste
by what she most desired to escape. What a sickness was
this ! What a devastating disgust !

" Shall I bear it ? " she asked. And she spoke the question
again and again, in a low voice but audibly as if it relieved her.
" Shall I bear it ? Shall I bear it ? "

That she *could* bear it—alas ! even now she knew. Already
the old excuses were beginning to marshal themselves for
Louis. What should she have done in his place ? What else
could he have done ? In the circumstances would it not have
been the most distressing folly for him to have acted otherwise ? And she herself was a party to circumstance. It was
only because of her extraordinary lack of imagination that she
now suffered so acutely. Nothing was altered.

Not only by her reason, but by her proved capacity for endurance she knew she might bear it. How she could revel

in the part of the oppressed and humble still! How she could hug to her bosom the secret jewel with its lustre turned inward, which is the inalienable treasure of the outcast! Was it not this that she had unwittingly coveted when for a penance she had kissed the blind beggar? Besides, did anything she had seen to-day make her need Louis less? And was it less true what he had said—" If you leave go of me, I shall be in the mire? "

She could bear it.

But would she?

It was not true that nothing was altered. Louis had been lowered in her eyes. She had seen him joined to his idols.

And where did the blame lie? In his weakness, or in her own dreadful endurance and humility?

This was what must be put to the test for his sake as well as for hers. Her lust for sacrifice should be gratified no longer. Would he also put his infirmity behind him? She had made her choice. He must make his. If the mire was his place, let him sink into it. It was cleaner than the stifling falseness into which she had dragged him.

Having walked about for nearly two hours, now in a sick fury, now in concentrated thought, she slowly returned to Chapel Court.

Her face under the rakish little hat looked pinched as if by illness. But as she was wearily opening the Moons' green door, she stopped, and a more hopeful expression came over her features.

Some one had begun to thump out the tune called *Simple Aveu* upon a neighbouring piano.

Vulgar and sugary air! How often in her early teens had Georgie wakened the household of a morning by practising it thinly upon her fiddle! The atmosphere now it conjured up was one of so utter, so unsuspectedly morbid a dreariness, that Joanna was forced to take comfort thereat. Whatever life might be now, it was a thousand times better than it had been then. Not before had she realized to the full the unhappiness of her teens. If she were at that moment, half so unhappy, she would certainly kill herself. But she had something better to do.

In the house a telegram awaited her. It was from Linnet.

V

It was a telegram of eleven words.

Joanna read it once. After a short, passive interval she read it a second time. After a longer, more active interval she read it a third time. But already at the third time she knew it by heart.

When she drew the thin, folded slip out of its envelope that she might read it a fourth time, she was seated in the night express on her way to Scotland. She still knew it by heart. For the past five hours it had been reiterating itself in her brain, even on her lips. What was more, the wheels under her carriage and the pulsing engine in front, had both got it by heart. They kept repeating the eleven words over and over in a kind of drone. But though this was so, though it had caused her to do so many things with collected swiftness ; though it had brought her to the station, and had put her into this train that swung and thudded northwards, perhaps it was all a mistake, a figment of her own tired brain ?

So she read it for the fourth time :

"*Mother not well don't worry but think you should come Linnet.*"

It was dated from the village where she had left her mother and Linnet. And it had been dispatched at 5.15 p.m. . . . A quarter-past five ! The hour upon the clock over the swing doors of the picture gallery ! Just as she had caught sight of Louis Linnet's message had started trembling along a wire in the North !

A long, long time ago it seemed. Far longer than five hours. And it was the telegram that had made it so. Because the telegram had compelled action. It had visibly and in an instant transformed her life, while that other had produced nothing but emotions. Under the violence of the new compulsion, Joanna was tempted for a moment to deny the importance of the earlier event. It seemed trivial beside the fact of her mother's illness. But she was growing honest and she refused the evasion. What had happened in the picture gallery was important, but it could be left. That was all. The summons from Linnet could not wait. Their mother was ill. When had she been taken ill ? He did not say. There had been no hint of illness in any letter. A week ago she had been well—particularly well. How ill was she now ?

" Don't worry," Linnet had said, and Joanna had dwelt on that part of his message in her hurried talk with Georgie before leaving London. They all knew that Linnet was helpless in the slightest case of illness at home. How much more so, away there in that remote village, and under such primitive conditions. It was natural that he should send for one of his sisters. And Georgie was not in a state to travel.

She was not to worry. Linnet had expressly said so. But Joanna lay awake all night in the train and knew that there was no hope. Linnet, when he telegraphed, had not known that there was no hope. She was sure of that. His telegram had told her what he himself did not or would not know.

Though she could not sleep, she lay down, trying to rest. The day had told upon her in an aching fatigue, and she must save the strength that remained for what was coming. Towards morning she slept a very little.

In Glasgow she found there was a coast train she might catch with a rush, and a later one which would give her time for some tea and a wash. "Don't worry," Linnet had said. But Joanna raced for the first train, and scrambled into it as it was moving.

On the steamer she swallowed some breakfast, though the thick, round oaten biscuits, which in childhood she had enjoyed, were as sawdust in her mouth. It was a rough, bright crossing. There was a band, to which the plunging paddle seemed to keep time and all the white, churned wake to dance. Everything recalled the unforgettable journeys of childhood . . . with piles of luggage, baths with straps round them, perambulators, bags of biscuits for the sea-gulls . . . their father pacing the deck springily, laughing with the wind in his beard . . . their mother falling asleep in a sheltered corner with a tired, happy face. But now all the blown people on the deck looked like ghosts.

Upon landing she was told that no coach ran till the arrival of the next steamer, an hour later. So she started on foot, leaving her bag to follow by coach. She set out at a good pace, but very soon her fears made the slowness of walking unbearable, and she broke into a run. She ran till her breath came in agonizing gasps and she was forced to walk again. She was not to worry. . . . It was probably only a bad cold, or perhaps another gastric attack like the one at the time of the removal—nothing really serious. But the question was,

would she get there in time ? If she went on walking she
would be too late. So she ran again. And so she kept
on running and then walking, and then running again—but
mostly running—all the way along the winding, coast road,
with her eyes continuously dazzled by the glittering morning
sea. She had about four miles to go.

At last. There was the cottage ! It was the very end one
at the far-away end of a row of small, white cottages, some
thatched, some slated, which stood only about half a mile
ahead round the bay. Everything looked as it had looked
on the morning, little more than a week before, when Joanna
had left for London. The peat smoke rose comfortingly from
the chimneys into the pale blue sky : dogs barked : children
were playing on the road between the cottages and the sea.

And there was Linnet !

He waved his hand, shouted, disappeared into the cottage,
and in less than half a minute came out again and began run
ning towards her.

Joanna waved and ran faster. It was all right after all
She need really not have worried. Linnet would not wave
and shout if mother was dead. He must have dashed into
the cottage just to tell her.

" I knew you would come,"—Linnet's first words clashed
with the sighing—" How is she ? " that came from his sister
as they both sped on without pausing a moment.

" She'll be as right as rain now you are here," he said
soothingly (but with what relief !) as he took the breathless Joanna's arm. . . . " She was so pleased when your
wire came." And he told how their mother had been well
—never in her life better—and in splendid spirits, till three
days ago when she had been taken ill in the night with bad
pains. In the morning she had been better, but worse again
towards evening. It had only been yesterday morning,
that he had gone, without telling her, to fetch the doctor.
Mother had been cross. She was positive a strange doctor
couldn't understand her constitution, but she had been glad
to see him all the same, and had taken his medicine. But
this morning, all of a sudden, she had seemed rather low. It
was good that Joanna had come to nurse her.

Joanna hardly listened to Linnet's words. She heard in a
heavy stupor of amazement his declaration that, though he
had sent for her, he had not been the least anxious till this

morning. But in her pocket she had his telegram of the day before giving her no hope. And for all his voluble reassurances he had not yet contradicted that message.

He waited in the tiny, littered sitting-room while his sister went through to her mother's bedroom beyond.

There was a dreadful, cottage closeness in the air that puffed out to meet her as she opened the door. And mingling with it came an abhorrent breath, which the girl recognized though it had never before blown against her face.

VI

On the bed, under a tumbled patchwork quilt lay Juley. Without changing her uneasy attitude she turned her face as her daughter came in.

"My own dear child!" she said, with a curious, difficult utterance. But her eyes were lit up.

Joanna put her arms round her mother, kneeling by the bed, and the tears rained down her cheeks.

"I came as quick as I could, my darling," she said, laying her head on Juley's breast. "And now I'll never leave you again."

Juley stroked her child's head in silence.

"How are you, dear? Are you better? Is the pain gone? Can I get you anything?"

"Quite gone. I'm better. No, nothing to drink . . . I'll soon be well . . . but I'm uncomfortable, and how untidy the room is."

"That's what I'm here for—to make you comfortable. This isn't like you, Mother," Joanna chided, drawing herself gently away and looking about the dark, untidy little room. "What a mess! Linnet *is* a bad nurse. Shall I tidy up a bit before the doctor comes, or is there anything I can get for you first?" She tried to speak with composure.

"No, dear. Tidy . . . I'd like th' room tidied . . . but leave the bed . . . no pain now . . . but must keep still . . . don't touch. . . ."

Joanna who was trying to open the deep-set, impossible window, looked round aghast. The sick woman beginning the sentence distinctly enough, was now mumbling like a drunken person, and at the end of the mumble there was a little, dreadful gulp. Running to the bedside the girl saw that a change had come over the face on the pillow.

"Linnet!" she called out loudly. "Fetch the doctor! And run! Run!"

As if he had been waiting for that word, Linnet sped from the cottage.

And now Juley's face had changed still more. She raised her strong, beautiful voice in what seemed urgent speech, but Joanna, to her despair, could not distinguish a word, not even a syllable in the sounds that came. She would have given her life to read the meaning in the eyes that gazed with such intentness of supplication into hers. But she could not.

She tried to find some comfort in the strength of her mother's voice. Dying people surely spoke feebly?

"Don't talk now, darling. It will tire you. I'm not going away. We can talk afterwards. Shall I read to you . . . the morning verses?" Joanna pleaded. And she held up the familiar, worn copy of *Daily Light* with its stamped leather covers and a star on the back, which had lain by Juley's bedside these forty years.

But Juley shood her head emphatically.

"No, no!" she said—"not now." And having clearly uttered these words she babbled off again, vehement but incomprehensible.

Then she stopped speaking, and a look of extreme surprise crossed her face.

Joanna, beside herself with helplessness, tried to give her water in a tea-spoon, tried brandy and water. But the liquid only ran down outside the unconscious mouth . . .

And the next moment Juley's face passed from surprise to profound preoccupation. She seemed to sink within herself, drew one long, terrible breath, and frowned intently. Joanna looked for the first time upon death.

VII

Linnet had not yet returned, and after the first panic and blankness, Joanna resumed her mechanical task of tidying her mother's room. It was the last thing she had been clearly asked to do. And as she did it she became gradually aware of a deep contentment which she could neither understand nor question. Soon she would be involved in the explosion of mourning. There was Linnet, poor boy! Georgie would have to be told. The doctor would come, and with him an unending, impertinent train of arrangements and condolences. But now, for this little while, she felt close to her mother as never before. Without speech they seemed to share the secrets of life and death. Soon enough would grief with its clumsy trappings and its real pain smash the exquisite prism. Then all would be chaotic and desolate again. None must rob them of this moment of union. It was infinitely precious and perfect.

So Joanna made the toilette table neat, arranged the bottles together on the crazy mantelpiece, and tried to make the room seemly as her mother had liked it to be.

But each time she turned away, the bed drew her back. And she came again and again to gaze at her mother. She laid her hand upon the forehead, and her flesh recoiled from the waxen coldness of that contact. This then was death. We must all die and be like this. No wonder little Ollie had cried. No wonder! Joanna was filled for the moment with a horror of anger against the physical outrage of death. She searched the immovable face, questioned it fearfully. We must all die. None could escape. But here was one who had been used to speak of death as of hidden treasure, to be waited for with patience, but to be coveted exceedingly. Now she had her wish. What was it to her? In that last profound withdrawal by which she had met it, had she been afraid, or joyous, or simply unconscious?

Though the frown remained a stern furrow between the brows, the puzzled look was gone; and now the face seemed full of judgment. Joanna had heard that the faces of the dead were peaceful. This face was set in a perfect stillness of indignation and judgment. Juley, the merciful, the striver, the stricken, had become the judge. And to her child she would not say one word. She lay there in grave, remote, inexorable understanding, in unrelenting judgment that would never be disclosed.

As Joanna was trying unavailingly to straighten the bright quilt over the already stiffening body, a printed card slipped from a fold of the patchwork into her hand. It was lettered in blue, with red capitals and gold underlining, and she knew it must have fallen earlier out of *Daily Light,* within the flaps of which it had been Juley's custom to cherish such things.

"These children are dear to Me," it ran. "Be a mother to them and more than a mother. Watch over them tenderly.

Be just and kind. If thy heart is not large enough to embrace them, I will enlarge it after a pattern of My Own. If these young children are docile and obedient, bless Me for it : if they are froward, call upon Me for help : if they weary thee, I will be thy *Consolation :* if thou sink under thy burden, I will be thy *Reward*."

The daughter, having read, leaned down, whispered something in her dead mother's ear, and ran out of the cottage blind with tears.

This was death. Not the cold forehead, the stillness, the sad, uncouth posture. But this—that the child could never again say—" I love you," and see her mother's eyes light up with joy ! How unimaginable it was, and how pitiful, that she should no w have to ask herself whether once in all these years of womanhood she had clearly and simply declared her love ! Now it seemed to her that all these years her mother had been supplicating for that alone. And now it was too late.

In the afternoon Joanna and an old woman from the village washed Juley's body and dressed it for burial.

The brother and sister took turns in sitting by the dead till morning. Sometimes they remained a while together, talking in low tones. Once or twice they laughed a little. They felt like plotters.

At dawn Joanna was there alone, and suddenly she could endure the room no longer. What foolishness to stay here when her mother had escaped—had gone like a bird over a lake—had fled and left behind all the tedious, daily matters she had so hated, the staleness, the fearfulness, the makeshifts, the heavy, dragging carcase of flesh !

Outside on the road before the cottage door, she drew a breath of the early morning deep into her weary body. After the night in that miserable, airless death-chamber, she knew how to savour the caller saltness of the sea-weed and wet rocks : she could detect by turning her face inland, that warmer yet as sharp fragrance of the bog-myrtle : and through eager nostrils she inhaled the homely pungency of the peat-reek. In her blood she could feel the stirring and upstanding of the millions of tiny plants upon the hillside. With her blood she knew them—the little spiky, spotted, orchises, the knowing fly-catchers with sticky leaves, the waxy heads of bell-heather, the small daisy buds—innocent buds that, like cherubim and seraphim, covered their faces, with all their narrow, crimson-tipt feathers. The sun was not yet risen, but the sky looked pearly, and far up some flakes of cloud, winging higher than the rest, were rosy with prophecy.

Then along the horizon a line of fishing-smacks came beating back to harbour after the night's catch.

A meaning, a cohesion in everything she saw, struck on Joanna's spirit as the opening bars of a compelling air of music strike on the ear. The freshness, the pulsing flight of some birds speeding inland, the faint stirring of the trees, the first thin, blue smoke rising from a distant cottage chimney—these were harmonies in a complicated yet decisive theme. They were full of solutions. They gave release to all that was cramped and tortured in the heart. And dominating all of them—like a thought, like melody, like the soul of man—went the tiny, indomitable brown sails, beating along home between the sea and the sky.

VIII

But the funeral and all connected with it was a progression of horrors.

On the steamer, the coffin having been slung on board from the ferry like any other piece of heavy luggage, Linnet and Joanna felt as if they were the sharers in a shameful secret. In Glasgow, the house stank with the sweetness of white flowers, most of them sent out of mere respect by old acquaintances of their father, so that to Juley's children the names on the cards were but names. And the rooms seemed always full of whispering people who would belie the dead by their praises. The only relief came from such of Juley's poor folk as came timidly to the door that they might look once more upon her face and weep. For to them Juley had been but goodness and mercy, and nought besides.

Georgie, in spite of her condition, had travelled north. Her grief was real and simple. Yet when she joined exuberantly with Aunt Georgina, Aunt Ellen and Mrs. Boyd in cataloguing her mother's virtues, Joanna turned away, feeling that the dead woman was deserted indeed. If only one of them would say the truth—" She failed," or " She went unfulfilled," or " In death alone has she come to blossom ! " But no. They would have it, perhaps for their own solace, that she had gone bearing her sheaves with her.

More loving than such love there flamed up in Joanna the desire for clear knowledge, for the deep and free admission, in which alone our failures may find their absolution, even their vindication. Oh, when she came to die, might there be one that kept knowledge of her, rather than many that self-sparingly loved, forgave, and so annulled her!

Mabel, though she was again at home, this time with her husband, did not come to Glasgow. Neither did she write to Joanna. But she was at some pains to explain both omissions in a letter to Georgie. She hinted at certain of "poor darling Aunt Juley's" confidences during her stay at La France Quadrant over a year ago. She was "awfully sorry" that under the circumstances, and as a sincere person, she felt unable to express the usual kind of sympathy with Joanna. And so, as she wished not only to preserve her own integrity but to avoid giving unnecessary pain, it was better, wasn't it, that she should not stand with them by the grave? She would be with them in spirit. Joanna, with her hatred of false conventionality, would be the first, she hazarded, to appreciate her genuineness. This had not been an easy letter to write.

And along with the letter, Mabel sent an anchor of violets, of which the too faint natural scent had been fortified by liberal sprinklings of *Ess. Bouquet*.

Joanna was grateful to Georgie for the wrath she displayed over both the letter and the flowers. The perfumed anchor was picked out of its box with the tongs and thrown upon the fire to frizzle. Georgie hugged her sister and swore she would never forgive Mabel, who after all couldn't help being a sneak, as she had been born so. But the cousin's accusation remained with Joanna and tortured her.

Unkindness . . . neglect . . . and was there something besides? Certainly Mabel had implied a more direct guilt. Joanna remembered the strange gladness she had felt during these few minutes alone with her dead mother before the world had broken in with its lying and vulgar clamour of lamentation. And now—it was true—except for a moment, to give and get assurances of love beyond all question, to give and get the kiss of perfect, clear-eyed understanding, she would not have her mother back. A thousand times, no! Was she then at heart her mother's murderer? Perhaps she was, But even so, coming from Mabel, the charge was foul. Mabel, who knew them all! Mabel, who with nods and smiles had from the very first, urged on the breaking of the household. O! Mabel, more hateful and destructive than any murderer, what degradation to be blown upon by such as you!

These miseries weighed so heavily on Joanna that at first she hardly felt the stroke of outward shame that now fell on the family. And when she did feel it, she inclined almost to welcome it as a distraction.

Yet in itself it was grave enough. On the division of the Bannerman estate, Linnet had had to confess to speculative follies of long standing. Only by foregoing the greater part of their portions, would the girls and the absent Sholto be able to meet their brother's debts and prevent his public disgrace. And this done, Mr. Boyd, as their mother's trustee, their father's friend, and Linnet's employer, insisted seriously on the expediency of Linnet's leaving Glasgow with the least possible delay.

Linnet himself, rather to everybody's surprise, made no objection. Sholto, he declared, had long ago invited his coming to Australia, and he was not forced to assume that Mr. Boyd had anything to do with the prompt but hearty renewal of that invitation which he now received by cable.

Joanna saw him off. To the end he maintained an admirable show of unconcern. He had been deucedly unfortunate, said his manner. And though his sister could not meet his eyes because of that in them which so belied his words, she had to love him for his refusals, to pay him tribute in that he neither cringed nor broke down.

Seeing her brother on the deck of his ship, waving his hat to her in farewell, and with his narrow, finely cut head bare against the grey morning sky, Joanna was confronted yet again with her most familiar image. Like a key the master symbol of her life heretofore was put into her hand. . .

> " Ev'n as a bird
> Out of the fowler's snare
> Escapes away,
> So is our soul set free! "

CHAPTER III

I

WHEN the ugly flutter of death had subsided, Joanna with mounting terror discovered that her world was changed. The mask of stability had been stripped from outward things. Inherent deathliness was everywhere made visible. Even her own firm self seemed to be crumbling within her.

Desperately, and with every subtlety at her command, she fought against the dissolution which threatened on her return to London. She kept the outer shell of her existence intact—the shell composed of work, duties, human contacts, the care of her room, her clothes, her body. And because all meaning had gone from these components—because her work (though there was more need now than at any former time, that she should bestir herself in making a livelihood) was loathsome to her, and seemed particularly useless—this was a kind of heroism.

Unhappily it was a heroism that demanded all her strength and emptied her of real courage. Under the strain of keeping up appearances her resolve to force a choice upon Louis melted quite away. Instead she turned frantically to him for help. Louis had never lied to her, thought she, never pretended. He had been frank in disbelief. In him might she not find at least a foothold of sure ground amid this quaking bog of death ?

Surely enough it looked at first as if she might get from him the succour she needed for life. Regarding the incident at the private view, he had that same day written to her; and this letter, full of love and self-loathing had reached her on the morning of Juley's funeral. At their next meeting, some weeks later a new flower of passion had blossomed between them. Now she longed for him bitterly all the hours they were apart, while Louis on his side laid caution aside in flying to her. But a fearful thing had happened between them. Now when she lay in his arms, there came always a vision of her mother's face, dying or dead—the heavy frown, the altered mouth, the long, dreadful breath. And when he left her she was cold as earth.

She could hardly bear it. Yet even the inner deathliness of his embraces still seemed better than the final outward rending of losing him. Did she not love him ? Her ideals were all for faithfulness in love, and her cowardice pointed the same way. Did he not still need her, still keep the power to make her tremble though with a touch, a look ? If that went, what was left ?

So she was beset on both sides by fear. And she survived from day to day, from week to week, by sheer stiffness of will.

II

Early in October Georgie became the joyful mother of a son.

Even before Juley's death Joanna had taken to spending much of her time with Georgie. The sisters had sat and sewed together many hours, making baby clothes. And they had spoken of all the things sisters would inevitably speak of on such occasions. The elder had been the more voluble, being, like Aunt Perdy, that kind of talker that needs little more than a listener. But Joanna too had borne her part, and one day she had come very near to a full disclosure about Louis and herself. She would certainly have made it so, had not it been for her continual and very sensitive consciousness of Max in the background. As it was, she left Georgie in no doubt that she had had the misfortune to love a married man and the temerity to make her love the pivot of her life.

Immediately after their mother's death the two, as was natural, saw still more of each other. Joanna was still able —spasmodically at least—to believe that her world was shaken by the ordinary course of bereavement. Her mother, she told herself, had stood, more than could have been guessed, for the external seemliness and the underlying coherence of things. And now that her mother was gone, these were challenged. But here was Georgie, herself soon to be a mother. Here was Georgie, eloquent and beaming—a very embodiment, if ever there was one, of the affirmation that all was solidly established as before. In Georgie's company Joanna was able to regard her own deathly knowledge as mere, sickly, grieving fancies. And this was what she frantically sought

Then in October the baby boy, the treasure of treasures,

arrived. And amid that wonder and rejoicing and piercing wistfulness of envy Joanna thought she perceived the way by which she might save herself.

Though it came to her apparently as a revealing flash from without, she had no sooner measured its importance than she knew it had lain hid in her heart for years past. Why else had she drawn such peculiar comfort from the presence of Ollie and Roddy in Chapel Court? Why had the tending of their bodies so deeply stirred her own flesh? Why now did the handling of this small, red bundle in Georgie's firstborn send so strange a quivering up her arms to her heart, and from her heart back along her limbs to the very hollows of her feet?

The answer, she thought, was clear. If only she might bear Louis a child!

Far from raising new problems in Joanna's confused and tortured life this idea offered her a well-nigh perfect solution. Not only did it promise an enforced consummation of her love for Louis, but the very material difficulties, which might have appeared as obstacles to another woman, were to her so many spurs urging her on. They attracted because they seemed to show the direction in which effort would be worth while. As for the immediate conventional bearings of the situation she had no fears. Her mother was dead, her brothers away, Georgie married and happy. And just because she was herself ready for all risks, she knew she could be prudent. Within the first hour in which she saw herself as a mother, a complete programme of action arranged itself in her mind. She would go, she told herself, to Aunt Perdy's mountain top to have her child. If Louis chose to cleave to her it would be salvation for him as well. If he dared not, she would let him go. There would be no alternative. Besides, with a girl-babe like little Ollie or a man-child like Roddy sprung from their love, she would have her place in that world which now was slipping from beneath her feet.

That Louis might refuse a demand at once so imperious and so reasonable as this seemed to her she would hardly admit. He must see clearly that it was no more than her right. Hers was the ultimate undertaking, his only whatever share in the responsibility he freely desired. To any other view she closed her eyes.

At the same time, even in her exaltation, some instinct warned Joanna to go cautiously to work. Men were so strange.

One never knew with what unexpected, incomprehensible prejudice a man might regard so perfectly straightforward a matter. And she was in this man's power. With every logical and passionate argument on her side, he could yet deny her the one vital thing left in life. This made her very wary, and she waited for her moment without saying a word to him of what filled her mind. Sometimes she thought he looked at her curiously.

III

But one day in the Christmas holidays, when Georgie's baby was three months old, the sisters planned a shopping expedition or. his behalf. Already he was growing out of all his clothes and would presently be ready for short-coating.

The night before, Joanna had lain long awake thinking and thinking of her mother. Was it after all her death that had changed the face of the world ? Was it not rather the manner of her death ? She had gone without once attaining the full stature of her soul, without once uttering clearly the word it should have been hers to utter. With all her struggles, her nobility, her sacrifices, she was unfulfilled. She was like the sides of an arch that fall in together in a heap because the key-stone is missing. Yet who had faith if not she ? What had been wrong ?

All at once Joanna turned in accusation upon her dead father. In spite of the unkind childish dream she had kept his memory all these years as of some one good beyond question, almost god-like. Nor had Juley ceased to foster to the last this ideal image in her children's minds. But now this with other security was gone from life ; and in that quiet midnight hour Joanna asked herself if he was not greatly to be blamed. Was it not their father who had failed them all ? Was the keystone of the arch of fulfilment not placed in the hands of the male ?

She condemned him pitilessly, as only a woman can condemn a parent. It had all been wrong, that apparently happy and peaceful marriage—wrong from beginning to end. There had been no beginning and no end. There had been only a confused and accidental issue of wrongness, of which she, Joanna, was a part. She remembered the words—" In sin did my mother conceive me." Why not—" In sin did my father beget me " ? And in her very bones she could feel at work that reward of sin which is death.

She blamed her father. But amid the heat and misery of her indictment, Sholto's face, so long vanished from earth, rose cold and sweet and patient before his daughter, and he refuted the charge. It was long years since she had shut the door against him in her dreams. Now it seemed as if he had been waiting and waiting there outside for her mature reproach. And was not this patience of his, his everlasting vindication? Oh, the patience—the heart-breaking, awful patience of the dead! Oh, that face with its sweet, sunshiny smile, and its eyes so puzzled and afraid, yet innocent, like the eyes of a child! Had not he also, he asked her, been denied fulfilment? If Juley's soul through him had suffered a tragic negation, what of his own extreme, irremediable pathos of incapacity?

Weeping, Joanna turned on her face upon the bed. And weeping she forgave her father and begged his forgiveness.

Next day she tried to discover her trouble to Georgie. She was almost speechless with shyness; but as they were sitting alone together at *Duntarvie*, drinking cups of chocolate before starting for town to buy young Sholto's " shortenings," she managed to put into poor words some part of her midnight thoughts.

The sisters in their black dresses sat facing each other across a small table in the green and white morning-room. Georgie, lolling back a little in her chair, showed all the pride of young and fruitful womanhood. Her eyes were absorbed and manger-worshipping, her face ruddy with health, her breasts large and sweet with milk. Joanna, as she rather painfully spoke, leaned forward—her elbows on the table and the tips of her fingers pressed against her temples as if the pulse there needed protection. And though she still looked very girlish, she was white-faced and harassed, with a faint shadow under each cheek-bone, and between her eyes the same sad, vertical line of perplexity which had been there at the time of Mario's death.

Georgie broke in upon her halting questions with such ready and emphatic replies that Joanna immediately regretted having spoken. Having spoken she would listen. But here was no help to be had. Georgie, as her sister now realized, was enclosed and impenetrably protected by the immediate experience of her own motherhood. She was set on seeing in their mother's death both release and happy fulfilment.

For any declarations of imperfections in this world she was ready with assurances of perfections in the next. Above all she was generously up in arms against each word that might be construed as criticism of the dead. She would remember, she insisted, raising her voice, none but the good and beautiful things about her parents: because only beautiful and good things were real. Faults and failures were best forgotten for the simple reason that they were of no vital importance. They had no lasting truth. They were but passing aberrations which, if we had more faith, we should not even see.

Was Georgie right? Joanna's beseeching eyes rested on her as she discoursed more and more eloquently upon the non-existence of evil. And the younger sister felt so greatly at a disadvantage that she was almost inclined to repudiate her own experience. Was truth not best proved by such a union of physical health and spiritual satisfaction? Was Georgie not happier, more useful, immeasurably fuller of faith and certainty than she?

Yet for all that she could only look blank and miserable, feeling as Georgie's spirit soared, that her own by that very action was being thrust further into darkness. There is a buoyant and genuine faith which, while ostensibly stimulating the faith of others, seems only to be able to swell itself at their expense. And while Georgie glowed and spoke of their mother, it was to Joanna as if the coffin lid were being screwed down afresh, this time more sacrilegiously on Juley's soul.

On their way to the shops, the elder sister, warm with the consciousness that she had given from her own rich store to one in distress, began rosily to sketch out her son's future and her plans for his upbringing.

She was, she declared, ambitious in the best sense of the word. In baby Sholto the fine religious motive of his grand-parents was to be mingled with his father's agnostic humanitarianism. But above all things he was to have absolute tolerance inculcated. From an early age he should develop grace of body and a sense of rhythm by means of the very latest method, the lamentable absence of which in Georgie's own childhood must entirely account for her own abortive musical attainment. (She stated now by the light of this new discovery that even in Dresden the teaching had been completely at fault.) Sholto was never to be punished or forced to act against his inclinations, but would gain his education in Nature's own way, by receiving full and truthful answers to his questions. Georgie herself might be a stupid failure—she laughed happily—in everything she had tried save motherhood. But what did that matter? All that mattered was the new generation, which was so wonderfully to profit by our mistakes. *They* would do, and do far better all that we had left undone.

It would have surprised Georgie could she possibly have known how every word of cheer she uttered struck a fresh blow at the last of her sister's hopes. Joanna herself did not immediately guess the collapse of that hope. At first she only knew that as she listened her heart grew more and more like lead in her breast, and she wondered vaguely why this should be when she had a fair degree of sympathy with Georgie's theories of education.

But in Regent Street, while they were buying little wincey dresses and woolly jackets and boots and cunning caps for Baby, it broke upon her so suddenly that for the space of about a minute the shop and all it contained whirled about her like a tornado.

Not for her that newly-springing and so fair-seeming hope that by her own achievement of motherhood she might make good! Not any longer for her! Here was Georgie turning each purchase over, again and again reminding Joanna of their mother as she tested its softness against her cheek. Ah! There it was! Their mother had done this for them, and her mother for her, always with the same eager and touching confidence in the next generation. And what was to come of it?

Nothing!

Nothing—because it was based on a lie. Nothing—because it was a shirking of the personal issue. Nothing—because it was the last, most exquisite cowardice.

Shaking all over, Joanna examined some white lute ribbon her sister had put just then into her hand, and she gave as her opinion that it would be quite strong enough for binding flannel pilches.

No! If the children, born and unborn were to be served fairly, one must utter clearly and fearlessly one's own word of truth in one's own lifetime. And against this utterance, hard enough in itself the whole world was combined in the most tyrannical of all combinations, the combination of the past with the future generation. What a plausible and cruel trick was there !

It gagged one (yes, that was the right shade of blue for a sash), stifling, if it could, even the word of failure. For failure might be one's word. All could not blossom. But all could reject the greater disaster of unacknowledgment. And this was what Georgie with her light talk of failure would not do. She would sooner deny meaning to their mother's life than admit its failure. She would deny her own failure by child-bearing and the expedient of shifting her fulfilment from her personal hands to the impersonal hands of the future. And this she would call by the name of faith. All round her she shed easy enthusiastic denial,' and Joanna shrank back forsaken and unsheltered. Such enthusiasm only increased the menace she felt everywhere. By the time Sholto's new sash was measured and cut her disbelief in that fair hope by which she had lately been living was complete. It was finished and hard in the darkness—a jewel of unfaith.

They left the shop. And as they walked, hugging their parcels, from Piccadilly Circus to their station in Leicester Square, she looked with strange, terror-stricken eyes at the faces of the passing people. There were the satisfied, solid ones, the flighty, knowing ones, the benevolent, the wicked, the careless, the merely anxious. How they had impressed her once, taken as a whole : and never so much as when her own course was most erratic ! Once she had believed that somehow, between them all, they possessed human truth and knowledge. To-day, for the first time she saw them as a flock of blind things, each one trusting implicitly, as she had done, in the corporate wisdom of all the other blind ones. . . . Louis blind . . . her mother blind . . . the sadness of it almost killed her. . . .

"Isn't life too gorgeous, . . . too wonderful . . . ? " exclaimed Georgie, breaking in upon her thoughts at that instant. And in her exaltation Georgie shouted, so that people turned their heads—some smiling indulgently, some with contempt, others with a peculiar frown of anger . . . "And I feel the whole time that darling Father and Mother, united now, are watching over us, rejoicing so lovingly over the progress of the next generation. Don't you, Joey dear ? "

The other did not at once reply. With the bitterness of

spears behind her eyeballs she saw again the strange indignation in her mother's dying features. Then—at the very last, when the poor tongue could only babble senselessly—had Juley not been trying perhaps to leave her special word of truth with her children? Anyhow at this moment, just as the sisters were passing the steps of the Empire Theatre, Joanna came by the absolute knowledge that if she did not give Georgie the lie here and now their mother's prayers had been in vain. In understanding and obedience therefore, she fell at her mother's feet. She would do it.

She was afraid, however, horribly timid of Georgie.

"I don't believe a single word of all you have said to-day."

Painfully as these words were wrenched out, and appalled as Joanna was by their clumsiness and crudity, they were spoken distinctly.

But the elder merely looked at her younger sister, first in astonishment at this unexpected rudeness, then, seeing the quivering lips, in affectionate pity.

Later, when Georgie began soothingly and deliberately to speak of trifles, Joanna knew that she was being humoured—probably by her brother-in-law's advice—as one in a morbid and overwrought condition.

IV

Joanna knelt by the hearth in the archway room, and piled up her fire between the hobs of the little dog-grate as high as she dared. It was bitter, cold January weather, and she expected Lawrence Urquhart in the course of the evening.

Since Juley's death Joanna's oft fading friendship with Lawrence had put forth fresh shoots. On her return from Glasgow he had appeared at her side with a quiet offering of understanding that could not be refused. As concerned love she believed (sometimes with a pang of which she was ashamed) that he had gone from her; but all the more readily did she admit and even cling to the new bond he had unobtrusively created. It was something different from the former spasmodic attraction, so that she no longer scrupled to make use of his steady kindness in any small practical ways which might relieve her extremity. Also he had become an acknowledged friend of the family. She often saw him now at Georgie's house where he seemed to enjoy talking with Max. And more rarely he would come to Chapel Court.

Earlier that same evening Lawrence had been called to the Bar. And at his invitation Joanna had gone to see the ceremony in Middle Temple Hall.

Its baldness had somewhat disappointed her. From her perch in the high, cramped cage of the gallery she had watched the little doll-like figures advancing in wig and gown to sign the roll as their names were called, and she had hardly been able to distinguish her friend among them.

When it was over, and she had squeezed down the cork-screw staircase in a press of womenfolk, she saw that Lawrence had already almost made his way to her through the crowd and the congratulations. It was then that she was surprised by quite a new view of him. The sculptural folds of the gown gave a dignity that his slight figure needed ; and beneath the formality of the white horsehair wig, all his features were sharpened into a more insistent yet sensitive maleness.

This she had seen, or rather felt. But she had felt also that Lawrence had never been so far removed from her as at that moment. He was gone utterly into the unknowable world of men. Nothing of her world could touch him. She was alien, even hostile to the strongly suppressed excitement in his face and movements.

For a minute they had stood talking together. The Call dinner, Lawrence said, would last till about nine o'clock, after which the other members of his mess would want to go to a music hall. He himself didn't much like the idea—for one thing he had been half-crazy with neuralgia all afternoon. Still it would be better than to return straight from the dinner to his rooms in Chancery Lane. And when Joanna in commiseration (she too had suffered of late from neuralgia) suggested phenacetin with tea by her fireside later in the evening, he thanked her gladly.

So she had stacked up the fire (for though her room with its windows vis-a-vis, was ideal in summer, it was searched by shrewd draughts during the winter) ; and she had lighted the candles on the mantel-piece, and drawn the curtains close, and set out the tea-things on table and hob. She had changed her day dress too for a thinner one of black silk of the kind that floats and does not rustle. All these festive and hospitable things she had done. At the same time her mood was despondent, and she dully regretted having asked Lawrence at all.

When ten o'clock came, however (it had been six when she left the Temple), and there was still not a sign of her visitor, her depression showed no lifting tendency. It was indeed considerably increased. A further restless quarter of an hour passed and she could settle to nothing. She had just made up her mind to go to bed, and was in the act of blowing out the first candle, when she heard the belated steps of Lawrence passing under the archway.

Was it the frost, she wondered when he came in, that had given him such a cheerful, unusual starriness? As they shook hands she realized that he was for once quite divested of his shyness, and so seemed other than himself.

While she busied herself with the tea, which she was making after the Russian fashion in tumblers with slices of lemon, Lawrence sat down and passed his hand over his hair as if he feared it might be disordered. But it was perfectly smooth, reflecting the candle-light almost as well as the polished stove.

' How is your neuralgia ? " asked Joanna observing the action but mistaking its motive.

" My neuralgia ? " He repeated the question as if at a loss for the moment. " . . . O ! It's gone, thank you . . . quite better . . . I had forgotten about it."

He refused the tabloids which she had laid ready for him, but drank her tea thirstily.

" It was good of you to ask me," he said happily, pushing his second empty glass aside, and leaning back in a posture of greater physical unconsciousness than was usual with him. " . . . I'm afraid I'm rather late, but it was impossible to get away sooner. Call dinners are long affairs."

" You were only to come if you felt inclined," Joanna reminded him. " I had almost given you up, and was going to bed."

" I wanted to come, you stupid," he retorted in calm good humour, and clearly without the slightest consciousness of rudeness. " I'm glad you didn't *quite* give me up," he continued not noticing her look. " . . . It's something not *quite* to be given up : isn't it ? "

As he seemed brightly unabashed to be waiting for an answer, Joanna murmured in a neutral voice that she didn't know It had struck her for the first time that perhaps he had drunk too much at dinner. This would account for the lyrical quality in his appearance.

"You are cheerful to-night," she said, staring at the flame of a candle she was snuffing. The room was lighted only by candles and by the splendid, leaping glow of the fire.

Lawrence might well have been warned by her tone ; but he merely recrossed his feet and looked more cheerful still.

"I am," he returned. "Why shouldn't I be ? I've had a good dinner. I'll never have to go in for another examination in my life. It's a pleasure to me to sit here by your fire with you. Why shouldn't I be cheerful ? "

"No reason," admitted Joanna. And having trimmed all four of her wicks on the mantelpiece, she sat down again and leaned her head back against her chair.

At that ever so slight but desolate movement Lawrence changed his own attitude. Now he bent forward, resting his elbows on his knees.

"But *you* aren't," he said. ". . . I'm afraid you're sad. It was all the kinder of you to ask me this evening. I wish I could cheer you up. Won't you tell me what troubles you so ? "

Complete silence and stillness were the only reply.

The young man looked his fill at the heart-breaking shape opposite—apparently so intimate in the firelight, yet really so far out of his reach—at the dear brown head outlined against the linen chair-back, at the disconsolate hands folded languidly in her lap. And though his immediate feeling was one of concern for her, he savoured at that moment both her soft dejection and her damnable obstinacy.

"Are you grieving very much for your mother still ? " he asked, kindly.

His beloved stirred slightly and looked at him.

"It isn't exactly grieving for her," she made answer. "I'm glad for her and for myself that she's dead. No. It's that everything else seems to have collapsed with her."

"Perhaps that's a good thing," said Lawrence after a few moments. "I can't help thinking it is."

Joanna's languor vanished as she sat up in her place. It was not the first time Lawrence had thus disturbed and upset her all of a sudden.

"It's all very well for you," she exclaimed resentfully.

"Why all very well ? I lost my mother too," he returned almost roughly.

"I know. But . . ."

"And I'll tell you what," he interrupted her with vehemence, using strangely enough a phrase which Joanna had long ago come to associate with Louis—". . . I loved her. But I never knew till she was dead what an injury she had done me. And I couldn't forgive her. I don't know if I forgive her now. She had drained me . . . all my life she had drained me . . . I can't think of any other word . . . of my manhood till it was almost gone. She lost me you. Don't speak. I know what I am talking about. She lost me you. You did right not to take me then. I doubt whether even you could have saved me. I had to have everything collapse round me too. You look doubtful. I tell you it was so. Carl could tell you."

"Still . . ." Joanna persisted, after a short, astonished pause. "You had your world of men to fly to, and you found it solid. That seems always left to a man . . . what you said once about being in the stream of things. Look at you to-night. You are quite happy. But what you have wouldn't satisfy me."

"Quite happy, am I?" asked Lawrence, appearing to examine the backs of his finger-nails with the greatest attention.

"You seem to be. A minute ago you said you were, didn't you?"

He raised his eyes at this. "I said no such thing. I said cheerful."

"I'm sorry. Is there so much difference in your case?"

With a violent gesture of his right hand, Lawrence jumped to his feet.

"*Why* are you so hateful to me?" he demanded—"so perfectly brutal and hateful? You know—no one better—that I need you. . . . Not for happiness . . . happiness be damned . . . but just for life. Yet you shut me out; and are vile to me into the bargain. You talk about the world of men. Don't you know it's only a makeshift without the other you won't give me?"

"I can't give what's not in my power."

"Ah! There you are. You can't *give*. No. I ought not to have asked you to *give*. You're much too fond of giving, Joanna : and your kind of giving, if you only knew, is sheer robbery. Give, give, give—to the poor man, when in reality it all goes to feed your own egoism. You are all self-will.

Try to take from a man for a change. Then perhaps you will learn really to give. Carl was right in what he used to say of you."

" What did he say ? "

" He said that in love you were like. . . ." Lawrence considered a moment. " . . . Carl's way of talking is apt to sound rude in anyone else's mouth."

" Never mind, what did he say ? " Joanna insisted.

" He said you were like a clod of earth trying to give itself to a seed, by shoving itself inside the husk. I believe myself," added Lawrence with growing animation, " that you work with all your strength for the very opposite of your nature's true desire."

" So I'm a clod, am I ? " asked Joanna, her eyes dancing with spite. " Once I was a juggler. Now I'm a clod. Shall I tell you what you are ? "

" If you like."

" You are . . . You've been drinking too much."

" True. But I am not drunk."

" Perhaps not. I didn't say so." Joanna spoke coldly. Her voice seemed to be holding her skirts round her as if they might touch him.

" I shouldn't have come here if I had been drunk. You know that," said Lawrence. " I did feel braver than usual, and thought it would be good to be with you feeling brave for once. Now I've begun, I may as well finish . . . I daresay that's nonsense about the clod—though remember that for the seed the clod has all the sky in it, and the rain and sun and sea and wind as well as the earth . . . Images, though, are apt to be misleading. Who knows ? Perhaps you are the seed and I the clod. I daresay. What I'm certain of, more certain than I ever was before, is that I need you. I need to hide myself and to lose myself in you. If you knew what my life is like these days ! All that can be said is that I have the grace to be sure it isn't life. And I do believe you need me too. My poor, hopeless pet ! . . . Let me call you that this once . . . If you were getting on well without me, I wouldn't say a word. But you aren't getting on."

" Whether I'm getting on or not doesn't help in this."

" Why not ? It should."

" I love some one else. You see it's no use. And you knew it before. Carl must have . . ."

" I don't believe it," he interrupted doggedly.

" What don't you believe ? "

" That you know anything whatever about love . . . yet."

She turned from him. " Perhaps that can only be proved by my faithfulness," she murmured—" and it shall be."

Lawrence groaned.

" Joanna, you are such a fool, I almost wish I didn't love you."

She pondered a moment. Then—

" You would soon stop loving me if you knew the kind of person I am," she declared. And to Lawrence's amazement she suddenly smiled as she spoke.

" Why ? What do you mean," he asked.

" I'm really bad," she said, a little more seriously but still with a peculiar, ungovernable flippancy.

" How bad are you ? "

" Just bad."

" Tell me."

She paused a moment ; and then looking steadily away from him, spoke in a different, quiet voice.

" So bad that I can be attracted by men I don't love at all."

It was the man's turn to smile now. But Joanna did not see him.

" Who says that's bad ? " he asked.

" Everybody—in a woman."

" Sometimes," said Lawrence, all the lines of his body expressing relief from strain—" . . . sometimes you shock me. You have always seemed so complete to me . . . so much a woman . . . and then you say a thing like that, which one would think could only come from a schoolgirl."

He waited, but there was no answering smile on Joanna's face. Instead a quiver passed over it, and the bright colour that had swept into her cheeks, ebbed quickly under his eye.

Would he never understand what she was trying to say ?

" I should have said . . ." she persevered clutching all her courage (and now indeed she was cruel in all conscience : now indeed she chose her words with merciless directness) —" . . . I should have said that though I *belong* to one man, and always must belong to him, I'm capable of feeling strongly attracted by others."

From the first word of this speech she had kept her eyes

immovably fixed upon Lawrence's which at the moment were intently regarding the flame of one of the candles. But a minute before, he had taken the candlestick in his hand, and with a match had been kneading the rim of hot wax into a scolloped frill all round. The small, erect flame illumined the irises of his eyes. Joanna could see how surprisingly light they were in colour—like peaty pools. She could even see the darker flecks in the iris, which made her think of trout in a burn. And not a flicker of the eyelids could have escaped her vigilance.

But she had said her say, and there had not been the faintest tremor. The hand which had been wielding the match became perfectly still. That was all. The eyes and face, still already, became stillness incarnate. Then he put the candlestick back in its place, and stooped so that his face was hidden. He stooped ostensibly that he might throw into the fire the match that had dropped from his fingers.

The instant she had spoken, Joanna felt happier. Lawrence's stillness was too extreme to deceive her. She knew by it for certain that her disclosure had been a disclosure indeed, and that it had hurt him. All the more had she been all this time to blame.

Now that was said which should in fairness have been said long ago. It was too bad that he should suffer. But she was thankful that he could take it like a man. Suppose he had winced and wept and reproached her, as on that last ride ?

When he faced her again, his lips shook but his words came composedly enough.

" I take back what I said about your needing me," he said slowly. " I was wrong seemingly. Please be generous and put it down to the fact that I had been drinking more than was good for me. I should perhaps have been wiser not to have come to-night."

" Perhaps. . . . Still I wanted you to know. . . . " Joanna's gaze was almost fawning on him now for a kind look, though, to do her justice, there was no appeal in her detached voice. It merely served her in the making of a true statement.

" If you are satisfied, that's something," said Lawrence, his eyes flicking her like a whip. " I think I'll wend my way homeward now," he continued. " It must be late." (Even as he spoke, he wondered at the absurdity of his using that absurd phrase now for the first time since his schooldays. Why " wend his way " to-night ?)

" My watch has stopped," Joanna said helplessly looking at her wrist. " But it's only about eleven I believe. The clock on the mantelpiece is slow."

He studied his own watch as if the time were a matter of real importance to him. " Five minutes to eleven, I make it."

As they said good night, both their voices plodded along the dead level of exhaustion.

But Joanna must go down the dark little staircase with her guest to see him off. Just as if their evening had been of the happiest kind, she must open the door for him and warn him of the three crooked steps. There was a moon somewhere low in the sky behind the tall houses, but the court was full of treacherous shadows.

Lawrence lost no time in parting from her. He made nothing of the steps. And almost before she realized he was gone, she heard the echo of his quick retreating tread.

When that had quite died away in the street outside, she went forlornly up to her bedroom as one who has lost a friend. An old-fashioned expression of her mother's came appositely into her mind. She felt, she told herself, " like a knotless thread."

v

For the next three months and more, Lawrence was not seen at Chapel Court. Even to the Garden Suburb he no longer came. A single accidental meeting which Joanna had with him about six weeks after that evening in January, served only to strengthen her conclusion that he had dropped out of her life.

It happened that Ollie's mother, Mrs. Garland, was ill in bed, and had asked Joanna to deliver some copy for her in Fleet Street. Until she was at the very door of the office, Joanna had not known that Mrs. Garland's paper occupied the same building as the *Sunday Budget* for which Lawrence worked. Still it seemed improbable that she would come across him. He was not likely to be there. And in any case the *Budget* office was on the third floor, while her errand was on the second. She was taken aback when, immediately after her handing Mrs. Garland's copy to the small imp at that moment in charge of the tape room, an inner, editorial glass door was opened, and laughing over some unknown jest, two men came out, one of the two being Lawrence.

With a sudden scarlet in her cheeks Joanna bowed uncertainly. But if Lawrence too was taken at a disadvantage he hardly showed it. Leaving the editor to melt back into his glass room, he came across to her, exhibited ordinary, friendly surprise at her presence, heard the reason of it, chatted a minute or two with cool detachment, and as soon as he could do so politely, ran back to remind the man within of some forgotten matter.

As Joanna descended the stairs she again heard his voice and the other's raised in exclusive mirth. She had hardly recognized her lost friend in this easy, keen, absorbed young man. Indeed and indeed men were to be envied in their work. Lawrence might protest as he liked that there was no satisfaction in it. No doubt while he was with her he had felt it so. But his face, both now and on Call Night had told a different story.

On her way home she was more than ever convinced that she had at last made a clean break between herself and Lawrence. Further she felt sure that Lawrence was not averse to her knowing it.

VI

So she went on with the bitter and deathly course which accorded with her ideas of faithfulness. She was upheld in it by her one conscious belief—the belief that she loved Louis.

When, one morning in May, Mr. Moon summoned her to answer a telephone call in the shop below, Joanna guessed it must be from Louis. His way was to telephone rather than to write, and it was five days since she had seen him. Always at the end of three days they were both restless for sight and sound of each other.

She ran downstairs, eager and trembling for his message as ever.

No sooner had she heard it than the familiar office, with its urns and its samples of stone and wood, spun darkly round her, and she had to hang her head for faintness.

Louis was going to Edinburgh next day. And he wanted her to come with him. Except for a peculiar, almost angry note in his voice, he might have been proposing that she should take a walk with him in the Park. Yet this was the

first time he had ever asked her to go away with him. Both
of them hitherto had fought shy of anything suggestive of the
ordinary intrigue. Wherever Joanna was Louis had known
he could come without fear or shame. And there had been
their country walks. But for anything else, Joanna had
instinctively waited till their going should be a real departure.
Tacitly Louis had understood this and had acquiesced. They
had let slip many opportunities.

But here was he all of a sudden asking her to take a real
journey with him, and at the very peremptoriness of the
request her heart cried out in hope. He could not well tell
her so much in words at this moment, but might not this be
his way of coming to what she longed and lived for ?

Half fainting she said she would go ; and they made arrangements for meeting. Baldly they fixed time and place. By
not a word did they betray the unusual nature of their decision.

It was her lover's plan for the next morning that she should
take an early train as far as Peterborough, and there wait for
the two o'clock express by which he was travelling. From
then on, they would be safe. In Edinburgh the following day
he would hurry over the event which was taking him North
—the unveiling of some panels of his, in which from their
earliest drawings Joanna had taken a lively interest. And
after that he would be free. They could go anywhere, do
anything, be all the time together.

As she packed her travelling-case, Joanna had to fight
down a certain nausea by pretending to herself that the whole
thing was an adventure, thrilling and sweet, above all rather
humorous and dashing. That she and Louis should go together
to Edinburgh of all places ! Was there not a nice irony in
that—a delightful stroke of defiance ?

But really, from the moment of agreement, her heart was
sick with apprehension. The crisis of their loves was at hand.
She knew it. And she was certain that Louis also knew.

VII

At Peterborough she had four hours to wait for the train
that was to bring Louis.

She tried to eat, but could not, so left the station.

Walking aimlessly in the unknown streets she found herself
looking about her and listening, like one who has never looked
or listened before. The experience of sight was intense,

almost like pain ; and each sound came unprotected to her ears as if thick veils had been drawn away between her and the world. Even the movements of people, the grouping of buildings, the ways in which the clouds were arranged, were like words or sentences piercingly spoken. Arrowy voices were aimed at her from all sides. She was a frail, silken banner, riddled and tattered by well directed shafts. She was more alive to the world of sense than would long be endurable.

Coming to a bridge, she stood leaning over the parapet as if to find a refuge in the steadiness, the simplicity, of flowing water. The air was laden with sun and dust. The leaden sunshine weighed everything down. Only on the water was it pointed with silver. From an opening far up in a flour mill, men were loading a barge with sacks. The sacks were sent flying down two very long planks which, bending under their own slim weight, reached from the high doorway to the deck of the barge.

When she had gazed awhile, still in that strange helplessness of receptivity, one of the men who was in the barge helping to pile up the sacks, noticed her. He rubbed the sweat from his forehead with his arm, smiling intently up at her ; and must have said a word to his mates, for they too looked up amid their cloud of flour and stopped working for a moment.

And Joanna, before she drifted on, treasured their gazes like a farewell. A dreadful sense of approaching death was upon her. She was looking her last on the world in which she had lived till now—was severing all human contacts one by one. Already her body seemed near to dissolution.

In absolute terror she entered a church and knelt down. She had not even realized that it was the cathedral. Mechanical with fear, she began to repeat the prayers of childhood. " This night I lay me . . ." she began : then prayed for her mother, for Georgie, Linnet and Sholto. " Bless poor Mario, bless my Louis, bless Lawrence. . . . Help me to be good ! " she murmured swiftly. And so that she might include enemies in her blessing, she tried to bring in Mrs. Pender's name. " May we all have what is best for our souls and bodies," she concluded, using a phrase she had heard a thousand times on her mother's lips.

Suddenly then, as she cowered in the dark and lofty cathedral, it seemed to Joanna that she saw the Lord on His throne. And that He was preparing to answer her prayer for herself,

not with His smile but with His sword. She could feel beforehand the stab that would destroy her. But she would not
shrink. Rather would she lift up her breast to receive it.
If it was God's will to slay her, then must she be slain. Not
for nothing was she Juley Erskine's daughter.

VIII

She had been more than half an hour in the station when
the train from London came in.

At the sight of her lover leaning from the carriage window
looking out for her, all her fears, all she had just gone through,
became absurd. Here was the old solid world claiming her.
She could still cling to it. She rushed forward, and Louis
came in his rather fussy way to meet her.

But when she had taken her place beside him, and the
crowded journey northward was resumed, Joanna knew that
she would have given anything not to have come.

It was not because there were other people in their compartment—a man and two women. It was not because the women,
who were evidently well disposed toward Louis, looked distrust-
fully at the newcomer. Joanna would not have minded these
things if only Louis had stood by her. She remembered the
many happy hours they had spent in trains, going out to
country places for their walks : and some of the most memorable had been merely enhanced by the presence of other people
as by every other fetter of circumstance. Louis when he
wished, could give her such a sense of the secret warmth
between them, that the very disadvantages which might
most easily have blown upon their pleasure added a zest.

Why then to-day, after the first flush of greeting, should he
lapse away from her in a strange, hostile exhaustion ? The
unexpectedness of it paralyzed her. His looks were like axes
that had been sharpened in secret to sever the bond between
them. And he left her quite exposed to the disapproval and
curiosity of these onlookers. Was it for this that he had
asked her to come away with him ?

It would have helped her somewhat if she could have accused
him simply. But beyond all easy argument she knew that
Louis no less than she was taken unaware. It was one of those
things, by no means simple in themselves, which happen
suddenly and, as it were, involuntarily. Louis, she was
positive, had invited her in good faith. But somewhere a

spring had clicked, and here they were, both in some cruel trap, baffling to him as to her.

For a while he made conversation. He had been up half the night, he told her, working at a belated drawing so that it might be in the publisher's hands that day. Up half the night . . . and yet had had to rise early this morning to finish it . . . such a brute it had turned out. . . . Now he was dead tired. Again and again he repeated how tired he was. "Dead tired . . . down and out . . . a dead beat old man. . . ." His reiteration chilled her. For he did not want sympathy. That he made clear. Persistently he used his tiredness not to draw her to him as he might have done, but to push her farther and farther away. That he was very tired she pitifully knew. His face was grey and lined with weariness.

Before strangers however they could have no real talk, and presently Louis fell asleep in his corner. Joanna then went out into the corridor and stood there a long time, seeing the flying landscape through sheets of tears.

For a part of the way the train ran beside the sea, and the tide was far out, leaving bare the great, clean stretches of sand. The tide—that was what Louis was like in his love! The shoreward waves had been so strong that she had not realized the ebb of the whole ocean of his being. He was too old. He had said it, and she had shrunk from it with closed eyes. He was too old—an ebbing, dying man. No power could alter that grievous, icy fact. She saw that now. And yet, and yet—she cried out that she loved him. If he would but allow her to share in this death of his, she would surely go through with it. She loved him so much. So much did she long to be faithful.

As the landscape darkened, however—the tears stiffening painfully on Joanna's face—and Louis still slept on in unconsciousness, she became subject for a time to less exalted feelings. What right, she asked herself angrily, had this man so to humiliate her? He need not have suggested her coming to-day. But having done so, whatever his feelings he should have deferred this treacherous blow. In the circumstances it was mean and shameful of him. She would not tamely submit to it. And she actually allowed herself to be beaten up into what is often known as "spirit," by remembering with what difficulty she had got together the money for her ticket.

This mood, the more wretched for being foreign to her nature, was aggravated by Louis's behaviour in the restaurant car during dinner. As always he revived, superficially at least, under the stimulus of food; but on this occasion whatever energy he thus gained was vindictive. Having glanced without remark at his companion's inflamed eyes, he proceeded to talk with a certain vivacity of their fellow-travellers. He pointed out the extraordinary likeness between the man in the corner and a bust of the youthful Nero in the British Museum. And had Joanna noticed the clear-eyed, pretty girl who had sat opposite to him?

Joanna had of course noticed her, and with that wistful admiration we accord, when deeply harrowed ourselves, to one who is as yet untouched by life. The girl in question was merry, quite young, and of a type essentially English. At any other time Joanna would have listened equably to any praise of her. But to-day there was an element in Louis which made his eulogy of this other unendurable. As clearly as his weary glance had earlier showed Joanna that her new way of wearing her hair with a fringe (impulsively adopted that morning) was distasteful to him, so clearly did he now seize upon this nice young thing's charm as an instrument of repudiation. At his pointed enthusiasm Joanna arose from her untasted dinner, and stumbled along the cruelly swaying corridor till she reached an empty compartment.

Here Louis followed her, though not at once. He was relieved to see that she was not crying. And indeed she had been struggling hard in the interval to gather some steadiness.

He sat down opposite to her without a word, only making a warmer gesture than he had yet used that day, as he bent forward and brushed some grits from her skirts with his bare hand

" What's wrong ? "

" I don't know."

It was wonderful though how his action freed her from all pettier exasperation.

" Louis," she said in a low voice innocent of resentment, " why did you ask me to come to-day ? You shouldn't have asked me. You needn't have. You might have told me you had changed toward me. When did you change ? "

Louis stirred unhappily before speaking.

" But I haven't changed toward you," he replied at length.

"That is, not that I know of. If I've changed as you say, I've changed somehow to myself rather than to you. I don't myself know what has gone wrong. It's true something seems to have broken in me—just gone *phut*. . . . I can't explain."

"You mean, now?" Joanna asked in mournful wonder—"All of a sudden, since this morning?"

"I have told you I don't know!" He was becoming restive again. "I certainly was unaware of it before. You must know that. . . . I wouldn't have . . . as I say, I can't explain it to myself. It's just one of these things there's apparently no accounting for . . . there seems nothing to be said. . . ."

Truly there seemed nothing. Or if after a time there might have seemed something, it was prevented by the arrival just then from dinner of the rightful occupants of the compartment into which Joanna had drifted.

She and Louis had no choice now but to return to their own carriage where the youthful Nero, and the pretty girl and her mamma were already reinstalled. And before many minutes were gone Louis lapsed again into that disheartening, jaded sleep.

IX

They stood for a few moments on the platform at Waverley Station, chilled and uncertain. Louis had already told her that an artist friend half expected him for the night.

"You had better go to him," said Joanna tonelessly. "I know you hate hotels, and you have a cold, besides being so tired. You had better go to him, Louis." And she shivered in the draughty place.

Louis too was miserably chilled after his cramped doze in the train. His cold felt many degrees worse. He hesitated with his reply: and she waited, not quite hopeless yet, in spite of her own suggestion. Was it possible that he should leave her now? Was it in common kindness possible? Yet she saw the callousness of his worn and clouded face.

"But what about you?" he asked. With so simple a question did he deal out death to her, finally, unmistakably. ". . . . What about you?" He repeated it stupidly.

Joanna received the wound without a sign.

"I'll be all right," she heard herself say. "I can get a room at the station hotel."

She remembered once seeing *hari-kari* enacted in a Japanese play—remembered the actor's queer silence when the dagger first ran into his body up to the hilt. It was a silence in which he had continued his beautifully ordered movements. Only when the dagger was withdrawn, had he lost control and expired in a bubble of blood.

Now she only wanted to be alone. Louis too, she could see, was longing to be gone from her. But he found it difficult to move.

" Joanna ! " he paid her his tribute—" You are a generous woman. The most generous I ever knew."

At that a smile twisted her mouth for a moment, and again they were standing, looking fixedly, strangely at each other. He had a moment of cowardly fondness, and took her limp hand. " After four to-morrow I should be free," he said. " I'll call or send a message the instant I can. I wish things were different. Do you see ? But, my child," he continued with a violent shudder, " the draught in this place ! It's icy ! The old man will drop dead in a minute. There's a cab. Hi ! There ! I'll be off. Till to-morrow, old girl. Take care of yourself."

They shook hands like acquaintances, Louis—comically, as Joanna had to think—lifting his hat. She saw him cross the pavement with a touch of his old jauntiness, and get into the cab. It rumbled away.

She walked carefully to the hotel. Unless she walked very carefully she must surely reel or fall down. It seemed to her that Louis had broken her right across with his hands. It would not do if people were to see that she was broken right across. She must keep upright till she got into a place by herself.

But even when the hotel attendant had left her alone in a great, high, inimical box of a bedroom, she continued to move with circumspection. When she unpacked her nightdress, she noticed an odd thing. The low neck was threaded with a piece of mauve ribbon taken from one of her mother's funeral wreaths. How it had ever come to be there she could not think. She must have used it unconsciously, not even knowing that she possessed it though now she recognized it at once. She let it be.

All night she lay a broken thing hearing the banging and shunting of trains. And her feet were like stones. Now and again a kind of ague took her. She could not weep, could not think, could hardly even feel. There was in her no real anger against Louis. The waves of fury that overwhelmed her from time to time were all from the outside and inessential. What really concerned her was that the menace of death which had been with her all these months was now fulfilled in her. Louis was no more than the instrument in a proceeding as far beyond his own control as hers.

x

Neither then nor afterwards was Joanna able to account for her actions of the following day. They seemed merely automatic. There was no real life left in her.

At eight in the morning, having dozed a very little during the last hour, she dressed herself, and with that factitious access of spirits, rather lightheaded, which comes to some people as one of the phases before collapse, she paid her bill and left the hotel. Louis would send his message, or more probably would come himself. And he would find her gone. That was something.

She could not think of London, however, while he was still in Edinburgh. So she walked stupidly about, always carrying with her, her bag which grew heavier and heavier.

It occurred to her that she had better look for a room. She began accordingly to make inquiries wherever she saw a card in a window. But in the district where she happened to be wandering, lodgings were of the cheap, theatrical sort ; and she fled time after time from the vision of a sordid, unmade bed, and an empty tumbler of the night before on a bed-side table covered with circular stains.

At length, returning to the other side of Princes Street, she found what she sought in a small and friendly temperance hotel. Here she dropped her bag with relief, then went out, bought a bunch of wall-flowers—dark red and yellow—which had caught her eye at a street corner earlier and put them in water on the dressing-table of her new quarters. A passionate gratitude welled in her for these warm, sweet flowers with their homely air. They were her only friends, and she wished for no others.

At luncheon time she followed the general drift into the coffee-room, and when food was set before her she was surprised to find she could not eat. She was more than surprised —she was suddenly afraid. She began to fear—as if it were something quite disjoined from herself—for her willing body. But though she tried methodically, her gorge rose at each mouthful and she had to stop. The bill of fare appalled her— boiled cod, minced "collops," corn-flour pudding. She wished there were some food she had never yet tasted—food with a new, unearthly flavour—food ambrosial that would melt into her dry, bitter mouth without effort.

She had been dimly conscious of a great many black coats in the room giving the place an atmosphere that was both familiar and depressing. Then scraps of talk came to her from the next table where sat a frizzy-haired young minister. He had just been assuring his wife that they were in ample time for their train.

" I'm sorry to miss the closing address to-night," he went on. " I doubt we won't see the old man again in this world."

" With that halo of snow-white hair, Dr. Ranken makes a very dignified Moderator," said the wife.

" But frail, frail," returned the husband. " It is a marvel to every one how he has carried through the ten days."

The month of May ! Black-coated figures everywhere, chattering cheerfully like a colony of starlings ! Why of course, it was the General Assembly ! Not since the year of her father's death had the General Assembly existed for Joanna, so that a bewildering cloud of reminiscence was evoked in her by the casual discovery that it was even now in progress, and an added sharpness was given to memory by the mention of Dr. Ranken's name. The General Assembly and Dr. Ranken as Moderator ! Looking at the hearty minis- terial feeders around her, Joanna felt more than ever a ghost.

Within the next half hour she was drawn back by an ob- stinate revival of hope to the station hotel. Here there was a telegram for her ; and she was further informed that a gentle- man had telephoned at breakfast time—had telephoned again later—had called at about twelve o'clock, but had left no message.

As she tore open Louis's telegram she was almost ready to come to life again. Was it all a mistake ? Was she a fool, so to have taken to heart a momentary state of fatigue ? She was at the mercy of a sickening back-wash of the life she thought to have parted from.

Louis asked her to meet him at half-past twelve. (There was only the bare request.) It was now half-past two.

She went out again, desperate to find him, utterly unable to comprehend her own actions of the morning by which she had brought this about. And in Princes Street, close by the Scott Monument, she was almost run into by a figure from which long scarves and picturesque mulberry-coloured draperies fluttered in the east wind. It was Mildred Lovatt.

"You here, my dear girl!" cried the little woman. "But why were you not with us? We have just given Louis Pender such a send-off! You knew his panels were being unveiled to-day at the new Nicholson Hall?—*The Seasons*—to my mind he's never done anything better. But I needn't tell *you!* I was not the only one to recognize the face and figure of *Spring!* After the unveiling we gave him a luncheon party; and as he had to go by the two o'clock train, we all went and saw him off. He had a frightful cold, poor man, but I think we succeeded in cheering him up a little. You should have been with us, Joanna. Fancy your being in Edinburgh. . . ."

Somehow Joanna excused herself and made her escape. Louis was gone. It was all over. No more hope. Though it had been by her own doing that she had not seen him again, she did not deceive herself on that account. If he had wanted to see her from any other motive than remorseful kindness, he would have waited longer. He must have remembered that he had mentioned four as the hour he would be free. Yet he had left no further message at the hotel. He had brought her to Edinburgh and had left her there alone. He had been glad, no doubt, to escape so easily.

That she could do anything else now than return to her hotel for the night never occurred to her. Louis was gone. But for herself as yet trains to London had no existence. The last grain of her initiative was gone. Immediate shelter was all she could think of.

Hour after hour passed till night came. Still she had not swallowed a morsel of food : and as she lay, once more sleepless, on a strange bed, with a labouring heart, and lungs unable to compass the top of a breath for all their continual, deep sighing, she was again beset by that sudden fear for her body.

It was full of strange pains. Suppose it were to take ill here in the hotel? Suppose it were to die? Two o'clock struck from a church outside . . . three o'clock . . . four o'clock. She lacked the courage to rouse strangers at this hour. Yet she felt so ill—so sinking all at once—that by the usual waking time she was sure she would be lastingly stricken. Without some outside help, she would be very ill, or mad, or dead by dawn. Her flesh would not hold out so long.

But why should it hold out? Was it not right that the vessel no longer informed by the spirit, should fly asunder? Would not its now useless particles be thrown back swiftly among the other broken potsherds, diminished not one whit for the unceasing purposes of creation? As for the spirit, truly one need never fear for that. The spirit could neither be defrauded nor added unto. It needed no salvation and no pity, returning always to its place till it should be breathed again into some new vessel, fashioned from the immemorial stuff of the old.

It was she only—Joanna—*She, Herself*—that would be no more if her body were now to perish.

Was this the Law? Was this what her mother had called the Will of God? If so she would yield herself to it, and in faith would even cease utterly to be. She had lived a little . . . her eyes had beheld the sun . . . *Un peu d'amour, et puis bon jour*! That was as Louis saw it. And not Louis only, but a great mass of the world's sages and poets. Was it not enough? Truly it was a good deal. Truly it had its beauty of pathos, its melancholy fascination, its own deathly-sweet flower of satisfaction.

But it was not enough. Not at least for her. It was no more enough for her than her mother's transference of fulfilment to another world of sheer spirit had been, nor than Georgie's relinquishment to the next generation. And was it indeed a thing ordained any more than they? Had it not been said " My Word shall not return unto Me void " ? What was oneself, if not a word? Oneself was not all spirit, as Juley had believed. No self could be, without the body, without the form of clay into which a puff of spirit had gone from God's mouth. In breath alone there is no word. The word comes by the conscious moulding of the lips, by that which gives a preconceived shape to the formless issuing forth of breath.

Grasping this, Joanna was yet more terrified. At first it had seemed to her that by the untimely death of her body, her proper self would cease to be. Now she saw that if her body dissolved into its elements at that moment she would more truly never have been at all. For that fusion between flesh and spirit in which alone is absolute being had not taken place in her as yet. The spirit had been in her : the form of the word she had been designed to utter had been hers. But the two had stayed apart, and now they would go their several unfertile ways. Here was annulment indeed ! Here was the empty returning of the word which God hated. Before ceasing to be, she must *be*. And to that end the disruption of her body must be deferred yet awhile. The flesh must be kept from its separate extinction till it had lived again and anew, interpenetrated by the returning spirit, and so serving its purpose.

The question that now grew every moment more urgent was how this might be done. How save her body when she could neither rest nor eat nor sleep ? While she did nothing but think, the unravelling was steadily going forward. Soon she would be too late.

As these fears swept her distracted being, memories of Aunt Perdy began to present themselves. Tentative at first, they became persistent. Aunt Perdy had spoken of fleshly renewal, of death, of a new birth. She had spoken much and with authority of unseen forces that were in the air about us ever in attendance to help or to hinder.

And what was it that Aunt Perdy had said about the body being as a string of beads ? . . . a shock of ripe corn . . . of its capacity for relapsing into a motion of such fine degrees that it was a kind of living stillness in which restoration came to it from every side ?

Joanna slipped out of bed. She could smell the wallflowers on the dressing-table. The room was not quite dark, but of a negative grey dimness filled with triangular shadows. As she drooped, and sank, and came limply to the floor like a heap of grain that is softly flung down, she thought involuntarily of a field in which the meek sheaves are bowed together. She herself had fallen into something of the posture of an Oriental at prayer. And as she had fallen, so she remained a long while at rest. Her lax thighs ached violently, and her loins were wrung with a new pain as if some poison had suddenly revealed its course. But gradually the ache grew less and less ; and when it was gone, instinctively as a woodland creature turns in its sleep, she let herself roll with a gentle heavy movement on to her back. Her limbs, all slack, went sliding and quivering their length upon the grey floor. Soon every inch of her lay there released. Not till that moment did she know how tightly strung she had been for the last forty hours and more.

Then how steadily and how strangely the deathliness of fatigue went rippling along her arms, along her legs, and away ! Here at least Aunt Perdy had been right. One thought wrongly of the body as of something single and upright. Truly it was no more than a handful of various weights strung loosely on a string.

Joanna knew that she was safe now from what had threatened her. Her body, still bereft, was safe. Her defeated brain was laved by the clear waves of nothingness. She lay and lay till time, for her, was not. Slowly her breathing altered. It grew deeper, milder, more regular, and at last in the sure knowledge of sleep she returned to her bed.

It was now that there sounded in her soothed ear a small, sweet forgotten voice of childhood. At Duntarvie, long ago, her bed had stood within hearing of the house cistern. Here in the same room with her, by a curious chance was the water tank of the hotel. It was hidden in a cupboard, and in the daytime she had only dully recognized a familiar presence by certain muffled thrummings and spoutings and sudden gushings. Through the night as yet she had marked no sound at all.

But now in this secret hour before dawn, when the rest of the world was asleep, and Joanna was waiting in quietness till sleep should come to her, the water began to speak. It started unaccountably out of the silence with exquisite precision.

Drip . . . dreep-dreep-dreep . . . drop, drop . . . dripeet, dripeeteet . . . drip-ipeet-ipeety !—went the tiny, silvern, interminable cadenza. Like silver its music tinkled—like seed-pearls, like icicles, so fine and clear and absolved that it was an ecstasy to hear—a keen ecstasy quite purged of any dross of excitement. Steadily the singing would go on for a bar or two, tone after perfect tone. Then like a rill that leaps under starlight it would scatter its drops in a spray of grace-notes. On it went, sometimes singing, sometimes speaking, modulating continually from one delicate, undreamed-of rhythm to another. And though it was a voice from childhood, Joanna had never truly heard it before. It was the still, small voice of a new birth, of a new life, of a new world. It was a new voice, but it was the oldest of all the voices. For it was the voice before creation, secure, unearthly, frail as filigree yet faithful as a star.

CHAPTER IV

I

$\mathbf{S}$HE had slept, and in the train next day on her way to London she was still able to rest. Her body was weak but safe. After the alternation of sharp, riving pain and dull stupor which had been her existence for the last two days, his was almost happiness.

In the barn-like Waverley Station wherein the passengers seemed like so many strewn grains from the threshing, she had slipped clear of her trouble. She too was now but a grain, a speck, whereas last night her heart had filled the universe with its heavy and clamorous throbbing. In this restored proportion she had only her infinitesimal part in the whole, and it was enough. Behind her lay great misery : before her in London she knew that more awaited her. But she might make of this journey a quiet breathing space—a narrow oasis in which for an hour she could forget the choking desert.

Having no stomach yet for everyday victuals, she had bought herself a little, rare basketful of fruit. Here was a knot of grapes the colour of glacier water, here were two granadillas—passion-flower fruits with their tough rinds full of luscious, translucent globules, here were almonds to crunch, a white-fleshed apple into which to drive one's teeth, a peach from which the velvet, scented skin came glibly away.

Leaning back idly in the corner of an empty compartment she watched the wheeling countryside. It was a poet's May morning, one of those mornings when white, white clouds are piled up and gleaming, and the sunshine lies like snow along the hedges. Young lambs that might themselves have been snow leavings, were scattered upon the emerald grass. A faint, low haze of hyacinths hovered in the bare woods. In one small station, through which the train passed without stopping, the steep banks were rich with crocuses that had already been spilt and ravished—with crocuses that were flaming their lives out like passionate lamps.

Joanna sat on that side of the train next to the corridor, and every now and then, passing between her and the Lothians, some passenger would blot out a whole brown woodland or amber-coloured field or bare hill of palest amethyst. To her at the moment one broad, obscuring back was like another. She hardly realized, therefore, that a particular pair of tweed shoulders returned again and again intil they came at length to a hesitating stand-still opposite the door of her compartment. Even when the door opened, and a man's brown face looked in with inquiring friendliness, and a lean hand was stretched out, and her name warmly uttered—even then it was several moments before she realized that the stranger was her old playmate, Bob Ranken.

"Joanna! It *is* you!"

"Why . . . Bob!"

He wrung her hand and sat down opposite, smiling—taking off his hat, looking at her with evident pleasure.

Joanna too looked at him. He was the same old Bob! After the first shock of shyness and strangeness she saw that he had not really changed. He was bigger, older, and certain marks of worldly assurance were as clear as the deep sun-wrinkles that surrounded his eyes. But the African sun had not burned away the spiritual indecision lurking about his attractive lips, nor informed the almost callow innocence of his gaze.

"Do come into our carriage," he begged her schoolboyishly. "My father is there with me. I thought and thought it must be you. But your hat hid your eyes and I wasn't positive."

"I wonder you knew me at all," said Joanna. "I am changed more than you, I think. Am I not changed?"

"Yes and no," he replied. "I felt a bit afraid of the dashing-looking female I first caught sight of. But now that I have a good look at you I can see the old Joanna. I wish you would take your hat off. Would you have known me?"

"Anywhere!"

"Yet you didn't when I first came in and stuck out my paw at you."

"No. I was half asleep."

"Asleep? You didn't look it!"

"Thinking, then."

"Ah!"

He searched her face curiously as she rose, and they went together to the other carriage where Dr. Ranken sat reading with one plaid about his shoulders and another over his knees. The old minister looked fragile indeed, but he had maintained a brittle alertness. He smiled his wintry yet rather sweet smile at Joanna, and made her sit by him while he asked about her doings, and about her brothers—mentioning both by name —and about Georgie and Georgie's baby. It was a clear and a pleasing point of vanity with him, this individual remembrance which he kept of each boy and girl who had ever had a place in his flock. And Joanna was the more surprised, as in their childhood he had never seemed to them to notice their existence. Certainly his former bleakness was gone Time, sometimes generous, had given him with his white locks, a distinction quite denied to his middle-age. And it was perhaps his own appreciation of this that made him genial.

" And your mother," he said presently,—" I was sorry, very sorry to hear of her death. Your mother, my dear, was a good woman."

" Yes," said Joanna.

" I never knew a better. And she had courage—a rare gift . . . a gift I esteem not less but more as I grow older. True, theologically we did not always see eye to eye, your mother and myself . . . " he twinkled.

So they talked mostly of the early days in Glasgow, of St. Jude's Church, of the Boyds, of this one's death, that one's marriage, the disgrace of that other. And the old man was lively in his interest. As for the young man, he sat smoking and watching, seldom speaking. In answer to Joanna's questions he told her a little about his work, and she divined that he loved the part of the world where it was. Laconically as he spoke, there was enthusiasm in his description of a certain high mountain which dominated the landscape visible from his bungalow.

But if Bob took no great part in the conversation, he was all the more intent in listening to every least remark of Joanna's. When they parted at King's Cross he was emphatic upon the strange coincidence of their meeting. He had meant, he said, the very next day to have sought her out at Chapel Court. Might he still come ? He was to be at the least a fortnight in London. Joanna could not but see that his eyes were full of eager reminiscence.

II

But at the Moons' house there was trouble.

Roddy, who had fallen ill suddenly, was to be operated upon next day. Edwin Moon was white with anxiety. Trissie was grey. He was bowed more than ever. She was more than ever upright. Dreadfully upright she was, with her shoulders thrown back and her desperate head held high.

They had " taken the liberty "—they told Joanna, upon her arrival when the bad news was poured out—of using her bedroom as the sick-chamber. It was the most suitable in the house, and they could not bear to have the child taken to a nursing home. Already the stripped walls were hung with sheets drenched in carbolic, and the scrubbed kitchen table stood shockingly in the middle of a bare floor.

During the week that followed, Joanna, sleeping on the sofa in her sitting-room, gave every minute of her time and every ounce of her strength to the racked household. She cooked, ran errands, found a substitute for Trissie at the laundry, interviewed customers downstairs for Mr. Moon, helped to tend the unwitting Edvina. And so long as all went well with Roddy she was content. While the distraction of illness lasted, her own essential life stayed apart, suspended. It was a respite.

And the operation was a success. Roddy emerged from it his entire, bright self. It seemed there was no further cause for anxiety. Yet Trissie's face remained tense and ashen as before, nor would Edwin leave the bedside.

That night, though she was very weary, Joanna lay sleepless. With Roddy out of danger her own troubles were again unleashed, and now like hounds they threatened her. She stayed broad awake till after sunrise. Then, when she had newly fallen into a drowse, came a touch on her shoulder. She sat up instantly. It was Trissie, who said a low word and was gone. Joanna leapt up, threw on her dressing-gown, and followed.

An hour before dawn—nearly twenty hours after the surgeon's work was satisfactorily completed—the child had begun to look strange about the eyes. Then he had slipped by slow, obstinate degrees into unconsciousness. Now he was in a coma. " Coma," was the word that had remained with Joanna when Trissie had spoken and vanished.

It was " a most uncommon case," declared the puzzled physician (the surgeon, having performed his task and being busy elsewhere, did not appear). But he thought they would " pull the little chap through."

Trissie's eyes widened in murderous disbelief till the white glared all round the irises, but she carried out every direction submissively and well, winning the doctor's praise. There never had been such a nurse. As for Edwin Moon, through each unfolding horror of activity around the bed, he only sat with his head hanging, looking on without hope, quite passive.

Twice in the course of the day they managed to rouse the boy so that he uttered conscious and natural cries of protest. And after the second of these times he lay awhile quiet, and was his composed self as if he would recover.

The father raised his head then and gazed into his son's open eyes. And Roddy, as if he had been waiting for this, smiled back at him contentedly.

So they would have remained, but the mother bent forward, thrusting herself between them in her terrible jealousy.

" How does my sonny feel now ? " she asked, curbing her frenzy with an effort that almost killed her, into a tone of gentle ordinariness.

At this, Roddy only moved his head restlessly, searching past his mother with feeble impatience for his father's lost face.

" How's my sonny ? " she repeated,—this time a fine jet of her agony breaking through in her voice.

" Much better, thank you."

Roddy spoke with the politeness he used to strangers. And again he sought his father's eyes.

Trissie turned away. Her face was like some crude, grinning mask of tragedy.

But the child had scarcely spoken, before consciousness flickered out again. An hour . . . two hours . of unbroken stupor followed, do what they would. And then the small, square finger tips began to curve strangely outwards like young leaves that are too near a flame. And he grew cold. And one long, long breath was the last he would ever draw.

The mother, her eyes wide and unseeing, stayed by the dead boy. And the father, having composed the small limbs. wandered slowly from the room.

III

It was on the night before the burial that Trissie found relief in a stream of incoherent speech which seemed as though it had been pent up for ages and now could never have an end.

Edwin, she told Joanna, had gone out, and he would probably walk the streets till morning, as he had done many a time before. This was not their first trouble. What else indeed but trouble had they known these many years?

She sat on the little rocking-chair in the archway room that midnight, and her story—or what she thought was her story—came from her in a bitter confusion of words.

When all had been said, Joanna knew little more about the Moons than she had already gathered half-consciously by living with them. She learned indeed for the first time that Moon was not their real name, and that the name they had forgone was one well thought of in a northern county where once they had lived prosperously. But what Edwin had done—saving that it had been an act of criminal folly by which he had nothing to gain and everything to lose— all Trissie's incontinence did not disclose. He had done it, declared Trissie, when he was not himself. For he had never been himself since the day when his pet Edvina, from being a lovely, lively child of two, had within an hour become the thing she now was. Was it any wonder if crazed by this blow he had thought for a time that certain babies were better not to be born into the world at all? Be that as it might, such thoughts had led to a disaster from which his life and hers had never recovered. Ill luck had dogged them ever since.

Here was the burden of Trissie's lament. Here, in the steady incorrigible tracking down by misfortune. It was Edwin whom the pursuing furies had marked for their prey. She, Trissie, had been born—she was sure of it—for good fortune. She had always been known as a lucky person, and was convinced she would be still, were it not for Edwin. If was Edwin who had spoiled her life, who had cheated her ot her happiness, who had brought upon her one trouble after another. And he had done it in all innocence. Therein lay his offence. Any wickedness—again and again Trissie wildly repeated this phrase—*any* wickedness, she could have forgiven him. For then she could have cut herself off from him. If he were a guilty man, she could have gone free, been happy (once, just before the birth of Roddy she had tried to leave him, and he had told her she was free to do the best for herself). But he was an innocent man. It was only that fate had marked him as a prey. And how could she leave this Jonah, this victim, this man set apart for vengeance, by whose side nothing could prosper?

So the wife raved and wept.

But on the day of the burial, Joanna came nearer to the true heart of the mystery.

In the church, and afterwards by the graveside, she saw how the strange couple clung each to the other. And there was that in their clinging which was more than the ordinary holding together for comfort of married mourners. To Joanna it seemed to proclaim their secret from the housetops. The Moons, like Phemie and Jimmie, possessed what she in her own unfulfilled being must envy.

IV

Now she would have to go back to her own life.

But the day before, it had seemed as if she might live only in Trissie's life and in entire devotion to Trissie's unhappiness. Now she knew that Trissie did not need her. The husband and wife had cast her out by the grave. She had no part with them. She must go on again alone with what was no longer a life, but only a dying and a denial.

So it was that in the weeks that followed, Roddy's death ceased to cause her any personal grief. It became merely another incident in the recession of all life from her. For days on end she was shorn of herself, shorn of the world, shorn of the old assured existence for which her mother at one end, and Louis at the other, had supremely stood. She was denuded even of the warm and exquisite fleece of memory. She had no past, no living present, no conceivable future. But under all her deathliness was one grain of faith that death must be fulfilled to the uttermost before any new birth can be. She lay abandoned, waiting in a perfection of emptiness.

V

But to die is not so easy—to die, that is, the death in which is clenched the seed of a new birth. There are pangs in it of false resurrection, dreadful like the return of Lazarus. As in the death of the body, the will revives time after time and fights. Appalled and faithless the consciousness struggles in the very act of dissolution to be again what it was—to escape its appointed re-entry into the dark womb of extinction.

In these weeks there were mornings when Joanna woke full of a gnawing malaise for Louis.

Then all her memories, fiendish, but clad like angels, would leap to their deathly work. All the old lies would raise their plausible, flat heads, denying the possibility of true renewal. Back, back, back she must go into safety; back to haven: back to the known system which swung securely between the psalm-singing, sunset faith of her fathers and the exquisite underworld of moonlight and falling leaves wherein Louis had his dwelling. Resignation, renunciation, sacrifice! These thrust forward their false, lovely faces; and all their pleadings were for the revival of self-insistence under the mask of immolation.

For even *in extremis* a choice is left, and the will has its part. Joanna had lost Louis. But there was still a way in which she might refuse to go from him. The very circumstances of their love which had kept them apart for months at a time, the fact that in her dealings with him she had been clear of pettiness, his assurance in the train that he had not so much changed toward her as broken down in himself— all these offered her that way of death in life which is chosen every day that passes by people of her nature.

She could be faithful to Louis. She could refuse to forget and to go on. With loyal obstinate submissiveness she could turn her life into a shrine. She had seen the faces of women who had done this. Was it not the best way when one had so deeply committed oneself? It was not the way of the new birth, but it lay at hand; it showed the sign post of authority; one could travel it and not yield up one's will.

Or on other days a different brood of devils would crowd in upon her. These had features less like Juley's than the last, and more like Louis's. They were full of pleasantry and mocking reasonableness.

Why take so tragically, they asked, what was probably only one of her lover's bad moods? It was a question of time and good sense, good sense being what she had chiefly lacked.

He had behaved badly no doubt. But she might have managed him if she hadn't been so painfully in earnest. She might still, with time, coolness and skill, win him afresh.

Or quite suddenly she would find herself caught up in a whirlpool of hatred and all-encompassing spite.

Why should Louis go free while she was thus tormented? she would then ask. Could she not make him suffer, persecute him, even kill him? Why not? As man to desperate woman, his would be the disadvantage. He was spared by her scruples alone, not by her fears. It was no matter what became of her so that she could wreak herself once and for all upon him. When she dragged him out before his world that he so feared, ranted forth her mind at him, showed him like a beaten cur to his wife and his sons and his son's wife, made the seemliness he so treasured, impossible for him forthwith, she could complete the work by killing herself. What was to prevent her? Nothing!

Nothing, save that in spite of all, she knew she was finely prompted in respecting Louis's obduracy. Something whispered that it was not all cowardice for him to have cast her off, that beneath the maddening incidents of their parting he had taken a step which was intrinsically decent. Was not his action in harmony with the unknown forces that had long been driving her out of his world? What if the break between them had sprung from his refusal to drag her further into his own long dying?

So she took no decisive action. And the only outcome of all her stormy hours was some letters. She could not help writing letters to Louis that were by turns exalted, self-abasing, passionate, reasonable, threatening, and simply appealing.

Louis replied by one letter only.

"You must allow me to act," he wrote at last, "as I think best. Believe me, I'm saving you from yourself, as well as, in another way, saving myself from you. I don't want to see you. I won't. It could serve no purpose except to hurt us both, and what's the use of that? I haven't exactly changed in my feeling toward you. I've meant every word and more, that I ever spoke to you. You know that well enough, I expect. There will never be anyone else to count. There never *was* anyone else that meant at all the same as you have meant (and I suppose, still mean) to me. It may seem strange to you when I say I care every bit as much as I ever have—

possibly more. I confess it seems strange to me. Certainly
I didn't expect anything of the kind when we began. But
something has gone dead in me, Joanna. I can't go on.
That's what I realized on the journey to Edinburgh when I
was so awfully tired. Quite suddenly, once and for all, I
realized it. I can't go on. And in this of ours, we must go
on or make an end. Don't you agree ? As I see things now,
it has been tug and tug between us this long time past—perhaps the whole time. If I'd had it in me I would have gone
off with you long ago. You always wanted that, I know, and
once or twice I have fancied that I could. But I know now
that I never could have. It would only have been a sickening disaster for both of us if I had tried. Perhaps I was too
old when you got me. You don't know yet what that feels
like and you ought to be thankful. Anyhow there it is.
It has wanted courage for me to cut loose from you and stay
behind. You must have the courage to cut loose from me and
go on. I believe you can do this. But whatever you do,
don't make things ugly and regrettable at the end by asking
the impossible of me. I'm sure I've done you no harm,
and I hope I may have done you good. Let me alone, my dear,
with my memories. Be sure a man never had sweeter
ones. Be sure I wish you well, and am for ever grateful.

" Your old lover,
" LOUIS."

If many a time, in his love-making, Joanna had been driven
to make excuses to herself for her lover, in his withdrawal he
rose far beyond any need of apology. If she indeed had it
in her to go forward into a new, unimagined life, here in this
letter would lie her dearest trophy from the old.

VI

During the futile weeks that followed, she even took to
visiting fortune-tellers. It was a tribe that had never before caught her attention. But the days must be passed
somehow.

Though she despised herself for it, and had little enough
money to spare from necessities, she would put down the preposterous fee eagerly for the false excitement it brought—
would wait trembling in the frowsy ante-chamber of the oracle.
And once, when some hag of the Edgware Road hinted at

what might be construed into a marriage, after many years, with Louis, she went home with a lighter step—to know within the hour that it was a shameful drug.

This however did not prevent her from repeating the same folly, and she continued fitfully to go from one soothsayer to another.

" I see a dark . . . no, a fair man . . . " droned the sibyl, (This time she was rich in her appointments, and herself young, large and comely as a stalled ox.) . . . "I see a *medium* fair man . . . still young . . . yes . . . the first love . . . his thoughts are toward you . . . there was a break . . . both were in fault . . . years have passed . . . but he has been faithful . . . and now his heart is set toward his first love . . . I see happiness . . . money . . . children . . . two boys . . . no . . . a boy and a girl . . . seas to be crossed . . . many storms in the past . . . but happiness close at hand ! " She sank back in her chair as if utterly exhausted, drew the black velvet over her glass ball and closed her eyes.

And Joanna was impressed.

During the last fortnight Bob Ranken had continually sought her company. Noticing her drooping spirits, he had insisted more than once upon her going out with him to dinner in town and had taken her to a theatre afterwards. And that very afternoon, on her return to Chapel Court, she met him coming dejectedly away after a vain call there. In a week he would be leaving England. So she had to allow him to turn back with her, and to sit talking in her room. She had only to look at him to know how very easily she might make the crystal-gazer's prophecy come true.

' She was tempted. She did not love Bob, but he had still the power to stir a curious tenderness in her. Also it was dangerously sweet and flattering, especially coming upon the heels of such humiliation as could hardly be borne, to have stumbled upon the fulfilment of an old dream. After all these years, Bob wanted her. There would not only be safety with him, but as well a kind of newness which promised much. What of the mountain he could see from his bungalow . . . the African veld . . . different skies . . . dark faces . . . yet another escape ? And with Bob, however fond a wife she might become, she knew that she would be able to keep her essential being intact, a shrine for Louis to the end.

But Joanna's will, which had so often served her badly, served her well in this ; and that day she put the temptation aside. Better never be than be so falsely, foisting at the same time falseness upon another.

So she turned from him, and denied him every chance of speaking. And the next week Bob left England as he had come.

VII

She visited no more palmists. She did nothing and went nowhere, neither worked nor read. The long-preserved shell of habit had crumbled at last. But although acquiescence might mean open ruin, she could only wait passively. She could not move without some vital prompting.

It was not till the middle of June that the first hint of direction came to her, the first faint summons bidding her live anew. And as once before, in the life that was now dead and discarded, it came in the shape of a letter from Aunt Perdy.

"I am passing," she wrote, "through a time of hideous, lonely suffering. The powers of darkness in the heavens above are doing all they can to kill my heart and brain. It is dreadful to be like me—open to invisible influences ; for by the same means I am both aided and hindered. Pray for Auntie, whose heart is almost breaking, and who is presently without love or hope of any kind, and feels *miserably conquered*. Come to see her if you possibly can."

To this Joanna sent no answer, but she moved out of her lethargy and made simple preparations for a journey to Italy. To raise the money she found she must sell some of her treasures, but she did so without a pang. Not that there was any excitement or expectancy in her as there had been when she responded to her aunt's first summons. Now she was simply obedient to the seeming accident through which her new, untried life could stir. Her will no longer rose hard and possessive, driving her hither and thither. Her will now was merely the helm by which her frail bark might once more be steered to float upon a stream of life. But what other power had urged her to respond, whither the stream might bear her, she did not ask.

Not that even now she was quite beyond the reach of a deathly backwash. In the late afternoon of the day before her departure, when nothing remained to do, she found herself overwhelmed once more by the old sadness.

There was the deep chair in which Louis and she had so often kissed and held each other : here was a case she had come upon while packing—full of his letters and drawings : there on the mantelpiece was the Tanagra figurine with blown out drapery which he had brought her from Paris, declaring it was like her. All the little room spoke of him and of what he stood for. And mingling with these passionate memories were thoughts of Roddy who was dead, of Ollie who was soon going to Canada to make the third in a patched-up reconciliation between her parents. Wrenched with sobbing she lay back in the shadowed room. She cried a long time, so that when at length she was done, the evening had drawn greyly in. But she did not stir to light the lamp, and even when rain began to fall, beating more and more heavily against the black window-panes, she had no thought of drawing the curtains. There seemed no reason why she should ever move again. From shaking storm she had lapsed into stillness. Never before had she been sunk so deep in the blessed wells of nothingness.

How many minutes or hours passed then, she did not know. But the room had long been quite dark, when a sound from downstairs made her slip free of her abandonment in the low chair and stand alert listening. Her ears served her so beautifully at that moment that she could separate each from each—as an embroidress might separate a skein of coloured silken threads —all the faint vibrations of sound in the house. She heard Trissie open the door and parley with a visitor. It was impossible to distinguish words, but she knew immediately that Lawrence's was the low voice asking if she was in, and she could supply the answer in Trissie's doubtful murmur.

The next moment she was leaning over the wide-topped old banister of the staircase.

" I'm here," she heard her own voice assuring Trissie. And almost before she had spoken, there was Lawrence standing before her.

On the little dark landing they could see each other's faces as pale blurs only.

" How wet you are ! " she exclaimed as he touched her hand with his, all cold with the rain, and she could smell the rain-soaked wool of his clothes.

"Yes. It is pouring."

He followed her into the room while she groped for matches and lighted the lamp. And now, instead of her ears, it was her hands that moved with a new perfection and certitude that almost frightened her.

The wick caught evenly all round, and as the twin flames sprang up bright and smokeless in the funnel, Lawrence's eyes were upon her. Her face, she knew then, must be ravaged and unsightly from her long crying. At any former time of her life—above all with Louis—she would have shaded the unmerciful light hastily, turning her face aside the while. But this evening with Lawrence she had no more impulse to conceal it than she had to display it for his sympathy. Raising her head she returned his look starkly, and thus they both stood for a long second with the revealing lamp between them.

"Yes?" Joanna asked him. That he would only have come to her on some urgent errand, she knew of herself. And if she had not known it, his white, fixed face would have told her that something decisive had happened to him.

But he had seen her now, and in his eyes his own trouble made way for hers.

"What's wrong?" he demanded, instead of replying to her question.

"Nothing is wrong. I've been crying. I'm all right now. I'm going to Italy to-morrow."

It seemed odd to her that he should show no surprise.

"To Italy, you are going?" he said. " . . . I'm going away too. That's what I came to-night to say."

Joanna was the one to be astonished. His way of speaking was strange.

"Where are you going?" she asked wondering.

"I don't know yet, nor for how long. North, probably. It really doesn't matter. Though I think I'm about due a holiday."

"I'm afraid you are ill. You look ill," said Joanna, anxiously. There was that kind of sharpness in his features which often presages severe illness.

But he assured her brusquely that it was only a cold hanging about him.

"How long will you be in Italy?"

She did not know. She begged him to hurry home and change his clothes.

"Good bye, then," Lawrence said, holding out his hand—"It was mostly to tell you I was going away that I came. 1 couldn't help coming and now I feel you are going South for the same reason that I am going North. You have come to an end—*really* come to an end at last. Is it so ? "

Joanna nodded. She was full of wonder, yet it seemed natural that he should know about her.

"I have been at an end now for ages," she said. "The thing is, is there any new beginning ? "

"For you I feel there must be : for me I see none," replied Lawrence. "I'm simply down and out ; last time we talked I was glib enough. I thought I knew what it was. But I didn't."

Would he stay ? Joanna asked him shyly. Would he sit down a while ? Would talking be any use ? But he shook his head, so she went downstairs to the door with him.

The yard was spouting with rain, and rivulets of rain coursed under the archway. As Lawrence and she clasped hands Joanna loved the sound of it.

"Endings have to be gone through by each one alone," said he, "but I doubt if ever a true beginning was solitary." And with that he was gone into the dark, slanting curtain of the rain.

As she went slowly back to her room, she dared hardly believe in the virgin jet of promise that bubbled tinily, limpidly up through her own nothingness.

CHAPTER V

I

" I TOLD you," persevered the voice of Irene's holiday governess, " that some seeds, and some fruits too, have wings.
Can either of you tell me the name of a tree that has a winged
fruit ? Come, Carola ! You try ! The rain might go off
if you would stop looking at it. . . . "

At one end of the long, country drawing-room she sat
with her two little girl pupils, filling in the slow half hour
before tea with a Nature talk. At the other end Irene
was having an argument with Aunt Georgina. And the murmur of the children at their lesson made a kind of droning
counterpoint for the more acrimonious voices of their mother
and grandmother.

"This is just a fad of yours, Irene," declared the elder
speaker inclemently, " about the children needing sea-air in
August. I never heard such rubbish. Compared with
these hills the sea is a nasty bilious place."

It was now two years since the widowed Lady Westermuir had left Edinburgh and come to live at the small
Perthshire estate from which her husband had taken his
judicial title : and in this June afternoon (the very same afternoon upon which her niece Joanna was speeding South on
the first wind of chance) she was seated by a window that
looked out upon the Grampians.

"A mere doctor's fad ! " she pursued. "They would be
far better here with me till October. Broadstairs, too, of all
places ! "

While her daughter crouched shivering by the fire, the old
woman herself had made no further concession to the weather
than by having thrust her feet into a deer-skin hassock.
She sat steely and erect on a straight-backed chair before
her desk in the deep window-bow that was her favourite
post, and this though the mountain prospect that she loved

was quite gone in mist. Mist, chill, heavy and sopping on
this day of summer, had left nothing for the disconsolate
eye to rest upon save a drenched garden terrace, some shrubs
weighted with the rain, and a broken regiment of tiger-lilies.
" My dear Mother," returned Irene in a tone of martyrdom
which her mother guessed was due less to maternal anxiety than
to her grievance at having had to leave London in the middle
of the season, " you surely don't imagine that *I* like our
summer arrangements. But you see for yourself that Carola
has had one cold upon another since we came here. And after
bronchitis so lately . . . "

" . . . Look ! "—went on the persistent undertone of the
lesson. " This is a seed of the ash—a single seed in a sheath
which is really a wing. It is called a *samara*. See the twist
that helps it to fly ! And this is a sycamore fruit with two
wings."

" Can it really fly, Miss Frew ? " asked Carola, the elder
child, suddenly taking some interest, " like a bird ? "

" It can whirl along on the wind for miles and miles."

" The child doesn't go out enough," announced Carola's
grandmother.

" . . . Suppose it fell on a stone, Miss Frew ? "

" Then if it lived long enough, it would have to wait for
another wind to blow it to a place where it could sprout and
take root . . . "

" Would you have her go out on a day like this ? "

" Most certainly I should. To hear you one would hardly
think you were a Scotswoman at all." A fine, metallic thread
of contempt was one of the strands in the withered old voice.

" . . . Suppose the wind blew it on to another stone,
and another stone—*lots* more stones, Miss Frew ? Or into
the sea ? . . . "

" I don't hold,"—Aunt Georgina still spoke—" with your
doctor's fiddle-faddle about bronchitis and sea-air and nonsense. However, I see your mind is made up, and after all
they are only my grand-children, not my children ! "

" . . . For one seed that sprouts, millions and millions
only rot every year."

" Do billions and billions rot," asked Phyllis, the younger
child, speaking for the first time.

" I supose so."

" And trillions and trillions, Miss Frew ? . . . "

"I dislike having the house to myself in the autumn, and most people have made their plans by now. Of course I might ask one of your cousins, Sholto's girls. It has been in my mind for some time to ask Joanna. Joanna used to be fond of the country, and has no home of her own to go to these days. That is one thing I will say for your poor Aunt Juley—she brought her children up to be hardy. I remember how they used to run about in all weathers like so many young colts. Yes, I shall tell Joanna to come in August and see her old Aunt."

II

At the moment when Aunt Georgina's invitation was being fastened in its envelope, Joanna, a little dazed by her long journey, stood once more by the widely spilled water of Torre del Lago. She stood looking across the white expanse that seven years before had marked the turning of her life from dream to reality ; clearly she now knew that turning for what it was—but a part of her inevitable progression towards death. She had lived out the dream, had embraced the reality, and now death was fulfilled in her. She saw that, however different might have been the circumstances of her travelling in it, for her at least there could have been no other progression. Now it might be that death was her portion, or it might be that out of her very recognition and acceptance of death, a new life might spring. It came to her that the world was walked by thousands who were dead and whose true deathliness lay in their continued assertion of life. Such life surely was mere putrefaction, and from putrefaction came no new life worth having. The phœnix could not rise anew but from its acknowledged ashes. Anyhow she relinquished all claim to the old life. She rested in the void and was content to bide her time without a single defiant reaching forth.

And while Joanna climbed the steep winding path to the cottage (since her last visit there was no change in the hillside save that now on every hand the cherry trees declared themselves from among the olives by their brighter fruit) Aunt Georgina—in her old age sometimes generous on second thoughts—was re-opening her invitation and inserting a cheque.

III

Though the door stood open, Aunt Perdy was not in the cottage. Nor was she in the garden. Aurora however—larger and handsomer than ever, with two babies grabbing at her skirts—was there cutting artichokes, and upon catching sight of the unlooked-for visitor, she uttered a cry of mingled surprise and welcome.

"But what! Of course she remembered the Signorina Scozzese! But the misfortune! The poor Signora del Monte, (it was by this name that Aunt Perdy was known to the district) taken ill suddenly, had only the day before been fetched away by the other Signora, her sister—doubtless also well known to the Signorina—who had at Turin the fine house and the distinguished family! At Turin for certain the Signora del Monte would be well cared for. Nor did Aurora expect her return for some weeks. What was to be done?"

Joanna did nothing and suggested nothing. She merely stayed quietly on at the cottage. While she felt no particular relief at her Aunt's absence, neither did she feel any disappointment; and Aurora seeing this, fell in with it unquestioningly. She waited on the niece as she had waited on the Aunt, as a matter of course; and Joanna with her return ticket safe, was able to eke out over some six weeks money that in London would hardly have lasted for one.

Between the garden and the orchard, with eggs and an occasional fowl from Aurora, she found food enough, and other needs she had none. Occupation there was for her in plenty. She washed and mended whatever of Aunt Perdy's she could find that needed repair, put the cottage in shining order, weeded and dug in the garden, and between whiles she lay for hours at a time on the garden's highest ridge from where she could gaze upon the wide, sparkling sweep of the sea. Often then she remembered those sea-going ships upon the Clyde that had nearly drawn the childish heart out of her breast. But up till now all her adventures had been inland. Only now was she loosed—if so be the capacity lay in her at all—for the true voyage.

But the will to shape circumstances or to force an issue was gone from her. She had become submissive to the uncomprehended current of events. She did not grieve or rejoice. She did not live. She only waited.

And when Aunt Georgina's letter reached her she accepted

the invitation. The wind had blown her South, now the
wind was to blow her North. Free as a flying seed,
she still was as is a seed, at the mercy of the winds.
When would she be driven to the place where she might
strike her roots and at last raise her leaf and her bud ?
She recalled Mr. Moon's legend of the bird of paradise. It
was one thing to die to the world, to devour the sweet spices
and so for ever lose your foothold. It was another to find a
resting place in some new way of life. She could still feel the
lake swallows digging into her palms with their frantic claws.
But of what use was their escape to them, if escape were all ?
Was Lawrence too, she wondered, without foothold in the
world ? It seemed to her that for a man the whole scheme of
things must be different. Yet he too, as she could not forget,
had conceived of his life as a seed foiled of its consummation.

IV

August was nearly over, when one evening she stepped down
from the train at a Highland junction to be driven ten miles
along wet, bog-scented roads to Aunt Georgina's house which
she then saw for the first time.

It stood, white-washed and four-square on its hill, with no
creepers to break its bareness—a typical Perthshire dwelling
of the severer sort, set in good, though not showy grounds.
And on its wide semi-circular steps, confronting the terrace
and the watery sunset, stood its mistress awaiting her guest.

Joanna, who first caught sight of the straight, unmistakable
figure from a turn in the drive, was surprised by a familiar
tremor. Since her mother's funeral, when all family relations were abnormal, she had not seen her aunt ; nor had
she slept under her roof oftener than twice in the last
ten years. And if, in middle age, Lady Westermuir had
been a person to strike terror into young bosoms, in old
age she was even more intimidating. True, at that
moment, in the yellow light that beat up against her
from the wet gravel, turning her widow's cap with its precise
goffering into a moulding of pale brass, she might from the
waist downward have stood to a sculptor for the figure of
Charity, the folds of her skirts—black now instead of prune-
coloured—flowed out so generously at either side, ballooning
slightly in the air as she advanced. But no *Caritas* ever kept
shoulders so erect as these under the brown and scarlet Paisley

shawl: and the triumphant clash of cymbals would better than any more Christian music have expressed these leonine features.

Yet Joanna's fear proved after all to be but the ghost of a bygone subjection. Being faced with its object it passed so wholly that it only served to mark the distance she had travelled. For without doubt she emerged unshaken from the stately embrace, the condescending greeting and the critical old stare.

Two days later the morning gave promise of sunshine—even of heat—after a spell of rain, and Aunt Georgina decided that she would pay a call upon one of her more distant neighbours, a retired sheriff, whose house lay a few miles from Perth on the further side. As she had not visited there before, a map was produced and laid open on the breakfast table. And that her younger eyes might be made use of, Joanna was seated before it.

It was only then that there came to her as a perfect astonishment, what she must long before have known, had her childish geography not been of the haziest and never amended—Westermuir lay within twenty miles of Duntarvie!

Incredible as it may seem, she had never thought of Duntarvie as having a place upon the map. Deeply shaken she traced the district with her forefinger. *Duntarvie.* And close to it upon the printed map—*Drumwharrie*, the farm where Alec Peddie had lived. Before her eyes were the names of villages, streams and hills, which till now had seemed names in a tale.

The cob had gone lame, and Lady Westermuir did not consider the small pony equal to her weight upon the steeper hills; but the fine day was not to be missed, so she would go by train. If her niece really wanted to re-visit Duntarvie, why not do so that day? They could travel together as far as Perth.

So it was. At Perth Joanna saw her aunt drive off in a hired carriage, and herself returning to the booking-office, she took her ticket to the village from which Duntarvie was but three miles distant.

Though she had nearly an hour to wait for her train, she could not leave the magic enclosure of the station. She was filled there—for the first time these many days—with the strangest expectancy; and even apart from this, she found pleasure in the bustling holiday sight. Kilted men with guns swung past her, followed by excited retriever dogs. Anglers in shabby homespuns carrying their rods and baskets, moved more philosophically. Everywhere trolleys heaped with kit-bags and golf-clubs blocked the way. Children clutching green butterfly nets hurried before their parents across the big, black iron bridge. They were fearful lest they should not find their platform in this widespread network of arrival and departure. How well Joanna remembered that trembling lest the others should lag and keep one back, and so one's heart be broken by the sight of a missed train. Duntarvie, Duntarvie! Would the stream still be flowing clear brown, and its furry stones be sheltering the spotted trout? Would the heron still have his nest upon the island in the upper pond? Would the blaeberries be ripe and the larches heavy with their swinging tassels?

In the refreshment room to which she was driven by a slight dizziness, memory was further assailed by a vision of her mother's unslept but ardent face of travel. It had always been part of the ritual of the long journey from Glasgow that Juley should take her children here to drink tea out of these thick, white cups that had the thrilling word *Perth* emblazoned across them upon a blue strap.

Having ordered tea, she went to a small table opposite the entrance. Above that was the clock; and even while she raised the cup to her lips, she could hardly take her eyes from the slow, jerking, minute hand upon the dial. Only twenty minutes now, and she would be on her way!

A traveller came pushing himself in between the swing doors. He wore a sporting suit of a loud and gay pattern of tweed, woven perhaps in Scotland, but destined for no Scotsman to wear. And slung from his shoulders was a bulging ruck-sack.

"Carl! Carl Nilsson! My dear, dear Carl!"

Impetuously Joanna started from her seat and ran toward the newcomer, all the other people in the restaurant looking up to watch the meeting.

Strangers will always watch with a good deal of interest what is clearly a chance meeting. On this occasion, one at least of the onlookers—a stout woman of unimaginative appearance enough—was so anxious not to miss a single clue, that she could spare no glance for the lump of sugar which she held suspended half way to her cup. She dropped it with a clatter on the marble table-top : and even then did not take her eyes from Joanna's face.

Indeed, Carl's queer clothes and foreign looks notwithstanding, it seemed to be Joanna rather than he that held the attention of the onlookers. Quite apart from dress and feature, Joanna had lately got that in her presence which put her apart and set people speculating. She looked young (not more, decided the stout observer, than twenty-five) yet she had already discarded that density which is peculiarly the mark of youthful flesh. Had she perhaps just recovered from an illness ? That seemed ruled out by the bounding movement of greeting with which she had run forward. Neither was she particularly thin. Yet there was a difference, a rarity—something that marked her out.

And how came Carl to be in Perth ?

And how Joanna ?

The better to talk, they sat down at her table and she told him briefly of her doings. It was more than two years since they had met, and Joanna could feel her friend's clever eyes noting the changes in her. In him, except that the last traces of red had vanished from the grey of his beard, she could see no difference.

When she seemed to have no more to say, he told her that he was even now on his way to meet Lawrence Urquhart. Lawrence had been ill. She had not heard ? Well, he was better now or nearly so, and together they were going to make what Carl called a " footing tour " in Fife. Carl had long wished to see the Fife villages which were said to be like villages in the Low Countries. Lawrence was also to see them now for the first time. . . . Cupar, Falkland, Auchtermuchty, Strathmiglo ! . . . such promising names as they had ! Did Joanna know any of them ? She did ? Good ! What now of the " ancient, royal burgh " of Auchtermuchty ? It was there he was going to meet Lawrence that afternoon. Was it a place to be sketched ? Had it, as the guide-book assured him, a beautiful town hall ?

After having declared eagerly that she well knew Auchtermuchty, Joanna discovered that she could tell Carl nothing definite about it. It lay little more than five miles from Duntarvie, so that she had been there many a time. She remembered the horse-shows there, the crowded country races her father had enjoyed in spite of his principles, the great July Fair where as children they had crunched bright pink sugar hearts and wondered if they would be kidnapped by gypsies. But as to the size of the town, its situation, its architecture—as to anything indeed which might have been of use to Carl and Lawrence she was so ignorant that she began to wonder if in reality she had ever been there at all. She was all the more anxious to go to Duntarvie—to make sure beyond a doubt whether a certain white-washed house and red-tiled steading had once stood in a fold of moorland.

But in the middle of her talk of Duntarvie, she became aware that Carl was looking at her with a thoughtfulness not caused by her words.

"Meet us at Auchtermuchty to-morrow," he said as she faltered into silence. "See your Duntarvie if you must. Look your fill. I see you have to go. But get your memories over and be done with them. Stay the night at your village, and in the morning walk across and join us. We shall wait for you. Here is the name of our inn. But you will probably find me sketching the town hall and Lawrence looking for Roman rubbish."

He watched her closely.

"I told my Aunt that I should be back in time for dinner to-night."

"O! La, la! The Aunt!" laughed Carl. "You send her a telegram."

"Do you think I should? But truly, Carl?" Her whole being seemed arrested, waiting for his answer.

"I have suggested it, perhaps wrongly. The matter is one you must decide for yourself," Carl replied after a moment.

"But I cannot decide anything these days. You must help me, Carl. Do, please help me!" she begged him most earnestly.

"Are you a free woman?"

At his so abrupt question a very billow of blood swept over her from head to foot, but she raised her suffused eyes and faced him bravely.

"Yes," she said. "I'm free—quite, quite free . . . but I know nothing . . . and I am so weak. I know nothing, nothing! I can't tell what I should do. I'm blown by any wind. There seems no life in me."

Carl took her shaking hand and patted it kindly.

" Go, send the telegram," he bade her as if it were a child he spoke to. " I'm heartily glad of what you tell me. More glad than I can say. Go send the telegram. I meet you at the train. It seems we go so far together."

Joanna lost no time, but she was not flurried. In spite of her grave face, her steps to the telegraph office were set almost to a dancing rhythm. Dear Carl ! Dear, good Carl. What had she ever done to deserve such a friend ?

A slight, but not a painful constraint arose between them upon the short journey. They had the musty compartment of the little puffing train to themselves, and she was hoping that Carl would tell her more of Lawrence and his illness. Nothing however seemed farther from Carl's intention. Nor could she bring herself to question him till the moment of parting was almost upon them. Instead, therefore, they spoke of Joanna's work in London, of changes in Glasgow, of Phemie's expected visit home that October. Yet Joanna was happier than she knew ; and as the train came nearer and nearer to Duntarvie, she grew eager in pointing out each well-remembered landmark. There was the tower which some people said had *not* been built by the Picts : there the church : there the queer, pointed hill that wore its fir woods as though they were a cloak and a plume of feathers, so that she had always thought it looked like a highway robber. Every moment established her belief that Duntarvie was a real place after all, and her companion's praise of the countryside gave her keen joy. These were hills and woods and rivers that she herself would never be able to see with the painter's eye, but she was loverly proud to have their beauty vindicated by one who could.

They were jogging slowly into the station which seemed even smaller than her memory of it, when at last she turned from the window and spoke with timid haste. Carl had said Lawrence had been ill. Did he mean that he had been seriously ill ?

Carl replied with a certain dryness that this was precisely what he had meant. Lawrence, he said, had quite unexpectedly turned up at his studio in Glasgow—early one morning in June it was—straight from a night journey. He was then suffering from a chill which was bad enough to account for the sharp illness that had followed. But what had made Carl more anxious was the wretched slowness of the convalescence.

There had been one unaccountable relapse after another—
the whole thing a regular break in health rather than any
specific illness. In his last letter, however, Lawrence had
declared himself fit for the " footing " tour. This sunshine,
if only it would last—and really to day it looked like it—
should help to set him up.

There was no time for more. A warm grip of Carl's hand,
a glance—grave and trustful on her part, smiling and kindly
on his, a renewal of her promise to meet them without fail
the next day, and Joanna was alone. She watched the tail
of the train carrying Carl off till it disappeared at leisure
round a distant hill-corner, then crossing the rails by the
footboard she walked up the lane, past the round tower
where an iron ring for the necks of felons was still fixed at a
height for misery in the stones, and so on into the village.

v

To her delight it was just as she remembered it—a little
smaller perhaps as the station had been, but otherwise unchanged. The single, wide street still straggled unevenly
downhill, keeping many levels in one width of its close-set
cobbles. And there, perched on its mound at the top of the
village, was Tweedie's, the post-office and principal shop. It
too looked the same as it had always looked. The same stiff
bunches of boots and breeches stuck out from its dark doorway. The same smell of cheese and porpoise boot-laces,
paraffin and bacon came forth from it. Not before she entered
(and Joanna did enter, for in Tweedie's she knew she would
learn whatever was to be known of Duntarvie and its present
owners) would she have discovered that old sandy-haired
Tweedie was dead, and that young sandy-haired Tweedie,
already a bald-headed man, was the master.

But this was as nothing to the news of Duntarvie that she
brought with her out of that cavern of boots and breeches.
During the last eighteen years, Tweedie had said, the house
had changed hands many times. It had been found too
solitary for domestic use ; too cold in the winter for the
poultry-keeping attempted by one tenant ; the soil was too
poor to make the place profitable for the ordinary farmer.
So for some years it had stood empty, till six months ago it
had been taken over by the parish authorities. Now it was
used for housing old and mindless paupers. There they

might indulge in their feeble antics in the sunshine without distressing their fellows.

Here was a change to be faced.

Joanna however recovered her serenity as she stood awhile outside and surveyed the basking village. If Duntarvie house, she reminded herself, was become a place of sadness, there was still the moor, the burn, the upper pond : and what were the mere four walls compared with these in her memory ? Save for its inmates who were quiet and never strayed beyond the lawn, Tweedie had assured her that the place was quite unchanged. After all perhaps a few poor old lunatics were less hateful as tenants than would have been some strenuous family who would rebuild the steadings, or some speculative farmer who would divide the moor into hen-runs.

She ate in the village, also buying food to take with her so that she might be free for her next meal. Then leaving the main road by a rough old short cut that was more like the dry bed of a stream than a path, she set out.

It was late in the afternoon when she gained a track that ran thread-like, high up around the flank of a hill ; and still she was but half way to her destination. But she would not hurry. She was kept loitering, partly perhaps by some dread of what might await her, but much more by the quiet new vitality which seemed to well, more and more sweetly, more and more surely in her with every step.

How still it was !—almost sombre, in the strong, late sunshine. The birds did not sing. The larger ones only called and called to one another, while the smaller—brown dunnocks, green and yellow siskins, finches and linnets of every variety—fluttered silently from bush to bush or twittered vigilantly in the undergrowth. The leafage everywhere was of that dark, lack-lustre green which is as different from the green fires of spring, as from the flaming red and yellow of later autumn. Yet was that mighty business of scattering, of which the scarlet banners of October only mark the end, already well on its way. Lying with her eyes shut among the bushes of broom and whin, Joanna heard all around her the tiny sharp reverberations of pods splitting in the blessed heat. Opening her eyes she saw a thousand acorns pushing out their blunt and glossy noses from beneath the dark foliage : she espied a million winged fruits, which from having long hung aimlessly upon the parent boughs, now lifted themselves in swarms, ready with every pinion spread for the wind : she held in her wondering fingers the purple-black, riven pods, that disclosed each one a row of ebony seeds embedded in silvery silken down. Fir cones that were now no more than empty hives, lay everywhere around her. Others, untimely fallen, would never yield up their fruits, but would sink tightly clenched into dissolution. The whole earth was strewn with the signs and wonders, the triumphs and the vast wastage of the year's fulfilment.

Even in the sun's decline it was hot, and Joanna, finding a knee-deep pool in the stream all overgrown at that part with elder and rowan trees, and hazels rich with nut clusters, stripped herself and bathed. With its pale, sandy bottom and moss-covered stones, and its little brown fall that gushed from above, it made a lovely bath. Half sitting, half lying in it the young woman let the water splash upon her shoulders and run in a rivulet between her breasts. For some minutes she stayed there watching the flecks of sunshine move among the rippled pebbles. Then feeling fresh to the heart she regained the main road and went more steadily on her way.

Duntarvie lay two miles farther on, still uphill, at the end of its own steep and rocky road which, being tree-embowered for the last fifty yards or so had always been known to the children as the "Avenue." Emerging from there to the open space before the house Joanna stopped and sadly looked. It was more forlorn than she had expected. Yet she was comforted also. For a faint wisp of smoke rising from the kitchen chimney, and some hens that picked about the scratched grass behind sagging palings, were the only signs of human habitation. She had dreaded the sight of strangers on the lawn.

Slowly, and with some backward looks, she passed on. She crossed to where the hunched-up, red-and-grey steading seemed to have settled so deeply into the earth as to have become one with it, stooped below the iron girders of the mill shaft, to which no horse had been harnessed these fifty years and more, and skirting the shrunken lower pond began to climb the slope beyond among the beech trees. Nothing suffers more from human abuse than water. And when Joanna had seen the well covered with broken boards and nettles, and the pond with its stream half choked and its banks a wide margin of mud, she trembled for the heron's pool which supplied the house from the summit of the hill behind. There, however, she must go that night. The moor could wait till the morning. She would cross it on her way to Auchtermuchty.

On her reaching the place, it seemed at first as if her worst fears were to be realized, and her heart sank heavily. Here were the trees all standing round on guard as she remembered them. There was no touch of spoliation anywhere. But in the cup below her she could see only unbroken greenness. Where was the water she had so loved, the water that had figured all these years as a kind of shrouded symbol in her life? Had it disappeared, or had it never been?

Then even as she looked, a breeze came running through the trees at her back, and stirred the rushes, and the pale green evening sky discovered for her as if by a spoken word, the living glitter of waters. There it was! There was its perfect circle as of old. There was the living, undespoilable spring that had been set here to spill and spill for ever from its far hidden source in the earth.

So after all one need not despair! Joanna remembered how, when her life had lain broken within her, the water had sung to her from its tank in the Edinburgh hotel bedroom. And it was this now silent, almost hidden water that had made hopeful music for her when she lay a child in bed in the house below.

" If I forget thee, may my right hand forget its cunning! " That had been the vague but fervent exclamation of her childhood in this spot. Indeed she had forgotten! All these years, in her striving for the world, in her keeping Louis Pender as her centre of energy with the whole force of her wits and her strongly disciplined will, she had been madly oblivious of the sweet hint vouchsafed to her in childhood. She had forgotten because she had never truly understood. And so it was good to have forgotten. One had to forget first. One had first to expend and lose utterly all the disastrous cunning of one's right hand, before one could at last simply *be*, as one was meant to be. Here surely was the new birth. Why it should have to come by such a widely circling and deathly route, why so much pain and wastage should intervene before one could start fair, was a vain question. Enough that for her at any rate there could have been no other way. She could look back now, without regret or sadness, to the beginning when her life had been as a seed enfolded in a double mesh of desire. On desire her life had fed these many years, imprisoned but ripening. A long agony it had been, for she had never known to which desire she must be given—to the desire of sacrifice or to the desire of pride. Each had asserted its sole claim : each had denied that the other had any right in her. And so she had turned from one to the other in a torture of ignorance and indecision. Only now that both had fallen away outworn did she come by the steady knowledge that both had been needed, that in the following of one alone there would have been sterility. Why then regret ? That period of life—conscious and striving, but blind—was past. She was free of it in knowing she could not have been free without it. Now her absolved self had its birth.

No moon rose behind the low, straight band of cloud that girdled the horizon, but the sky had become a dark-belted cupola of stars. Joanna wandered through forest clearings and across the open country where the dew-slippery grass showed like a grey web among the black bushes of whin and heather. She sat on a high stone dyke, ate some biscuits and raisins, and wondered where she should sleep. The idea of sleep became suddenly overpowering. But it was too wet to lie in the open, and she could not bring herself to knock at the doors of Duntarvie. Here and there in the distance from her high perch she could see the tiny lights of farm houses, but none seemed within a mile of her, and she felt too tired to go so far.

She bethought herself of the steading below, and went back there quickly. Her desire to throw herself down in some dry, dark place and sleep, grew upon her with every step.

The barn was locked. She could hear the sleepy rustling and fluffing and clucking of the enviable fowls inside. So was the old byre door locked. But to her joy, the latch of what in her childhood had been the stable, yielded under her thumb.

It was dark inside, for there were only a few small panes of cobwebbed glass among the tiles of the roof ; but she groped about and soon found her bearings. Clearly the place was used by the present owners as a byre, for there was no mistaking the warm, sweet redolence of cows, and these were no horses that sighed and snuffled in the two stalls. Joanna's relief was all the greater when she stumbled up against the old stable bin in its accustomed place, standing a little way out from the wall so that the lid could be propped upright. Best of all, it was full to within a foot of the top with some kind of chaff mixture. It was a great metal box, long as a coffin and far deeper, and saving that it was rather narrow, a better bed could hardly have been found. Throwing off her hat and shoes, and spreading her short coat over her as a cover, Joanna climbed in. The chaff yielded comfortably to her hips and shoulders. In five minutes she was asleep.

She slept fitfully however, being straitened for room, and woke again and again to long, albeit peacefully enough, for the morning. Her deepest bout of sleep was the last, which carried her far past dawn, and she sat up half in fear to the long-drawn pipe of a starling on the chimney outside. Fine as the bird's whistle, a gold rapier of sunlight lay across her body in the corn bin. She looked at her watch. Six o'clock—so late! The wonder was that no one had come from the house yet to see to the cows. She felt hungry.

When she had put on her shoes, shaken her clothes free of the chaff bedding, and gone out into the pearly morning she could see no sign of anyone stirring. Her good fortune seemed assured by the kitchen blinds being still drawn, so hastening back to the byre she laid hold of a metal dipper which had been in the bin, and with soothing words she approached one of the cows.

To her relief the beast looked round at her, mildly wrinkling a velvet neck, and did not low. Joanna's experience of milking was limited to a few half playful lessons in childhood in this very building, and she was unsure of herself. But she crouched down resolutely and grasped the two near teats. So, so, so, so! One must go on tugging firmly and with a fearless rhythm. That she knew. She laughed as two sudden, hard, white spirts came sideways at her like arrows, striking warm to her knees through her woollen skirts and thence dribbling to the ground. Soon the milk was coming bravely. The only difficulty now was to direct it from the slippery teats into the small and awkwardly shaped vessel beneath. For once that the criss-cross darts went hissing into the dipper, three times they would slither over the byre floor, blackening the cobbles, forming small white pools upon the hard earth between, or driving skewer-like into the soft round heaps of cow-dung. But Joanna persevered, and by the time she was warm through and through, and her fingers cramped with clinging to the heavy, freckled udder, there was a good cupful for her breakfast. Splendid it was too—clover-fresh, and sweet, and warm ; and with the last of the biscuits it stayed immediate hunger.

The next minute she was out in the sunshine. She crossed the stream at a bound, climbed over the squeaking wire fence, and was straightway on the old moor. The morning, for its freshness, might have been the first of creation. Small gleeful birds whistled in the whins which were bound each to each by a thousand radiant spiders' webs ; and Joanna, as she broke through them, loving what she must destroy, stooped to pick handfuls of bloom-grey blaeberries. She could still hear the strange, long, satisfied cries of the starlings on the steading roof, and magpies and whaups went circling and calling in the further fields. A lark flew up voiceless from her feet, a weasel darted behind a boulder. As she got higher, she saw that the greater part of the moor was now a plantation of baby pines and firs and larches. In ten years' time it would be a moor no longer, but a forest. As yet, however, the little sturdy conifers—few of them over two feet in height—had not interfered with the heather, the high-growing blaeberry plants, or the tufts of long, needle-like grass interspersed with clumps of wild thyme which lay between. It was happiness just to pass between these young trees that sprang everywhere with such a delicate, balanced strength, and were so dew-covered and innocent. Already the moisture was being sucked up so swiftly by the sun that it could almost be felt flying skywards in an ecstasy. And when, after some wandering, Joanna came to the corner she sought, she found the ground almost dry. Here at the boundary of the moor, where dark old woods lay beyond the lichen-covered paling, the hollow of grass and heather received the sun as if in a chalice.

Choosing a springy tussock of heather near some rocks she sat herself down in great contentment to wonder what she should do next. It was still too early to start for Auchter-muchty. To Duntarvie house with its forbidding decrepitude she would not return. She began to trifle with the idea of making Drumwharrie farm away to the south. Perhaps they would give her breakfast there before she went on her way over the Fife border. Surely at Drumwharrie there would still be

some one who remembered the Bannermans ? To Drumwharrie she would go.

Presently—that was ! . . . Not quite yet. . . . The
sun was indeed getting at her in this sheltered cup. It was
getting most gratefully at her very marrow : and now a drow-
siness swam along her limbs and drew film after film over her
eyelids. She had slept in the corn bin, but not enough for
her need. Now her eyelids fell, and her head sank toward
one shoulder. Her last conscious movement before yielding
utterly was a pushing and insinuating of herself as far into
the bush of heather as she could get. With a comfortable
sigh she settled yet more deeply. On all sides she was supported by the springy stems, yet she was so far sunken out of
sight that the warm, dry, rustling flowers nearly met over her.

When she was wakened by the abrupt cu-uck . . . cu-uck
of a cock-pheasant quite close to her ear, it was her firm belief
that she had slept but a few minutes. Yet it was past ten
by her watch, and the sun had mounted high in the sky. Had
it not been for the shade of a larch bough, its rays must have
beat her eyes open long ere then. As she rose stretching herself, leaving such a deep impression of her body in the heather
that it would be days before the fine grey thongs would stand
again upright, the cock-pheasant stalked out of sight. His
gait declared that he was prudent, but that he refused to
be hurried. Two young rabbits nibbling near the fence were
less careful for their dignity.

Perching on a boulder higher up, Joanna shaded her eyes
and searched toward the south for a sign of Drumwharrie.
It was with a touch of incredulity that she recognized, well
within a mile from where she stood, the dark slate gables
and the high old smoke stalk which in childhood had seemed
a day's journey across the steeply curving hillsides. She was
about to descend from her rock, facing a little the other way
to avoid the sun in her eyes, when something made her gather
herself back into intent, balanced stillness. Away on the
moor a jerkily moving object caught the sunlight. It was the
bare, black head of a man who was otherwise hidden by
rising ground and whins. It moved along quickly ; sometimes
bobbing up and down as its owner ran a few steps or leaped
over the knots of heather ; sometimes disappearing completely
behind a hillock ; but always widening the distance between
itself and her.

Now it had gone, and Joanna watched for its re-appearance with a feeling in her heart different from anything she had ever known before. Now it came again into sight, followed rapidly by the shoulders and the man's whole body, as he mounted a little hill perhaps two hundred yards away. She knew then beyond all doubt that it was Lawrence and no other that was here on the moor with her. And it was only then that she was pierced through and through by the clue of her own new-born life. Clear as the starling's whistle, piercing as the first ray of the morning, she knew her happiness and hailed it.

But he had not seen her. He did not know. He was not even looking for her ! As fast as he could, he was walking away and away. Soon—in a moment—he would be gone.

He must not go.

Every thought, every desire, every invigorated cell of Joanna's renewed body leapt on the instant in unison with this declaration of her spirit. Lawrence must not go. She must stop him. She had never known anything as she knew this. She had never experienced living knowledge till now. Lawrence too must be pierced with this new, dazzling ray of knowledge or there would remain only darkness.

She started running at top speed. First she went pelting down her hillock, losing all sight of him ; then, zig-zagging like a hare along the clear passage of grass that wound pale yellow between the whins, and springing over the sapling pines, she breasted the longer hill in front. She could see him again now. If only he would turn round. But no ! He stared sometimes a little to the right or to the left, but never turned his face enough for any movement from behind to catch his eye. And not once did he glance back. What breeze there was on these heights was contrary, and so would prevent the sound of her running from reaching him till she should come up close. Once or twice she thought she could hear that he whistled to himself as he walked. He looked young and care-free, with his coat off and thrown over one shoulder, and though the breath was failing her, a spend-thrift laugh escaped her when she saw him go flying over a particularly wide obstacle of rock and heather.

She had reached the top of the second hillock between them, he meanwhile climbing also, when her plight began to seem desperate. The last push up hill had made her breathing fearfully ragged, and she had reached the top just in time to avoid falling. She realized also, what she had not grasped before, that her task was not merely to cover the stretch of uneven ground between herself and Lawrence, but to overtake him as well. If she could not gain seriously on him by the next plunge down hill and across the intervening shallow dip, before he was again descending at a helter skelter pace, she was done . . . she was lost. She would have to sink mute upon the earth while he would go on whistling and unknowing. It was too late to attract his attention by calling. Even if she had tried to shout earlier, with the wind as it was, it would most likely have been mere waste of precious breath. Precious breath indeed! Now it was too late for the weakest cheep of a *hoi-hoi!* Soon she would have no breath left for anything, not even for survival.

She plunged down the hill, not zig-zagging now, but jumping and stumbling straight forward, sometimes falling on her hands and knees. The braid of her skirt was torn into festoons and her knees trembled shockingly. It was even worse going downhill than up. But she went on, and across the amber-coloured dip which was full of quivering air. Only twice before in her life had she run so. Once, it had been up the Glasgow hill to her first meeting with Louis, under the dread that he would be gone. And once it had been along the winding shore road to the West Coast village where her mother lay dying. She remembered these times now. . . . " Once for love, once for death ". . . . Her blood took up the refrain with its bursting throbs. . . . "Once for love, once for death . . . this time for life ! " It was life that she ran for now. Life . . . few there be that find it. Life . . . that for her Lawrence held in his keeping . . . and was carrying swiftly away.

Again she had lost sight of him, and the knowledge that as she was crawling up this next slippery hill, he was going pellmell downwards, nearly killed her. She uttered his name now in gasping, voiceless breaths, though she knew it was worse than useless. But she could not refrain. If only he would stop for one moment. To die on one last, short breath in his arms would be better than to recover in solitude. There was no real recovery for her but in his arms. If she fell short of him her heart would break. It was breaking now. She had to keep her hand pressed over it. Why did he go

on so fast and never stop ?   A fury of anger against him
ran parallel with her desire.   She loved him, needed him,
hated him, all at once.

With the tears pouring down her scarlet cheeks, and all
her features convulsed like a frantic lost child's, she got somehow over the brow of the hill and looked for him.

He had stopped.   He had turned round.   She heard him
shout . . . saw him come running towards her ; and she
tried to raise her arm in a signal.   Though she was saved,
she could not have stopped running now—not if she had
known the next step to be her last.   But soon they were only
a few paces apart, and Lawrence, becoming suddenly unsure,
stood still.   He uttered some inarticulate sounds of question and welcome, but knew that he must wait for her.
There was a treacherous looped root of heather in the turf
between them, and Joanna was no longer able to lift her
feet, nor to look where she was going.   With her eyes
on Lawrence's face she tripped badly on the root, and as he
darted forward to save her, she pitched forward right upon
his breast.

For what to both seemed a long time, no word was spoken.
Joanna clearly was quite unfit for speech.   Her breath came
and went in painful, sobbing gasps, do what she would to allay
it, and her tumultuous heart-beats shook her body through
and through.   As for Lawrence, silence was his better part.
He could only hold his love to him in fearful happiness.

But as soon as she began to draw away from him, he let
her go.   She still panted, her hair was fallen in a lump on
one shoulder, her moist face blazed like heather flowers in
September sunshine after a rain shower.   She groped in her
skirts and in her bosom.

" I must have lost my handkerchief ! "

Lawrence pulled out his—a comfortable male square of
linen—and put it in her hand.

" Thank you . . ." she murmured fervently.   And when
her face was a little comforted, she added seriously—

" l ran after you."

Lawrence threw back his head and laughed to the
sky.

" You did that ! " he replied when he could speak.   Then
—" See, sit down here," he went on, as if he were coaxing some
panicky animal.   " Here's a good seat.   Take your time.

You must have run ever so far to get yourself in such a state. Why didn't you shout on me?"

"The wind was against me . . . then my breath was gone," said Joanna. She was recovering, but still had to heave great sighs, and she pressed her hands to her flaming cheeks.

"Rest a bit," urged Lawrence as she tried to rise. "Could you drink some cold coffee? I have some here, see . . ."

He knelt beside her, unfastening his ruck-sack, while Joanna tried to twist up her hair.

"All my hair-pins are gone," she complained.

"I'm afraid I can't help you there."

"No, I shall just have to plait it."

With practised fingers that seemed to her companion to accomplish a miracle of skilfulness, she made a long braid of her hair and doubled it up under her soft hat.

"I think I'll never be cool again!"

"Not up here, certainly," agreed Lawrence. "Shall we go down among these trees? There should surely be a burn there?"

She nodded. "There is. *My* burn. Let's go." And she scrambled to her feet.

"But first here's your coffee," he said, giving her a cup, and she drank gratefully.

As she handed him back the empty cup their eyes met, and it was as if each now saw the other for the first time. Only now did Joanna clearly note the marks of his recent illness in his face; but it was no more this that kept her eyes so long upon his, than it was her morning freshness that made Lawrence gaze on as if he could never look elsewhere. Never before had their primary flames of being leapt up so nakedly. And they were full of recognition, each for the other. There on the moor that vibrated with noon-day, he was Adam to her Eve. There among the broom bushes whereon the dark seed pods went *crack, cracking* in the strong sunshine, the past was shed from both of them like a garment. Nor did any future as yet exist for them. They were " in the beginning " of their new creation.

"Did you see me on the rock?" A question leaped at last from her. "Were you trying to get away when I ran after you"?

"I didn't see you," he replied, "Not till I turned and

you were quite close. How can you ask ? I would never run from you. I must always follow you for ever."

Joanna had never listened to words of such penetrating sweetness.

" If I hadn't caught up on you," she said, " I should have died."

" And I," said Lawrence, " should never have lived."

They went for shade down to the burn, and there they sat to talk. They talked till the afternoon drew in, but it seemed to them that they could never be done disclosing to each other the so widely differing courses of their two lives which had yet converged at last.

Joanna told about Gerald, her first love who close by where they sat had skinned the wild birds, and about Alec Peddie's offer in this very spot (how Lawrence laughed at that !) to show her what lads were for. And she talked of Mario and Italy and Aunt Perdy. Of Louis she found she could not yet speak plainly. The reminiscent misery of that was still too raw. But when she told, as she did, of the secret garden door of La Porziuncola, and of all that love had meant to her . . . escape . . . adventure . . . excitement . . . . learning . . . possession of the world . . . she found that Lawrence understood. She knew well that no corner of her life would be—or need ever be—kept from him.

And when in turn he told her of his life, she listened amazed. Where she had been as a field under the harrow, never left in peace, he had lived folded in upon himself. She knew now what he (and Carl too) had meant when they reckoned him as the seed and her as the clod of earth. For in her had lain his one means of escape, and she had denied him. Elsewhere he had been able neither to give nor to take in any vital way. His essence and his treasure had lain hoarded up for her alone.

In an interval of their talk she laved her face in the stream and they squatted gaily to share the food Lawrence had brought in his rucksack. When thay had eaten it all they fell silent at last. Joanna rested, leaning slackly against a beech trunk. Her hat was off so that the long unfastened braid of her hair hung fallen behind like a schoolgirl's, and round her forehead the smaller locks clung to the skin in damp rings. Except for the bright patch of sunburn where her linen blouse fell open at the neck, and a vivid stain on either forearm, she now looked cool as satin.

"How old are you?" asked Lawrence out of the quietness.

"Thirty."

"I suppose you are!"

"Why?" She answered the wonder in his tone. "How old do I look to you?"

"No particular age. But you look just such a *lassie*!" he said.

"Not weary and worn?"

"Not now at any rate."

"But sometimes . . . eh? When I look like a juggler? You remember!"

"Yes. I've seen you so. And you looked horribly beautiful. All the same, I like best for you to be as you are now. You were meant to be all freshness."

"Yet one has to grow old and even middle-aged. And thirty is a good way towards it?" she questioned wistfully.

"My love. You needn't be anxious! There is more youth in you —more real youth, than in a girl of seventeen."

"I believe that is true. Yes, somehow I know it here with you now," she agreed simply, all her face bright. "How old are you Lawrence?"

"Twenty-eight."

"So much younger than I! And yes: you look it. Alas!"

"Do you mind?"

"Not really. I don't think so at least."

"You shouldn't," he assured her. "There was a time when I *was* too young for you . . . heaps too young. But I have made up since then. Soon I shall be far older than you, though I hope not too old. Compare the shape of our heads! I am of an older race. What you have come through would have made tatters of me long ago. Physically I might have held out. (I have a toughness of fibre —I found that out when I was ill.) But not a bit of freshness would have been left. If I had spent myself as you have, I could never have laughed as you laughed a moment ago. I'm a frail sort of being beside you, Joanna!"

"You do make me sound a tough old thing!" she protested.

"Not tough,—sturdy!" he corrected her, ". . . like one of those sapling firs up there that shoot up all the stronger for being buffeted about by the wind."

Later they climbed the grey dyke and went swinging in

true lover's rhythm down the hilly road toward the village where Carl would be waiting. As they came near it, they passed with their happiness between the new-scythed shocks of wheat that bent in their places meekly as if praying.

"Happy ? " asked Lawrence, breaking a long unconscious silence.

Joanna laughed quietly in response. "I haven't thought," she admitted.

"But I have, though," said he, "and I know you are, by your voice."

"It is true, Lawrence," she replied. "I think my heart never felt light till now."

"Nor mine either."

"See ! The moon ! "

Together at Joanna's cry they wheeled to look. Amid the flock of little clouds behind them, a young, mis-shapen moon had been speeding up unseen. Now each cloud, holding fast its own seed of darkness, floated apart in a pale, transparent spume of light.

"Like the seeds of a passion flower, aren't they ? " murmured Joanna.

"Ay. No need to ask the moon if she is happy ! " Lawrence mused. "She looks fulfilled . . . like a web of ripe seeds that has this moment been scattered."

THE END

Other VIRAGO MODERN CLASSICS

PHYLLIS SHAND ALLFREY
The Orchid House

SYLVIA ASHTON WARNER
Spinster

MARGARET ATWOOD
Bodily Harm
The Edible Woman
Lady Oracle
Life Before Man
Surfacing

DOROTHY BAKER
Cassandra at the Wedding

JANE BOWLES
Two Serious Ladies

KAY BOYLE
Plagued by the Nightingale

ANGELA CARTER
The Magic Toyshop
The Passion of New Eve

WILLA CATHER
Death Comes for the Archbishop
A Lost Lady
My Antonia
My Mortal Enemy
The Professor's House
The Song of the Lark

BARBARA COMYNS
Our Spoons Came from
    Woolworths
The Vet's Daughter

ELIZABETH HARDWICK
Sleepless Nights

EMILY HOLMES COLEMAN
The Shutter of Snow

TILLIE OLSEN
Tell Me a Riddle
Yonnondio

GRACE PALEY
Enormous Changes at
    the Last Minute
The Little Disturbances of Man

STEVIE SMITH
The Holiday
Novel on Yellow Paper
Over the Frontier

CHRISTINA STEAD
The Beauties and Furies
Cotters' England
For Love Alone
Letty Fox: Her Luck
A Little Tea, A Little Chat
Miss Herbert
The People with the Dogs

SYLVIA TOWNSEND
    WARNER
Mr Fortune's Maggot
The True Heart

REBECCA WEST
Harriet Hume
The Harsh Voice
The Judge
The Return of the Soldier

ANTONIA WHITE
Frost in May
The Lost Traveller
The Sugar House
Beyond the Glass
Strangers

VIRAGO MODERN CLASSICS

The first Virago Modern Classic, *Frost in May* by Antonia White, was published in 1978. It launched a list dedicated to the celebration of women writers and to the rediscovery and reprinting of their works. Its aim was, and is, to demonstrate the existence of a female tradition in fiction which is both enriching and enjoyable. The Leavisite notion of the 'Great Tradition', and the narrow, academic definition of a 'classic', has meant the neglect of a large number of interesting secondary works of fiction. In calling the series 'Modern Classics' we do not necessarily mean 'great' — although this is often the case. Published with new critical and biographical introductions, books are chosen for many reasons: sometimes for their importance in literary history; sometimes because they illuminate particular aspects of womens' lives, both personal and public. They may be classics of comedy or storytelling; their interest can be historical, feminist, political or literary.

Initially the Virago Modern Classics concentrated on English novels and short stories published in the early decades of this century. As the series has grown it has broadened to include works of fiction from different centuries, different countries, cultures and literary traditions. In 1984 the Victorian Classics were launched; there are separate lists of Irish, Scottish, European, American, Australian and other English speaking countries; there are books written by Black women, by Catholic and Jewish women, and a few relevant novels by men. There is, too, a companion series of Non-Fiction Classics constituting biography, autobiography, travel, journalism, essays, poetry, letters and diaries.

By the end of 1986 over 250 titles will have been published in these two series, many of which have been suggested by our readers.